CAESAR

The Life Story of a Panda-Leopard

&

HUSSEIN

An Entertainment

PATRICK O'BRIAN

HarperCollins*Publishers*

HarperCollins*Publishers* Ltd
1 London Bridge Street,
London SE1 9GF
www.harpercollins.co.uk

This paperback edition 2019

1

Caesar first published by G.P. Putnam's Sons 1930
Second edition published by the British Library 1999
First published by HarperCollins*Publishers* 2000

Hussein first published by Oxford University Press 1938
Second edition published by the British Library 1999
First published by HarperCollins*Publishers* 2000

A catalogue record for this book is available from the British Library

ISBN: 978-0-00-833737-7

Set in Minion Pro

Printed and bound in the UK by CPI Group (UK) Ltd, Croydon CR0 4YY

MIX
Paper from
responsible sources
FSC
www.fsc.org
FSC™ C007454

This book is produced from independently certified FSC™ paper
to ensure responsible forest management.

For more information visit: www.harpercollins.co.uk/green

Contents

Foreword

It is a curious experience looking back from a distance of more than seventy years at the little creature who shared one's name, bones, and indeed a good deal of one's essential being, as far as it can be made out at all objectively. Curious and by no means entirely agreeable: I doubt if my present self would have liked the twelve-year-old boy who wrote this tale — he was certainly not very popular among his brothers and sisters. Nevertheless, that remote being and myself, his aged descendant, are linked by a common delight in reading: the boy read voraciously, often in bed, by the light of an electric torch. And when he was very young his stepmother, the kindest of women, took him to see her sister, who gave him the Reverend Mr Wood's *Natural History*, a mid-nineteenth-century edition illustrated with a fair number of engravings. Since he was already something of a naturalist (an admired, much older brother had practically invented birds), the boy devoured the book, which was written by a sensible, well-informed, scholarly man. The boy was also something of an invalid, which interfered with his education and worried his father, a bacteriologist in the early days of vaccines and electrical treatment: the young fellow (pre-adolescent: a sort of elderly child) therefore spent long sessions in the incubator room, sitting at a glass-topped metal table and doing the simple tasks set by his tutor. But the tasks left a good deal of time unoccupied, and since it was obviously unthinkable to bring a book to read, the boy, by some mental process that I can no longer recall, decided to write one for himself, thus discovering an extraordinary joy which has never left him – that of both reading and writing at the same time.

It may seem absurd and pretentious, above all apropos of this piece of juvenilia, to say that writers, once they have experienced this intense delight, live fully only when they are writing fast, at the top of their being: the rest of the time only the lacklustre shell of the man is present, often ill-tempered (deprived of his drug), rarely good company.

I cannot remember the genesis of *Hussein* with great clarity, but I rather think that it derived from a tale I wrote for one of the Oxford annuals, to which I contributed fairly often: Mr Kaberry, an amiable man who ran the annual, said that it would be a pity to publish no more than the abbreviated form I showed him, and suggested that I should expand it to a book.

This I did: I was living in Dublin at the time, in a boarding-house in Leeson Street kept by two very kind sisters from Tipperary and inhabited mostly by young men studying at the national university with a few from Trinity. What fun we had in the evenings: the Miss Spains from Tipperary danced countless Irish dances with wonderful grace, big-boned Séan from Derry sawing away at his fiddle and the others joining in as well as they could. On Sundays we would go to a church where, without impropriety, the priest could say his Mass in eighteen minutes; then we would ride to Blackrock to swim; and all this time the book was flowing well, rarely less than a thousand words a day and sometimes much more. I finished it on a bench in Stephen's Green with a mixture of triumph and regret.

Although I had known some Indians, Muslim and Hindu, at that time I had never been to India, so the book is largely derivative, based on reading and on the recollections, anecdotes and letters of friends of relations who were well acquainted with that vast country; and it has no pretension to being anything more than what it is called, an *Entertainment*. But it did have a distinction that pleased my vanity: it was the first work of contemporary fiction that the Oxford University Press had published in all the centuries of its existence.

It was fairly well received, and in the writing of the book I learnt the rudiments of my calling: but infinitely more than that, it opened a well of joy that has not yet run dry.

PATRICK O'BRIAN
Trinity College, Dublin 1999

CAESAR

One

 First you must understand that I am a panda-leopard. My father was a giant panda and my mother a snow-leopard.

I will begin my story at the first things that I can remember.

My early days were spent with two brothers and a sister in a large cave, high up in the side of a mountain.

Of my father I remember little, except a hazy recollection of a very large shape which brought food to my mother in the first few days of the opening of my eyes.

The first thing to make any great impression on my mind was the killing of my sister.

It happened like this – the day was very cold, we were huddled together for warmth, and mother had gone for food, when I heard a scratching noise outside, and somehow it frightened us, for the others had heard it too.

Then a head appeared in the mouth of the cave. It was that of a large black bear.

The face seemed to split almost in half as the bear roared, and this sent us into the back of the cave, all except my sister, who sat petrified with fear in the middle of the floor.

The bear came right into the cave, and then shot out one of his great paws, and struck her a blow which laid her dead at our feet.

Then he picked her up and went out growling terribly.

Scarcely had the bear gone, when mother returned carrying a tough old pig.

She smelt around for a little, and seemed worried. Then she noticed my sister's absence, and with a low growl she went straight out of the cave, following the tracks of the bear.

She came back late in the evening with her white fur splashed with blood, both her own and the bear's, and in her mouth she carried two bear cubs, both quite dead. She was very tired as she had kept up a running fight for miles before they had reached the bear's lair, where mother had killed him.

We ate the bear cubs.

Next day passed uneventfully, but I missed my sister in a dim sort of way. We played as usual, but I noticed that one of my brothers stayed out of our games and seemed unhappy.

As the night approached he was more uneasy, and mother licked him to soothe his whimpering, and this calmed him; but by nightfall he was howling and crying, as if in pain, and mother looked anxious.

We tried to make him play, but he just sat still, not even retaliating when I bit his tail.

Soon after this I went to sleep, as there was no fun to be got out of him.

Next morning we found that he was gone, and we saw

by his tracks that he had gone straight out of the cave, down the mountain-side and over the frozen stream at its foot. Here we saw the signs of a struggle. A hyena had got him.

Two or three weeks passed quite happily, but the snow did not melt, and food was getting rather scarce, and then one day mother took us out to hunt.

We went down the mountain-side and on to the stream which was still frozen stiff, and here my brother and I slipped and fell many times before mother showed us how to walk on ice.

On the other side we rested, for our little legs soon got tired, and then we went on again.

A snow-hare jumped up about ten yards away, and I, wildly excited, set off after it, but the next moment I received a cuff on the side of the head that sent me sprawling as mother shot by me after the hare. She secured it in a few seconds, and we ate it where we were, as it was only a small one.

As we were eating it I took my little piece behind a fallen bough, and after I had finished it I looked at the branch more closely.

I poked it and rolled it over, and then all at once a lot of bees came buzzing out. One stung me on the nose, and I fled howling dolefully to mother.

She licked the place, but she did not seem to think, as I did, that I was in any immediate danger of death.

Soon after this incident we went home, as my brother and I were quite tired out by our exertions, which chiefly consisted of getting in the way and eating the food which mother had killed.

About a month passed before anything happened. We

were quite well and growing very fast, when my brother began to behave rather strangely, and his moping put me in mind of my other brother, who had run away a long time before.

One afternoon when I was teasing him to make him play. I received a blow from mother that sent me sulking into a corner for the rest of the day.

This seemed to cheer my brother somewhat, and he ate a little piece of the goat which mother brought in that night. After this he made one attempt to run away, but mother brought him back before he had got beyond the stream, which had thawed.

Next day mother brought in two little grey apes which we ate, but they did not agree with me, however, as I had horrible dreams all through the night. I have never eaten apes since.

On the following morning my brother was sick, and after this he got rapidly well again, being a strongly constituted young animal.

I awoke rather late in the day and found that mother had gone out, my brother killed a mouse and was immensely proud of it. I thought that it must have been both blind and paralysed, but it made no difference to his pride.

Mother soon returned, carrying with her a sambhur faun, and we ate some of it. Then mother took us out for exercise. We took the same path as before, but almost immediately after stepping out of the cave I missed my footing and started to roll down the slope, gathering speed as I went, but mother caught me before I had rolled any distance, and set me on my feet. I was quite giddy and sorry for myself, so when my brother suddenly pushed me from behind, I tripped and started rolling off towards the stream, into which I fell with a loud splash. As all the ice had melted I found nothing to hold on to, but instinct made me strike out – but not, however, before I had consumed what seemed half the water in the stream.

I swam towards the opposite bank, but the current washed me out into mid-stream and I went under again. Then I heard a splash behind me, as mother jumped in.

She soon had me by the scruff of the neck and swam ashore with a few powerful strokes. Once on dry land she shook all the water out of her fur, and I copied her. Then we trotted down the stream, and as we went I wondered why water was so wet, and why one could not breathe in it. Also why it was cold and unpleasant. I was very puzzled by the time we reached the ford, where mother stopped and walked in. It only reached to the top of her legs in the middle, so I plucked up my courage and followed her. Looking round I saw that my brother would not come in, so when mother and I had got to the other side and walked up the bank, she went back through the water, and taking him by the loose skin on the back of his neck, she carried him in; but when she had got to mid-stream, she lowered him in and he gave a dismal howl, which, however, was choked by water.

After this, he kept his head above the water and walked with her. As he scrambled up the bank, I remembered how he had pushed me down the slope, and I knocked him back again. He soon scrambled out, and after mother had licked us we set off again into the forest, mother leading the way.

We went in single file, mother leading; and my brother

kept nipping my tail until we came to an opening in the trees, where I fell upon him and mother separated us.

She showed us a lot of short, cropped grass in the clearing, and taught us that it had been eaten by deer. Then she showed us a little piece of fur on a thorn, which she made us smell and taught us that this was the smell of sambhur. We found the trail, and here and there a little fresh-cropped grass. After we had followed this trail for about a quarter of a mile into the forest we saw a cross track, a lot of little double-pointed footprints, which smelt different from deer. Very silently we followed the trail, which was quite fresh. The trails crossed and inter-crossed it, but the peculiar scent always distinguished it.

At last we came to a big, muddy clearing where a sounder of wild pigs — as a large family is called — was feeding. The sentinel pig saw us, and gave the alarm. The sounder fled at once, but with one bound mother caught up a little sucking-pig, and tossing it into the air she broke its neck. She picked it up in her mouth and began to go home. I very much wanted to chase the pigs, but it was not to be: I got a few steps after them, when mother picked me up and drove me in front of her. When we reached the ford, mother carried us over, as we were very small and tired.

When we got home we just had the energy to consume the pig, and then my brother and I went fast asleep.

———

Two

About one month later I saw my first human being. Mother had taken us out as usual, but we returned rather late. Imagine our surprise when we saw five things that looked like big apes in our cave, all gathered round something that was smoking and smelling under a lot of sticks. I did not understand it, but I feared the smoky thing, instinctively. The effect it had on my mother was extraordinary. She crouched on the ground with her ears flattened back and her tail twitching. She was growling terribly.

Then instead of charging the apes (humans) as I fully expected, she turned round and went down towards the stream. We followed her, and together we went upstream away from the ford; and soon we found ourselves at the mouth of another cave in the side of the bank of the stream, which had cut itself very deep.

Here we halted and mother went into the cave. I heard a roar, followed by the sound as of a scuffle, and two jackals shot out howling. Then we went in, and after snuggling down in the dried fern in the back of the cave we went to sleep.

At about midnight I awoke shivering. I heard mother growl uneasily, then the wind blew into the cave and I knew why I had awakened. It was the smell of fire. My brother soon awoke, and together we left the cave. All the forest on our left was blazing, and behind us and on our right the shrubs and long grass were burning furiously. The fire which the humans had made had spread and caught was to run south. So we ran.

After about five minutes we had caught up and passed many animals. There was a family of wild pigs led by a splendid old boar, and many goats who had come down in the evening to drink at the stream, and who had been caught by a wing of the fire.

We also passed two leopards, innumerable rats and mice and one old bear. How many animals there were to the left and right of us and in front I would not care to say, but there must have been thousands.

At last we found ourselves well in the van, the only beasts in front were the deer. Then my brother stepped on a porcupine, and filled his paws with quills. The startled beast lashed out with its long tail, filling my flank with the sharp points. We waited while we got most of them out.

But meanwhile the fire was fast overtaking us. About half a mile in front of us could be seen the waters of a lake shimmering in the moonlight. Not a large lake, but big enough to stop the fire. If only we could get there we would be safe.

Many animals were in the water already, but there was room for hundreds more. We put on an extra spurt, but we cubs were very tired and were getting rather too large for mother to carry. Soon the sparks were falling on us, and I felt almost suffocated by the smoke. My brother stumbled and fell, I ran on but mother stayed and lifted him, then I turned and between us we got him nearly to the lake.

By now the trees were burning all around us, and with a crash a burning pine-tree came down. I had barely time to leap for my life when another fell across my mother's back, pinning her down. Then the fire swept over them, and I was forced into the lake.

Three

After the death of my mother I naturally had to fend for myself. Of course, mother had shown me how to kill and how to hunt properly, so I managed fairly well for some time.

At first I only got rats and small deer. I also put up with lizards, but soon all food became very scarce as all the grass for the game had been burnt by the fire.

At first the larger animals moved south, and after them all the smaller ones, the process being gradual; but in about three weeks I decided to change my quarters, so early one morning I set off up the stream. After following it for five miles I found myself going up a considerable hill. At last I got to the top, and there I saw a large plateau stretching in a grassy plain in a circle of about three miles in diameter. Here I saw no traces of the fire whatever. But in about the centre of the plain I saw a number of things that resembled very large boulders, and there were creatures moving around them. Then the wind veered in my direction and blew their scent towards me, and I knew that they were men. I also caught the scent of goats and pigs, and I saw that there was a large herd of them in a small copse of trees about a quarter of a mile away.

As the wind was favourable I approached them, taking advantage of all the cover there was. I had very little difficulty in getting quite close. Then to my dismay I saw that there was a man with them.

Being very hungry I decided to take a risk, and as a small pig came unsuspectingly almost to my nose, I sprang on to his back, breaking his neck. Unluckily, the pig had time to squeal, and this attracted the man who, with a cry, picked up a stone. His arm went back and the stone flew towards me like a bird. It hit me on the nose and hurt me more than the bee-sting which I had had when a cub. It hit me on the same tender place which had never quite got better, and it angered me beyond words, and dropping the pig I charged, running low along the ground. Then I sprang straight at him.

With a shriek of fear he struck at me with a stick, and missed. We fell together, but his skull was cracked like an egg-shell. It was ridiculously easy to kill him.

Then something inside me made me want to roar, and tell the world that I had killed a man. So I roared for the first time. I was almost frightened at the sound I made, and the effect I made on the pigs and goats who had not already disappeared was magical. They ran for the boulders like the wind, and I never thought there was such speed in a pig until I saw them run that day. It was wonderful.

Then I looked down at the man. He had the strangest skin I had ever seen. It was loose and of all colours. Later I got to know that they were clothes, but at the time I was puzzled. He also smelt very strongly, so I left him and went to seek the pig which also smelt of men, but not so badly.

But I was hungry and made no bones about it. I dragged it under a bush and made a good meal, but before I had got half-way through the pig I observed a number of men coming out of the huts — for such were the boulders. It was evident that they were coming to investigate the cause of the sudden return of the flocks.

I saw that they were too many for me to deal with, so dragging the pig into some bushes, I made for a cluster of rocks which would hide me and yet allow me to see what was going on. Once among the rocks I was quite safe, for my coat matched the dull grey perfectly, so I lay in a sort of natural tunnel in which I was invisible. But through a small hole in the farther end I could see what was happening.

The men approached the body of the herdsman, which I had forgotten to hide. This seemed to anger them, and then they examined my tracks, and one old man, a hunter I believe, followed them as far as the place where I had left the pig. It was plain that these men were very foolish, for the wind was blowing from me to them. And if they had had any sense at all they would have smelt me at once.

They found the pig, or rather half of it, and set up a chattering like a lot of frenzied monkeys. They appeared more concerned about the pig than about the man.

Then they held a consultation like I have seen the monkeys do, all speaking at once.

Finally, however, two of them ran back to the village, and after about five minutes returned with five large animals that looked rather like wolves — I found out later they were dogs. The creatures were led to the place where the pig had been found, and they then picked up my track.

Slowly but surely they got nearer and nearer to my retreat, until they reached the first of the rocks. When they got as far as this I turned round in the tunnel and charged out. I took them by surprise, killing one dog and scattering the rest.

Once past the dogs it was plain sailing, for none of the men cared to follow me, even if they could. The dogs pursued me but had little chance of catching me, for though they could run nearly as fast as I, they could not keep it up. I shook off the dogs in about a quarter of an hour, all except one which was of a different breed from the rest, having longer legs and a slimmer body. After running at a breakneck speed for about four minutes, I suddenly leaped into the air, and on landing spread out all my feet and stopped suddenly. The dog could not stop and went careering on in front of me. Then in a few moments I had him pinned down, and despatched him at once. Then I made for the stream to put off the scent, and swam awkwardly down it for a little way.

On getting out I decided to go back to the old cave where I was born, but on reflection I thought that the cave in the side of the bank was more comfortable and nearer the herds. I went towards it, but I had forgotten the jackals who lived there, so I got a shock when on entry they mistook me for something small and set upon me. They soon discovered their mistake, however.

One fled for the stream, and reaching the bank he could not stop and plunged right in, nearly getting drowned. The other got his neck in the way of my teeth, so he made no more mistakes.

That night I slept well, but I woke feeling very hungry, and I thought of going up to the village again; but on reflection I decided not to, as they were sure to be waiting for me. So I decided to go up the mountain, where I knew there were plenty of ibex to be found, and also mountain sheep.

On my way up I passed the old cave. About three hundred feet above the cave the grass ended. Then I was in the part of the mountain which the ibex favoured, where I saw the tracks of a troop of about twenty of them. The tracks led upwards, and soon I found myself in the region where the snow began. I was on a ledge between a sheer face of rock and a drop of six hundred feet, a ledge about a yard wide between the bare rock and destruction. After I had got about one hundred yards, a part of the ledge on which my two hind legs had been resting gave way, and I had barely time to jump forward when about six feet of the thin ledge behind me fell down with a terrific crash.

Now it was impossible for me to go back, as I dare not try to jump, so I went on along the ledge. Soon I came to a corner, and round it I thought I saw one of the ibex disappear. The ledge became a little wider, so I put on a spurt, and rounding the corner I came face to face with a man.

Four

 The first to recover was the ibex, who turned and bolted towards the man, going straight between his legs. The man quickly recovered, and stood staring at me in terror. We stood thus for fully ten seconds, when an eagle above us screamed. The man started and looked up.

I saw my opportunity and took it. He only looked up for about a second, but I had time to knock him over the edge, and he went scrambling over the side. As he fell he threw out his arms and obtained a grip on the ledge, and there he hung.

Slowly the fingers began to slip, then his right hand lost its hold. His face assumed a horrible expression, and with a despairing cry he slipped, and when I looked over I could only see a heap, which didn't move.

Then, feeling rather sick, I followed the ledge along and at last came out on a high, bare plain, which was just below the region of snow, where a flock of mountain goats were feeding on the sparse vegetation.

I took advantage of all the cover that there was, but the goats were up-wind of me, so they got my scent before I had time to get very near. The sentinel gave the alarm, and off they went like the wind, going straight up the mountain-side on to the rocks that I couldn't reach. I caught a kid, however, and picking it up started the return journey. Before I had gone one hundred yards, however, I felt something like a sharp-pointed thunderbolt in my rear quarters. I turned to face this new enemy, and I saw that it was the kid's mother.

Dropping the kid I awaited the attack of the furious goat. I knew how strong the mother-love was in goats, so I knew that she would fight to the end.

She charged with her long horns lowered. I darted to one side, and with my paw I got in a blow which ripped her open to the shoulder-bone. Then wonderfully quickly she turned and gored me in the side. I leaped clear, and we stood panting and looking at each other for a second. Then I charged, and leaping on to her back I broke her neck.

Then I took up the kid again, and set off home, but by another route. On my way I found my wound was beginning to hurt, so I rested and licked it awhile, thinking as I did so that it was rather curious that I should be wounded by a goat.

I did not notice, however, that the sky was rapidly darkening, so when I started again I had to hurry, for I knew there was about to be a storm. Everything was very quiet, and I was vaguely alarmed, for I had not experienced anything like it before.

Then a cold wind began to hum through the pines, and I began to run as fast as I possibly could towards home. The pain in my side increased, and so did my terror, when I suddenly came within sight of the old cave.

Then the storm broke with a blinding flash of lightning and a formidable roll of thunder.

I was not more than twenty yards from the cave, but I was soaked through before reaching it. In the cave I found three hares and a faun, which all darted out when they saw me. Then I lay down and watched the storm.

That night I was lulled to sleep by the swish of the rain, which came down in sheets. When I awoke in the morning it was coming down as hard as ever; the dark sky was lighted by flashes of lightning, and the stream below was converted into a broad, roaring torrent.

I felt very hungry, and then I remembered the kid which I had put in the back of the cave. I dragged it out and made a good meal. He was very tender, if a little stale.

Then for the rest of the day I licked myself until my fur shone. There was nothing else to do except watch the rain. As the day wore on the lightning and thunder became worse, and several trees were struck. Forked lightning was particularly beautiful, as it played almost incessantly.

The night passed uneventfully. But in the morning I noticed that the stream was swollen to five times its previous size, and every now and then drowned animals floated down. I felt very unwell on account of my wound, which I could not easily get at to lick, and it had begun to fester and throb painfully.

Then suddenly the rain stopped, and there was silence like that which preceded the storm. Soon I heard noises as of animals and birds beginning to move again, and I got up to go down to the stream. Before I had gone far, however, my wound and my weakness through lack of food forced me to stop, and I lay down quite dizzy.

I soon was able to get up and go to the stream, which was very swollen. Here and there on the banks I could see drowned animals, such as goats, pigs and small deer, on whose dead bodies a number of jackals and hyenas were already feeding. But they fled on my approach.

I had a drink and felt better for it. Then as evening was coming on I ensconced myself in a heap of debris which had been washed down, in the hope that some deer or goats might come down to drink. My hopes were fulfilled before I expected, for no sooner had I hidden myself when a half-grown sambhur arrived. It had got separated from its mother in the storm.

I crept up behind it quietly, but it saw me, so I had to charge quickly. I broke its neck quite easily, but my wound had torn open, and I crept back to my shelter carrying the sambhur and bleeding profusely. I lay down for some time, very weak for want of food and loss of blood, and felt very dizzy and soon went into a kind of sleep. I dreamt for the first time. My dream was about the fire in which my mother perished, and I saw her quite plainly just before the pine killed her, and I felt very sad.

I woke with a start, and I observed several jackals in front of my shelter waiting for a chance to snatch my kill. They retreated hurriedly when I got up, but to prevent them taking it when I slept I made a meal there and then, and took the rest up to the cave.

My wound had closed, but I knew that any sharp turn or jerk would bring it open again, so I took quite a long time getting up there. I felt strangely weak and shaky about the legs, and I thought I was going to die. But after finishing the sambhur and having a good rest I felt much better, and next morning I was quite myself again.

I went down to the stream, which had subsided a great deal, and had a drink, which was against my usual custom, for I nearly always drank in the evening like the other animals. But the loss of blood had made me thirsty. After that I wandered down to the ford, which I could not wade as usual, so I swam it.

To my no little amazement, I found that if I kept my body under the water instead of trying to leap out after each successive stroke, I could swim quite well without much effort.

On reaching the opposite bank I struck into the forest, and wandered rather aimlessly away from my usual haunts. By noon I had gone farther than I had ever gone before, and when the sun became too oppressive I ascended a tree and rested in the crotch, about twenty-five feet from the ground; and I watched the insects and animals settling down for the midday siesta.

The monkeys made quite a noise for some time, even after the buzz of the mosquitoes had died down. Soon, however, everything was quiet, and I slept with the rest.

Five

 I was awakened suddenly by a stinging pain in the tip of my tail, which I switched up with a start.

Looking down I saw a large party of ants crawling up the bole of the tree, and the front ones had just reached my tail. They covered the whole of the front of the tree in a crawling mass, but in orderly ranks, guarded by warrior ants on either side, in the front and at the back. These warriors had very large jaws, out of all proportion to their size, and one of them was biting me. I whisked it off and went farther up the tree. Soon, however, the ants reached me again, and I went higher this time accompanied by four frightened monkeys and two small pythons.

The behaviour of these beasts reminded me of the way the animals acted when running from the forest fire. As a rule the pythons would have taken the opportunity of a meal in the form of the monkeys, to which they are particularly partial. However, they just ascended the tree in a panic-stricken sort of fashion.

Then one of the snakes half slipped on a rotten branch,

and did not recover till he had fallen nearly three feet. He fell in among the front ranks of the ants. In a moment he was covered with them. They swarmed over his body; he opened his mouth to hiss, and they poured down his throat. They bit away his eyecoverings and blinded him, and before two minutes had passed they had killed him and were taking him away in small sections to their nest.

When they had gone I thankfully descended. I could have gone no higher as the branches were getting thinner, and they would soon have broken beneath my weight.

Having descended I made a bee-line towards the village, as I was feeling too lazy to track deer. In about two hours I reached the edge of the plateau. The flocks were there just the same, but there were six men also.

Stealing up to the edge of the herd, I sprang up a tree with low-spreading branches. The leaves afforded excellent cover and shade, and I remained there unobserved for some time, awaiting my chance for an easy kill.

After half an hour had passed I dozed off to sleep. In a few minutes I was awakened by the sound of humans chattering below, one of whom was pointing to my tail, which I had allowed to drop during my sleep so that it hung down through the branches.

The chattering ceased and one of the men took a bright kind of stick, and resting it on his shoulder pointed it at me. Then there was a tremendous report and a flash of fire which frightened me so that I nearly lost my balance, and then something terribly hot hit me in the shoulder, making a searing gash right to my shoulder-blade.

After that I remember nothing but a blind, unreasoning wave of fury which overcame me, and confused shouts

– and my claws and teeth sank again and again in human flesh.

When I calmed down enough to stop the useless killing, I found myself alone covered with blood, with two dead men. I dimly felt sorry that I had needlessly killed these two useless things, for though I was hungry I could not bring myself to eat these smelly men.

I went to a small pond in the wood and had a drink. All the animals had disappeared, so I went downstream, homeward. On the way I was lucky enough to see a small pig which had wandered from the main herd. Fat and well fed, the pig could not run like a wild one, so I caught it with great ease.

I reached home, and while I was washing myself preparatory to eating the pig, I found that I had a large cut on my back, evidently from one of the sharp, shiny things which the men carried. It was not deep, however, and healed in a day or two. The pig, as I have said before, was fat and well fed – so I slept well. For three days I laid up in the cave, contenting myself with small deer that came down every evening to drink at the stream.

In this way I soon got over my wound, except for the old wound in my shoulder which left a permanent scar. I avoided the plateau for about fifteen days, but on the sixteenth I went up to the edge of the plain, and lying down in the rocks I formed a plan. After about a quarter of an hour I circled round the herds – always keeping up-wind of them, until I was within a furlong of the village itself, when I advanced towards the track which they always followed when going into the village. Here I concealed myself in some dense brushwood – awaiting their return.

———

My plan was this – when they were half way past me, I would spring out roaring, and in the confusion disappear with a buffalo calf, if I could get one, or at the worst a large pig.

I had not long to wait, and soon the foremost horned sheep passed me – but I let them go. Soon the men came, but they did not notice that the pigs and goats seemed a little frightened when they passed me. But the wind was blowing well in my direction, so they did not bolt or give notice that they sensed that I was around.

Soon, however, the pigs and sheep had all passed, and then the great water-buffaloes came by – first the bulls with their great needle-pointed curved horns and wicked-looking red eyes. I did not venture to pull one of these giants down in the sight of the rest.

For though the bulls might have stampeded, the cows would have killed me in an instant, for a buffalo cow with calf is easily the most dangerous beast in my fancy. So I changed my plan and waited for the stragglers.

The main body soon passed, and the stragglers began to arrive. I selected a half-grown bull buffalo and charged – roaring. In an instant all was pandemonium, and the main herd stampeded towards the village, which was what I wanted.

The calf seemed petrified with fear, and I sprang on to its shoulders, and in a moment my teeth had met in the back of his neck.

He fell, but from behind some bushes a small cow buffalo – his mother – came charging. I stood my ground over the little buffalo, being furious at my mistake.

When she was about six feet off I sprang, but not high enough, and she got in a blow with her horns which sent me three feet in the air. Luckily the points missed me, and I twisted in the air and fell on her back, and there I stayed. She dashed through the bushes trying to dislodge me, but I stuck on.

Soon, however, the loss of blood which was streaming from her sides weakened her, and as she slowed up I broke her neck, and she fell with a crash.

Slowly and stiffly I got up; my claws seemed on fire from the strain they had endured, and my back was scarred by the marks from branches.

Looking around I saw that we had left the village far behind, and I was near the great pile of rocks where I had been tracked by the dogs before.

I tried to drag my kill towards them, but I quickly realised that she was too heavy for me. I dragged her a little way, but after twenty yards I had to desist. Then taking her up again I succeeded in getting her to the rocks. The great weight was a reminder that I was not yet fully grown, for I remembered seeing my mother carrying a big buck sambhur with ease.

Once in the rocks I made a good meal, for I knew there was no time to lose. Running back after about half an hour, I picked up the little buffalo.

In the village fires were flaring and a terrific hubbub was going on. Taking it by the neck in my mouth and slinging the body over my shoulder, I set off at a rapid trot for home.

This time I did not attempt to cover my tracks by plunging into the stream.

Far behind me I heard the baying of the dogs, but soon I came to the rocky foot of the mountain, which I knew would leave no tracks.

Gaining home, I slept almost at once.

Next morning I wandered off towards the south until noon, when I slept as usual. Instead of a tree, however, I selected a broad slab of rock over a small stream — overhung by the branches of an aspen. Being tired I slept on and on, little suspecting the danger beneath me.

Six

I awoke with a start fairly late in the afternoon, with a sense of danger near me. Seeing nothing, I began to stretch myself and wash.

But I was interrupted by a low hiss, and turning I looked into the face of a large king cobra, which was coiled for a spring, not at me, however, but at something behind me, and towards the left.

Turning sharply, I saw a little brown man crouched like a monkey in some long grass. Then the cobra struck, its head shooting over my tail like a whip-lash. It missed, for the man had dodged to one side and had hit it on the back of the head with a bent stick, and the snake lay motionless on the ground.

All this only took about half a minute, however, but I had time to back out without being seen, for I had never seen any animal like this who could dodge the fastest thing in the jungle.

From my place up a tree which I climbed, I saw him follow my tracks round the rock towards me. Then I lost sight of him, but feeling uneasy I left my tree and concealed myself in the rushes.

Soon I saw him come out of the brushwood, bent double and staring around him. Then he saw a place where I had put my foot in a little patch of mud. He ran to it, and after inspecting it some time he rose with a little whistle of surprise, and disappeared again in the bushes.

Soon after that I came out, feeling hungry. As I have said before, the rock on which I had been lying was over a small pool, and now as it was evening I hoped that some game might come down to drink. So, hiding near the banks, I waited.

In about half an hour there came a sounder of pigs led by a vast boar. Having had some little experience of these boars I knew that it would be better not to touch him or his family, so I let them alone.

Then the pigs began to drink. A few minutes passed, and with a roar a large tiger leapt out of the bushes opposite to me, and the pigs scattered.

One little one ran straight to me, and I secured it without any noise. All the pigs fled except the boar, who stood facing the tiger who, after circling around for a moment, charged.

The boar with great speed leaped to one side, at the same time getting in a blow with his long tusks which opened up the skin from the tiger's shoulder to half way down the ribs. Then before he could recover the boar had swung round and gored him again.

The tiger roared and began to circle round slowly and cautiously – and then he leapt. The boar was too slow, and lost part of his right shoulder. The tiger retreated and continued these tactics for some time, circling and dashing in and back again.

After a while the boar was a sorry sight; all his head and shoulders were bleeding and the blood obscured his vision.

The tiger suddenly leapt in again, but he over-reached himself, missing his mark as he struck, and the boar, with a grunt, lowered his head, and with lightning speed ripped up the tiger.

As he fell, the boar with one great raking thrust completely disembowelled his adversary, who lay kicking on the ground. The boar drew off and soon the tiger's struggles ceased and he lay dead.

Then the boar crawled away into the bushes opposite me, and soon after I saw two jackals near the place. In a few moments five more had come, and from the sky the vultures and crows were coming.

Soon I had finished my pig, and I walked out into the open.

As soon as they saw me the cloud of crows and vultures rose and settled on all the trees around. I looked at the tiger's body and saw beside the main wounds innumerable others all over him.

Having inspected the tiger I went farther south on the trail of some deer. I followed this trail along through what seemed like a beaten track or path until I came to a kind of cross-roads, where another set of deer tracks converged on to the main one. Further along still, I found some more which led into it, and I could tell by the scent that I was coming near to the deer.

Then quite suddenly the sun set and the afterglow set in, and after about five minutes the darkness began to close in.

A month ago I would have been looking for a sleeping-place, but now, oddly enough, I took little notice, for I was growing up and knew that the hunting time for the big carnivores is the night.

I saw the fireflies dancing in among the grasses in front of me, and vaguely I wondered where they got the light from. As I travelled along the deer trails I began to notice a scent in the air which I did not recognise, and as I progressed the smell grew more powerful, until at last I knew I must be very near the beast, whatever it was.

Then breaking through some bushes (I had left the path in my curiosity) I emerged into a clearance, where I saw a huge black shape standing still in a corner.

It was an elephant, and what is more it was a rogue elephant, or a mad one which had been driven from the herd. It raised its trunk as it caught my scent, and seemed puzzled.

Then the moon rose and showed me up. He saw me, and I saw that his little red eyes glittered in the pale light, which also shone on his huge tusks. All at once the great beast came at me with its trunk curled in the air, as fast as the forest fire and as silent as a snake. With its great ears spread wide it was on me before I had time to spring properly, and I received a shattering blow in the side from the powerful trunk which knocked me into a thorn bush.

I roared with pain, but I had barely time to scramble to my feet when the elephant turned and charged again. This time I managed to claw my way on to his great broad neck, and there I endeavoured to tear him to small pieces.

I had reckoned without the trunk, however, which flicked me off like a mosquito, and I fell to the ground with a thump. Feeling very dazed as I struggled to my feet, I heard the elephant charge on for a little way. Then he stopped and, turning, began to search for me.

I kept quite still, hoping that he would miss me. As the elephant came nearer I noticed something moving in the bushes near me, and the elephant saw it too for he turned off towards it with a rush.

A large black panther leapt out into the clearing, his tail switching his sides.

I knew there must be something wrong with him. Then in the moonlight I saw that his flanks were full of arrows. The two mad beasts stood glaring for a second, and then the elephant, trumpeting shrilly, charged. The panther sprang straight up at his face, but was seized at once in a grip of iron by the elephant's trunk, whirled aloft, and dashed with a sickening thud against a tree. The elephant then knelt on the body, breaking every bone in it, and gored it with his tusks, which showed red in the moonlight.

I did not stay any longer, but slipped noiselessly away. The wind was blowing in my direction, and I knew that he would not scent me.

I quickly regained the path made by the deer, and feeling very stiff and bruised I sat down under the cover of a bush and licked myself all over, pulling out many thorns from my body, after which I felt better and continued to follow my original trail.

After some time I came to a large river where all the tracks disappeared, and I saw that the herds must have crossed here.

I did not feel up to crossing the broad stream, so I turned back along the path by which I had come until I came to another track which crossed the main one. This I followed up, and at last I came upon a sambhur doe sleeping; and creeping round a tree near her I climbed it, and I was able by crawling along an overhanging branch to spring straight on to her back, and I despatched her at once.

I made my meal where I was, and having gorged my fill I reascended the tree, and finding a comfortable crotch about twenty feet from the ground, I watched the glowing eyes of the jackals close in round the remnants of my feast.

Seven

Some weeks passed quite peacefully after my elephant adventure before anything noteworthy happened. I was living in my cave at the time and feeding to a large extent upon the villagers' herds.

They increased their guard, but the men were afraid of me, and most of them ran on seeing me; also, they had no sense of smell, and as they themselves smelt quite strongly I had a great advantage over them.

But they were able on their part to pick up stones and make them fly in rather a puzzling manner, though the worst of all were the arrows which I often broke off short, and the points remained in me and rankled.

At last it appeared that the head man of the village became so angry at losing his cattle that he sent for the white men who lived in a small town twenty miles south. He had asked them to kill a tiger, for none of them had seen me for any length of time. So when the beaters and elephants came upon me in a lot of elephant grass they were evidently surprised to find me so large (as I had been growing very fast and was as large as a very big tiger).

On seeing the elephants I was much alarmed, but seeing there was no possible means of escape I charged the nearest, hoping to take him by surprise.

I sprang high on to his shoulder, and there I saw the little brown man who had tracked me nearly a month ago. He struck at me with an iron rod, but missed, and I knocked him off the elephant's back.

Then I heard a terrific bang, and turning I saw another man in a kind of hut, and in his hands was one of the shiny sticks with which I had been hurt before.

This man was quite white, rather like a dead man, and behind him was another, pointing his stick at me.

I sprang at him. I saw the flash and heard the deafening boom again. Then something hit me on the top of my head, and the world seemed to spin round and I heard the trumpeting of the elephant very faintly, and then I remember nothing more.

When my sense returned I was stretched on the ground, and there was a circle of white men standing around me. One said: 'A queer sort of tiger, isn't it?'

'I think it's a sort of overgrown snow-leopard myself,' replied the young man who had shot me.

Then I moved and they were much alarmed. 'Look out — the things only stunned,' said one.

'Get those bear nets — take it alive,' rejoined another.

I half rose — giddy and sick, but a man behind me brought down the heavy end of a stick on my head, and I lost consciousness again in a world of stars.

When I came round again I was enveloped in yards and yards of stout net tied at the top with a rope. I kicked and bit at the nets, but it was of no use, so I stopped.

Some men approached me with long poles. I struggled

to get at them, but they were not in the least alarmed. And coming nearer they thrust the poles under the net, and each man taking hold of one pole-end they carried me roaring and struggling towards the place where the elephants were standing.

This caused me considerable alarm, but the elephants, who actually appeared to be obeying the men, took very little notice of me, except one of the little elephants who was trumpeting.

I was conveyed to a small thing that resembled a box mounted on circular discs which went round, and I afterwards found out it was a cart.

After a while I lay still, and after that I smelt some bullocks, which the men were driving towards me. Soon the cart began to move, to my surprise, for I saw no legs on it. However, the mystery was soon solved, for I twisted round and saw that the bullocks were dragging it along.

We soon came to a village, and hundreds of people came out to look at me. They retired hurriedly when I roared.

Soon they became bolder, and one young man got a long stick and poked me with it, and another threw a stone at me.

Presently, however, one of the white men came out of a hut and drove them away.

Then the journey recommenced, and I was jolted over about ten miles before we came to a halt again.

Night was approaching, and I was beginning to wonder if we would ever stop when one of the men who was leading the bullocks trod on a dust snake and expired on the spot, to my great glee.

The party stopped, and as night was falling they drew

up all the carts in a wide circle, in the centre of which the elephants and bullocks were put, evidently for protection against tigers or panthers, which were very abundant in this region.

Over my cart they fastened several logs, so that it was impossible for me to get out. However, I tried till morning, flinging myself against the sides and the logs, and I roared myself hoarse, so that the ten men who were posted by the cart appeared somewhat concerned for their own safety.

Once I cracked a board in the side of the cart and the effect was magical. Men left me in a body, going to the tents and huts which they had erected, and they set up a chattering which would have done credit to the largest band of monkeys.

Finally they came back with more pieces of wood with which they strengthened the sides of the cart.

When they had done this they retired still chattering.

When morning came I was very hot and tired, and when the cart began to move again I felt very bruised and battered, and as we journeyed until midday I was feeling remarkably savage when eventually we stopped in the street of a large village.

Here the party scattered, and I was driven with the elephants to the house of one of the white men, where many people came out to look at me. Soon the men with the poles reappeared, and after untying the logs they got me out. After carrying me past the house they went into a large courtyard, where they dropped me heavily and banged a huge door.

This courtyard was paved with stones and it had walls

on every side rising twenty feet. One of the walls was also the side of the house, and had holes in it, at all of which were faces of people looking at me.

I struggled with the nets for quite three-quarters of an hour with no success before I saw the gate open, and the young man whom I had attacked on the back of the elephant came in with a long stick at the end of which was a knife, which he stretched forward and with which after a few moments he managed to cut the ropes, after which he retired hurriedly.

In about five minutes I disentangled myself. After pacing round and round the enclosure I tried to jump the walls, but it was impossible; so after knocking myself about a good deal I stopped, feeling extremely angry.

Soon I saw some men at one of the holes and they were holding a small pig which squealed, which they lowered down with a rope, and it ran round and round my enclosure.

I killed it almost at once, and taking it to a dark corner I consumed it, as I had had no food for two days. After which I snatched a little sleep and then felt calmer.

I was soon awakened by the chattering of some monkeys on the walls, after which night fell and I dozed off.

I did not sleep at all well, however, and I dreamt of elephants and guns in which my mother seemed mixed up.

Just after daybreak a number of children began throwing stones from one of the holes in the wall, and this made me exceedingly angry, and roaring I jumped up at the holes. I had never jumped so high as I did that time, and although I did not actually reach the hole I alarmed them so that they did not appear again.

In about an hour I saw two men with a small pig again, which they lowered, which, however, was tied this time by one leg. I darted at it hoping to snatch it away before it had time to recover.

As soon as I reached it, however, a net fell over me which was drawn rapidly together by a cord from the bottom, and I was trapped again.

Eight

 Then the door of the courtyard opened and the brown men with their poles came in. They carried me through into the house along several passages and at length into a great hall down the sides of which many cages with animals were placed, and one of the animals saw me — it was a panther.

He roared and I roared back at him, and then a brown bear joined in, and in a few moments the whole place was in an uproar. But above all I heard the mocking bellow of an alligator.

They carried me to an empty cage and pushed me through the door, untying the net through the bars. I was between a bear on one side and a grey ape on the other, both of which renewed their noise immediately. I was almost too dispirited to answer, but I showed what I thought of them quite plainly.

Soon, however, the noises died down, and retiring to a heap of straw I slept, for I was quite worn out.

On the next morning I awoke with a start, expecting to see the sun as usual coming through the open door of my cave, but there was no light at all in the cold grey room, and I despaired of ever seeing the sun and feeling the cool wind again.

To pass the time I began pacing up and down my cage, up and down with just the same number of steps, and the monotonous regularity of the bars in front of me whichever way I turned appalled me.

My impotence and wretchedness filled me with a mad unreasoning rage, and I tore round and round the cage roaring like a mad beast.

The other occupants of the room were all aroused by the din which I made, and together we created a horrible uproar which, however, soon subsided, and I resumed my pacing up and down.

I noticed that the ape in the cage next to me was climbing up and down a rope and swinging to and fro. I stopped and watched him for a while. First he climbed up the rope, poked his hand out between the bars, and took some straw from a box which was balanced on the top of the cage. Then he came down again and put his handful on a heap which he had already collected. He did this several times until he had gathered enough to make a comfortable bed into which he burrowed, only to come out again in about five minutes and move the whole lot to another corner.

My attention was soon drawn from the ape as a man came in pushing a little cart in front of him, on which were some large pieces of meat.

When the man entered all the animals began to get very excited. They ran up and down and roared and growled. I saw the man take one of the pieces of meat and put it on an iron hook and thrust it into the panther's cage, then he shook it off. Then he passed down the line of cages, feeding all the animals. He began to get nearer to me, and I saw the bear in an absolute frenzy of anticipation. The man opened a little door in my cage and thrust in a piece of meat.

I hurled myself at the bars trying to get at him. The meat was hardly eatable, it smelt strongly of man and had hardly any blood in it.

The man passed on to the ape and gave him some food, then going back to the end of the hall he opened a little door in the back of the panther's cage by pulling a little rope in front. The panther went out at the back.

Having done this to nearly all the cages he came to the bear, who went out as if used to it; and soon his cage was clean. The man passed by me and went out at the end of the room, returning shortly with a little cart with bowls of water. When he gave me mine I hurled myself so violently against the bars that I knocked it into his face, and he hurriedly passed on to the ape.

Later the man brought in a great deal more straw, which he put into the cages. I could not see where the animals went, and most of them seemed to have so little spirit that none of them attempted to escape.

Three days passed and precisely the same thing happened. On the second day I ate my meat, which was not really so bad, but in the meanwhile my cage was becoming almost unbearable. On the third day, however, three of the white men came in and looked at all the animals, and when they came to me I recognised the man who had shot me, and I growled and spat at him through the bars. Then they all made a noise somewhat like that of a hyena just before a meal.

———

One of them called for the man who fed the animals, and they chatted together for some time, at the end of which he went out and soon returned with a little cart.

Then the young man — whom I shall call my master from now on — came up to my cage and made encouraging noises. But I was suspicious and growled unceasingly.

But he moved about in an even sort of way and didn't jerk about and alarm me. Then he opened the back of the cage and I slipped out and found myself in a pleasant open space about twenty-five feet square, which was completely enclosed by iron bars which prevented escape. It was carpeted by grass and had a large broken tree in the middle. I hadn't seen the sky for some days and I was remarkably pleased to be in the open with the sun shining on me again. Then in the longer grass at the end of the paddock I saw a very large rat, which I killed at once. It was much nicer than the bloodless meat which the men gave me.

Soon I heard a noise behind me and, turning, I saw the door rise. I was determined not to go back to the smelly cage, so I remained where I was. Soon the direction of the wind changed and I noticed a somewhat familiar scent which was that of an elephant. The scent became stronger, and an elephant with a man on its back came walking along the path in front of the open cages.

I thought of my first elephant, and perceiving that discretion was the better part of valour, I darted through the door, which banged behind me. Once in the cage I roared my defiance at elephants and the world in general. Then I remembered that the elephants were tame and obeyed the men, and this must have been a tame one.

I looked round the cage and saw to my relief that it

had been cleaned; some fresh water was in my trough and some straw had been thrown into one corner.

In the front of the cage, just between the bars, was a large piece of meat, and I saw that the bear was straining to get his paws through the bars to get my meat. Thinking that if I didn't get it at once I shouldn't get it at all., I took it to the back of the cage. It was very juicy and obviously was fairly fresh. Leaving the bear in a furious rage, with one paw firmly wedged between the bars of his cage, I consumed it slowly.

After eating half of the meat I washed and regained my sleek appearance. Then I lay curled up in the straw till night came, when I was awakened by the sound of footsteps.

I jumped up and saw my master approaching from the entrance; he was carrying a basket in his hands, and I thought that I smelt some animal.

He walked straight down the rows of cages until he came opposite to me, when he stopped and began to advance slowly. I growled.

He advanced to the front of the cage, making soothing noises. I retreated as far as possible feeling very apprehensive, and for a few moments he continued his silly noises. Then he took from the basket the carcase of a jack rabbit and threw it to me.

The sudden movement which he made in throwing it made me start; however, he made no other movement, and I think if I had not just had a large meal I would have taken it, but as it was I left it lying and snarled and spat at him.

Soon he left to my great relief, for my nerves were all on edge. After he had gone I ate the rabbit, which was very nice and did not smell of man as much as the ordinary food.

Then having licked myself all over very thoroughly, I paced up and down my cage for the best part of an hour. Then I lay down in the straw and slept for a while, only to be awakened by a sharp pain in the tail.

Jumping up, I saw that the ape had seized my tail and was pulling it. I jerked it away with a roar.

I mention this as an example of things which I had to put up with.

At length night fell and I slept well.

Nine

For many weeks my master continued to clean out my cage and feed me, and gradually I got so used to his presence that I even forgot to growl at him.

But when anyone else came, such as the native who cleaned the other cages, an ungovernable rage seized me and I hurled myself against the bars until I was sore.

One day my master stayed away, and then I realised how unpleasant it was to be without him to clean out my cage or feed me, for no one else would come near me. Next day, however, he returned and I had fresh straw and a clean cage; but when he was cleaning the cage and I was in the paddock I accidentally trod on a thorn which, with a small branch attached, had blown from a tree near by. With a snarl I broke off the branch and thought no more of it until the next morning, when my foot was painful and it made me limp.

But by midday the paw had become twice its proper size, and it throbbed very painfully. My master seemed to notice it, but he did nothing, as I was so angry that I would have killed him if he had entered my cage. By evening I felt so unwell that I did not even retaliate when the ape pulled my tail, who soon left me alone, or when the bear, nearly tearing himself in two with the effort, took the meat which I hadn't touched, having no appetite. I got very little sleep that night and I felt as if I did not mind what happened to me.

Next day my master did not come until the evening, when he stood outside my cage for some time making his usual silly noises. Then very slowly he opened the cage door and came in. I growled and half rose, but he showed no signs of fear and continued to approach. Then bending he lifted my paw. I growled, but I did not snatch it away as I hardly had strength to do so.

With a quick tug he pulled out the thorn – and I snarled at the pain, but I had the sense to see that he was trying to help me. Then he squeezed the paw gently and a lot of matter came out which at once relieved the pain. He tied a piece of cloth round it, and backed out of the cage, shutting the door.

Soon after that I dozed off into a refreshing sleep. I slept well all night, and next morning I woke up feeling much better and also extremely hungry. I could move about quite well, and after a time I worried the bandage so much that it came off, and I licked my paw, until I saw the native attendant coming in with his little cart, and I so far recovered my spirits as to roar lustily at him. Then I lay down in a corner of my cage where the sun could shine in and idly watched the ape swinging on his rope.

After about an hour I began to doze, but I was awakened by the sound of my master's voice, who was standing outside the cage with the basket which he always carried when he came to me. I was pleased to see him, partly because I knew that his coming meant a good meal and partly because I had some feelings of gratitude towards him.

He smiled and pulled the rope that opened the door at the back of the cage. I went out and heard him enter. Soon he had finished and I came in again, expecting to find my piece of meat. But there was not a vestige of food in the cage. I went to the front of the cage and there he stood outside with a piece of meat in his hand. He cut a piece off, and I wondered whether he were going to eat it.

He did not eat it, however, on the contrary he threw it through the bars at me. It landed at my feet. I sniffed it suspiciously, and then finding it all right I snapped it up. Then he threw another piece, this time a little nearer to himself, then another and another, until at last I was almost feeding from his hand.

Curiously enough I felt no alarm. There was one more piece, and this he held just between the bars and did not throw it. I wondered if he would suddenly hit me if I took it. Then I saw what a juicy piece it was and my hunger overcame my fear. With a quick snap I took it out of his hand and jumped back to the end of the cage.

To my surprise he showed no signs of anger, merely smiled, and withdrawing his hand went away.

I paced up and down for some time, thinking how curious it was that I should take my food from the hand of a man, and that I could have cracked that man's skull like a bird's egg, and that I should permit him to enter my cage to extract a thorn.

The idea, however, did not anger me as it would have

done a month ago. I merely thought it to be curious and dismissed it from my mind, and started to wash. I had little else to do.

Later in the day a diversion occurred in the form of a small grey monkey who had come in from one of the paddocks when the cages were being cleaned.

He had remained in the cage of a very old panther, who did not find him for some time. The monkey squeezed through the bars at the top of the cage and raced up and down the top of the other cages, until he came to the tank where a huge tame alligator was kept, almost opposite to me, where he missed his footing and fell. The alligator, who had been as still as a log all day, suddenly reared out of the water and caught the unfortunate monkey in mid-air.

It took several minutes for the pandemonium to die down again. Later on in the day I caught a large rat which was amongst my straw.

Ten

Six uneventful months passed, during which my master and I got to know each other very well. I for my part understood that he did not mean to hit me nor shoot me, and he was always very kind and fed me and cleaned my cage.

One day he came into my cage as usual and opened the door at the back. I went out, but instead of hearing the door close I turned round and saw to my surprise that he had followed me. In his hand was a large ball. 'Here, Cæsar,' he said (he always called me Cæsar). Thinking for a moment that it was alive, I pounced on it and caught it in my teeth. He seemed pleased, but when I began to worry it he made a noise and patted his knee.

He seemed to want something, but I could not quite understand what he meant, though I saw dimly that it was to do with the ball. He bent down and flicked his fingers, then in a flash I understood that he wanted the ball. Picking it up I took it to him and put it at his feet. He seemed pleased, and scratched me behind the ears, which I liked.

He took the ball again and rolled it to one corner of the enclosure, saying at the time, 'Fetch it, Cæsar.'

Seeing that he wanted me to get it again, I went and fetched it, but I thought that he was rather foolish to throw it away if he really wanted to keep it. Then after we had done this for ten times he observed that I was getting tired of it, and he went in to clean the cage while I lay in the sun pretending to be asleep, but really watching a large lizard creeping along in the grass. Its beady little black eyes were taking in everything. As soon as it came near enough I suddenly shot out my paw, but of course I was not nearly quick enough, and almost too quickly for my eye to follow, the lizard had darted across the enclosure and out between the bars, leaving only a little dust and its tail behind it.

I went back into the cage and saw that my master was tying the ball so that it was suspended about three feet from the floor. After he had gone I happened to bang against it, and seeing it swing as if it were alive, I turned to look at it and it hit me on the nose. I struck at it but it swung just out of my reach. I kept on patting it for some time, then I went to sleep for a while, but some mosquitoes woke me up. Feeling bored I patted at the ball again, just to see it swing, and back it came, and I pretended it was a living animal and growled at it.

On the back swing it seemed to be running away and I patted it again, this time from the side, and it went round on a circular course, like a bird; in fact, I was having quite a game with it when my master came back with my food and water, which was rather late. He also had a specially tasty little piece of meat, which I took from his hand as usual. Nearly every day for some months he had brought me some special thing, and on every seventh day a pig – a whole pig.

I started playing with the ball again, and I was amazed to find how fat and out of condition I was. In fact, after about half an hour's exercise I was quite tired and perspiring freely. However, it did me good, for I slept better that night than on any other occasion.

Next morning I was a little stiff, but with a fine appetite. Soon my master came and we went out into the paddock together. He had another ball, which he threw to me as before. In a short time we were having quite a game with it. He pretended to throw it one way and threw it another. I pretended to be very angry and growled. In the end I unfortunately bit the ball in two. So he went in to clean my cage.

While he was doing this a small bird settled on the ground near me, and I tried to catch it but I was too slow. Then I saw how fat I was really getting, and I decided to exercise my body more by means of the ball. So when I got into my cage about half an hour later I knocked the ball about quite energetically, and by midday I had invented a game. I stood on the side of a crack in the stone floor of my cage and the ball hung just over it, and if on the back swing it got past me, it had escaped – if not, I had caught it.

During the next three weeks I learned how to bring the ball when I was told. We had long games with the ball sometimes, and I became very adept at catching it. As the days wore on I began to look forward to the time when he came to feed me, and I was quite anxious if he was late; and I also became so used to my cage and ready-killed food that I hardly believed that I was the

---

same panda, who could pull down a water buffalo and think nothing of it. I do not believe that if at the time I had been set free I could have supported myself comfortably.

One day when I was in my paddock, as the door had been left open all day, the air suddenly became colder and the sky dark, and I had a horrible feeling that something terrible was going to happen. The other animals who were also in their paddocks (as their cages were being cleaned) seemed very frightened. The bear next to me started running round and round uttering a curious whimpering noise, and on the other side the ape was leaping about and chattering as if demented. Everything was as still as death, not a breeze enough to move the aspen trees on the path outside, and not a sound other than that of the animals. Then all at once the sun seemed to go out like a dead firefly and a chill that sent a shiver down my back came with its going. Now all the animals were quiet and not even a gnat buzzed, and in the distance I heard a dog howling. One would have thought that the world was dead.

In a few minutes my master came out, and after looking up to the sky for a few moments he came over to me and put his hand over my eyes and stroked me. I was badly frightened and trembling, so I snuggled my head under his arms, and he said in an even voice: 'Keep calm, old boy – it's only an eclipse.'

I did not know what he meant, but anyhow it was very soothing. In a few minutes after that the sun seemed to light up again.

Eleven

So far I have only mentioned the pleasant side of my life in captivity, but there was quite another side.

Can you imagine the utter dreariness of the long hours between the times when my master came and fed me and the night? If so, you will be able to understand my intense hatred for all men, except my master and a few others.

Men had taken me from my home, from the jungle with its infinite variety of life and colour, and had put me in a cage with bars and a cold stone floor. A paddock or small plot of withered grass was my jungle and the barred cage was my lair.

For a flowing stream to drink from I had a small stone trough, and instead of the pleasure of tracking, stalking and then killing my prey, I was given at a regular time every day a smelly, stale and bony lump of flesh with no blood in it.

That which I missed most of all was the killing of my own food. It is true that I was always given enough. But what could compensate for the thrill of the charge, and then the last wild gallop before I reached its neck and it fell dead? What could rival the warm blood and juicy meat of which I was particularly fond?

However, on the whole I was not too unhappy, and the ball which had been hung up was a great consolation, and in a few weeks I knew every curl that it would make.

My dislike of the brown man who cleaned the other cages grew in intensity as time wore on.

One day after my master had fed me and cleaned my cage this little hyena of a man came with a long slender stick of bamboo and tormented me with it. In vain I tried to catch it and crush it to pieces, for I could not move with any rapidity in the tiny space I had, and he lashed me again and again with it, laughing all the time. I hated that mocking laugh, which was as if a hyena had got into a man's body.

At another time he snatched my pig from my cage, having driven me into a corner with a spiked iron rod. As I have said, my master brought me a pig every seven days, and I looked forward to this as they were always very fresh and tender. Besides, I had always been very partial to pig.

At another time he purposely upset my water, so that it ran out of the cage. He always did these things after my master had gone, so as not to be found out. I was always hoping that my master would come back and catch him.

As the months drew into a year I became very attached to my master, who seemed to understand me and I him. He also seemed to know how I felt and behaved accordingly. For instance, if I was feeling poorly he would sit down and stroke me quietly behind the ears and talk to me; or if I was full of spirits we sometimes pretended to fight. It began by my refusing to give up the ball with which we often played, and then he pretended to be very angry and rolled me over on my back; and I roared and snarled as if I would eat him, while he rolled me over and over as if I was a little cub. As for hurting him, I would have perished before doing so.

He taught me to obey him and, among other things, to carry and fetch, and to even leave my food when he told me. I could not understand why he made me do this, but there was a reason.

One day he brought into my cage a steel chain and a collar of thick leather. The leather collar had a leather buckle which fixed it to the chain. He opened it and calling me to him fastened it round my neck, and we went out into the paddock where he fastened the chain to it.

At first I disliked it, but within two weeks I had become quite accustomed to it. He also trained me to stay still and not move until he called me.

One day when he had finished the cleaning of my cage he fastened the chain on as usual, but instead of going out into the paddock, to my great surprise he opened the cage door and led me out. At first I did not like to come, but when he said 'Come on, Cæsar,' and tugged the chain, I jumped down to the floor by his side.

How curious it was to feel different ground under one's feet, for in one year I had grown to know every stone in the floor in my cage and almost every blade of grass in the paddock.

My master led me down the passage between the cages, and out at the entrance and through two rooms, and out into a large enclosure in which there was a large stretch of green, very short-cropped grass. The walls of this pad-dock were made of brick, and they were about ten feet high. At the foot of each of these walls there was a space in which the earth had been turned up and flowers were growing in orderly rows.

I wondered how they got there, and I came to the conclusion that the ants must have put them there, for the ants are very fond of going about together in lines. Also I had seen when turning over an ant-hill in search of a rat that the ants had several of the small things from which the plants grow stored up.

I did not have much time to wonder, however, before my master said, 'Here, Cæsar – meet my wife,' and turning I saw a female who evidently was my master's mate. I growled at her.

But he stopped me and said, 'Down, old boy.'

The female was without fear, and put her hand on my head, and at once I felt that she was friendly towards me. My master said, 'This is your mistress, Cæsar,' so hereafter I shall call her my mistress. Then my master took the chain from my collar and the ball from his pocket, with which we had a fine game in which they threw it from one to the other and I tried to catch it.

After we had finished my mistress sat down and made a great fuss of me. I saw that my master was pleased so I permitted her to stroke me to her heart's content. Besides, it saved me the trouble of a wash. Soon he put the chain on me again and we went back to the cage.

After he had gone the native whom I hated came with his bamboo rod. Inserting this through the bars he suddenly hit me on the nose. The blow stung and I roared.

This is what he wanted, and, laughing, he struck at me again.

Leaping to the back of the cage I observed that my master had left his hat on the floor. The man had not seen this, however, and continued to torment me, while I hoped against hope that my master would come back for it.

Soon I saw the door open as he entered and, roaring, I hurled myself against the bars to attract his attention. Just then the wretched man gave me a particularly vicious crack.

In a few strides he reached the man, and seizing him by the shoulder, he said in a quiet tone: 'What is the meaning of this?'

The man said something which I did not catch. My master with great speed drew back his fist and dealt the man a blow on the jaw, knocking him off his feet into a corner. I thought that my master would now kill him, but he let the man lie. Then he came into my cage, and after giving me the cane, which I tore to fragments, and stroking me, he took his hat and left.

Soon after this two natives came and took my tormentor away, who was almost stupefied but had just enough energy to shake his fist at me as he was taken away.

Next day another native cleaned the cages out, but he kept clear of me, to my very great content.

Twelve

 A few days later my master took me into the garden again, where I saw his two young children, which were quite like him, only very small. They smelt the same. I was very proud that he should trust me so much and determined not to hurt them, for evidently he liked them, though they would have made a tender and juicy meal.

My mistress stood guard over them and appeared very anxious, very like my mother was over me. They were not in the least afraid of me, to my surprise, and made rather pleasant gurgling noises.

Then my master took one of them in his arms and held it quite near to my face, and it chuckled, putting one of its podgy hands on my head, and I realised that these were quite pleasant little creatures. Very soon, however, they were removed and my master and I went through the garden gate. We emerged on an open court-yard in which there were several stables in the walls, all of which were empty except one, and from this I caught the scent of some animal that I did not know.

Then my master attached the end of my chain to a

ring in the wall, and said very slowly and impressively: 'Stay there, Cæsar'; and I knew from long weeks of training what he meant.

He had taught me to obey him absolutely, and I would have as soon thought of flying as of disobeying. Then he went to the occupied stable and led out a great beast like a buffalo, but taller and less thick. Its tail was composed of long hairs and its head was bent at right angles to the neck and it had no horns. This extraordinary animal was evidently tame.

On seeing me it reared up and made a loud noise, and I growled, but my master said: 'Be quiet, Cæsar.' The animal would not be calmed, so he got it back with difficulty to the stables. Then he came to me, and after he had unfastened the chain, he said:

'Well, Cæsar, and what do you think of my horse?'

I did not understand what he said, but afterwards he said 'horse' a great many times, so I concluded that the creature was called a horse, and I wondered what it was for.

When we reached the cage I went in as usual after he had removed the chain, and he remained a little while outside talking to me. I did not understand what he said, but I liked the sound of his voice. The word horse kept re-occurring, and I thought he was trying to make me understand something about it. Although I went over all my ideas of his words I could not get his meaning. Soon he went away and left me to puzzle over this animal.

Before nightfall I came to these conclusions:

First, the beast was tame;

Second, my master had shown signs of liking it;

Third, he had stopped me from hurting it by chaining me up.

———

On the following morning after cleaning the cage he took me to the courtyard, and after fastening my chain to the ring in the wall he brought out the horse, and after a while he took it back again, and then we went back to my cage. This happened on the next day and on the one after that, and so on until I lost count.

At the end of all this time the horse and I got quite used to each other, and at last I comprehended that my master wanted me to like the horse, and he also wanted the horse not to be afraid of me. Then after a month had passed the horse didn't fear me any longer, and I no longer wanted to kill and eat it.

Then one day my master brought out a kind of seat made to fit the horse's back, and after strapping this on he brought from the stable a piece of metal and some leather thongs. The piece of metal he passed under the horse's tongue, and the horse, who seemed quite used to it, stood still. Then to my amazement he jumped on the horse's back, which by means of the leather straps was entirely under his control. Then they went out of the gate, and he said to me:

'Stay there, Cæsar.'

Soon he returned, and after he had put the horse back we went back to my cage.

One day in the next week we went out through the garden to the horse's stable, and when my master had put on the harness as he called it, he took a longer chain and fastened it to my original one; then he mounted the horse, and taking my chain in his hand he rode out of the gate and I followed. At first the horse was very excited and tried to get away from me, but he soon calmed down, as my master spoke to him soothingly. We emerged on to a grassy plain, extending in short bushy folds as far as the eye could see.

How good it was to have the crisp grass under my feet and to see an uninterrupted horizon all round. As we went I reflected on the remarkable conditions under which I was existing, and observed to myself how strange it was that anyone like myself should be found fastened by a chain to an animal of which he should be making a good meal, and obeying every word of a man seated on the back of this horse.

My reverie, however, was cut short by a hole in the ground, in which I half tripped. My master laughed, and saying 'Come on, old boy – keep up,' made the horse gallop, and we tore along at top speed for a while, which was very pleasant because for a whole year I had not really exerted myself. Having covered three-quarters of a mile we stopped, and I looked at the horse with new respect for it did not appear in the least fatigued, whilst I was panting and sweating a little.

Meanwhile my master had climbed a tree, very clumsily I thought, and was looking round and round as if search-ing for something, and he came down looking as if he had not found it. Just then the wind changed a little, and I smelt game. My master must have seen it, for he looked pleased and pointed in its direction.

Then an antelope came into sight, feeding on the short grass, and my master crouched down at once so as not to be seen. Then he unfastened my chain and said to me: 'Fetch it, Cæsar.' I understood what he meant and determined to show him what I could do. I was off in a moment, wriggling through the bushes in my most skilful fashion. At first I was so clumsy that I was afraid the creature would see me, but soon all my old cunning returned and I got within killing range.

The antelope saw me and I charged. Though the beast was very fleet, and I had to exert myself to my utmost speed, I soon secured him. Having broken its neck, I began to lap up the warm blood; but in a few moments I was checked by hearing my master's voice calling: 'Leave it, Cæsar.'

Thirteen

Looking up I saw him standing about twenty yards away, looking at me steadily.

I thought: 'Why should I give up my kill to this man?' Then a remembrance of all his past kindness made me hesitate to disobey; but a smell of warm blood was wafted up from the antelope and almost killed my better feeling.

Then the habit of implicit obedience which I had formed came uppermost, and I picked up the animal and going to him laid it at his feet. He did not do much; he just said 'Good, Cæsar,' and patted me on the head, but I felt amply repaid for my sacrifice.

After this he picked up the antelope and went back to the horse which had been tied to a tree. Having slung it on to the horse's back, he mounted, and we went back to the house. When he had put the horse back into its stable we went back to my cage, and my master gave me a large piece of the antelope's shoulder, and I remembered that I always used to begin my meal at the shoulder of my prey instead of at the haunch, as I had seen some animals doing.

———

After I had eaten every scrap I paced up and down my cage pondering over the curious chain of events which had made up my life so far, and I wondered why I did not escape when I had the chance. In a way I was glad that I had not, but on the other hand I thought how pleasant it would be if I were back again in my old cave where I was born and going wherever I wished and feeding at my own time. But on reflection I thought it would be even better if my master were with me.

My thoughts occupied me until nightfall, when my tail was suddenly seized by the ape, who had thrust his hand through the bars of both his cage and mine and got a grip on my tail when I turned during my walking up and down. I tried to jerk it away, but the ape had a firm hold, so I whisked round and before he could withdraw, my teeth had sunk to the bone in his arm.

Pandemonium ensued, and the ape raced round and round his cage chattering and shrieking. After about ten minutes he burrowed into a large box of straw at the back of his cage, from which he did not emerge for a whole day, but gave out dismal howls and moans which interrupted my sleep somewhat.

In a few days' time he was moved up the row away from me, and a cage with a little mongoose, who took no notice of me, was put in his place.

In about a week's time my master took me out again. This time, however, we met a native who fled towards the village. I set off after him with a roar, but the combined strength of my master and the horse pulled me up. My master appeared very angry, and I sulked for a short while, but I soon recovered my spirits, observing to myself that one man did not matter, and anyway he would not have tasted nice. I suppose my master felt bound to protect his own kind, but at the time it seemed rather unreasonable to me.

We went on and on, past the place where I killed the antelope and about ten miles south-east until we came to a place which my master and the horse seemed to know. Here we stopped, and as we were all a little fatigued we had a short rest.

Then my master took the horse to a small hut which was hidden among some trees and shut him in. I suppose this was as a protection against wild animals; then he led me by my chain and we went down to a small pool, where I saw some fairly fresh pig-marks. Here my master looked round for some time and at last found some of the more obvious tracks, and I wished that I could have communicated with him in some way to make him understand the bent pieces of grass, a little splash of mud on a stone and, above all, the faint smell of pig in the air, so that he could translate all the signs that pointed to the fact that pigs had been there a little while ago.

But it was no good. All my growls and scratchings he mistook for signs of pleasure, so soon I gave it up.

When he had found several footprints my master took me to them and, selecting a very large one, said: 'Fetch him, Cæsar!' I felt a slight sinking of the heart as I saw that it was that of a remarkably large boar, probably the chief of the sounder. But nevertheless I followed the trail along a stretch of very difficult country, all stony with only a sprinkling of grass here and there.

My master followed, still holding the chain, but soon he took it off. He made such a noise in walking and he smelt so strongly that I was afraid we would never get near enough to catch any of them.

However, things turned out better than I had hoped, for after not more than ten minutes of stony ground we reached a lot of long green grass which held the scent, and I could see that the grass had been crushed in places.

Now I went very slowly, for as the scent was very fresh here I felt that we might come on them suddenly. We crept on through the grass, my master crawling with his hands like a rational beast, and we soon found the pigs in a grove of bamboo, eating the tender shoots.

The great boar was feeding with the rest, and as the sentinel pig had not seen us, I hoped to be able to dash in and kill the boar in the confusion.

Then my master sneezed, and in an instant the fat sows and the tender sucking pigs were in full flight. Only the boar stayed to block my path, to let the others escape. He did not think that I was after him, for who would prefer a tough boar to a fat and tender sow?

However, I charged in directly and got my shoulder laid open for my folly, and remembering the tiger whom I had seen killed before, I contented myself with circling round and looking for an opening. I rather wished that my master had had better eyes when he picked out this pig's footprints, but for all that it promised to be a grand fight.

Suddenly I saw an opening as the boar had turned a little too slowly, and I darted in, rolling him over and tearing his flank in my endeavour to pin him down. But in a flash he had whipped round his head and with his tusk had cut into the pad of my right forepaw. Then as I released my hold he rolled over and got on his feet again, aiming a wicked thrust at my unprotected stomach.

With a roar I sprang out of range, and as he was carried on a little way by the impetuosity of his thrust, I leaped in and gave him a blow which smashed his skull in, and he fell kicking feebly. But he was dead almost as soon as he touched the ground.

I am glad that I was able to finish him when I did, for as I was lamed by the cut in my paw I could not have lasted very much longer.

As soon as the boar fell my master came from his hiding-place and walked towards the boar, saying, 'Leave it, Cæsar – good boy.'

This time I did not hesitate, and left it at once, and went over to him, looking up for approval.

On seeing my blood he knelt down on the grass and took up my injured paw, talking kindly all the time. The place was bleeding fast and hurting abominably, so he tore a large piece from his clothes and wrapped it round the wound. I tried to walk on the paw, but the pain made me desist. Meanwhile my master was covering the hog with a heap of stones. Evidently he did not mean to carry it with him.

Then he set off towards the hut where we had left the horse, and I walked slowly on three legs, and he tried to help me along, but the march back to the hut was the slowest and most painful that I have ever made.

At last we reached it, just after the sun had set.

A panther was prowling around, attracted no doubt by the scent of the horse, which I could hear snorting angrily. The panther cleared off, however, at our approach. The horse, being down-wind of us, caught our scent, and I heard him whinnying with pleasure.

On reaching the hut my master went in, and after searching round for a little while, he brought out a metal box, from which he took a blue bottle containing some brown fluid, which he poured on to my wound.

It stung horribly. At first I thought that he was playing a trick on me, but the thought was foolish, so I dismissed it from my mind at once. Having done this he bound it up again and reentered the hut and brought out the chain, with which he tied me up to a post, and then he went back to the hut saying, 'On guard, Cæsar.'

Fourteen

 I understood what he meant and I prepared to have a sleepless night. I felt sure that he would not have said 'on guard' if he had known how tired I was, and all night I paced up and down, and sometimes lay down, but I never went to sleep, in case a panther, or perhaps a leopard, should come along.

Once or twice I heard the coughing roar of a panther, and again I caught the scent of a leopard, but neither of the creatures attacked me, for which I was extremely thankful, as I could not have held my own against either of them with my paw in the state that it was.

But at last morning came, with one of the most beautiful sunrises that I have ever seen.

Then presently my master woke up, and after harnessing the horse, he set off towards the place where we had left the boar. After taking my chain off, and telling me to have a good sleep, he shut me in the hut.

I heard the noise of the horse die away in the distance and then I went to sleep. Hardly had I closed my eyes, however, when I was awakened by a soft hiss, and starting up I saw a large sized python surveying me with glittering eyes.

I jumped up, and either my eyes were deceiving me or something, for between me and the terrible snake I clearly saw my mother. She looked pale and smoky, but perhaps that was the sleep in my eyes, and I thought I saw her baring her teeth in a snarl at the snake.

The snake glided out of the door, which was slightly ajar.

Then the thought that perhaps she had lived through the fire flashed through my mind, and I started forward with a purr of delight to meet her, but to my horror and amazement there was nothing there. I had gone right through her.

Turning round – I thought perhaps she was hiding, but after searching the hut I was convinced that I must have imagined the whole thing, in a sort of waking dream. But there were still the snake marks in the dust on the floor to explain away, but not the faintest scent of her or a footmark except my own was in the hut.

Greatly puzzled by this incident, I walked up and down trying to solve the mystery, but then almost at once my master came in, with the body of the boar, which he had fetched with the horse.

I suppose he put down my agitation to my wound.

As the cut was practically closed, we set off for the house, and going rather slowly we reached it by midday.

When I was going to my cage I trod on a sharp flint, which opened the cut again, so feeling rather angry and upset I let my master bind it up again, but I soon worried the bandage off as I was feeling rather peevish.

Until nightfall I wondered how to explain the fact that

the snake had not appeared at all alarmed at my mother's presence.

All my explanations to myself that it was a dream were swept away by the fact that the snake marks were so obvious that there was no mistaking them.

As I was unable to come to any satisfactory conclusion, I dismissed the matter entirely from my mind and went to sleep.

Early next morning I was awakened by my master calling to me from outside the cage, and he was carrying what seemed like the shoulder of the boar, which he gave to me. After I had consumed it he came into the cage and inspected my paw, which was healing nicely.

After this I went out into the paddock while he cleaned my cage. My master did not take me out again for nearly two weeks, during which time my paw had quite healed and I was feeling very fit.

Then one day a lot of white men came and looked at me. My master was with them, and he brought one old white man into my cage. I was feeling very happy and good-humoured, so after the stranger had got over his first fears I permitted him to stroke my head, very nervously, with the tips of his fingers, standing as far off as possible, while my master was encouraging him. I looked round and caught my master's eye. He smiled and nodded and our amusement was mutual.

Soon the little man became rather boring, and as I wanted to play with my master, I decided to get rid of him, so suddenly springing up I gave a frightful snarl, showing all my teeth, and he left quite hurriedly.

After he had gone my master burst into a roar of laughter, and after producing the chain, we went to the garden, where he told me to stay while he harnessed the horse.

I had just jumped up into the lower branches of a tree which was in the corner of the garden, so as to be in the shade, when I heard the voice of our visitor raised in a somewhat agitated manner. Evidently he was walking down the gravel path outside which led to the garden gate.

Then I heard it open, and into the garden walked my mistress and the old man, who was saying, 'I tell you the beast is not safe. It will be escaping some day and eating somebody.'

Then I jumped down from the tree to meet my mistress, who always made a fuss of me. The old man let out a bellow like a bull buffalo in pain and disappeared with remarkable speed, leaving a cloud of dust.

My mistress appeared a little flustered at first by her guest's curious behaviour, but just then my master reappeared, and they talked together, and then they both laughed, and my master and I went to the horse, which was getting impatient, and then we went out on to the plain.

This time, however, luck seemed to have deserted us, for in a whole day we sighted only one antelope, and I bungled the stalking of it so badly that it was able to get down-wind of me, and it was off at once.

I thought that I could run it down and set off after it, but I failed dismally, and after I had gone nearly a mile at top speed, and in the end had lost it, I turned and went back to my master, who consoled me with a large piece of the meat which he was eating from a bag.

It had an extraordinary taste, rather interesting, but

like no animal that I had ever killed, and there was no blood in it at all. I afterwards found out that men have a curious way of putting their meat over a fire and destroying its delightful original flavour by many quaint devices. Why they did this I could never discover.

Then after the midday siesta we searched for game and followed up many trails but with no success. At last we heard a frightful noise coming from behind a small hill about half a mile distant.

We reached it in a few minutes. Meanwhile the extraordinary noises increased in volume. They mystified and frightened me, and I was wondering what strange beast this might be which howled so horribly, when suddenly we came upon a white man squatting in front of a box which gave out these terrible roars and whines. The beast was evidently imprisoned within it.

The man was not in the least disconcerted by our sudden appearance and continued to belch out smoke from his mouth at intervals. Then he said to my master in a curious kind of voice: 'Say Bo – taking the cat out for a run?'

My master laughed and they talked for a little while.

Then he tethered the horse, and together they went over to a kind of cart which was standing about twenty feet away.

Up to this time I had been so utterly petrified with amazement that I had stood perfectly still by the horse, but then the animal in the box gave a particularly violent and high-pitched howl which hurt my ears, so I roared at it to silence it.

My master laughed and then said to the man: 'I'm afraid Cæsar has no ear for radio music.'

Then the stranger came over to the box and either killed the beast within it or something.

Then my master and the stranger began to do something to the cart. At first I thought that the man had lost the bullock for his cart, but when it suddenly gave out a menacing roar I altered my opinion and roared back at it, thoroughly frightening the horse, who plunged and kicked till my master came over and calmed him.

Soon after this we left the man to his roaring and howling companion and went homeward. Before we had got far, however, I heard the cart give a violent roar which I answered, but it easily outroared me, and it never seemed to pause for breath. When I began another roar my master stopped me by saying, 'Perhaps motor-cars don't agree with you, Cæsar – but you needn't tell the whole world about it.'

Fifteen

 For the next months we did a lot of hunting with various success, mostly the smaller antelopes, who sometimes came quite near the house.

Once I killed a small Nilgai or blue bull, after a struggle in which I got rather nastily gored, but my master intervened and shot the creature with his revolver.

During this time I saw quite a lot of his children. They grew rapidly, and I liked them almost as if they were my own cubs. But one day I missed them, all except the smallest, and then I remembered having seen them start on a journey.

My master seemed rather silent and sad after they had gone, and when my mistress and the youngest went a week after he became quite melancholy, and spent most of his time with the horse and with me, sometimes going great distances up to the mountains, where I caught some fine ibex and bharals and we saw some red pandas.

My master always appeared very surprised at the way I could follow even the fastest in this very rocky and dangerous country, but I thought it was scarcely surprising. Most of my food during my life had been derived from mountain goats and wild sheep, so that I was adept at hunting them.

Speaking of red pandas, I have seen many more of them than of my own type, which is so much larger than they are.

Besides, who would have a silly red coat instead of a clean white one, with such fine black ears?

My indignation was great when my master caught and tried to tame a nasty smelly red panda, spending quite a lot of time with it instead of with me.

However, one day it poked its head through the bars and made foolish noises at me, trying to make friends, no doubt. But, to punish its impudence, I bit its head right off, and so stopped its idiotic chauntering.

My master was very angry and took no notice of me for three days, but I had the satisfaction of knowing that he could no longer like the red panda.

As I have said, my mother was a very large snow-leopard, and this accounts for the fact that I was growing so very large. Also, my legs, unlike those of most great pandas, were growing quite long, and I could run very fast.

About this time the spring was coming on and my summer coat was growing. I noticed a lot of blackish spots on my new fur which I thought greatly enhanced my appearance.

A week after I killed the red panda my master took me out hunting again. This time we went on for four days right up to the foothills of the great range of mountains, which I had seen from my cave and which was about eighty miles to the west.

———

After we had stayed there for two days, hunting sha and bharal, we ascended half-way up the nearest of the mountains. It was hardly a mountain, but really only a large foothill, being the top of a long ridge, which extended right and left, before we came to the real heights. We left the horse tethered near the tent in which my master always slept.

On reaching that part of the mountain where the snow always lay I killed an ibex, which my master skinned and cut up, putting the very best pieces into his knapsack and giving me the rest. Then we went still higher up, and I noticed my master was breathing with difficulty. So we stopped, and after looking all round at the vast extent of land below us, we began to descend. I stayed behind, finishing the last pieces of the ibex, and after a few minutes my master turned and called me.

He did not appear to be able to see me until I moved, and for the first time I saw the use of my white coat, which made me quite invisible against the snow. After about two hours we reached the horse, which was feeding on some of the scanty grass which was the vegetation. He was pleased to see us, and, as he had broken his rope, he trotted up to my master, who patted his neck, and I felt rather jealous but did not show it.

When night fell my master made a fire and cooked the pieces of ibex in a pot full of melted snow.

Then next morning he put the tent down and we all ascended the mountain side. The horse was a lot of trouble, but at last we got about half-way up. He put the tent up again behind a huge boulder where there was no snow. It was hard for him to fix the tent pegs, but at last he found a patch of ground with a little grass on it.

———

Soon he had a fire on the bare rock, where he cooked some more of the ibex, some of which he gave to me.

Later in the day he shot a goat (which I had missed) which had darted up a pinnacle of rock. This was the most remarkable piece of rock which I had ever seen, jutting straight out into the air over a precipice of about two thousand feet. The goat, on being shot, bounded into the air and luckily fell our side of the precipice.

As the cold was intense my master made a coat from the skin of this goat and the ibex, which he wore with the fur inside. At the time I remember I thought human skin must be very poor protection against the cold.

On the next day, as I was following a very large goat up a sharp incline towards the peak, it suddenly disappeared from view behind a rock. In a few minutes I had reached the place, but the goat was nowhere to be seen. Then I observed a narrow fissure in the mountain side through which it must have gone. I thought I had him now for certain, as in his terror he had fled into a blind alley.

This was not so, however, for on investigation the fissure proved to lead into a roughly circular tunnel, down which I could dimly see the goat.

Its hoof-beats echoed and re-echoed till it sounded like twenty goats. I followed it for some way, but it seemed to know the twists and turns of the tunnel, and after turning a corner, before I had time to see where I was going, it darted off into a side turning leading off the main one.

I ran on for some little way and passed several tunnels which led off the one I was following. I think I passed five before I came to a place where the main passage split into four. Rapidly selecting one, I darted down it and charged full tilt into a very chilly and deep stream. Scrambling out I pursued my course until I realised that the goat must have escaped me.

I began to retrace my steps, and after crossing the stream I came to the place where the tunnels converged, and I wondered which one I had come by. I chose one, of course the wrong one, but I followed it until I saw a glint of light at the end.

Soon I emerged, but instead of finding myself on the familiar ground about half a mile from the tent, I was standing on the top of a pleasant grassy slope going down with a gentle incline to a small lake, fed by the stream into which I had fallen, which gurgled out into a little waterfall to my left.

About ten miles across this valley the real mountains extended in a vast unbroken line as far as I could see.

Then I understood that I must have gone right through the mountain, which was no doubt honeycombed by these tunnels. The idea came to me that if I could get back I could lead my master through by this way and save him the painful and slow ascent of the mountain, as he obviously intended to get over to this side.

So, turning, I went back by the path I had come, and I noticed that all the way it sloped upwards, which accounted for the lowness of the far end of the tunnel. As I went I thought it would be a good thing to follow my own tracks backwards and thus find a way out. The rock held the scent very badly, and as I was very used to my own smell I had a lot of trouble in following it.

Presently I came to a place where the paths met, and as I was determined not to go wrong again, I carefully noted all the distinguishing marks of the passage along which I had just come.

Then I cast around for my tracks again, and after finding them I wondered if these might be the ones that led to the stream or not. However, I took the chance, and following them up, I soon discovered that I was wrong again, and I felt quite lost.

Sixteen

 After wandering round and round the seemingly endless series of galleries and caves, and several times recrossing my tracks, quite suddenly I found myself at the entrance again.

The time was late afternoon, but I noticed that the sky was dark and I could not see the tent in the gloom which surrounded me.

I began to trot down to where I thought the tent would be about half a mile further, and as I went the sky became darker and I grew alarmed, for though I had been wandering for a long time in the tunnel, it was not nearly night time yet.

Then suddenly the wind rose, and a few flakes of snow fell in my face, and then all at once down came the snow. The wind blew a flurry of snow into my eyes and I was temporarily blinded, so brushing my paw over my face I pushed on.

I could hardly see a yard ahead, and the wind which was blowing into my face howled like an angry wolf, carrying away the sounds which I made to attract my master.

As I had twisted and turned so much in the tunnels I had quite lost my sense of direction which was usually so infallible, so after about twenty minutes struggling with the wind, I found myself at the brink of the precipice, still further from my master.

By now the wind had reached a terrible force, and for a little while it was all I could do to prevent myself from being blown over the edge.

Presently it abated a little, and I soon gained the shelter of a protecting boulder, and I sat down under the lee of it. The wind, however, returned with still greater force and the snow utterly shut out all the light, so I stayed behind the rock, but a powerful eddy of air kept covering me with snow, and if I had not been continually shaking it off I would have been buried in a very short time.

At length the day must have merged into night, but I noticed no difference, either in the light or in the fury of the storm.

Soon the snow heaped up in a huge drift on the other side of the rock, and at what I would judge to be about the middle of the night, the great drift became over tall and a small avalanche entirely buried me. I was almost suffocated before I had time to scramble out, and on doing so the wind raised me up into the air in spite of all my efforts to keep on my feet.

After carrying me a little way the wind dropped me into another snowdrift which had heaped up on the wind-ward side of an even larger boulder. I burrowed through the snow to the other side, which was somewhat hollowed out like a shallow cave and gave excellent shelter.

The place seemed very familiar, and I wondered where I had seen it before – when suddenly I remembered this was the place where the tent had been, and looking round I saw the marks made by the tent pegs. I searched for the remains of a fire, but it was outside the little semi-circle of protection and was buried.

It was evident that my master had gone without me, but where, I wondered, had he gone – up the mountain? If so it was unlikely that he would survive such a storm. If he had gone down the mountain, sheltering among the smaller foothills, he might have lived through it; but then it would be impossible for me to find him. I thought of going back to the house if the storm ever finished, which seemed hardly likely.

It must have been nearly a hundred miles either south or west to my master's house. I tried to recall our route on coming up to the mountains, and all the different ways which we had gone in four days, sometimes going on trail after game, and more than once making detours round lakes, but it was too much for my memory. After striving to collect my thoughts and failing, my senses left me and I sank into a sleep of utter exhaustion.

I did not wake up until the middle of the next day. The storm had ceased, and I started up with the intention of joining my master at once, but to my horror there was no track or traces for me to follow, for of course the snow had obliterated all of them for miles.

As it was freezing, a firm crust had formed over the top of the snow, so if I kept my feet well splayed out I could travel about with ease; but I feared that my master, with his boots, would sink into one of the deep drifts and never be able to get out. I searched for the least clue of his whereabouts all day without success, as I was afraid of going too far from the camp site, in case he might return.

Towards nightfall I became aware of my extreme hunger, so when I observed a troop of wild goats and mountain sheep coming down one of the dangerous paths (which they seemed to prefer) towards me, I ensconced myself in a hollow which I rapidly scooped out of the snow, and when they passed I darted out and seized a small fat one, which I took behind a small rock and there consumed.

When evening was coming on the sky became threatening and dark, and as I feared another storm I went up towards the entrance to the tunnels and went in. I was determined not to get lost again, so I only went as far as the place where all the tunnels met, and there I chose a dark corner of the square.

To my surprise I found that the place was littered with a lot of dry ferns and grass, and there was a scent about the place which I could not recognise. I thought perhaps I had lain down here in my wanderings the day before, for the scent was very like my own, but on second thoughts I saw that it was too fresh to be mine.

However, I did not worry about it, but fell to thinking what a safe place this would be to live in when one got to know all the passages and caves.

Then I wondered where my master was, whether he were still looking for me or whether he had lived through the snowstorm. I feared he would not, for his skin even with all his clothes was scarcely sufficient protection against such severe cold. I also wondered whether we should ever go hunting again together, or whether I should ever see my mistress or the children again, or if I should ever play with the ball any more.

———

In the middle of all these melancholy thoughts, how-ever, I fell asleep, and did not wake up until the next morning, when I got up, and after washing myself I went to the stream and had a drink. In the tunnels there was twilight all day and utter darkness at night.

I roamed all round and round the passages which honey-combed the mountain and soon found the exit again. At first the dazzling reflection of the sun from the snow quite blinded me, but I regained my sight and continued to search for my master.

As the hours passed without any signs of him, and I felt quite sure I should never find him again, my loneliness can hardly be imagined, for after a year and a half of his company I had got so used to his voice and presence that I could hardly believe that I was parted from him.

The great white stretches of pure snow broken by occasional bare rocks comforted me, however, and the exhilarating air of the mountains felt strange in my nos-trils after the thick air of the plains.

Then I ascended to the very highest reaches of the mountain, and I thought I saw some smoke coming from far away to the south. But I was not sure, for a bank of cloud rolled in, obscuring my vision.

I did not leave the mountain for fear that I was wrong and that my master might return to the site of the old camp in my absence.

At midday I returned to the cave and I slept until night, when I came out, and after about half an hour I had a fat goat. After eating it I went down to the stream for a drink. I thought I saw another animal just leaving on the other side but was not sure, so soon I went back to my cave and presently went fast asleep.

———

Seventeen

 For the whole of the next fortnight I searched for my master, even going down into the plains, but I never found even a trace of him. Then I began to lose all hope of finding him and turned to hunting. I spent more time in exploring the tunnels, which I soon began to know quite well.

They consisted of two main caves, one above the other, each with a great many tunnels leading off them, and they were connected by one main tunnel.

In the top one there were quite a lot of holes in the sides which let in light, but they also let in snow and water, so I always lived in the bottom cave. Also in the top there were images of men squatting on great flat stones, which frightened me. Some of them had six arms, and one of them had an elephant's head, and they were all very much larger than any live men that I had ever seen.

On the sides of some of the passages there were some pictures which looked something like men, but I could not be quite sure. And in one of the tunnels which led nowhere there were a lot of skeletons of men, but there was no meat on them, as they had been dead many years and some of them were falling to dust. Often I thought that I saw a creature of some sort, but I was never able to catch it, and I did not think it ever saw me, or if it did, it never attacked me, so I did not worry about it, as there was plenty of meat running about on the mountains.

One day, however, as I was going into my cave I heard a growl from the corner, and turning in its direction, I saw a pair of green eyes staring at me, and in the pitch dark of the corner I could not make out what it was at first, but when it bounded towards me I observed that she was a snow leopard nearly as big as myself.

She appeared very thin and hungry, and evidently she was trying to frighten me away from the goat which I was carrying, and I saw that she was wounded in the right forepaw. Then she saw that I was no enemy and she made friendly noises.

In a short time we had made friends, and I let her have some of my goat. It appears that she had wounded her foot on a porcupine a week before, and had hardly been able to get enough food, as it hindered her running powers.

I think she had lived in the tunnel nearly all her life, hunting in the valley and between the first range and the main mountain. As I was feeling very lonely we played together, and in the morning we went out to hunt.

When she came out into the daylight I saw how beautiful she was, with her white coat and the black line on her ears which extended down to her forehead and made her look very fine. She seemed to know this and also admired my spots, and I saw that she had quite a lot of intelligence.

When we sighted a solitary sha, which was feeding behind a rock, I felt that here was a chance to prove to her how clever I was.

So pushing her into a snowdrift I set off after it. It sighted me sooner than I expected, so I gave chase, running at top speed, and killed it just in front of her. She pretended to be looking the other way, but I could see that she was much impressed, and I drew myself up with pride at my fine size and strength for her benefit.

Hearing no appreciative purr, in answer to all my fine postures, I turned and saw that she was sitting with her back to me and was starting to eat the sha.

I was justly enraged as I saw that she was eating the best part, which is, in my opinion, the shoulder. So stealing up behind her I gave her a sharp nip in the tail, and she relinquished the shoulder to me.

After this we went down to the lake, and I saw a red panda, who made off on seeing us.

Then she showed me a rock from which one could catch fish, and she tried to do so by crouching on the rock which overhung the water with one paw hanging down, but with no success.

As I had done this once or twice in the stream outside my first home I thought that I could show her how it was done, so I got on to the rock, and after waiting for some time I saw a fish. Then I darted down my paw to scoop him out, but I over-reached myself and fell in, much to her amusement; in fact, the foolish thing made quite a noise, as if it was funny. I also saw the red panda on the other side of the lake looking highly amused.

———

Presently we went back to the cave where we slept. As night was coming on I woke up before she did because she kept grunting and rolling in her sleep, so for a joke I suddenly jumped on her and roared in her ear, but curiously enough she didn't see the joke, though it was very funny. She appeared quite offended and cross. Some leopards, I thought, can never see a joke against themselves.

Soon she recovered herself, and as one small goat was hardly enough for a whole day, we went out, and between us surprised a small troop of sheep and goats and secured a large fat one.

I picked it up and began to go home, but my greedy companion thought that I was going to make off with it and tried to snatch it away. I calmed her, and when we reached the cave I let her have the shoulder, to her very great content.

Eighteen

 For a year we lived together hunting in the valley and living in the main cave of the tunnels, and in spring our four cubs arrived.

At first my wife would not let me see them, but as I hunted nearly all day and night for food for both of us, at last she showed them to me. I have never been so proud and happy all my life as when I saw the four little cubs.

They were the most beautiful creatures that have ever been born, of that I was firmly convinced.

Their eyes were not open then, but I thought they looked even better for that. They could hardly walk, and as they went sprawling about they made the most delightful little noises.

Soon my wife drove me away, however, and as I did not sleep in the main cave for fear of disturbing the cubs, I went out into one of the side passages and slept for a few hours at a time.

I woke up suddenly with a sense of guilt, for I thought she might be wanting something to eat. So I went very quietly through the cave and out into the open. I encountered a large wolf, who was looking down the tunnel, but he cleared off as I came out.

Then I went up towards the big mountains, where I knew most of the game had gone. As it had been a very hard winter, which was continuing into spring, I had driven off all the goats within miles of the cave. I had to go farther afield, and recently a large wolf pack which usually hunted twenty miles down the valley had come up nearer to us, also some snow leopards. Both helped to clear off the game. So as my wife was very fond of bharal meat I had to go right over the valley for it. As I went I thought that if the spring weather did not come soon we should have to move our quarters, which might be bad for the cubs.

Presently I reached the usual path down which the bharals used to come to get to their favourite feeding-place, but I was forestalled by a snow leopard.

It was plain that he had not seen me, and by the code which my mother taught me I should have left them to him, but I thought that my cubs' health was far more important than that of the snow leopard, who had no family.

So I concealed myself behind a boulder and waited for the bharals. Presently one came along, and I thought that if I let this chance go it might get the scent either of the snow leopard or myself, so I jumped out, but it saw me at once and fled towards the snow leopard, who seized it and then stood growling at me. I thought for a few moments and then, seeing that he was not very big, I charged.

We closed, and the leopard, after a few minutes'

struggle, managed to get a grip on my throat with his teeth and slashed at me with his long claws. But I got one paw under his head and I pushed with all my strength.

For a few minutes I felt the claws raking into my flesh, but then there was a ripping sound as the skin and fur that my enemy was holding gave way. His head slipped back and I sank my teeth deep into his neck. He gave a coughing roar and blood spurted all over me, and he fell to the ground with his limbs twitching.

Presently, when my fury died down, I became aware of the horrible pain of the cold on the bare flesh of my throat, and the blood streaming from the wounds in my flanks.

I was too exhausted to do anything, so I lay down in the snow for a little and watched the blood of the leopard flowing down the slope in many little streams, melting the snow as it went. I picked up the bharal and went towards home.

When I reached the cave my mate smelt my blood, but she did not leave the cubs, but she purred to me when I put the bharal down. Then she licked me all over, and after the pain had subsided I went to sleep.

In a short while the smallest cub began to crawl over to me and woke me up.

I growled sleepily, and received a sudden bite in the ear from my wife as a reproof.

Nineteen

 In a few weeks my wound healed, but I had to hunt far and wide for meat of any sort, as the winter did not break, and even the goats went farther down to the warmer slopes. Meanwhile the cubs were growing and had opened their eyes, and soon they would be needing meat.

My wife was quite strong now, and she could have helped me only she would not leave the cubs in the cave alone, in case they would hurt themselves or get lost, or anything which she seemed to fear might happen to them.

They were going to be very big, and I hoped the spring weather would come before they wanted meat and got their enormous appetites, but it did not come. Every day I had to go farther, and stay longer, until sometimes my mate grew quite anxious.

Then one day the largest cub ate a piece of ibex and my wife felt proud of it. At first he sniffed it and played with it, then with a gulp he swallowed it whole. He choked and coughed as if he would burst, but he got it down at last.

In a few days the other cubs followed his example, and

I worked myself to skin and bone in getting their food.

One day my wife came with me, when they were all asleep, and we got enough meat to satisfy their extraordinary appetites. They gorged themselves until we had to stop them.

But this was a lucky day, for on the following two days I was unable to get anything except one half-starved goat, and the cubs were quite unsatisfied.

Next day I went out early in the morning, and I went right across the valley to the lake, over which I crossed, as it was frozen stiff. On the other side I found a porcupine, but though he had tender meat, I thought I could do a little better than that.

So I went on, and presently I came to the bottom of the range of mountains which formed the other side of the valley, and they stretched up into the sky with their peaks hidden in the clouds. I went straight up, for I hoped to find a pass through which I could reach the farther and still loftier mountains, where there was sure to be food.

After the first gradual incline of the grassy slope I reached the snow-line, where I felt more at home, with the great bare boulders sticking up into the firm snow, looking as I thought rather like the ears of a huge panda. Soon I reached the place where the crest of the mountain could be seen, with its tremendous height thousands of feet above me, and I felt very small.

While I was looking up I nearly fell down a crack in the mountain side, so I proceeded more carefully, and I looked around for a pass, but I could see none, and it looked as though I should have to climb right up to the place where the peak detached itself from the main range. But this meant the loss of nearly half a day, so I looked very carefully for any means of shortening the distance.

The district over which I was now climbing was almost perpendicular, with many deep and dangerous ravines, and littered with many huge rocks, one of which started rolling as I passed by, as its base had been so worn away that the slightest push started it off. It gathered speed as it rolled down, taking huge bounds when it met other rocks, and on its way it moved many more, which went thundering down.

I watched them until they appeared no larger than pebbles, then I continued my course, thinking how like a panda's life was the course of the boulder down the mountain side.

At this point of my thoughts I nearly fell down another ravine, so I concentrated on climbing.

The cold here was intense, but I did not mind that so much as my inability to find the pass. Then all at once I saw about five hundred feet above me a deep cleft in the mountain side which would lead to the other side.

Soon I reached it and saw its remarkable formation. It looked as if the whole mountain had cracked and made a rift nearly a thousand feet deep. I quickly got through, thinking how horrible it would be if a rock got loose up at the top and fell on me. On the other side of the mountain I found myself on a gentle slope of snow going down about twenty yards before ending in a precipice of terrible depth beyond which there was a high icy plateau extending for miles to the north, and beyond that fold after fold of the great mountains as far as I could see. On the other side of the precipice I could see some ibex leaping from rock to rock.

I ran along to the place where the plateau joined the

mountain and I crossed. Having stalked the ibex for the best part of an hour I at last separated one from the herd, and after a thrilling chase I killed it very near the edge of the precipice.

Being ravenously hungry I was just about to make a meal when I remembered why I had killed it, and picking it up I took it back to the pass homewards. Soon I reached the valley, and when I got to the lake I rested and looked at my ibex, which was very fat and no doubt tender, but I refrained when I thought of the cubs.

As I crossed the lake the ice cracked beneath me, but I was glad, for I thought the warm weather would soon come. I also saw some very small green sprouts on the banks.

As I reached the other side the wind changed, and I heard a distant howling of the wolves. I went slowly onwards and heard the wolves more clearly and thought that they had been lucky enough to get some big animal who was putting up a fight. I knew that only eight of the pack had survived, as all the weakly ones had been killed, and the remaining eight were the largest and strongest.

Then I wondered when the ice would break up on the lake, but my thoughts were interrupted by the roar of my wife. I answered, and started forward at a trot, then rounding a boulder I made for the opening of the tunnel, from which I could hear the roars of my wife, mingled with the howls of the wolves. Dropping the ibex, I rushed forward, and on entering the tunnel I saw what was happening at a glance.

The wolves had attacked my mate in the cave, and while five of them engaged her the rest were catching the cubs, one of whom was already dead.

With a roar I charged, and three of the wolves came

to meet me. One leaped at my head, but I dodged him, and in a moment I had him by the neck and he died, but in the meanwhile one of the others had seized my leg and was pulling me down. I roared to my wife, and then more wolves heaped themselves on to me, biting and clawing wherever they could reach me.

I fought in silence now, and only managed to keep my feet with difficulty, as they kept trying to pull me down. I shook myself free, and then broke the neck of one who held my leg. But he seized my neck in his death-throes, and before I could recover the others swept me off my feet and another got at my throat. I could hardly move, but when I got a chance I struck into the mass of fur under which I was buried.

Once I managed to kill a wolf with one stroke of my back leg, as the others pushed him on to me, but the one at my throat hung on, though I clawed and bit him almost to pieces.

I could not draw my breath properly and my head swam. I regained my feet and caught an unwary wolf as he leapt up and broke his back with one bite, but with a rush they overwhelmed me again, and I felt bite after bite all over me, and I gasped for air, but the wolf at my throat never relaxed his grip, and there were black dots in front of my eyes.

I felt that I could hardly struggle any more, but then I heard my mate come back to the fight. She attacked them from behind and killed a pair of wolves in quick succession. This only left two, one of whom escaped and darted out through the tunnel, and the one who held my neck fell dead from his wounds.

I staggered to my feet, gulping down the air, then my

leg gave way and I sank down, almost fainting from the pain.

My wife was hardly wounded at all, but the bone of one of my hind legs was broken through, and from a terrible gash in my chest poured out my life's blood. She sat down by me and licked my wounds, and soon the pain subsided.

I felt a growing weakness, and a beautiful sleepiness came over me. Then I saw three of the cubs come from the side tunnel. They were quite well, but the fourth, who was the largest, lay dead under the heap of wolves; but my wife never turned to them, and she licked me frantically, trying to stop the blood, which poured from scores of my wounds.

The light seemed to be fading, though I knew it was only afternoon, and I felt curiously aloof from my body and felt no pain.

The mist in front of my eyes was getting worse, and I heard the whimpering of the cubs, as if they were very far away, and my poor mate continued to try and stop the bleeding, but I felt it was useless.

My strength was ebbing fast, and I was weak like a little cub again. I looked at my wife, but I could not see her so clearly, and I thought of the eclipse and of my master, and I glanced up for the sun, forgetting where I was.

I looked at her again, and she seemed very far off and misty, like my mother was when I saw her in the hut years before.

Then a terrible pain shot through me, and when it died away I could only just feel her licking, and I sank into a wonderful dream, in which everything seemed far off, and I thought I saw my master, and then——

———

HUSSEIN

One

In the Public Works Department of the Government of India there are a great number of elephants. It is the custom for one mahout to stay with the same elephant throughout the years of his service. One of these elephants was called Muhammed Akbar; his first mahout was Wali Dad. When Wali Dad grew old, and was pensioned off, his son Ahmed became Muhammed Akbar's mahout, for he had grown up with the elephant.

Time went on, and as Muhammed Akbar was reaching the prime of his life, Ahmed took a wife, who presently died, giving birth to a son.

The child was brought up by his grandfather and Ahmed. Ahmed had loved his wife very wholeheartedly, and he felt that he could not take another woman, although his food was much the worse for the want of a wife. She had been a small, delicately-formed girl of fifteen when Ahmed had married her – a grown woman by the standards of her people. But before the first year of their marriage was gone, she was dead, so Ahmed, who had not had time for disillusionment, carried a sweet memory with him always.

———

From his babyhood the boy, called Hussein after the father of his grandfather, who had been a great mahout in his day, was brought up among the elephants. His grandfather was very fond of Hussein, and he taught him to walk by looping an elephant's picket-rope about him, and trailing him very gently to and fro.

The very first thing that Hussein could remember was his grandfather trailing him round in the shade of a pipal tree, while an elephant — probably Muhammed Akbar — rubbed himself with a grating noise against the bark of the thick trunk. What fixed the incident in his memory was a brilliantly blue butterfly that hovered quite near, but which he could not catch; while he was trying to, he suddenly discovered that he could run by himself.

At first an aunt looked after Hussein, but while he was still quite a baby the elephants were moved to Agra and she was left behind, so Hussein grew up without any women. As soon as Hussein was old enough to learn, Wali Dad taught him the Mohammedan confession of faith — La illah il Allah, Mohammed raisul Allah — there is no God but Allah, and Mohammed is the Prophet of Allah — that, with a few vague remarks about Paradise, which was only to be reached by those who did not make a noise when their elders were talking, and a good deal of rather bitter comment on the undesirability of bût-parasti like the Hindus, completed his religious training: after that his education was confined to the elephant lore accumulated by countless generations of mahouts, and passed down by word of mouth.

Both Wali Dad and Ahmed told him all that they had been taught about elephants, and all that they had found out; they also taught him the hathi-tongue, in which the mahouts speak to their elephants. It is a strange language, quite unlike any other; only the mahouts know it, and they keep the knowledge carefully among themselves. The elephants understand it, and there is a tale that when the moon is eclipsed they speak it to one another.

Hussein absorbed the knowledge easily, for he was a born mahout; his ancestors had been mahouts as far as history went back and beyond: it was in his blood.

He grew up to be a strong boy, tall and slim. Muhammed Akbar was very fond of the boy, and taught him, in his own way, more about elephants than he could ever have learnt from men.

Now in the year when the great pestilence went up and down India, killing by thousands, and by hundreds of thousands, they were at the great city of Agra, which was crowded at the time for a certain festival. The monsoon had delayed in its breaking, so that the people were crying out for rain to all their gods. But it did not come. The weather grew hotter and still hotter, so that everything withered, and men died from the heat alone.

Then the cholera came. People died in the streets, and in the temples: there was a famine all through the land, so that men were distraught, and died like flies from cholera, starvation, and fear of both.

The mahouts in the Government elephant lines did not fare so badly, for they were fed and made to keep clean.

All through the hot days and stifling nights the Hindus prayed in the temples of their bloody-handed goddess, Kali, but she would not hear them, although the conches screamed and blared without ceasing.

The dead were thrown into great pits, for there were so many. The Government did all that it could, and trains came from the south with food and doctors. It is said that men of the IMS died from overwork and exhaustion and nothing else.

One day Ahmed was sent out with Muhammed Akbar to take an official through some rough country for a day's journey. Ahmed did not want his son to be out of his sight at a time like this, so he asked if Hussein might go with him. The official, a kindly Englishman, agreed, and they set out at daybreak. It was a depressing journey, for men lay dead in the roads, with none to bury them. They passed through villages that had been busy with people a month ago, and that were now quite empty, the people having died, or run away to find a place where the cholera was not. All that should have been green was brown or grey: the air was heavy and still, and the heat seemed to beat up from the iron-hard ground as well as from out of the sky.

When they got back, Wali Dad was dead. He had sickened and died before nightfall, and he was already buried. Mahmud Khan, an old friend of his, had stayed with him to the last, in spite of the danger. He had given Wali Dad enough opium to ensure that his passing should be clean and painless, which was a very good thing; Mahmud had also given him an honourable burial. In that great heat a man had to be buried almost as soon as the breath was out of his body.

Ahmed tore his clothes, and cast off his turban, pouring ash and dust upon his head. Hussein did the same, and they mourned for a long time. For days Ahmed took no food, and only a little water; but Hussein fed more heartily, although his grief was sincere. Six more mahouts died in the next week, and new ones were sent from other parts to replace them. Among them came Mustapha, the husband of Ahmed's sister. Ahmed went to him and said, 'Peace upon your house!'

'And upon yours,' replied Mustapha; 'may you never grow tired.' For some time they talked about indifferent subjects before Ahmed came to the question that had brought him.

'If anything were to happen to either of us,' he said, 'what would become of your wife and children, and of my Hussein?'

'Allah is merciful,' said Mustapha, who was a mild, dreamy man, and something of a scholar.

'Without doubt,' replied Ahmed, 'but perhaps it would be as well if, in the event of certain things coming upon either of us – (he would not mention cholera, for it was so near, and naming calls) – we were to agree that the other should take care of those who would be left.'

'This is an excellent suggestion, and on my honour, and by the Beard of the Prophet, if such a thing should come about – which Allah forbid – I and my wife will look after Hussein.'

'And for my part, by my father's head, I will do the same for your wife, my sister, and for your children.'

And so it was agreed; after that the talk drifted to unimportant things. The same night Mahmud Khan was struck by the cholera; Ahmed stayed with him all night, doing all that could be done, which was not much. Towards the end Mahmud asked for opium; Ahmed gave it to him, and he died a little before daybreak.

———

Ahmed was worn out with grief and with nursing his friend. As he was very weak from taking almost no food since his father died, he stood no chance when the cholera struck him at noon; he was buried before sunset. Hussein, when they told him, was dazed: he had never thought it possible that his father should die — he had seemed so strong, and so essentially permanent. Even when he was buried, Hussein could not believe that he was gone for ever. It all seemed like a bad dream, from which he would presently awake to find everything as it used to be. Within an hour of his father's burial, Hussein was unconscious in the high fever of black cholera. Mustapha kept his word to Ahmed, and carried him to his own house, where his aunt nursed the boy. He lay on a string bed, his body distorted with the furious pain; it wracked him so that he could scarcely breathe the heavy air that seemed to weigh down on him like a stifling blanket.

Zeinab, Mustapha's wife, sat by Hussein all night, sponging him now and then with lukewarm water. He was still living at dawn, but as the day wore on he lapsed into a coma.

'It is all over now,' said Zeinab.

'El mektub, mektub,' replied Mustapha with a sigh, 'what is written, is written — his fate was on his forehead, and there is no escaping it.'

At dawn, however, a little breeze had sprung up, and by noon it had risen to a strong wind, and the people on the housetops could see the great banks of cloud driving down from the north. All day thunder roared, and a little after noon the monsoon broke at last. The rain fell out of the sky in great solid sheets, and the scorched earth drank it with a hissing sound. The mud splashed up waist-high, and the rivers swelled as one watched them. Ceaselessly the rain roared down, making a great noise like the thunder of traffic in a great city magnified tenfold. The air freshened within a few minutes of the coming of the rain, and Hussein stirred from his coma. The clean air revived him a little, and before nightfall Zeinab was able to feed a little soup to him from a spoon. By the time a week had passed the cholera had left the city — it was washed away.

Hussein lived, and after some time he was on his feet again. At first he kept forgetting that Wali Dad and Ahmed were both dead, and each time that it came suddenly to him, his grief broke out afresh. At such times he would go to Muhammed Akbar, and lie between his fore-feet, with his head in the dust; but while Hussein tended to become used to it, the elephant did not. Indeed, Muhammed Akbar grieved so bitterly and so deeply that since Ahmed died he would hardly eat anything at all. Only Hussein could persuade him to take a few plantains now and then. The great beast wasted away, and his skin hung in folds on his flanks.

All the mahouts understood, and they did not trouble him. In a little while Muhammed Akbar became so weak that he could hardly support his own weight. One day Hussein found him leaning against the pipal tree in the compound. The boy was carrying some plantains for the elephant: he sat between the great round forefeet, and began talking gently. Suddenly he stopped, for the elephant was not making those little throaty gurgles of response by which he always used to show that he was attending. Hussein slapped the hanging trunk to wake the elephant, but there was no response; he started to his feet, and looked up; then he understood, for Muhammed Akbar was dead.

Two

Mustapha, Hussein's uncle, was a quiet, dreamy man, and although he was by birth and breeding a mahout, he was also a considerable scholar in the old Islamic tradition. He knew the greater part of the Q'ran by heart, and he had even begun a commentary on Al Beidâwi, the great commentator of the Q'ran. One of the first things he did when Hussein was convalescent was to teach him to read. His own sons — he had three — had reverted to type, and they were simple mahouts, blood and bone, so that he had long ceased trying to hammer any learning into their thick heads. But Hussein was more quick, and he wished to please Mustapha.

Mustapha had all the scholar's enthusiasm for imparting his knowledge, and after a few months Hussein could struggle through most of the Q'ran. Among those people it was no little distinction to be able to read, for not two in a hundred of the common people could understand the written word. Mustapha's three sons were all considerably older than Hussein, and they thought him too young to quarrel with at all seriously, so they got on very well together.

Zeinab was particularly good to Hussein, for she was a good-natured motherly woman, and she felt the need of someone to look after now that her own children were almost grown up.

The elephants were soon moved away from Agra, and after a little time they were stationed at Amritsar. In this town Hussein began to lead a new life. To begin with, the people spoke a different tongue, for they were mostly Sikhs, speaking Punjabi. Hussein could generally make himself understood in Urdu, which is spoken all over the land, but very quickly he learnt Punjabi so well that he thought in it. His grief, which had died down to a dull ache, seemed to leave him with all these new things coming into his life, and although it returned sometimes when he was unhappy or alone, yet as time went on it faded out of his conscious mind.

They all lived in a hut in the elephant lines, which consisted of a long row of flat-roofed buildings with little gardens. There was a broad maiden that sloped down to the river, which was dammed in order to make a pool for the elephants. The town was some little distance from the elephant lines. In the evening the mahouts used to give their elephants over to their sons, and they were taken down to the pool. Hussein often used to take his uncle's elephant, who was called Jehangir Bahadur.

When they came to the pool the elephants would walk slowly in and squirt themselves all over with the cool water. They all had different habits, and it was Jehangir's custom to go out into the deepest part, where he could go right under, only leaving his trunk out to breathe. Then he would come out to the shallow part where Hussein was; he would suck up a trunkful of water, and squirt it all over himself, while Hussein scrubbed him with a coir brush. When they were back on the bank, Hussein would search Jehangir's broad feet for thorns, and also his ears, which were rather tender, becoming inflamed very easily.

The water at the dam made a perfect swimming pool, as no crocodiles ever came there for fear of the elephants.

In the garden outside Mustapha's house there was an old piece of wall that stood by itself; for no particular reason it had never been pulled down, so Mustapha made a sloping bed against it for melons. Hussein was very fond of melons, and he had made these his special care, for being rather far-sighted he reasoned that the more they were looked after as plants, the better they would be as melons.

He was squatting idly on the top of the wall when the heat of the day had passed, gazing at the ripening melons. In the elephant lines he heard a tumult, but he paid little attention, for the mahouts often quarrelled, making a great noise without ever coming to blows; therefore, thought Hussein, it was not worth while running to see two men shouting at one another, with other people joining in to make more noise. Actually the hubbub was caused by Jehangir, who had gone mûsth, and had knocked another elephant over. It was a mild attack of that form of madness that is peculiar to elephants: it is often caused by an elephant being given too much bamboo in its fodder, for this makes its blood so hot that a very little will upset it and drive it mûsth.

All the mahouts were trying to separate the elephants but they could do nothing. As the noise increased Hussein climbed on to the flat roof of the hut to see what it was all about; he hoped that it would be Imam Din pulling

Daoud Shah's beard, as he had often threatened to do. The mahouts got out two of the biggest elephants to force Jehangir away.

Hussein was in two minds about going to find out what it was all about: the sun was still too hot for it to be worth while running to hear two of the mahouts' wives abusing one another, but, of course, it might with luck be Imam Din carrying out his threat. From the roof he could not see anything but a confused crowd, because of the dust and the heat-haze.

Before the big elephants had been brought on the scene, Jehangir's mood had changed. He rammed his opponent once more with all his force, and then went away to look for something to destroy, for his temper made him feel like destroying things.

No one dared to get in front of him, so he trotted off down the lines towards the larger huts where the married mahouts lived. His one desire, that was by now an obsession, was to crush something: his head was aching splittingly, and his madness had driven all the goodness out of him for the time. He came quickly down the dusty road, and Hussein, on the roof, recognised him at once by the glint of the silver bands round his tusks, which were cut short. He had no idea that Jehangir was mûsth; indeed, he had never seen an elephant in that state, and he only knew of it by hearsay. He called out to the elephant, but he was rather surprised when Jehangir came charging at full speed towards the mud house; Hussein thought that he was only playing, as he had often done before. But Jehangir did not pull up; he blundered right on into the brick wall, smashing it down with his forehead, and quite ruining the melons.

Hussein gasped, and then shouted, 'Oh, soor-kabutcha kasoorneen, what have you done?'

The elephant stood still over the wreckage of the bed; he had knocked his head very hard against the wall, and that had cleared it a little. If he had been left alone the madness would have clouded his brain again, but Hussein came scrambling off the roof, catching a heavy bowl which was there to catch rain, and he leapt from the top of the verandah on to Jehangir's neck, crying, 'Oh, son of a great pig, what have you done to my fine melons?' He beat the bowl furiously on Jehangir's head, so that it broke.

It did not hurt the elephant particularly, but it brought him to his senses. Suddenly he saw what he had done: it was as though he had awoken from a bad dream. He was horribly afraid that he might have injured Hussein, for he was very fond of the boy. But Hussein kept banging at his head with what remained of the pot, so he saw that there was no harm done.

'Go straight back to your picket, you clumsy, toad-like oont; I shall never speak to you again. The melons were almost ripe, and now they are quite ruined. Worthless earth-worm that you are,' shouted Hussein very angrily. By this time a pursuing crowd of mahouts with five huge tuskers and chains had come up, and as soon as they were within ear-shot, a man shouted, 'Have a care, have a care, he is mûsth.'

Hussein heard this, but he saw that the fit had passed. Very quickly the two biggest elephants came up on either side of Jehangir to pin him, so that a rope could be passed about one of his legs; but Hussein saw his opportunity, and cried, 'Leave us alone, we shall not hurt you.'

Everyone gaped, as Hussein had hoped they would, and

Mustapha said, 'But what is this? Jehangir has gone mûsth.'

'It is a small matter, I have dealt with it. He was only a little troubled with the heat, so he came to see me. I shall take him to the pool.' Hussein carried it off perfectly, and they went down to the water, where Jehangir squirted water all over himself, and then plastered his head with cool grey mud.

But the next day Jehangir was punished in the only way that an elephant can be. He was chained firmly to a tree, and each of the other elephants was given a good length of chain. They all filed past him, and each gave him a great blow with the chain: they went round three times. Jehangir was bitterly ashamed of himself, and he trumpeted in the night, but Hussein came and comforted him until the morning.

Hussein gained a great deal of credit, and it was prophesied that he would become a famous mahout when he grew older. The Englishman in charge of the mahouts sent him twenty rupees, for he said that anything might have happened if Jehangir had not been caught. The khitmutgar took fifteen of the rupees by way of commission, but even so, it was great wealth for Hussein while it lasted. For a little while Hussein was quite unbearable at home, but Mustapha beat him one day, and he returned to normal.

Jehangir became even more attached to Hussein after that, as he felt that he had saved him from doing horrible things.

Zeinab was the only person who saw through Hussein's pretence of having known that the elephant was mûsth, and one day, when she suddenly taxed him with it, he was too flustered to deny it. She used to blackmail him in a mild way, so he paid more attention to Mustapha's teaching than he would have done otherwise, and he kept the garden in much better order; but she was a kindly soul, and did not plague him at all, so he loved her none the less. Although she had a long tongue with a shrewd edge to it on occasion, she was as good as a mother to Hussein, and she treated him just as well as her own sons, and perhaps a little better, for she knew that she would never have another young boy of her own. Zeinab was also a surpassingly good cook, which made her household love her more than any amount of beauty would have done. It was firmly held by all those who had tasted it that the saffron stew she made from the tail of a fat-tailed sheep was equal to any food this side of Paradise. She had inherited the recipe for this dish from her mother, who in turn had had it from hers; it had come with her to Mustapha, being of great worth. Indeed, it was this stew that had brought Mustapha to her in the first place, as he had eaten it one evening in the house of Wali Dad, and had asked who had cooked it.

Mustapha's three sons, Amir Khan, Yussuf, and Abd'allah, were also kind to Hussein in that rather condescending, offhand manner that very young men use towards boys, because they wish it clearly to be understood that they are on two different planes — that they are quite grown up, and that anyone younger is a great deal younger, and not a man at all.

Amir Khan had a moustache, of which he was inordinately proud, and which he oiled assiduously; he was the mahout of a cow elephant called Kali, because of her temper. He was a weak, good-natured youth; handsome, and rather vain. He was very proud of his elephant, who, to tell the truth, was a singularly dull and vicious brute as elephants go, and often he would tell Hussein of the wonderful way in which she understood him, and of the things she could do if she were not so highly strung.

Yussuf and Abd'allah were twins; they were very much alike – both tall and well set; but apart from their inherent understanding of elephants, they were stupid; but they were simple and good-natured, and Hussein got on very well with them. Being rather young to be full mahouts, they were employed to cut fodder in between taking out any odd elephant that had no regular mahout. They spent a good deal of their time playing soccer football, which had been introduced by the English soldiers. It was extremely popular, particularly among the young Mohammedans. They played in bare feet, and their game was very fast, as the ground was nearly always as hard as asphalt. Hussein played quite a lot, but he was very light, so he did not get much of a game, the barging being rather heavy; but he was quick on his feet, and when he could get hold of the ball he could generally do something with it.

The Sikhs at Amritsar were also keen footballers, and one of the younger English officers in the PWD had organised a match between an eleven of his men and a team drawn by his friend, a lieutenant in a Sikh regiment.

The game was played on Thursday, when there were no parades, and the soldiers turned up in great force. All the mahouts came with as great a muster of elephants as they could bring for the honour of their side.

The match ground lay near the regimental barracks. None of the senior officers of the Sikhs or the PWD liked to be spoil-sports, so they all turned up. The Mohammedans played in white turbans, closely tied for greater security, and the Sikhs in blue turbans. Yussuf and Abd'allah were both playing as half-backs, and Hussein was watching with Mustapha on Jehangir.

The match was very fast from the beginning, and the ball was all over the field before a few minutes had gone. The audience was very much worked up, and the Sikhs were howling in Punjabi to encourage their men.

At half-time there was still no score: the barging had been a trifle wild, but it had been perfectly clean. After the change-over the game was still faster, and presently Abd'allah, the left half, took the ball from one of the Sikhs, and ran up the field with it. He tricked three men very neatly, and he had just swung the ball in to the waiting centre forward when one of the backs charged him very heavily. He had already passed the ball when he was knocked flying; the Sikh had used his elbow, and Abd'allah was carried off the field. A penalty was awarded against the soldiers, and immediately afterwards the PWD side scored. The penalty was unpopular with the non-Moslem part of the crowd, and the goal made it even more so. The Sikhs began playing rather wildly, and their opponents met them fully half-way.

Before long a Sikh was knocked out practically in the goal mouth; his turban came off, showing his long hair – a great shame for a Sikh. But the game went on and no penalty was awarded, although half the crowd howled for one.

Then the outside left of the PWD team broke away, running right up the touch-line with the ball. The inside left was backing him up. They were on the side away from their supporters; two men converged on the outside left, but he tricked them both, and passed the ball to the inside left, who had gone ahead. Instantly all the Sikhs shouted 'Offside!' but the referee did not blow his whistle.

No one quite saw what happened next, but there was a scuffle as some of the onlookers surged on to the ground, and when they went back the inside left was lying unconscious over the ball.

Then someone knocked a Sikh's turban off, and pulled his long hair. A Sikh hurled his knife-edged steel turban-quoit at the referee, cutting his head open. Then all the Mohammedans rushed as one man from their side on to the ground, and the Sikhs met them in mid-field. Their elephants were a tower of strength to the mahouts, and although they were outnumbered, the PWD team were collected, and carried off to safety by their supporters.

The Hindus in the crowd joined with the Sikhs against the Mohammedans, and soon a budding riot was growing on the football-ground.

Fortunately some of the senior officers had guessed what would happen a little after half-time, and they had called out the guard from the barracks. The Sikhs' discipline soon re-asserted itself, and what might have been a very ugly riot fizzled out after a round of blank cartridge. Nevertheless, three people had managed to get killed, and a great deal of religious fanaticism had been stirred up, which meant an anxious month for the Indian Police. The unfortunate young men who had organised the game were given exceedingly undesirable posts. The PWD man was sent out to investigate wells in the Bikaneer desert villages, and the Sikhs' officer was attached to a Madrassi regiment of infantry. The mahouts were moved, with the elephants, to a place right away in the Deccan, where they were building a road. The elephants, with their mahouts, travelled with the baggage-train of a south-bound regiment.

Three

They marched all the way, as there was no urgent need for them. The journey took several weeks; Hussein and Mustapha stayed with Jehangir, and on the way Mustapha recited long suras, in a high chanting voice, so as to improve Hussein's mind. Sometimes, when Mustapha dozed on Jehangir's neck, Hussein would slip off, and go back through the dust to the slow bullock carts where Zeinab sat among the pots and bundles. At each stopping-place she made a little fire, and prepared kebabs, which she wrapped in cool leaves for Hussein to eat on the way. Every day was like the one before. They marched, with halts, from dawn until sunset, when the soldiers pitched their tents, and a complete camp sprang up within an hour. Hussein and his cousins slept on a great soft pile of fodder that smelt sweet and fresh, like new-mown hay.

Before dawn the bugles went, and the tents disappeared like snow in summer. By sunrise they would be on the march again.

It was a splendid journey from Hussein's point of view – there were always new things to be seen, and new people to talk to. On one memorable evening some villagers tried to creep into the camp and steal a rack of rifles, but they were caught, amid great tumult and shouting; once a leopard took a straggling goat; and once Hussein lay down on a fat snake in the fodder heap.

But at last they came to the place where the regiment was stationed, and the mahouts went on alone. They had an escort of the Indian Police, as they were going through a very wild part of the country, where there were bands of dacoits. One night they camped half-way through a great forest, and in the night they heard the trumpeting of wild elephants. The tame elephants trumpeted back, and Kali, Amir Khan's elephant, broke her picket-rope and vanished into the forest; she went for ever, and though most of the mahouts thought it a good riddance, Amir Khan was inconsolable. He wandered into the jungle calling for Kali, and he got lost. They spent a day in finding him; he had stumbled into a wild bees' nest, and he was in a lamentable state.

At length they came to Rajkot, where the road was being made right through the jungle. The hills nearby abounded in game, from wild elephants and tigers to sand-grouse. The young 'Stant Sahib' who commanded the Police was a very keen shikar; and Hussein soon developed a great admiration for him.

He was a big, red-headed man, with a face burnt brick-red by the sun. This prevailing redness gave his blue eyes a startling intensity which impressed the natives tremendously; in fact, there was a rumour current that he had a tail, being a sort of djinni. Hussein used to gaze at him for long periods; he had never seen anything like it before. 'I wonder', he thought, 'whether his tail is red, too?'

He often used to hold the Stant Sahib's pony, so as to look at him more closely, but he never saw a vestige of a tail, red or otherwise. After a while the Englishman began to notice Hussein, and sometimes he spoke to him. At this time Hussein was a tall, thin boy of about sixteen — a young man by Indian standards.

One day the Stant Sahib, whose name was Gill, heard of a leopard that had made a kill about half a day's journey into the jungle. According to the report the leopard was a very large one, which had been harrying the cattle in a little Ghond village in the jungle for some time. Gill wanted to pot a good-sized leopard, but the journey would have to be made on an elephant, as it would take much too long to cut a way through the virgin jungle. So he went to the Englishman in charge of the mahouts, and asked him if he could spare him an elephant.

'I can let you have an elephant all right,' said this man, 'but I'm afraid I really can't spare a single mahout; you see, four of my best men have gone on leave for some damned funeral or festival or something, and I need every man I can lay my hands on for this tricky stretch of road by the stream.'

'That's a pest, because I particularly want to get out to that part of the jungle — it isn't so much on account of the leopard, but because the dacoits have been rather busy in that direction, and I've an idea that a bit of reconnoitring might do some good.'

'I'm awfully sorry, old man, but no can do. I've got to get past that awkward patch before the big-wigs come out and make remarks about inefficiency and lamentable lack of drive.'

'Oh well, I daresay I can make it on a pony, but it'll

mean carrying a hell of a lot of kit. I suppose you're coming over for bridge to-night?'

'Yes, of course; look here, I tell you what, perhaps you can get hold of a chap who knows which end of an elephant goes first, and then I can let you have one, if you'll take full responsibility and all that.'

'That's definitely an idea. I daresay I'll be able to get hold of someone, if it's only my syce – an elephant will make all the difference. By the way, don't forget to bring over some sodawater to-night, I've run clean out of it.'

The next day Gill's khitmutgar went among the mahouts to find someone who could take the Englishman's elephant. After a good deal of discussion a man suggested Hussein.

'He is very young,' objected the khitmutgar.

'Yes,' said Mustapha, 'but he knows Jehangir almost as well as I know him myself, and moreover, he handled him when he was mûsth, which not many would have done.' All the mahouts supported him in this.

'He would have to take a lesser wage,' said the khitmutgar, 'on account of his youth.'

'And a certain khitmutgar would get a larger share of it,' replied Mustapha.

'No such thought entered my mind,' said the khitmutgar, 'for I am a virtuous man; he will get eight annas, which is a princely sum for a youth.'

'Allah! Behold this virtuous khitmutgar – he would sell his grandmother's shroud! Hussein shall have one rupee and four annas, not a pice less.'

'These Muslims! I am fallen among thieves! Fourteen annas and two pice.'

'By no means; one rupee and one anna.'

———

'Very well, one rupee.' They haggled a little longer, and at length Mustapha got one rupee two pice for Hussein, who had not said a word. He had a curiously exalted feeling in his heart, as he had never officially been in full charge of an elephant before.

He wanted to have a howdah on Jehangir, that he should look the more glorious, but Gill only wanted a pad. Long before dawn Hussein prepared Jehangir. He scrubbed the great forehead, so that it seemed grey against the blackness of the rest of his body, and he polished the silver bands about the fore-shortened tusks. Zeinab wrapped up some chupatties for him, and Amir Khan lent him an ancient iron ankus.

At daybreak he brought Jehangir round to Gill's bungalow. Gill had his breakfast while the khitmutgar and Hussein put his things on the pad. He only expected to be gone three days, so he had cut down his baggage to the minimum. When everything was ready, Jehangir knelt so that Gill could get up, and they set off down a little thin path.

The sun had not yet come up over the trees, and there was only a curious greenish light. It was quite cold. A slight silver mist floated about the tall grass and the trees. Everything was quiet.

Jehangir made very little sound as he went along; his great round feet were padded like thick rubber, so that he seemed like a moving shadow. Presently Hussein, who had been awake nearly all night, fell asleep as he sat a-straddle on the elephant's neck. Gill was not sufficiently used to the elephant's rolling walk to be able to sleep, but he dozed now and then. It was rather like being in a boat when there is a swell on the sea, and the tall, waving elephant grass rippled like water. At length they came to a place where the path joined three others: Jehangir stopped for guidance. Hussein awoke with a start; he turned to Gill, who was looking at a sketch map on the back of an envelope. It showed a vague path – indicated by a wavy pencil line – that led to the Ghond village.

'Hm,' he said, 'it doesn't show any other paths. Still, the place lies almost dead east of the road-head, so we had better steer by compass.'

According to the compass none of the paths would do, so they struck into the jungle. It was not long after the rains just then, and the jungle was very thick, so thick that a man on the ground would have had to go down on his hands and knees to creep through it in places; but Jehangir made his own way.

Hussein carried his cousin's ankus with him, so as to look like a great mahout; but he never used it, because his grandfather had said that the best mahouts never needed to – but it looked well. He had soon got tired of holding it, and had put it down behind him, just in front of the compass by which Gill was going. Naturally the iron affected the compass, so that by noon they found themselves before a river that ran between a hillside covered with bamboo and a great reddish expanse of rocky hills that faded away into thin jungly country in the distance.

'This is all wrong,' said Gill. 'We are miles out. This river isn't shown at all on the map.'

'It is the Jhelunga, huzoor,' said Hussein.

'You're right; I remember it now; I was here for pig-sticking some time ago. We'd better have lunch now we're here.'

———

Hussein tapped Jehangir on the forehead, and the elephant knelt. Gill got off, and they pitched a little tent, for the sun was at its height. Gill fed from a tin of peaches and some biscuits, while Hussein retired behind a rock and ate his chupatties and some cold lamb's tail, carefully wrapped in a vine leaf by Zeinab. Jehangir found a flowering mimosa bush, which he ate as far as the roots. Gill slept for a while in his tent, and Hussein wandered about until he found a wild mango. He called Jehangir, and was lifted up into the tree; he threw some mangoes down for the elephant, and had a few himself; then he swam in the river. It was a swiftly flowing stream, with a gravelly bed, so there was no danger of crocodiles. He swam about until Gill awoke and called him.

'We had better cross the river,' said Gill, after they had folded up the tent and got underway again; 'if we strike due south we may get in by about moonrise.'

So Hussein led Jehangir down to the bank: there was a little sandy beach, and the elephant went over it very cautiously, for he knew that if once he got into a quicksand nothing would save him. As soon as the water was deep enough for him to swim, the elephant surged along at a surprising rate: Hussein swam beside him, for he knew that Jehangir must be feeling nervous. The strong current swept them down-stream quite a long way, but they got over without any mishap.

As Hussein was scrambling up the bank he cut his foot on a sharp-edged stone; Gill, on the elephant's back, did not see it, or he would have put iodine and a bandage on it. They had followed the river for some way when they saw some black-buck feeding under a clump of trees. They were up-wind of the elephant, so they had not smelt the men. Gill whispered to Hussein to make Jehangir kneel, as he wanted to stalk one for the pot. Hussein was to wait with Jehangir by the river, where he could easily be found. Accordingly, as soon as Gill had slipped away among the bushes, Hussein turned Jehangir back to the river. He went along the bank until he reached a grove of bamboos. Here he got off Jehangir, and plucked some broad leaves, which he wrapped round his foot, to cool it.

Then he wandered in the shade, vaguely looking for fruit trees. Jehangir went back to the river, but Hussein knew that he would come back at a call. Quite soon he found a very large mango tree standing among the bamboos. Its smooth trunk stretched high up without a branch within reach, so he had to get up by means of a rather shaky bamboo that was growing beside it. He was waving about alarmingly at the top of the bamboo by the time he reached the lowest branch, but he managed to reach it in safety. The mangoes were very good, but monkeys had eaten most of them. Hussein climbed to a comfortably broad crotch, where he lay along a branch with his head to the trunk. The deep green shade of the myriads of leaves was very restful: millions of insects buzzed, making a deep, steady note all together.

A mynah came and whistled in a branch over his head, but a small grey monkey chattered at it, and it flew away. A brilliant green tree-frog clung to the underside of a broad leaf above him: it looked as though it had been glued there and painted. Suddenly its neck swelled, and it made an utterly disproportionate noise like the yapping of a small dog. Hussein threw a mango stone at it, and it vanished to another leaf, where it yapped again. Another mango stone flew, and it was quiet. Far away he could hear Jehangir splashing in the river, and once he trumpeted, perhaps to a wild elephant, for they lived in those parts. A sowar of wild pig grunted among the fallen mangoes for a while, but soon they went. A minute, gem-like beetle crawled laboriously on to his big toe, and flew away. Hussein slept.

Away by the bank where they had crossed, a dhole sniffed at the stone on which Hussein had cut his foot. The wild dog put back his head and howled. Another dhole answered him, and soon there were half a dozen of them on the little beach. Now and again one of them would raise his muzzle and give the calling cry to the rest of the pack. Far away, from among the red sandstone of the caves, where the pack lived, an answering howl came back.

More dholes came, and they followed the scent until it became confused at the place where Hussein had mounted Jehangir. The wild dogs scattered, and cast about until one of them picked up the trail again at the spot where Hussein had wandered off by himself. The dholes came together again; the scent of blood was easy to follow, so they ran along the trail. They were fierce red wild dogs – bushy-tailed, stoutly built, and rather smaller than wolves. They hunted in much larger packs than wolves, and there was nothing that could withstand them; a tiger or a wild boar would run from them, and even an elephant would turn aside when they passed.

Hussein heard a sound in his sleep, and stirred uneasily; then he yawned, and opened his eyes. In the open space beneath the tree there were about a dozen dholes. More were coming quietly through the undergrowth: they were all watching him.

———

He started to his feet, and instantly the nearest dhole leapt up at him, snapping his teeth just under the branch. As they reached the end of the trail the wild dogs had kept silent, but now they gave tongue. Several more leapt up, but fortunately for Hussein the branch was about a foot out of their reach. Many more came through the bushes and sat beneath the tree. Hussein counted fifty of them.

At intervals they howled; it was something between the howl of a jackal and that of a wolf, but more fierce than either. Hussein reached up and grasped a branch above his head; he swung himself higher, and the dholes stopped jumping up at him: they sat in a wide circle round the tree. They were quite capable of waiting there until he dropped from exhaustion.

Hussein heard a sound like an old rusty watch ticking very loud and fast: with a shock he realised that it was his own heart beating. He climbed higher and higher. Every time he seized a higher branch he felt a wave of fright go through him; he had never felt anything like it when he had been climbing before, but now his nerves were upset by the certain knowledge that if he lost his hold and fell, the dholes would be there. At length he crept out to the end of a long branch from which he could see a part of the river, and he called, 'Ohé, Jehangir.' His voice was rather squeaky and wavering. He waited a moment, and then called again, 'Hitherao, hathi-raj. Ohé Jehangir!'

The dholes howled beneath him, and suddenly he felt giddy: he lay flat along the bough, and gripped it with all his strength. He shouted until his voice grew hoarse, and at length it failed him altogether – when he shouted only a croak came; but he saw no sign of the elephant. He crawled back along the branch, and sat with his back to the trunk, a-straddle the crotch.

Hussein pulled himself together, feeling rather angry at his weakness; but, indeed, the great circle of dholes, all glaring up at him with furious eyes, and all lusting hotly to eat his flesh, was enough to make the bravest man shiver a little.

A strong musty odour drifted up to him — the smell of the dholes — and he spat down at them. He called again — his voice had come back — and this time there was a despairing note in his cry, and the dholes sensed it: they howled.

Four

Some time before, while Hussein was asleep, Gill had come back to the river with a small black-buck over his shoulder. Jehangir, standing shoulder-high in the stream, had seen him, and had come out on to the bank; they waited for Hussein in the shade of a twisted tree among the rocks. After some time the Englishman blew on his whistle; Hussein, in his tree, heard it, and shouted back. But the wind was in his direction, and although it carried the sound of the whistle to him, it carried his own voice away. Nevertheless, he felt rather better now that he knew where Gill was, for the sound obviously came from the river bank some way to his right. Hussein stopped his ears with a piece of bread that he still had in his dhoti, so that he might not hear the howling of the dholes, for it seemed to melt the strength from his bones, and he climbed down to a branch that touched a limb coming from another tree that lay towards the river. As he crawled out to the thin end of the bough, it bent down and swayed so much that it just brought him within reach of the leaping dholes for a moment: one of them, snapping at a twig growing

---

from the branch, hung there as it swung up again. Then the dhole scrambled on to the branch and rushed at Hussein. Luckily the rounded branch gave the dog no foothold, and it fell to the ground before reaching him. Before the branch swung down again, Hussein had caught hold of the other one; he swung himself on to it. Although it was much stouter, it still swayed up and down a great deal, so that one moment he was practically in the jaws of the dholes as they leapt up, and the next he was far above them. The wild dogs were furiously excited: the noise was appalling. As soon as he could steady himself, Hussein scrambled along the branch to the trunk, where he rested, and pulled the bread from his ears, for his first panic was over, and he felt master of himself again.

There was a dead creeper on the tree, and he broke off lengths of it, throwing them at the dholes. They sat down and waited, with their red tongues hanging out, their ears pricked, and their thick tails brushing to and fro.

From this tree he could see his way plainly for about the spread of five large trees and a few smaller ones. After that a confused mass of greenness blocked out everything else. There were innumerable creepers joining the higher branches. Hussein saw a big grey langur running swiftly along them, and he decided to go by the same way. He found that they were easily strong enough to hold him. Grasping one of the thickest of the lianas he walked gingerly along.

In the middle, where the supporting branches were far apart, the monkey's road swayed a good deal, and one or two dead creepers fell in long strands; but it held, and he quickly made his way through the trees, holding the thinner lianas with his hands, and walking along on the great cable-thick parasites that grew all over the biggest trees, and crushed the smaller ones to the ground. He was practically hidden among the leaves and blazing crimson flowers of the giant creepers, and he was high above the ground, so that for the space of two trees the dholes lost sight of him. His heart leapt, and he ran along the twisted stems: there was a chance that they would wait under one tree, while he could get away. But he went too fast in his eagerness, and missed his footing; he almost fell, but he snatched at a long liana that ripped away from the rest, and swung him hard against a branch. He grasped it, and was safe; but the noise had brought the dholes to the tree, and they crowded round it, howling like demons.

He rested awhile, as the fall had shaken him; his ribs were bruised, and he felt them tenderly. Nothing was broken – the leaves had checked the speed of the swing, but it was a nasty knock, and it had winded him. When his breath came back he went on, but soon he came to the last big tree. A sea of waving bamboos stretched away almost to the river. There was no large tree standing among them, and there were no creepers: he saw that he could go no farther.

He climbed as high as he could among the dark green shadows: nearly at the top of the great tree he poked his head out of the leaves. At first the sun blinded him, but when his eyes got used to the brilliant light he could see the river plainly, and by the place where they had crossed he could see Gill and Jehangir.

There were several kites circling above him; they were following the dholes for a share in their kill. Hussein unwound his turban and waved it, shouting as loud as he could. He could hear Gill whistling impatiently: the white man saw nothing, and Hussein saw him sit down on a rock; but Jehangir, who had been vaguely uneasy for some time, turned his head from side to side, with his great ears outstretched, and his trunk held straight out, sniffing the wind.

Then he shuffled quickly away towards the trees; Gill saw that something was the matter, and ran after him. The elephant paused and looked at Gill, considering whether he would be useful or not. He made up his mind quickly, and unceremoniously took Gill about the waist with his trunk, hoisting him up on to his back.

Hussein saw them coming, and climbed quickly down the tree. About half-way down he stepped right on top of a fat snake that lay coiled under a cluster of leaves; it fell, without striking him, and hit the ground squelchily. Hussein saw that his luck was in that day, and took heart of grace. As he came down lower the dholes greeted him with a deafening howl. He put on his turban again, and waited for Jehangir. He heard a crashing sound among the bamboos — Jehangir was making his own path. The dholes heard it too, and they looked this way and that: they were clearly puzzled, but they stayed under the tree.

At the edge of the clearing Jehangir paused for a moment. Gill was seated astride his neck, with a shot gun in his hands, and the HV rifle, which he had brought for the leopard, across his knees; he had grasped the situation when he heard the dholes howling. Jehangir was thinking for a moment, trying to decide the best method of attack: the dholes stood motionless, the hair upright on their backs.

'Call him to you and jump on to his back,' shouted

Gill, who had found that nothing he said or did had the least effect on the elephant. 'I'll pepper them with the shot-gun until we get clear.'

Hussein nodded and came down lower; the dholes leapt up at him, two and three at a time. He called gently to the elephant, 'Hitherao, Jehangir.'

Jehangir came out from the bamboos with his trunk curled up: Gill blazed away into the dense, reddish-brown mass of the wild dogs, and in another moment Jehangir had passed under the branch, and Hussein had dropped on to his broad back. They were out of the clearing before the dholes had time to follow what was happening. But the wild dogs, though they were confused, were not daunted, and giving tongue they streaked away after the elephant. None of them was killed or even seriously injured, as the gun was only loaded with shot for partridge or sand-grouse.

Jehangir crashed through the thick bamboos as if they were grass; the stems struck the men on his back like whips.

The dholes wriggled through the undergrowth, yelping like young hounds in a covert. They came out into the open, and Jehangir began moving really fast. The wild dogs were strung out on either side, with a bunch just behind him. Altogether there were between fifty and seventy-five of them – a very formidable pack. They ran silently, keeping their distance, and waiting for a lead. Gill and Hussein changed places, a very difficult thing to do on the elephant's swaying back, and Gill tried to pick off some of the dholes with his rifle; but Jehangir, going at full speed, rolled like a ship in a heavy sea, so his shooting was rather wild.

'Shall we cross the river?' he asked.

'No,' replied Hussein, 'for they swim well; moreover, even Jehangir likes to take his time over a crossing and, being worried by these scum, he might be injured.'

As they were speaking one of the dholes running at the side came in and snapped at the elephant's flank; he hung there for a moment, and dropped. Several others followed his lead, and soon the whole pack was close behind. Jehangir stopped suddenly, so that Gill was almost jerked off; then he turned very nimbly; the dholes fell away on either side, but he stamped on two of the slowest, destroying them utterly.

Then he went on, rumbling a little to himself in his throat. For a little while the pack kept its distance, but soon they were snapping behind him again. Gill was getting more used to the rolling now, and he wounded one of the leaders severely. In a moment the wounded dhole was torn to pieces; he had been the leader of the pack, and was very unpopular with the younger dholes. The pack swept on, leaving him for the following kites.

At this time they were passing through the bare rocks where the dholes had their lairs. Some of them ran ahead to a rocky defile where a ledge overhung the path. They leapt down as the elephant passed. Three of them got a footing on Jehangir's hind-quarters, and they came at Gill. Hussein knocked one off, and Gill another, but the third got the Englishman's arm between his teeth, and hung on. The heavy, thick-set brute had Gill half off before Hussein caught up his ankus (he had tucked it into the pad) and beat the dhole so hard on the head that it died at once. But even then its jaws stayed clamped, and they had to prise them open.

Gill recovered his balance as Jehangir turned again and

stamped four times: at each stamp there was a short gasp as a dhole was flattened into the ground. But this time the dholes did not scatter: they leapt up all round, worrying the elephant's legs. Jehangir plucked them off with his trunk, and hurled them against the rocks, but more came on. Some scrambled up to the ledge, and jumped down at Gill and Hussein. They were prepared, however, and knocked them off with clubbed guns. Jehangir stamped twice more, and broke away.

The chase began again, and for quite a long while the wild dogs kept a good distance off. Gill was firing rapidly, and he managed to pick off one or two now and then. They went on and on: the river was left far behind, and they were in a very desolate country with bare, reddish ground thinly covered with thorn trees. Gill's left arm, just above the elbow, was badly torn, and it made his aim very unsteady after a while. He kept on firing, however, as he thought that the noise might keep the dholes off, even if it did not hit any of them; but soon they took very little notice of it.

Every now and then Jehangir turned, but the dholes were intent on tiring him out, so they fell back, and would not close with him.

The elephant was limping with his off fore foot now – a long thorn had lodged in it. The pace was telling on him, and his speed grew less and less. He stumbled, but recovered and went on. Imperceptibly the dholes drew in. They were silent now, and they ran with their tongues hanging out. When they were fairly close, Gill and Hussein took the rifle and the shot-gun, holding them clubbed, for there would be no time to load if all the dholes rushed them together.

Jehangir stumbled again; he fell to his knees, and stopped. He turned and faced the dholes. They spread out in a wide circle; they were panting fast by now, but they were still good for half a day's running, whereas the elephant, with his heavy load and his lame foot, could not go much farther. Suddenly the circle contracted, and they were surrounded by a seething mass of dholes. Some scrambled with amazing agility on to his back; Gill guarded one side and Hussein the other, but they could hardly keep themselves from being pulled off. The elephant slipped to his knees again as he stamped on a dhole, and several of them came over his shoulders. They were beaten off, but one seized Hussein's foot, and another tore Gill's coat from his back. They all drew off for an instant, yelling like fiends: it was obvious that they were going to make a concerted charge. In a second they rushed all together. In desperation Hussein shouted, 'Break away, hathi-raj!'

Jehangir grunted, and heaved himself out of the mass of dholes. He shook his great shoulders, and stamped again and again; he stumbled twice, and nearly went over, but he broke away. Dholes hung on to him all over, like leeches: Hussein and Gill beat them off. It was clear that he could not go much farther without a rest, and without having the thorn pulled from his foot. Before they had beaten the last dhole off, the elephant crossed a path. He uncoiled his trunk and sniffed the wind: then he turned along the path. The wild dogs followed.

'By the mercy of Allah', said Hussein, 'he has smelt a village.'

'If only he can reach it,' replied Gill, 'everything will be all right.'

———

They swept on, the dholes running silently. Behind them, at the place where Jehangir had almost fallen, the kites and jackals, who had followed at a distance, closed in on the dead or dying wild dogs.

Jehangir was going along at a good speed, but his breath was coming short, and he faltered now and again in his stride. The dholes were less confident now; they came on just the same, but none of them was anxious to give the lead in attacking the elephant.

By a fluke Gill shot two of them with two successive shots, killing both. But just then the path dipped into a little valley. There was a muddy stream at the bottom, and as Jehangir came to it he hesitated, and the dholes crowded behind him, howling with new ferocity.

Hussein bent over his head, patting him and urging him on; at the bank he stopped dead, and several of the wild dogs leapt; one caught Jehangir's tail; the sudden pain startled him, and he shot forwards: they were across the slow stream in a flurry of spray before the elephant realised it. The dholes swam across. There were only about thirty heads bobbing in the water now, but the pack was still quite large enough to be very dangerous, as all the weaker dholes had fallen back, and only the biggest and fiercest ones remained.

Jehangir smelt that the village was not far away, and he put on an extra spurt. After a little while a dense patch of thorns appeared; the path led in and out to the mud walls of the village, which was quite near now. Jehangir took no count of the path; he went straight through the thorn bushes; they crackled as he smashed through them.

The dholes were losing ground as they picked their

way among the bushes. As they came nearer and nearer to the village many of them stopped.

Only one was near the elephant now: this one, with a prodigious effort, leapt up and snapped his teeth on the heel of Gill's boot. It snarled, and bit clean through the heel; then Gill killed it with the butt of his rifle.

To their amazement they saw that the gates of the village were shut. Two or three shots rang out from the walls, and the bullets hummed unpleasantly close to their heads. But Jehangir was determined to get to the village, and nothing short of heavy artillery could have stopped him now; he rolled up his trunk under his tusks, bent his head, and putting on an extra burst of speed he fairly flew at the gates. Gill and Hussein crouched flat on his back. There was a rending crash; a cloud of dust flew up. When it faded they saw that Jehangir had destroyed the gates and half the thick mud wall as well; he was now standing in a deserted square surrounded by huts. A man crept from beneath the wreckage.

'What the devil did you mean by firing on us?' shouted Gill.

Hussein pointed, and whispered, 'Ismail Khan.'

Gill said, 'You're right,' and to the man, 'Put your hands up.' He covered him with his rifle, for he recognised Ismail Khan, a notorious dacoit.

The man salaamed. 'Pray do not threaten a poor honest thief, huzoor,' he said; 'we will be peaceable.'

'Then call your men out one by one, and tell them to lay down their arms: if anything else happens, I'll shoot you as you stand.'

Ismail Khan obeyed: as each man came out from his hut Hussein covered him with the shot-gun. They laid down their weapons — ancient blunderbusses and match-locks for the most part — in a pile by Jehangir, who stood quite still, breathing heavily.

'We should have been able to entertain you more like men,' said Ismail Khan, with a grin — for he held his hereditary and ancient profession to be no shame — 'if we had not run out of powder. Will it be a hanging or only the jail-khana?'

'That depends,' said Gill; 'now you will get me a very long rope. Let no other man move. Hussein, follow that man, and shoot him if he tries to escape.'

Hussein followed Ismail Khan, scowling fiercely to show that he was not at all afraid. The dacoit led the way into a hut where there were various jars of grain and stores. He paused for a moment, and Hussein raised his gun.

'That jar is full of rupees,' remarked the dacoit.

'Get the rope,' replied Hussein.

'Handsome young mahouts can do a lot with a jar of rupees.'

'That is true, but I do not believe that there are any there.'

'Look and see for yourself — I am very liberal to my friends.'

'Yes, and put my gun down: I am not quite a fool,' said Hussein.

The dacoit turned the jar on its side: a stream of silver coins came out on to the mud floor. 'Help yourself,' he said. Hussein said nothing.

The dacoit showed another jar — smaller this time. 'Gold,' he whispered, opening a leather bag from inside the jar, 'you understand?' Hussein nodded; the dacoit threw the bag, and Hussein caught it in one hand, keeping his distance from the dacoit.

'Now look the other way,' said Ismail Khan, 'so that you can swear by the Beard of the Prophet that you did not see me go.'

'No,' said Hussein.

'What in Jehannum?'

'I said no; now get that rope.' He pointed the gun at the dacoit – he had tucked the little bag into his dhoti.

'O son of Eblis – incredibly base leper . . .'

'Silence, soor-ka-butcha. Get the rope.' Hussein scowled ferociously. With no more words, but with an evil look, Ismail Khan brought out a coil of rope. Coming out of the door he made a rush at Hussein, flinging the heavy coil. Hussein ducked, and jabbed the dacoit in the stomach with the gun – he was not sure how to fire it. When Ismail Khan got his breath again, he picked up the rope and walked back quietly to the square where Gill sat on Jehangir, guarding the other prisoners. Gill dismounted and took the rope: as he put his rifle under his arm to take it, someone threw a knife: it knocked his topi off, but did no harm. Ismail Khan gathered himself together for a spring, and Hussein clubbed him from behind with the butt of the shot-gun. Before his topi had reached the ground, Gill fired from his hip, killing the man who had thrown the knife.

After that the dacoits were quite meek. They stood in a line with their hands behind them, and Hussein bound them, linking them all together.

They bound Ismail Khan and put him across Jehangir's back. Before the dacoits were bound it had been touch and go whether Gill and Hussein would get out alive; but no man cared to be the first to move, although if several had attacked together they would have been certain of victory; yet no one wanted to be the first to get shot. Also, they were cowed by the ease with which Jehangir had crushed their wall, and some even made remarks about people who employed djinn to fight for them.

Now Gill, having discovered the dacoits' village by accident, did not wish to remain in a part of the country that might be swarming with their friends, nor did he want them to have time to recover from their despondency, so he asked Hussein if it were possible for Jehangir to make the journey back again at once.

'Yes,' replied Hussein, 'when I have got this thorn out, and provided he is given a great jar of arrack; I saw some where the rope was.'

'Go and get it, then,' replied Gill.

Hussein went, and returned with the jar: his dhoti seemed curiously swelled, and he clanked gently as he walked.

Jehangir lifted up his foot, and Hussein soon got the thorn out. Then the elephant sniffed at the jar, picked it up with his trunk, and emptied it down his throat. He flapped his ears, and seemed brighter in a few minutes, for the immensely powerful spirit gave him heart. Leaving Hussein to guard the bound prisoners, Gill searched the huts, finding nobody until he came to the last and biggest. He opened the door of this one with some effort, for it was being held closed from within. He poked his head in; there were piercing screams. He slammed the door. 'Oh Lord,' he said, 'women.'

There was a passable horse in the village; he commandeered it, so as to relieve Jehangir, and rode out with his prisoners over the ruins of the shattered wall. They were tied in a string, and as he had forbidden them to speak, they were quite easy to manage. As they were crossing the Jhelunga they made a faint-hearted effort to escape when Gill's horse became skittish and nearly threw him in, but a shot over their heads quietened them at once.

By keeping them at a sharp trot, Gill managed to reach the road-head before nightfall, which was fortunate, as they would have had more chance to escape in the dark. It was a very good thing to have got them all at once, as this band had spoiled the countryside for years, and in spite of the most determined efforts of the police, their hiding-place had never been found.

The villagers were really grateful, and they showed it by sending messengers for miles to Gill to report remarkable heads of deer, or good-sized leopards.

When he got in, Gill sent his policemen back for the women, and got his arm bound up. Then, after food, he went round to the elephant lines to see Hussein and Jehangir.

The elephant was surrounded by a crowd of mahouts, all dealing with his hundreds of small wounds with their strange remedies.

Mustapha was attending to Jehangir's tail, and Gill asked where Hussein was. Mustapha guided him to their hut, where Hussein was squatting before a great pot of steaming saffron stew, made from the tails of sheep, and between mouthfuls he was telling the tale to a gaping circle.

Gill paused outside the door, in the shadows.

'And so,' said Hussein, 'I plucked a branch from a tree, and cleared my way through these dholes, thus rescuing

Jehangir and the Sahib, who were beset on all sides. Then I guided them to this village, and – with a little help, it is true – I overset the walls of it. After a long fight – I killed some four of them, I believe – we subdued them, and having tied them cunningly, one after the other, I brought them back, the Sahib being unconscious from a blow on the head. He only recovered just before we arrived, and he pressed gold on me: I would have refused, but he said that it might seem to imply that his life which I had saved (or so he was good enough to say) was of no value.'

'Inshallah! But surely the youth deceives us?' said a young man, enviously.

'Yes, where is the proof?' asked another youth, still more desirous of confounding Hussein.

'Here is the gold,' said Hussein, simply. He poured it in a shining heap from the bags in his dhoti. From all around there were admiring cries. 'Bismillah! He is another Rustum,' said someone.

Gill crept away unheard, for he would not spoil a good tale, and besides, Hussein had really saved his life at least twice that day.

Five

The road pushed its way slowly on and on. They cut through the jungle, and filled in swamps: they bridged two rivers, and blasted through solid hills of rock. All through the year Gill spent all the leave he could get in hunting: he knew that he would probably never have such opportunities again, and he made the most of the time: as often as he could he took Hussein and Jehangir.

On one occasion, when they were after a leopard, Jehangir brushed against a tree in which there was a wild bees' nest. They came out in a furious black cloud, and Hussein had to run for it — Gill was some distance away.

He got as far as a stagnant pool, and he stayed there, only bobbing his head up to breathe, until dark, when the bees left him.

At another time, when Gill was going into one of the Ghond villages far away in the jungle, they camped in the forest about half a day's journey away from their destination.

Hussein put a long piece of grass around Jehangir's leg to show him that he was not to go far away in the night.

The moon came down through the trees, making singularly delicate patterns on the ground: a few langurs howled and a leopard coughed far away. The men slept. Their fire glowed a dull red.

Jehangir stood motionless, half of him silver in the moonlight: he was not asleep. Far away there was a noise to which he had been listening for some time: it was not the hunting leopard, nor the dismal howling of the apes, but a distant crashing sound. His trunk moved to and fro as he sought for a hint of a scent on the still air.

A high pealing sound, very faint, came through the trees, and Jehangir spread his great ears. He looked at Hussein, who lay with his head on his arm by the fire, fast asleep; then he moved slowly away into the trees. Never a twig stirred as he faded into the shadows: he moved his great bulk as though it were no more substantial than a shadow itself.

After a little he moved more quickly, but still silently. Elephants have a way of suddenly being there, without one having had a suspicion of their approach — rhinoceroses are the same. Again he heard the noise — the distant trumpeting of a wild elephant. He raised his trunk and trumpeted back. In the camp Hussein stirred, but he did not awake.

Deep in Jehangir's mind was the memory of the free days when he had followed the elephant herd with his mother — a half-grown young calf elephant. In the days of his freedom he had fought with other young elephants in the light of the full moon.

He had heard the great bulls trumpeting to one another, and the crash as they joined in fight; and now the moon and the distant trumpeting combined with the forest to awaken his buried memories of the life he had led long ago – so long ago that three generations of men had passed since he was captured.

An hour's swift travelling brought him to a great open clearing in the trees. In the silver light two huge bull elephants were fighting: in the shadows the rest of the herd watched them.

With their trunks intertwined, and their tusks locked, the elephants strove together with their foreheads together. They pushed, grunting, and their feet slid on the torn-up ground.

For two full minutes they stood quite still, their forefeet clear of the ground. The strain must have been tremendous. Then there was an incredibly quick twisting of their trunks, and all at once the one nearer Jehangir crashed over on to his side. Instantly the other knelt on him, and thrust forward twice: he got up, and his tusks dripped red. The fallen elephant scrambled to his feet, and shuffled into the shadows.

The other stood alone in the clearing: he raised his trunk, and sent out his challenge. Jehangir moved out from the shadows: there was a wild tingling in his blood; he trumpeted back.

The elephant in the middle of the clearing spread his great ears, and glared at Jehangir with his little eyes: then he backed to the opposite side of the clearing. He trumpeted a shrill note of defiance, and charged. Jehangir met him half-way. The ground shook as they met head-on in the centre. They backed a little, and charged again.

This time his opponent swerved a little as they met, and one of his tusks gashed Jehangir's side. Jehangir, whose tusks were cut short, saw that he was at a disadvantage,

---

so he closed. The other elephant sought to catch Jehangir's trunk with his own, but Jehangir had a trick worth two of that, and as they struggled, forehead to forehead, he curled his trunk about the other's left forefoot, suddenly jerking with all his strength. His opponent was taken by surprise, and fell heavily on to his side, but before Jehangir had time to kneel on him, the other got to his feet and broke away. For a few moments they watched each other across the clearing. Then Jehangir trumpeted and charged. The wild elephant dodged and thrust at Jehangir's shoulder with his tusk: his thick hide was ripped open, but the wound did not go deep, and in another moment they were in the middle of the circle again, with their trunks intercoiled, pushing with all their strength.

Jehangir felt himself being forced back, and he thrust forward with even greater force: he felt his skull almost cracking before the other yielded a little. He pressed his advantage, and shoved the wild elephant back and back. Suddenly the wild elephant tried to break free, so as to use his tusks; but as he stepped back to do so, Jehangir launched his whole weight on him, and he slid back several feet; then Jehangir, with all his strength twisted his opponent's trunk. The animal collapsed on to his hindquarters, and then, as Jehangir thrust again, crashed over on to his side. He kicked wildly, but before he could rise, Jehangir was upon him, first knocking the breath out of his body by butting him in the stomach, and then kneeling on him.

The wild elephant squealed like a huge pig, and Jehangir backed away. The tusker gasped twice, got up, and staggered away to the other edge of the clearing. There he turned and looked at Jehangir, who trumpeted again, and advanced a few steps. The wild elephant turned, and went crashing away through the forest, followed by all his herd, with the exception of the younger cow-elephants, who stayed to caress Jehangir with their trunks.

Before dawn Jehangir was back in the camp, looking very innocent; but his wounds betrayed him, and Hussein beat his toe-nails, scolding him all the time.

For the rest of the journey two of the she-elephants followed them at a distance, but Jehangir took no notice of them at all.

The road pushed on and on: the men blasted through solid rock, and filled in swamps; they threw bridges across three streams, and at last they came to the village where the new road joined another, and their work was done.

All the people were scattered to different parts of India: Gill was promoted to a better post in the hills – the result of his action against the dacoits. He wanted to take Hussein with him as his syce, and he offered good wages. For three days Hussein thought it over; Mustapha would not advise him, saying that it was his own life. In the end he felt that he could not leave Jehangir, so Gill went away without him.

The elephants were sent to Haiderabad, where they worked on a great new embankment. By this time Hussein was a mahout in the Government service, and he rode a young bull elephant called Amurath. Amurath was an unintelligent beast as elephants go, but he had a good-natured, phlegmatic way about him, and Hussein got along very well with him.

Jehangir was exceedingly jealous of Amurath, and he made the smaller elephant's life quite a misery whenever they were alone together.

When they had been some time in Haiderabad,

Mustapha stiffened quite suddenly. They gave him a pension, and he retired.

Hussein had Jehangir after that, and Amurath was left in peace.

Mustapha spent his days in pottering about the elephant lines, and sitting in the sun before his house. He was happy in a mild way, but he was utterly lost without his work. He aged very quickly, and after some months his memory began to fail him: he called Hussein Ahmed, and sometimes he sat for hours in the sun with a book upside down in his hand.

Zeinab, who was always active, was disturbed. She had never thought of herself as an old woman, for the business of feeding and caring for five men had always kept her very much alive. She said, with a puzzled smile, that it was very like having a baby in the house again.

One night Mustapha died in his sleep. All the mahouts rent their clothes, and they gave him a great burial, with the elephants all trumpeting the Viceroy's salute. The women came to comfort Zeinab, but she did not seem to need any comforting. She sat quite still: she seemed dazed, and she did not answer when they praised the dead Mustapha, neither did she loose her hair and wail in the dust: she did not even seem very unhappy, but that night she swallowed enough opium to ensure that her passing should be swift and clean. They buried her beside Mustapha the next day.

Mustapha's sons and Hussein mourned long and sincerely, with dust and ashes on their heads in the old eastern way.

When their first grief had abated they came together to decide what they should do.

———

Mustapha had always said that Hussein was to be regarded as one of his own sons, so Amir Khan, who, being the eldest, divided the inheritance, placed the money (in a jar buried under the floor) in four equal heaps, one for himself, one for Yussuf, one for Abd'allah and one for Hussein. It was difficult to divide the rest of the things, but after some time they settled it fairly among themselves. Hussein got all the books. For the full period of mourning they lived on together in Haiderabad, but after Ramadan the elephants which Yussuf and Abd'allah rode (they were all mahouts now) were ordered away to another part of the country. They were very unhappy at the parting, but they had to go. An uncle and three cousins were among the other mahouts who went with them, so they were not without friends. Amir Khan and Hussein moved to a smaller hut, for the older one was melancholy with no one in it. After a little while they began to notice that there was no sort of restraint upon them, and that they could do pretty well what they pleased. Although this was pleasant, there was something very sad in having nobody to tell them not to do things.

Amir Khan, having little sense, took up with a fast set of young bloods, and he borrowed money from a bunnia: soon he found that he could not pay it back, and he took to borrowing money from Hussein to pay the interest. Hussein put up with it for some time; indeed he did not make much of a fuss even when Amir Khan took his money without the formality of asking for it.

Sometimes he made tentative suggestions to Amir Khan that he was hard up too, but his cousin would say quite truly that Hussein did nothing in his spare time but moon about with Jehangir or read, so that he wanted no money to spend, and as money was only a danger when it was hoarded, it was much better that one who could enjoy it should spend it.

'Besides,' he said, 'some day when you really need it I shall undoubtedly repay you — in fact, it is much the same as if you were to save it now, for I am a man of my word.' Then he twirled his growing moustache and borrowed three rupees from Hussein.

For more than a year they lived together in the Haiderabad elephant lines, but one day when neither Hussein nor Amir Khan had any money to pay the interest that was due, the moneylender hauled Amir Khan before the court to make him repay. In the court he became excited and tried to state his case in his own way. Two lawyers tried to restrain him, and he banged their heads together: then a policeman seized him, but he thumped him on the floor of the dock and kicked him in the stomach, for he was a stalwart young man.

In the tumult he escaped, and came running to his hut, where he hid under Hussein's bed, meaning to fly into the country during the night. But the police found him and he was sent to prison, after putting up a tremendous fight, in which all the mahouts joined so that there was almost a riot.

Hussein wrote to Yussuf and Abd'allah; they took leave and came back to Haiderabad. On the appointed day they all went to see Amir Khan in the jail-khana: he was cheerful because he had acquired great izzat by his hardy resistance, but he did not know what to do when he should come out, as the PWD would not have him any more.

They talked for some time, and then Abd'allah and

Yussuf had to go back, for they only had two days' leave. After a few weeks had passed they wrote to Hussein saying that a friend of theirs could secure a place as a mahout for Amir Khan on payment of Rs.100: they said that they could raise Rs.62 between them if Hussein could supply the rest: he did, by clearing his hoard right out and by pawning Amir Khan's turquoise-studded ankus, which he had hidden when the bunnia came to take possession of Amir Khan's other things, so that when his cousin came out of prison he was able to go straight to Sialkot, where his brothers' friend was waiting.

He parted very affectionately from Hussein, promising by his hope of Paradise to repay him, and borrowing another five rupees just before he went.

When he was gone Hussein felt more lonely than he had ever been before, and he turned still more for companionship to Jehangir.

However, he had made a good many friends among the younger mahouts, many of whom had been children with him, so he was not lonely, except when he wanted to be, as he did sometimes; for he had rather a powerful imagination, and there were times when he loved to be by himself, or with Jehangir, filled with a gentle, exquisite pity for himself, for no very obvious reason. When he felt like this he could sometimes go out beyond the elephant lines into the sand dunes, where he would thump on a tom-tom for hours at a time, singing that melancholy song they sing in Peshawar, of which the refrain goes 'Drai jarra yow dee.'

Now the chief of the mahouts had, among other things, a daughter. This daughter was as beautiful as a spotted sand-quail: her name was Sashiya.

———

Most of the younger mahouts were enamoured of her, and she had been betrothed as a child to a certain insignificant young man, who kept accounts.

Hussein's friend, Kadir Baksh, was particularly loud in his praises of her beauty: one day Hussein asked him whether she could be seen in any particular place.

'Yes,' said Kadir Baksh; 'every Friday she and other of Ghulam Haider's anderun go to the cemetery. They sometimes stay to play with the children among the mounds where there are no graves. I have often hidden with others among the trees, and I have seen her veil blown aside no less than three times.'

'Then', said Hussein, 'to-morrow we will go to the cemetery.'

They went and concealed themselves in a bush among the trees at the deserted end of the cemetery. For some time they waited: Hussein began to get impatient when ants began walking over them, but Kadir Baksh assured them that it would be worth it.

At length some people appeared among the tombs; they walked slowly towards the green mounds where there were no graves, and Hussein saw that they were women, with a few children among them. They all wore chudders, but Kadir Baksh pointed out one who wandered some way to the left of the main group. 'That is she,' he whispered.

'She walks like a gazelle,' said Hussein.

'But a gazelle has four feet.'

'Quite.'

Sashiya hopped from one mound to another. 'It is too hot for a veil,' she said, taking off her chudder. Most of the others took theirs off, for they had no idea that they were watched.

Sashiya sat on the top of a little green mound, hugging her knees. Hussein felt a shock go through him, as if he had swallowed a large piece of ice.

His mouth opened and he protruded his head from the bush. One of the women saw him and in a moment they were all gone.

Hussein turned to find Kadir Baksh regarding him coldly. 'I wish I had never told you about her,' said Kadir Baksh.

They went home without more words, and parted in silence, each wrapped up in his own thoughts. Next week they each went separately to watch Sashiya, but she did not come. They met on the way back and quarrelled, each being in a bad temper. The house of the chief of the mahouts was in Haiderabad: he lived with his brother, a merchant in the town, who had built a large house with a garden on the roof.

The women of the anderun used to spend most of the day up there during the hot weather, so that Hussein, coming to see Ibrahim, the chief of the mahouts, about a matter to do with the elephants, saw Sashiya leaning over the edge. She was gone in a moment, but he had recognised her.

The same evening he spoke with an ancient woman who sold herbs nearby. She said that she had often been into the house to see the womenfolk. She told him about the garden on the roof, but she could not remember whether there was another roof near to it or not, until Hussein gave her a rupee, and then she recalled a tree that was growing in the courtyard of a neighbouring

———

house: this tree, she said, hung over the parapet of the roof garden. Furthermore, she said that she could get messages into the house, as her sister was one of the servants; so Hussein sent several cardamom seeds and certain flowers, which being interpreted showed that he would be on the roof garden an hour after sunset.

He spent the rest of the day beautifying himself, and then he went into the city.

The courtyard where there grew the convenient tree was surrounded by a low wall. There had formerly been stables leaning against the wall, but these had fallen into disuse: indeed the whole place was practically deserted, as it had been bought up as a speculation by a merchant who had been unable to let it, since it was commonly reputed to be the habitation of a peculiarly malignant ghost.

Hussein, wrapped in a sombre cloak, got over the wall and climbed into the lower branches of the tree. The night was pitch dark and there was no moon, so he went up the tree slowly.

Just as he was hauling himself up on to the branch that overhung the roof, he bumped into a large soft body crowding against the trunk. It was Kadir Baksh on the same errand. 'What are you doing here?' he whispered.

Hussein was rather at a loss to reply to this, so he grappled with Kadir Baksh, meaning to throw him off the tree. They creaked to and fro on the swaying branch, cursing each other in fierce whispers.

Sashiya watched them interestedly from the parapet. She had often seen her lovers fighting in the courtyard below, but never before in the tree. Hussein wrenched Kadir Baksh loose from the trunk, and pushed him over, but the other seized Hussein's leg as he fell. They hit the ground together with a muffled thump; they rolled over twice; Hussein came out on top and he seized Kadir Baksh by the throat.

'Go away,' he whispered, 'or I will kill you.'

'How can I go away when you hold me by the throat?'

'Swear by the Prophet that you will go if I release you.' Kadir Baksh swore in a choked voice. Then he got up, feeling his neck tenderly, and disappeared over the wall. Hussein scaled the tree again: he found Sashiya sitting on the parapet.

'Well?' she said.

'I have come,' replied Hussein.

'So I see.'

Hussein could hardly make any reply to this, so he came creeping along the branch, and he would have dropped on to the roof, but she said:

'You had better stay where you are in case anyone should come, and then you could duck under the parapet.'

Hussein felt quite nonplussed: he had expected something entirely different. He hardly knew just what he had anticipated, but he felt that this was unconventional and not at all the right thing.

'I have composed a song,' he said, 'about your eyebrows.'

'Well, you can't sing it now,' replied Sashiya, 'or you will wake everybody up. But what is there that is so remarkable about my eyebrows that you should make a song?'

'They are like thin black bows bent in perfect symmetry above pools of unfathomable depth,' said Hussein, quoting from his song, which he had taken from the works of Hafiz.

'Aha?' she said. Hussein felt that this was more like the real thing, and he went on.

After the third verse he said, 'Even the finest poetry cannot be recited with any effect in a tree, you know, let alone such poor doggerel as I can turn out.'

'Well, if you come here you must promise not to make the least sound, or I don't know what will happen to me if that cat Fatima comes up . . .'

'On my head and heart,' said Hussein, pulling himself on to the parapet.

'You may go on with your poem,' said Sashiya hastily.

When he had finished, she said, 'What a pity I have read Hafiz too!'

Hussein was very much taken aback, but he did not show it. 'How singular!' he said. 'So you can really appreciate him. Do you know "The Gazelle of Quarasmia"?'

'By heart: and the "Rose of Frangistan".'

'Bismillah! But you are fortunate. I have never been able to get the "Rose".'

They talked for a long while, until the moon came up, and then Sashiya had to go.

'When may I come again?' asked Hussein.

'Next week, perhaps.'

'Oh, before then, please. To-morrow at the same hour?'

'Well . . . it will be difficult: you will wait in the tree if I am late?'

'All night, if need be.'

She found him quite stiff with waiting in the tree the next night, but she rewarded him with the 'Rose of Frangistan'. They talked only of themselves that night:

—

strangely enough they found it extraordinarily interesting.

In the morning Jehangir sniffed at Hussein and gave a little discontented rumble deep in his throat. As he lifted him up on his back the elephant gave him a little squeeze and shook him.

'Jealous, old fat pig?' said Hussein, pulling Jehangir's ears, and the elephant muttered again.

The next night he came to see Sashiya, and the next and the next: each time he liked her more than the last time.

Jehangir became really jealous, and he swallowed the 'Rose of Frangistan' because it smelt of Sashiya.

One evening, as Hussein was climbing over the courtyard wall, he was suddenly jerked to the ground and his head was enveloped in a cloak. A hearty blow stunned him, and he remained unconscious for nearly an hour.

When he came to himself, he was only aware of a violent headache, and he thought for a moment that he must have fallen from the tree.

Then a voice said, 'He is awake.'

Hussein opened his eyes and looked around: he was in a small low room with four men in it. They all had their faces covered.

'We had better peg him out,' said someone. Hussein was seized, and his hands and feet were tied to stout pegs driven deep into the ground. The four men gagged him, and then without saying a word they beat him very grievously indeed.

He could only grunt and strain at the ropes. The men said nothing: the only sound was that of their panting breath, and the heavy thud of the lathis.

At length the pain grew so intolerable that Hussein

ceased to move, in the hope that they would think him to be dead; but they went on and on, so that he writhed again. Then one of the men, missing his stroke, hit Hussein on the head, and he was stunned. He came to himself on a heap of rubbish near the elephant lines: the sun was beating down on him: he was entirely stiff, but his wounds had stopped bleeding. He could hardly move for his extreme soreness, but little by little he managed to creep into the shade. Time passed, and the shadow slid away from him: he lacked the strength to crawl after it now, and a host of flies tormented him cruelly. Some people passed fairly near, and he tried to shout, for he was still just conscious, but he could only achieve a cracked groan that went unheard.

High up out of human sight a vulture swung on motionless wings: it was watching the rubbish heap intently. There were other vultures watching it too. One of them rolled over on to its side and dropped towards the earth. The others followed. Suddenly there was a rush of wings as the first vulture perched on a nearby tree: it looked meditatively at Hussein, with its head on one side, wondering how soon it could safely get to work. At intervals the other vultures joined it: three crows came. For about a quarter of an hour they all stared unwaveringly at Hussein, who stirred now and then.

Several more crows came, and they began to quarrel among themselves. The noise they made attracted some people who were passing. A child ran to see what they were squabbling about, and he found Hussein twitching gently, just enough to keep the birds off. The little group soon became a crowd, all gaping at Hussein, but far too busy talking to do anything for him. With real Indian ineffectiveness they wondered shrilly how he had come there, while he was very nearly dying in front of them.

Their chatter attracted the mahouts, who came running from the elephant lines to see what was happening.

In spite of what he had been through they recognised Hussein, and they carried him to the Englishman who was in charge of that section; then he was taken into the hospital in Haiderabad.

———

Six

 After a week it was obvious that he had come by no permanent injury, and in no long time he came out of hospital quite whole again.

Jehangir received him with great joy; the elephant had become thin and anxious, for although Hussein had been away from him before for more than a month, he had felt that something was wrong, and had gone off his feed.

Hussein went to his hut; it was just as he had left it, except that a letter lay on the floor. He ran to it, hoping that it might be from Sashiya. All that it said was: 'If you go to see Sashiya again we shall beat you more seriously.'

The writing – it was in Urdu – was not that of anyone he knew. It looked like that of someone who was accustomed to writing, and that narrowed things down a bit. For a long time he meditated, lying on Jehangir's back while the elephant wandered slowly about by the banks of a pool, picking out tender branches from among the bushes. Suddenly Hussein had an idea.

'It is probably a letter-writer,' he thought. There was one of these always seated by the Temple of Hanuman, near the elephant lines. He was a fat Bengali: Hussein showed him the letter. 'I might know something about it,' he said, 'but of course I could not tell you anything – my work is most confidential.'

Hussein dropped some money negligently: the scribe covered it with his foot, trying hard to feel how much it was before imparting any information.

At length he said, 'Now that I come to think about it, it seems to me that that is the writing of Abd'Arahman, who writes in the Krishnavi bazaar. Yes, I feel quite sure of it.'

Hussein went into the city, to the bazaar of Krishnavi, and he found Abd'Arahman the letter-writer sitting before his pen-case and paper.

'Peace upon your house, Imâm,' he said, squatting in the dust.

'Salaam aleikum, hâthi-wallah,' replied the old man courteously, who knew Hussein well.

'A friend and I,' said Hussein, 'have had a dispute about the Q'ran. Now we have agreed to seek the arbitration of one whose judgment is infallible and whose learning is as deep as the well Zem-zem. So I have come to one who is not only a hadji, but also an Imâm.'

Abd'Arahman stroked his long white beard: he swelled with pride. 'What little learning I may have,' he said, 'is always at the service of the Faithful.'

'The point, then, of our disagreement is in the Sura called "The Ant", wherein it is related that Suleiman ibn Daoud (on whose soul be peace) desired to know who among his followers would fetch him the throne of Balkis, Queen of Saba, and two answered him. Then it is related that the throne appeared instantly before him, but it is not said by whom the miracle was performed; is it not so?'

'Assuredly.'

'Now I contend that it was performed by the Wazir Asaf ibn Barrachia, the true believer, who answered saying, "I will bring it unto thee, in the twinkling of an eye". Whereas he obstinately holds that it was done by the Djinni Dhakwan, who said, "I will bring it unto thee, before thou arise from thy place".'

'You are both wrong. It was performed by the Suleiman himself. As Al Beidâwi says in . . . And so I have shown, neither the Djinni, who was an Afreet and an unbeliever, nor the Wazir, who was a man full of evil, being a politician, performed this wonderful exploit. Allahu Akbar!'

'I hear and am dumb,' replied Hussein, awaking from his doze. 'By the name of Allah, I wish that my friend had been here that he might have been confounded, for I fear that he will close his ears against me when I tell him that he is wrong, being an obstinate creature and full of all manner of vice.'

The Imâm smiled. 'But you may still defeat him, O excellent Hussein, for I shall write my conclusion with ink upon a fine piece of paper, that you may show it to him.' The old man did so, and Hussein poured forth his thanks.

'It is but a small matter — a nothing,' said the old man.

'Now in the name of the Merciful, the Compassionate,' said Hussein after a little, 'but I could swear that I have seen this distinguished writing before: a friend showed me a letter that you had written for him — some little thing about Sashiya bint Ibrahim: now who in the name of Shaitan was he . . . Jafar? . . . No, my memory must be going.'

———

'Surely you mean Kadir Baksh?' said Abd'Arahman.

'Of course, Kadir Baksh: it is strange how one forgets names.'

'Inshallah! Now when I was a youth there was an ancient man in Haiderabad who remembered the days of the Company, when the English were small in the land and there was a Maharajah whose memory . . .'

While the old man rambled on Hussein was thinking furiously. So it had been Kadir Baksh: he wondered whether the other three were hired badmashes or other lovers.

Suddenly he was aware that the old man had stopped and was laughing, so he laughed too, and said, 'Aha! that was a good tale. Have you never thought, Hadji, of writing these tales in a book, so that your descendants shall say, "Verily, our great-grandfather was a scholar and a wit: one worthy of honour and remembrance? Others with less to write have done so, and they are honoured to-day.'

'By the Beard of the Prophet, I have never considered the matter, but it is a surpassingly excellent idea. Come and break bread with me, and we will discuss it.'

Hussein had nothing to do, for he did not intend to go to Sashiya before dusk, so he went with Abd'Arahman to his house. The old man was delighted with the idea, and from his inexhaustible store of memories he told scores of stories, inquiring anxiously if they should be included. After a little while, however, he saw that there was something abstracted about Hussein's replies.

'I perceive,' he said, 'that there is something troubling you: do not think me intrusive if I observe that I am a very old man, older even than Wali Dad, your grandfather, whom I knew, and from my experience of life I may by chance be able to give some advice that might help you.'

Hussein, charmed by the old man's scholarly courtesy, hesitated a moment and then told him everything.

'I told the lie concerning the Sura of the Ant not from idle impertinence,' he wound up, 'but because it is a point on which I really have thought a great deal.'

The Imâm thought in silence for some time, then he said, 'You have done very well to tell me about it, if I may say so without appearing to boast, for I write so many letters for so many people in all kinds of trouble that I have a certain experience in dealing with it. Are you certain that she does not look upon this Kadir Baksh with more favour than you?'

'Quite certain,' replied Hussein, without the least reason.

'How do you know?'

'Well ... I feel quite sure ...' said Hussein, feeling rather foolish.

'You say that you know Fatima the herb-seller, who can get messages to her for you?'

'Yes.'

'Then we had better ask Sashiya straight out, or perhaps find out in some more devious way.'

'But I am going to see her to-night. I will ask her myself. I shall know, whatever she says.'

'In spite of the letter?'

'Assuredly.'

'Well — I was once a young man too. Tell me about it to-morrow after the evening prayers, if you are still alive. No man may escape his fate ...'

'What is written is written, but I am going to-night.'

———

'Take the blessing of an old man with you. I had a son very like you — long ago, before the cholera . . .'

Hussein went by a roundabout way to the courtyard: he also carried a long curved knife.

He found rather more difficulty in climbing the tree than he had expected, for he was still somewhat feeble. When he was about three-quarters of the way up, he heard a whisper, 'Catch this!' and something brushed by him: it was a couple of sashes tied together that Sashiya had thrown down. He caught at the sashes and she pulled on the other end, so that he was drawn upwards like a fish on a line.

'Oh, Hussein!' said Sashiya rather tremulously, 'and they told me you were dead.'

After a little while Hussein said, 'Tell me just one thing, Heart of my soul: do you love Kadir Baksh?'

Sashiya looked at him, sitting sideways on the cushions that she had brought up; she let her veil fall and looking him full in the face she said, 'No, I hate him.'

Hussein blushed; he was silent for a while.

'He killed Daoud Shah, whom I loved a little once,' Sashiya went on, 'and I feel certain that it was Kadir Baksh who beat you. If he kills you I shall die.'

Hussein told her all about Abd'Arahman.

'I know him. He is a lovely old man. He did my horoscope once, and wouldn't let me pay him.'

The sky was full of stars and they began to count them. Hussein told her a great deal about the stars, eking out a few facts with a great deal of fiction: it was all one to Sashiya.

When the time came for Hussein to go, they leant together over the parapet and lowered a lantern by a long

———

string to see whether anyone was waiting below to waylay him again. They saw nothing, but when at last Hussein really went, and was half-way down the tree, she saw a head bob up over the wall; it was Kadir Baksh. She gave a low whistle to attract Hussein's attention, and beckoned him back again. They went to a place in the roof garden from which they could see over the wall. In the shadows there were three men, while a fourth walked up and down at the end of the blind alley to see that no one came.

'You must go by some other way,' said Sashiya.

'But how can I get through the house – and especially the zenana – without being seen?'

'Perhaps no one would hear you if you went very quietly!'

'But what about the watchman at your uncle's gate?'

'I had not thought of that.' She paused a little while, wrinkling her nose. 'I know,' she said: 'several of the women are going to the Mosque of Imâm Din for the midnight prayer. I will go too, and I will give you a thick chudder and a big cloak, and you can pass out with us.'

'You don't think that someone will notice that there is one too many?'

'No. I will get Fatima – not the old herb-seller, but my cousin – to stay behind. She will do what I ask without any questions, because I know all about her and Faiz Allah, and she knows I know, so that will be all right.'

'What a pearl without price is a woman with brains! I have never met your peer, even among men, although . . .'

'Without doubt, Best-beloved, but they will be going in a little while, so I will get you the things.'

———

In a few moments Hussein was transformed into the shapeless tent that is a Moslem woman when she goes out.

'Now remember to take little steps, Hussein; if you stride like an ostrich we shall be undone; and remember to bring back that yashmak in a bundle; it belongs to Oneiza, and she will raise Eblis if it is lost.'

'On my head and heart.'

After a little while they went down the enclosed staircase to another courtyard, where about a dozen women were waiting.

Without much talk they filed out of a little side door, past an ancient man with a sword – the watchman – and into the street. It was quite deserted except for a few prowling pariah dogs.

A few of the women talked in low voices, but Sashiya and Hussein, who were at the end of the group, kept quiet. Only once, when Hussein strode right over a large puddle, Sashiya whispered 'Ostrich!'

Hussein had not the vaguest idea of how a woman should behave at prayers, as he had never been at a mosque when they were there: he wondered how he could leave the party without disgracing Sashiya.

At length they came to a passage that was so narrow that they had to walk in single file. As they came to a sharp corner, Hussein, who was at the end of the row, took Sashiya's hand: she looked round; he whispered 'Good-bye!' and as the women went round the corner he stayed behind. None of them but Sashiya noticed anything.

He ran back along the way that he had come, for he did not know the city very well; but he knew how to get to the elephant lines from Sashiya's house. He soon reached it, and as he passed the top of the alley leading down to the courtyard he saw Kadir Baksh walking up and down, with his three men still waiting in the shadows.

When he was out of the city and near the elephant lines he stripped off his veil and cloak, wrapping them into a bundle, and he went to his hut.

On the next day Hussein went to see Abd'Arahman. He told him everything that had happened.

'We may be certain that it is none other than Kadir Baksh, then,' said the old man meditatively. 'Let us go to a place where we can talk in peace. I have written seven letters to-day and that is enough.'

They went to the Mosque of Al Beidâwi and sat in the courtyard.

'Perhaps, if he were to be beaten?' suggested Hussein.

'Yes: but if he were not killed you would be almost certainly within a few days, and if he were, you would be involved in a blood-feud with his people — he is of Pathan stock, you know. You might have him poisoned, but that is very dangerous these days, and you would have to bribe one of the women of his house, and you never know how long women will keep a secret, even if it is to their own advantage.'

'I might be able to stab him myself as he leaves the elephant lines at night.'

'No. You would be suspect at once. We must think of something more subtle.'

They sat thinking for some time: the Imâm in the Mosque called the Faithful to prayer from the minaret.

'La illah il Allah. Mahommed raisul Allah!'

———

Abd'Arahman and Hussein prostrated themselves towards Mecca.

'I have it,' cried the old man, as they got up: 'we will have him cursed. By my father's head, that is the solution of the whole matter.'

'Perhaps something a little more definite?' said Hussein dubiously.

'Eh, but you have never seen a man wither and die under a thorough curse by a fakir who really knows his business: in these degenerate days there are not many such men — but I know one — a red-headed fakir who sits daily on a bed of nails, a very holy man.'

'I know the one you mean,' said Hussein; 'he has one arm continually raised.'

'It is the same man. I know him well. Now I shall go and speak to him. Come back here with all the money you can bring at the hour of the midnight prayer, and I will tell you whether it can be done.'

'I will see Sashiya again this evening: if she thinks well of it, you and I will go to the fakir.'

'It is not wise to tell a woman of a plan before it is accomplished,' replied Abd'Arahman, 'but I am quite sure you will. Be very careful to-night.'

That evening Kadir Baksh was at a big Pathan feast outside the town, and his hired badmashes did not trouble to stay awake half the night with no one to watch them, so Hussein found nobody in the alley when he went over the wall to see Sashiya.

He told her all about the letter-writer's scheme, and from the first she thought it a very good one.

'He deserves anything', she said, 'for beating you, and for murdering poor Daoud Shah.'

———

'Did you love Daoud Shah?' asked Hussein anxiously.

'Just a little; but then I thought I loved Kadir Baksh a little too at that time.'

'But you don't now?'

'I hate him more than I can say. I would poison him if I could. Once I dropped a stone on him when he was climbing up the tree, but he only laughed because it missed.'

'You love me a little? As much as Daoud Shah?'

'No.'

Hussein looked unhappy, and Sashiya laughed.

'No,' she said, 'ever so much more – with my whole heart!'

For a long while they said nothing, but sat side by side, their little fingers linked.

A little after the midnight muezzin, Hussein found Abd'Arahman in the courtyard of the mosque.

'He will do it,' said the old man, after Hussein had told him that Sashiya liked the idea, 'and if you come here to-morrow at noon I will take you to him. Can you get away then?'

'Yes, there is no work done just now, after the heat becomes too great, and the elephants are not used much.'

'Good. You should bring all your money: he will probably do it for twenty rupees, but it would be very unwise to anger him by haggling.'

The next day they went to see the fakir: they found him in a very small, dirty hut leaning against the back of a house. He was squatting on a bed of nails, for he expected them. He was very thin and his body was quite thickly covered with dirt, which was cracked where he bent, like enamel. He had no clothing besides a mat of hair and a loin-cloth. For the last twenty years he had held his left arm up over his head, so that now it was immovable, and very thin like a dead stick. The nails were peculiarly long and twisted. He lived principally on bhang, which gave his red-rimmed eyes a very strange expression. Altogether he was a singularly pious and respected fakir, with a deep knowledge of hypnotism in its more curious applications, and a well-founded and widespread reputation for curses.

Hussein, after suitably respectful greetings, to which the fakir did not reply, but only laughed in a disconcerting way, stated his business.

'So you want him cursed? This is all very vague: is he to die of leprosy, small-pox, or by strange, hideous dreams?'

'Well, I am a poor man . . .'

'Oh, no you are not: you have thirty-two rupees there and a steady salary.'

'How do you know?'

'I know everything,' said the fakir magnificently. 'Now for those thirty-two rupees down and twenty next month I shall put a horror into the mind of Kadir Baksh, so foul that he shall wither for want of sleep and die mad within a month. I know him and I hate him: he spat at me some three years ago, and refused me alms; that is why I will do it so cheaply and, above all, so thoroughly.'

'But this is a great sum for such a humble man as I am: and also what proof can I have that the curse will be effective?'

'How did the babu Surendranath die? And Dhossibhoy Chatterji, Krishnaswami the Merchant, Wali Din, and Nichols Sahib the Englishman? You know,' he said, turning to Abd'Arahman, 'even if this impious and irreverent youth does not.'

'All mad,' replied the letter-writer.

'Of course. But come in this room behind, and I will convince you. Will you come too?' he asked Abd'Arahman.

'I am an old man: I know your powers. I will remain in the sun.'

Hussein crawled into the little dark room after the fakir; there was a brass pot with a fire burning in it that gave out a suffocating stench.

'Sit there, and do not move,' said the fakir. 'Hold this. It contains a hair of the Beard of the Prophet. If you loose your hold upon it your soul will die, and probably your body also.'

Hussein felt sweat running down behind his ears. He sat still, gripping the amulet.

The fakir moved about in the darkness, muttering. Presently he stopped, and Hussein heard, with an indescribable feeling of dread, a whispering noise that came from all around the room, like the noise of wind among trees. The horrible part of it was that there were several voices in the noise, each muttering, so that distinct words could be heard now and then. It rose and fell, like a breeze: the smell from the brazier grew worse, and the fakir threw something on it that flared up with a green flame. The voices sniggered.

The fakir muttered a question. The voices quavered an answer. Something that was not the fakir moved in a dark corner.

Hussein had to hold himself from panicking.

The fakir burst out into a long incantation: the voices

followed him, and sometimes they moaned. Then he blew a tongue of red flame from his mouth, and wiping his lips with his long, henna-dyed beard, he said to Hussein:

'Look firmly and without cease at the light in the ring on my left hand.'

Hussein stared at it for some time: the voices died down to a gentle murmuring, but that was worse than before, for the sound seemed to hold in itself an incredible malignancy.

Hussein felt his neck stiffening as he kept his eyes on the spot of light. The fakir muttered some words that Hussein heard half-consciously. Then, after a while, he said, in a loud voice:

'Look at my left arm.'

Hussein transferred his gaze to that, and the muttering went on. The voices rose to a loud chattering, and the fire burnt up with leaping green flames. Then Hussein saw the fakir take his withered left arm with his sound right hand and break it off at the elbow: he even heard it snap with a brittle sound, like a dry stick.

Seven

The last thing of which Hussein was conscious was the hardness of the amulet, which he gripped with such force that it broke his skin: then he was aware that he was in the front room, with Abd'Arahman splashing water on his face and the red-bearded fakir leering down at him.

The withered arm was still in its place.

'Now,' said the holy man, 'do you believe that I can curse?'

Hussein did not speak a word, but laid his thirty-two rupees on the ground, and staggered out, leaning on Abd'Arahman's arm.

'What happened?' asked the old man.

'All Jehanna,' he replied, and went away to his house, where he neither ate nor drank, but only slept for several hours.

For some days Hussein had to go away with Jehangir to take an official over some plantations, but before he went he saw Sashiya for a little while in the cemetery. She had slipped away, unobserved, from the other women to the trees, and he told her all that had been done.

When he came back he found a boy squatting before his hut: the boy said the red-bearded fakir wanted to see him, so he went at once.

He found him sitting in the sun against the wall of the temple of Hanuman. Hussein could hardly take his eyes from the distorted arm that stuck straight up from the fakir's curiously twisted shoulder.

'I have begun the curse,' said the fakir, 'but now it is essential that Kadir Baksh should know what is coming to him. You must see to that.'

'But how can I do that without incurring the blood-feud if he dies?'

'If he dies! In the Name of the Compassionate! What do you think my curses do? But you must let him know. I do not care how. Go away. I wish to think.'

'But . . .'

'Go away, or I shall curse you too.'

Hussein walked slowly away, thinking. The boy followed him. The fakir used this boy for gazing into pools of ink, and other things.

'I know how it can be done,' he said.

'How?'

'Give me four annas, and I will do it for you — I have done these things often.'

'But how?' asked Hussein again.

'Four annas first.'

'Two now, and two when it is done.'

'As you say.'

Hussein squatted by a fountain — they were in a public square — and gave the boy two annas. 'Now how will you do it?' he asked.

———

'I will go to Kadir Baksh — I know where he lives — and tell him that there is a message from a woman waiting for him at my master's hut.'

'But will he come? Surely he will suspect something?'

'I will leer meaningly at him. He will come like a hawk. It always works with these Pathans,' replied the boy.

'You are right. Allah's curse on all unbelievers and Pathans!'

That evening Hussein met the boy walking through the elephant lines with Kadir Baksh. The Pathan spat as they passed: so did Hussein. Before he had gone many yards a stone sang past his head.

Abd'Arahman was sitting, as was his custom, in the Krishnavi bazaar when Hussein came again into town.

'I have a message for you,' he said, when he saw Hussein. It was a note to say that Fatima was ill, and Sashiya could not see him because she had to sit by her cousin.

So Hussein spent the evening with Abd'Arahman, helping him with his book, which was rapidly coming into being. It was an amusing evening, for the old man had a wonderful store of memories, and hundreds of highly-seasoned stories.

The next day all the elephants were being used in a procession through Haiderabad for the greater honour of a visiting Rajah, come to pay his respects to the Viceroy, who happened to be passing through the town.

As the gorgeously caparisoned elephants went between the lines of soldiers that kept the people back, Hussein, on Jehangir, caught the eyes of the fakir's boy, who dodged under a soldier's arm, gave him a quick nod and slipped back into the crowd.

Hussein looked forward through the swaying howdahs

to where Kadir Baksh sat on his elephant, immediately in front of the Viceroy himself: he had half expected to see his enemy withered already, but there was no visible change.

Nevertheless, Kadir Baksh was far from at peace within: he had gone to the fakir's hovel as the boy had predicted, expecting a message from someone – he had hoped that it might be from Sashiya – and he had been told by the boy to wait in the front room.

After a little while the boy came back and said:

'She will be a little while yet,' and he gave Kadir Baksh some coffee.

Kadir Baksh woke up – still in a dazed state – some time later, to find himself in a dark room. He had been drugged.

Meanwhile the boy, anxious to earn his two annas, had persuaded the fakir to attend to the Pathan himself. So in a half-dream Kadir Baksh heard someone being cursed with hideous thoroughness; then he got used to the dim light, and saw a red-bearded fakir sitting before him. Suddenly he realised that the person who was being cursed was himself. He vaguely remembered having seen the fakir before.

While he was still dazed and unable to move, horrible things happened in the room, so that he was not sure whether he was awake or in a ghastly nightmare.

He awoke a second time, leaning against some railings in a deserted garden. He could not remember how he had got there, or what had happened, but he rather thought that he must have been drunk.

While the procession wound its slow way through the town, Kadir Baksh pondered over what had happened to him, trying to piece together the fragments of memories that hung about his brain.

He felt curiously depressed and anxious, as if something were going to happen.

That night Kadir Baksh drank heavily – he was anything but a strict Mahommedan – to raise his spirits. Because of the drink he slept well at first, but a little after the moon had risen he woke suddenly: he was wide awake; in a moment his head was perfectly clear, and he was conscious of a singular causeless dread inside him.

For some time he strained to catch a sound which, for some reason that he did not know, he expected. Then he heard a sort of murmur behind him. He twisted round, but he saw nothing. From another corner of the room there came a gentle, incredibly malignant chuckle. Kadir Baksh glared into the darkness: he thought he saw something move across a thin shaft of moonlight. For a long while he stayed quite still, listening. He heard nothing more for a period that seemed like hours, and at length he grew so stiff and cramped that he moved, and having settled in a more comfortable position, he slept again.

Almost at once, it seemed to him, he entered into a nightmare world so hideous and foul that he awoke screaming, damp all over with cold sweat. His dream had been of a loathsome amorphous black thing, so extraordinarily evil as to be well-nigh indescribable.

Mixed up with this dream was the figure of a fakir with a straggling red beard, whose left arm was withered and fixed above his head. As he awoke he heard the same chuckle: for some reason it seemed to deprive him of the power of movement, so that he lay tensely still, waiting for the next sound.

Nothing happened for a long time, and he felt himself going off to sleep: he dreaded the idea of having that hideous dream again, so he took to pinching himself to keep awake. At last the pinches became too few and far between to keep him from sleeping, and he dozed off. At once he was in the nightmare again: this time it was even worse than before. The same loathsome black thing and the same fakir took part in it, but there were other things, vague shapes, small and large, that kept up a continual rapid muttering in the background.

He awoke in an even worse state than before, and again he heard the gloating chuckle from a far dark corner.

Kadir Baksh managed to keep awake for the rest of the night: all the time he stared fixedly into the corner where he thought that he saw a dark thing move from time to time. He felt that if once it moved out of the corner something appalling would happen to him, and somehow he knew that he could only keep it there by a great effort of will, and by watching it continually.

An age seemed to pass, and the thin moonbeams moved slowly over the floor. Then a thin grey light filtered through the window. Kadir Baksh had never been so glad to see the dawn. The grey light grew stronger, and the shadows in the corners melted away. He staggered out into the open: in the daylight he felt safe.

Towards noon he felt inclined to treat the whole thing as a dream caused through drinking too much, and he swore an oath to himself not to drink any more for a week. But a little fear stayed in the back of his mind, although he assured himself again and again that he was a fool to have been frightened of a dream, like a child.

Strangely enough he did not tell anyone about it,

although two or three people saw that he was looking unwell.

By sunset the fear in the back of his mind had grown and grown, so that he could hardly bear to be out of the company of other men. He lived ordinarily in a hut in the elephant lines, but the idea of what might be awaiting him when he returned became so awful to him that he decided to spend the night at his brother's house in the town. His father, two uncles, four brothers and several cousins lived in a huge rambling house on the outskirts of Haiderabad. Technically it belonged to his eldest brother, but any member of the family would stay there as by right, for they were Pathans, and they held almost feudally strong ties of kinship among themselves. Most of them were horse copers, some did nothing at all, and others were frankly professional thieves. They came of a tribe of hereditary thieves and cattle-lifters, and this was the effect a town had upon them.

Kadir Baksh sat up as late as he could, playing dice with some of his cousins; but at last they all went to bed and he felt ashamed not to go too. As long as he could he kept awake, and he fixed a pin so that it would prick him into wakefulness if he lay down. But it slipped sideways, and he slept and writhed again in the grip of the hideous dream. He awoke to find two of his brothers and an uncle standing over him.

'What were you screaming for?' they asked.

Kadir Baksh did not reply, but stared past them into a dark corner, from which he heard the chuckle that he had expected and dreaded, and where he saw the dark thing move gently.

'Keep it back, for the love of Allah!' he shrieked.

They all turned; they saw nothing.

'What is it?' asked the eldest brother, but Kadir Baksh could not answer for the trembling of his teeth. After a little while he calmed down, and still staring into the corner he said:

'I am not very well: would you stay with me to-night?'

They thought it was a touch of fever, and his eldest brother pulled a string bed into the room and stayed with him. He was about to blow out the light after they had talked a while, when Kadir Baksh said:

'Put the lamp in that corner, will you?'

His brother looked at him curiously, but he did so, and went to sleep.

He was awakened shortly afterwards by an inhuman howl: it was Kadir Baksh doubled up in what looked like a fit. He was twitching violently, and there was froth between his lips.

People came running in, and they all tried to rouse him, but in vain: he lay unconscious till the next day, when he came to. He was very queer to speak to, but he seemed fairly well otherwise.

Towards nightfall he became more and more uneasy; he refused to go to bed at all, and spent the whole night surrounded by lights in the courtyard, walking about to keep awake. For several nights he did this, until he was almost dead from lack of sleep. Hussein saw him one day: for a moment he hardly recognised the Pathan, his face was so altered, but when he did he chuckled grimly and went to tell Abd'Arahman.

That night towards dawn Kadir Baksh slept in spite of the lights. His dream was even more terrible than before; Daoud Shah, whom he had helped to murder some two years before, came and joined with the devils who tormented him. His waking terror was horrible to see. After that he refused to be left alone for a moment, and he grew steadily worse. He would not speak, for he feared the sound of his own voice, and he would not take food. Some days passed and Kadir Baksh seemed hardly sane. Hussein, whom he had meant to kill, joined with Daoud Shah in his dreams, which came upon him now even when he was awake. He thought that he had killed Hussein. He grew very thin, and only spoke to mutter incoherent things about Hussein, Daoud Shah and a red-bearded fakir, and to shriek dreadfully if a shadow moved.

They sent for a hakim. This doctor was famous for his strength of mind; he treated all his patients with a purge and an invincible determination to make them do whatever they did not want to do: thus he made fat people take exercise, and the thin ones take more food. He applied this type of remedy always, and on the whole it worked well.

The relations of Kadir Baksh told the hakim that he would never leave the company of other people, and that he hated the dark; so the doctor caused them to prepare a quiet room, which was carefully darkened with shutters. Then he saw Kadir Baksh, and told the relatives that the patient was delirious and should be left in peace in the dark, quiet room.

'The patient', said the good hakim, 'might become a little violent — it is only natural in this delirious state. Of course, he does not know what he is doing, so we had better strap him down in his bed, lest he do himself some injury. You should take him a little light food three times a day, until the fever has declined, but otherwise you must leave him quite alone. Pay no attention to what he says, even if he shouts and screams – it is only light-headedness arising from certain humours in the spleen.'

So four men, one for each limb, took Kadir Baksh and strapped him on his bed. The hakim covered his face with a cloth to keep the flies away, and they left him in the darkened room.

No one bothered about the really appalling sounds that came from the room, and when they ceased after one dreadful long-drawn scream that died away with a choking moan, they nodded their heads, and said that the hakim was quite right, for Kadir Baksh would be sleeping peacefully now.

After some hours they went with food to the darkened room: Kadir Baksh was lying in a very strange position in one corner – he had broken his thick straps – with his hands over his head, as if he were protecting himself from something, which was manifestly absurd, because there was nothing there, as everyone pointed out. Nevertheless there was an expression of unutterable horror on his face: he was quite dead.

On the evening of the same day the fakir sent for Hussein, who came as soon as he could. He found the fakir lying in front of his hovel, looking utterly exhausted.

'It is all over,' he said, when he saw Hussein; 'he is dead and damned now.'

'Allah be praised! Are you sure?'

'Don't ask me if I am sure, clod. I have said it, it is therefore so. I have sent for you to tell you to keep your tongue from killing you. Never mention Kadir Baksh's name. Go away.'

———

Hussein went, with joy in his heart. The boy caught him up.

'It is true,' he said. 'Can I have my two annas?'

At the house of the Pathan the hakim was looking at the body.

'This is by no means an ordinary death,' he said, 'otherwise my treatment would have prevailed. Had he any enemies?'

'Many,' replied one of the listening circle.

'How many would desire his death?'

'Allah alone knows — perhaps five, perhaps ten.'

'There was a certain Daoud Shah,' said the hakim: the men smiled unpleasantly. 'Had he any relatives?'

'None who would take up a blood feud against him.'

'Now I saw a death very like this,' said the hakim, after a pause. 'It was a babu called Surendranath. The tale was that he was cursed.'

'Bismillah! my son muttered concerning a certain fakir, if I remember rightly,' said the father of Kadir Baksh.

'Yes — a red-bearded fakir, I heard him. Also, he cried out in his sleep against Daoud Shah,' cried a cousin.

'That is what he would do if he had been cursed in a certain way, known only to a very few. Again, he feared sleep and darkness worse than death; that also points to the same thing.'

That night Hussein and Sashiya sat on cushions in the roof garden.

'We might have been a little less drastic, Best-beloved,' said Sashiya, 'but he did deserve it, and anyhow, it must have been his fate, and he could never have avoided that.'

At the same time Amir Khan, the cousin of Kadir Baksh, was saying to his assembled relatives, 'There is only one red-bearded fakir that I know of in Haiderabad, and he sits daily near the Temple of Hanuman.'

On the roof garden Hussein said, 'We have better things to talk about. Tell me, this Wali Din, to whom you were betrothed, did you ever care for him?'

'So far as I know he is a pleasant, harmless little creature – hardly a man though. I have only seen him perhaps a score of times, and then only when I was a child, but as for loving him, by Allah no! I only look on him as a future husband.'

'Then if I were to talk to him, and persuade him that he could find a more suitable wife, do you think that your father would look on me with any favour?'

'Are you a Sufi or a Shiah?'

'Whichever you like – a freethinker. Sufi, really, I suppose.'

'Well, you must be a Shiah of the most orthodox sect. My father is a most strict Moslem; he hates the Sufi heretics worse than unbelievers.'

'Do you see that very bright star – no, that one? Well, if it were not in Hafiz, whom you know better than I, I would say that it is just like the light in your eyes. Do you know, I once saw an English sahib whose eyes were blue.'

'Blue! Bismillah!'

'It is true, on my soul: blue as that turquoise on your belt. I must tell you how he and I took a city full of dacoits . . .'

'I love a man who is a man,' said Sashiya, after some time – Hussein swelled – 'but do you fear mice? Rustum did, and so do I.'

'Mice! Why, I have subdued an elephant that was

mûsth, and that when I was a child – but I love a woman who is a woman. Women should fear mice.'

'An elephant! Oh, Hussein!'

'Well, it is true that I had no idea at all that Jehangir was mûsth, but I never told anyone – no one but you. Do you know, Jehangir is very jealous of you.'

'Silly old pig, but I understand him . . . Why did you tell none but me?'

'I don't quite know; but I feel somehow that I don't ever want to tell you lies, even if you could never find out.'

For a long while they talked about the exact state of their feelings for one another in the peculiarly unoriginal way that lovers have of expressing themselves. But to Hussein and Sashiya it was new and wonderful: they thought sincerely that they would never change, and they said so quite often.

For several days Hussein lived in a private paradise in his own mind, inhabited only by himself and Sashiya. He had never known that he could be so happy.

Jehangir became more resigned, but he cherished a secret hatred of the person who was taking Hussein's heart from him, although he did not know who it was.

One day Abd'Arahman came to him in the elephant lines. The old man was very agitated; Hussein took him to his hut.

'The worst has happened,' said the letter-writer.

'What? In the name of Allah, tell me at once.'

But the old man only moaned for some time.

'They have bribed the fakir's boy,' he said at last, 'and they have sworn a blood feud against you. Old red-beard wants to see you at my house to-morrow.'

———

That night, when Hussein came back from seeing Sashiya — he told her nothing — he found his hut burnt to the ground.

The news had spread among the mahouts with extra-ordinary rapidity. Nearly all his friends avoided him, as they had no wish to be mixed up in so deadly a matter. He slept in a small unused hut at the end of the lines. A little before dawn he heard a movement in the darkness: he reached silently for his knife.

'Sh! It is Mahmud,' said the man — one of his oldest friends. 'I have come to tell you that they say in the bazaar that the family of Kadir Baksh have discovered that you cursed him to death, and they have sworn a blood feud against you,' he whispered.

'I knew this afternoon,' replied Hussein.

'You have no hope against so many, and half of them have killed men before. You should be gone before day-light. For the love of Allah tell nobody that I warned you.'

Hussein promised, and his friend faded away into the dark. He thought for a long while, and decided to wait until he had seen the fakir.

There was no work for the elephants the next day, so Hussein went into the town, where he thought that he would be safe.

As he was going down the Krishnavi bazaar to find Abd'Arahman, a stone fell at his feet from a house-top. It was big enough to have killed him if it had hit him.

After that he kept in the middle of the lane. Suddenly he thought that he might endanger the letter-writer if he were seen with him, so he turned aside into a mosque to wait until noon, when he would see the fakir. He kept thinking of the way the stone had splintered when it hit the ground, and he knew that his knees were trembling. He felt desperately alone.

In the mosque he looked keenly at the other men there, for he knew that the Pathans would not mind where they killed him so long as they could do so without danger, and there were many dark alleys about the mosque, but he did not see anyone who looked suspicious. Nevertheless he kept in the open, under the sounding-board, where there were aged hadjis arguing.

After a while one of the old men turned to Hussein as an unbiased hearer and said:

'These two foolish old men maintain that it is unlawful to eat a crab on one's pilgrimage, saying that it is not a fish . . . incredible obstinacy!'

'What am I, to argue with white hairs?' replied Hussein. 'But it seems to me that in the Sura called The Table it is written, "It is lawful for you to fish in the sea and to eat what you shall catch" . . .'

'Just so,' cried another of the hadjis, 'but the crab comes on to the land, and to take it then is the same as hunting, which is unlawful during the Haj.'

'And again,' said the third, 'if one were to catch a drowned pig in one's nets, would it therefore be lawful to eat of its flesh? By no means! Undoubtedly the verse only refers to true fish, and a crab is not a true fish, by reason of its coming on to the land.'

'But Malek ibn Ans says . . .'

They argued hotly for some time, and Hussein was really enjoying himself when he saw three men come in. They looked about the mosque, and one of them pointed towards the group under the sounding-board: Hussein saw this from the corner of his eye.

Two of them sat down by the door, and the third strolled towards the arguers: he was a tall hawk-nosed man – obviously a Pathan. Hussein had not seen him before, and he felt sure that the Pathan did not know him for certain. He thought quickly for some time while the talk flowed past his head. Suddenly an idea came to him, and when there was a pause he said:

'Now I am no scholar at all, but my friend Hussein the Mahout, who is a very Imâm in learning, told me that Jallal'udin distinguishes clearly between true fish and crabs. But then some say the Jallal'udin himself was a schismatic, and therefore of no account; indeed my friend Hussein holds that he is little better than a Kafir, an unbeliever.'

He said this in a loud voice, and he saw the Pathan turn his head quickly, and go back to his friends. He saw them talking together: two of them were shaking their heads, while the third seemed to be disagreeing with them. After a while another came walking slowly by the old men; he gave Hussein a long, searching stare as he passed.

Hussein recognised him at once: it was Jafar, the brother of Kadir Baksh. He knew that his ruse had failed, for the Pathan had often seen him when he was friendly with Kadir Baksh.

He remained talking with the old men for some time and the Pathans settled down by the doorway. Towards noon several men came in for the mid-day prayer; then from the minar there came the great cry of the muezzin: everyone knelt, forehead against the earth, towards Mecca.

Hussein crawled backwards towards a corridor that led

to another door: no one noticed him, and he was gone when the Imâm's final 'Allahu Akbar' died away in the echoing mosque.

He ran to the house of Abd'Arahman: the fakir was waiting for him.

'Well, you are still alive,' said the fakir. 'I thought they would have got you by now . . . in my young days you would have been a corpse . . . inefficient lepers! I have got an amulet for you against their curses. You are lucky to be still alive: you must leave Haiderabad to-day. They are very powerful amongst the bad-mashes here; you will never have a chance.'

'To-day?' said Hussein. 'Well, I must say goodbye to Jehangir, and sell what I cannot carry, and then I will go. I will try to rejoin the service when the elephants go to some other place.'

'You do it at your own risk,' replied the fakir, 'and you need not sell anything: you owe me thirty rupees, but I will take what you leave in payment. Come back as soon as you can, and I will have a plan ready.'

Hussein wondered how the fakir knew that the few things he possessed would be worth the debt, but he said nothing. He went back to the elephant lines, keeping to the crowded streets; but for all his caution he was nearly run down as he crossed a street by an old Ford that had been creeping along by him for some way. He knew that the old wreck belonged to his enemy's cousin: if it had had a better turn of speed he would have been run over.

He drew all the pay that was due to him, and collected one or two debts among the other mahouts: then he told Jehangir that he was going away for some time, but that he would come back. Jehangir grasped that, so Hussein left him fairly contented.

He went back into the town with one of his friends who was taking an elephant in, and he came safely to the fakir again.

There was a gaunt old man there with him, whom Abd'Arahman introduced as Feroze Khan, the story-teller.

'How much money have you got?' asked the fakir, without any preamble.

'Only a very little,' replied Hussein cautiously. 'I am but a poor man.'

'It is of no use trying to deceive me. What is the sum?'

'Forty-three rupees and three annas.'

'Well, give me ten for myself, and Feroze Khan twenty; he will take you with him.'

Hussein saw that he could not object, so he said nothing and handed over the money.

'We had better change his appearance,' said Feroze Khan.

Hussein stripped, and the fakir gave him some old clothes of the sort worn by poor men in the north: the story-teller put a peculiarly folded pugari on his head and stuck a black, curling beard on his face. The fakir said that he could keep the clothes, as they would probably come in useful for someone else, and he gave Hussein some bhang to alter his eyes.

When they had arranged him to their satisfaction Abd'Arahman gave him a mirror: a new face looked up at him from it.

Feroze Khan gave him some heavy covered baskets to carry, and they left the house: at the door Abd'Arahman caught Hussein by the sleeve.

———

'Here is something from Sashiya,' he said, 'and this is my poor gift to you. Go in peace, and Allah go with you. Write to me and I will send you letters from her.'

Hussein knelt and patted the old man's feet: he felt strangely moved. Abd'Arahman leant on his shoulder a moment, and stumbled back into the house.

'I fear he will come to an evil death,' he said to the fakir.

The holy man belched cynically. 'What matter?' he said, 'he has no more money.'

'But he was a good youth, and very like my dead son.'

'No fool like an old one,' muttered the fakir.

Outside the house Hussein asked Feroze Khan what was in the baskets.

'Snakes,' he replied.

'But why snakes?'

'I will tell you everything in the train. We are going to Jubbulpore. There is no time to lose in idle talk.'

On the way to the station they passed the house where Sashiya lived: there were three evil-looking Pathans lounging about outside. Hussein lowered his head, and walked past them as nonchalantly as he could. They did not even glance at him twice, but until they were far behind he felt his heart thumping almost painfully.

At the station they sat down on the ground with a great number of other people. Feroze Khan left Hussein by the baskets and vague bundles while he got the tickets.

Every time a train came in there was a rush of peasants, who clamoured to know whether it was their train: many of them waited for hours with their baggage, eating their meals where they sat, for fear of missing their train. Some of them, also, hung their tickets about their necks as charms, but these were only the simple country folk: most of the people were quite accustomed to the railway. Feroze Khan was one of these: he told Hussein that he never waited more than two or three hours for his train – they had two hours to spare now – and then, in spite of the ceaseless tumult, he went to sleep.

Meanwhile Hussein investigated the little bundles that Abd'Arahman had given him: the first was tied up very intricately in a piece of spotted silk. When he had got it undone, Hussein found a letter, seventy-three rupees, a gold bangle and a broken mohur on a cord for a keepsake. Sashiya had written in a great hurry, rather incoherently, but she conveyed her meaning so well that Hussein wept. No one took much notice of him: they thought that he had lost his ticket.

A tall Sikh, who was eating in the midst of his bundles just behind Hussein, reached over the sleeping Feroze Khan and gave him a chupatti, saying, in bad Urdu, 'You will doubtless find it: look in the baskets.'

'Many thanks, Guru-ji,' replied Hussein in Punjabi, 'but my grief was for another cause.'

'Wallah! You speak like one from my own Amritsar. It is a comfort to hear a civilised tongue again. Women are not worth troubling about – eat another chupatti.'

'Why do you think I weep for a woman?'

'What else does a young man weep for? Money and women – that is all. Even an unworldly man is troubled by them.'

They talked for some time, and then the Sikh rushed away in a cloud of rich Punjabi oaths to catch his train.

Hussein undid the second bundle: it was the manuscript

of Abd'Arahman's book. He knew how the old man treasured it, and he almost wept again.

At last their train came in, and as they sat in it with their bundles, Feroze Khan explained to Hussein what he did.

'Often I follow the regiments as they march to and fro in the land,' he said; 'with the snakes I entertain the sahibs and the common soldiers, and I tell my tales to the followers in the evenings. Sometimes, when there are fairs, I leave the regiments, and tell stories throughout the day wherever the people come together in numbers. You will take round the bowl when I stop at the more exciting parts, and I will teach you how to manage the snakes.'

'May not I also tell tales to the people?'

'By no means: it is an art known only to a few. The mystery lies not so much in the telling, as in the choosing of the tales. Now I can tell at a glance what kind of tale is suitable. For instance, the peasants of the Punjab — many of them are of the Faith — love to hear of Sohrab and Rustum; and again, the unbelievers of the South desire to hear of the great emperors and warriors before the English came, or of the deeds of their strange gods. But it entirely depends on so many things that only one such as myself can be sure what story will extract most money from those who listen.'

They came to Jubbulpore, and Feroze Khan went to the house of a friend, where several men came to see him. Hussein was sent out while they were talking, and he spent his time in writing a long letter to Sashiya, which he enclosed with one to Abd'Arahman.

When Feroze Khan came from his friend's house he hurried Hussein away again to the station, and soon they were swinging away towards Agra. Hussein wondered vaguely why the old man did this, but he was too much concerned with his own affairs to worry over those of Feroze Khan.

In Agra there was a festival, and the story-teller made his way with Hussein to a market-place, where he found an empty corner, and sat down, beating on the tom-tom, and crying in a loud voice:

'A tale! A marvellous tale! Listen to a story-teller who has delighted Rajahs,' shouted Feroze Khan. Several people stopped; some of them squatted down. Hussein beat on the tom-tom, and the old man began.

Eight

'Now in the days of the great Shah Jehan there was a certain man who dwelt in this city: he was (here the story-teller's eyes swept his audience – all Moslems) a true believer. He was a merchant – an upright man who had, nevertheless, accumulated a great store of precious things. Among all these things, such as the teeth of elephants, rubies and tears of the sea, he valued none so much as his only wife, in spite of the fact that she had borne him no children. She was of a singular beauty, comparable to the light of the moon on desert sands.

'Now the merchant, whose name was Mahsud Khan, had always been a pious Moslem, and from his boyhood had cherished a desire to make the hadj to Mecca. So at a certain season, when his affairs were in an excellent condition, and there was peace in the land, he decided to fulfil his desire. His brother, Mustapha the Wazir, was high in the favour of the Shah Jehan, and to him Mahsud confided the care of his great possessions, his lands and his wife, Oneiza. Then he joined with a company of merchants and pilgrims who were going to the holy city, and they set sail, it being an auspicious day in the correct season, from Karachi, and after some days had passed they came, with the help of Allah, to Muscat.

'Here Mahsud found a great host of the Faithful who were waiting for a caravan to set out. He passed many days in the company of the great merchants of the city, with whom he had traded, but he was careful to observe the whole ritual of the hadj, and he offended in no way.

'At length a caravan was formed, and the pilgrims set their faces to the West.

'Mahsud bought camels for himself and his servants and he joined the caravan. Many of the other merchants went by sea in ships to Jeddah, but Mahsud had a loathing of the sea, for it stirred him evilly and incessantly within, so he preferred the arduous pilgrimage by land, although two months were consumed thereby.

'Meanwhile, Mustapha the Wazir had not prospered. The Frankish merchants were coming into the land: fierce men who measured their cloth with their swords.

'Mustapha perceived that they were Nassani, an abomination to the Faithful, so he entreated them harshly, the more so because they bribed the lesser officials well, but the Wazir meanly.

'Now the Franks of that day were by no means the same as the slow sahibs of these times: they were crafty men — at a later time their Clive Bahadur out-tricked even Omichaund the Merchant and won great fame — so they conspired with certain enemies of the Wazir, and together they poisoned the ear of the Shah Jehan against him, by means of venal officials.

'At this time the great ruler was almost mad with grief

at the death of his queen, so when he heard the tales that they told against the Wazir, he flew into a violent passion, crying aloud that there was no truth in any man, and that as he had raised up Mustapha, so he would cast him down.

'On the following morning Mustapha was trampled to death by an elephant before the whole court, in the ancient way, and his enemies triumphed openly.

'The whole of the unfortunate Wazir's property was forfeit, for after he had been executed, he was tried, and being — naturally — unable to defend himself, he was found guilty of plotting against the Peacock Throne.

'The treasurer of the King made no difference between Mustapha's own property and that which was left in his charge, so all Mahsud's wealth was swept away like the dry leaves in the evening. Oneiza and other women of the anderun of the Wazir were taken to the royal zenana, and as Oneiza outshone the rest as the moon outshines the stars, the Chief Eunuch considered her for a long time.

'Shah Jehan, with his heart gnawed incessantly by the scorpion of memory, was wont to seek distraction among his female establishment, but so far he had found no ease, and the Chief Eunuch feared for his head. Therefore he observed Oneiza the more closely, and he noted that she always wore a melancholy aspect. Again, he noticed that the other women were always cheerful of countenance, and yet the Shadow of the Lord was displeased with them.

'Oneiza was filled with bitter grief: her heart was, as it were, a pitcher beneath a fountain: again and yet again it brimmed over, as she wept for Mahsud, her husband, the light of her days: moreover, she knew certainly that

---

there was a child within her, and she was sorrowful beyond all words that the child's father would never see it. Yet she dared not say anything, for the other women of the zenana hated her — they feared her beauty — and the eunuchs if they knew, would undoubtedly cause her to be killed, for such was the custom.

'At this time Mahsud was going on and on through the djinn-haunted sands towards Mecca. The caravan had accomplished half of its journey in safety: the wild tribes had been pacified with presents; the oases had appeared regularly and there had been sweet water, according to the will of Allah, the Merciful, the Compassionate.

'Indeed, Mahsud had prospered exceedingly, for among the pilgrims he had met merchants from the Islands of Spices in the east, and he had arranged to trade with them, greatly to his own advantage. This was largely because he had, in Muscat and elsewhere, given alms freely, particularly to deserving tellers of tales. Strange and wonderful things were to happen to him, but now a bowl will circulate among you,' said the teller of tales, looking at his audience, who sat in a tightly-wedged semi-circle before him, 'and the discriminating may place in it what they choose in the shape of a coin.'

Hussein passed the bowl around the company; most of them threw in a few pice or annas, and one even paid a silver rupee on top of the heap.

'I see,' said Feroze Khan, 'that there is at least one of infallible taste among us.' Later, however, the rupee was found to be bad.

When the last pice had rattled into the bowl, the teller of tales raised his voice, and began once more.

'In spite of the pious alms-giving of the good Mahsud,

———

misfortune overtook the caravan, owing to the presence of some accursed lepers who hunted during the pilgrimage – the most unfortunate thing a man can do. These people (who were to perish miserably) were of the type who listen avidly to the efforts of a story-teller and who refuse even a single pie:' Here he glared at those who sat on without paying: two of them looked abashed, and threw coppers to Hussein. 'But to resume,' said Feroze Khan. 'One evening they came to the camping place, and behold! the wells were dry. They had to drink the water stored in the goat-skins. On the next evening the watering-place was, as it were, obliterated, for the Djinn of the desert had covered the whole oasis with sand.

'Certain of the pilgrims, being crazed with thirst – they were town-dwellers – insisted on making for a small town surrounded by palm trees, that appeared hazily in the distance. The guides sought to dissuade them, saying that it was a mirage, a phantasm. But they, afflicted of Allah, cried out against the guides, and went away over the sand. They perished miserably, tormented by devils in the form of a whirling dust.

'The caravan went on, and the next day they found a little water, brackish and foul, but it seemed like the water of Zemzem, the well of Paradise. There was not enough for the camels, who grew thinner.

'On the day's march from this place, the pilgrims beheld a host of Bedouin, who were all armed. The Bedouin did not attack, as the caravan was large and well-protected, but they suffered it to pass only on the payment of a huge sum. Each man had to contribute according to his store, and Mahsud paid seventeen purses of gold.

'Then for three successive days the wells failed them.

The guides, being Arabs of the desert, could go without water nearly as long as their camels, so they sold that which they had stored. On the second day the water cost its own weight in fine silver, and on the third day, its weight in gold.

'The poorer pilgrims died; the rich and the guides lived. Then the camels began to die. Mahsud bought another with a great sum; this combined with the cost of water left him with very little, but he comforted himself with the thought that there were a hundred merchants in Mecca who would lend him all that he could desire.

'They left a trail of dead men and camels until they came to the oasis called Bab el Hameda — the Gate of the Desert — after which there was a dreadful march of four days without any hope of water. Then there arose a great contention as to whether they should go through the worst part of the desert or turn and go back to Muscat.

'That night while they slept the problem was solved for them, for the host of the Bedouin came with the setting of the moon. Those whom the Bedouin did not slay they carried away into slavery, and among these was the unfortunate Mahsud.

'Mahsud was slung like a sack on a camel's back, for he had been stunned in the short fight. He was in a better state, however, than some of his companions, who had to run behind the camels on the end of a rope.

'For many days the Arabs travelled swiftly northwards until they came to el Bareida, where they met a caravan of slave merchants who were bound for Baghdad. These merchants bought all the captives, and marched on towards the City of the Khalif. The slaves were treated well, for the dealers wished to get a good price for them.

———

For a long while Mahsud comforted himself with the thought that soon he would come among the great merchants, who would know him, and from whom he would be able to borrow enough to buy his freedom; but when they came to Basra the dealers bought more slaves, among them a man from Agra, who told Mahsud the news of the death of the Wazir. Then Mahsud tore his beard and cast off his turban, pouring dust upon his hair, and Shaitan moved him to curse Allah, but the uprightness within him refused, although he was well-nigh demented from excess of grief.

'They asked him what it was that troubled him, for he had not disclosed himself, but he only said, moaning, "That which I was, I am not." And in his sleep he would start up and cry "Oneiza!" When they reached Baghdad he was nearly dead, so he was sold for a mean price to a Jew from Cutch: this completed his abasement. Arriving at Cutch, he was so ill that even the Jew could get no work from him, but as the unbeliever desired above all things to get value from his purchase, he caused a doctor to tend the unfortunate Mahsud, whom he won back to life with a rare preparation of toad's flesh: no one was more surprised than the good hakim that the patient recovered. Indeed, so pleased was the doctor that he offered to buy Mahsud from the Jew, so that he might show the result of his medicine to the public. After some haggling the Jew agreed, and Mahsud joined the household of the hakim. His work was not particularly arduous, as he was an educated man and the doctor used him as a secretary. But Mahsud thought incessantly of Oneiza.

'One day a teller of tales came to the courtyard of the doctor; in payment for treatment he told stories at the doctor's table when there were guests. He came from Agra, and Mahsud engaged him in conversation.

'Now Mahsud had told nobody what he had been, for he was a proud man, and he plied the story-teller with questions about the fate of the Wazir, and of the Wazir's zenana. The story-teller knew a great deal, for he had assiduously gathered all the gossip of the bazaars, so that perchance he might weave it into a story. Mahsud learnt that Oneiza was spoken of as the most beautiful among the women of the Shah Jehan, and as one who might become the great power when the Moghul's grief had abated, and when the Taj that then absorbed the Emperor's attention was built.

'A little after this a friend of Mahsud's, a merchant, came to the doctor, and he recognised Mahsud, who drew him apart.

'The unfortunate man besought him in the name of the Most High and for the sake of their old friendship, to buy him from the hakim, and the merchant, whose name was Ismail Abdurrahim, said that he would if he could, for he was indebted to Mahsud in many ways.

'The next day the hakim told his secretary that Ismail was his new master. Mahsud's heart leapt with joy: in two days they were in Agra again.

'It chanced that a friend of Ismail was making a present to the Moghul of several female slaves and some eunuchs.

'Mahsud had explained to the merchant that the great desire of his heart was to see Oneiza again, even if he were to die. Whereupon Ismail Abdurrahim sent for a certain fakir, a man famous for the extreme austerities that he practised, such as swinging by his flesh from hooks, and sitting upon live embers, and rolling himself along the ground for great distances. It was reputed that nothing was impossible to this dervish.

'Ismail asked him whether it would be possible for a man to be made to look exactly like a eunuch without actually being made into one. The dervish said that it could be done so that the imitation would at least pass the palace examination, and remain undetected for perhaps a week: more than that was impossible.

'So they shaved Mahsud, taking off his whole beard. Allah, what will a man not do for a woman! And they gave him certain drugs, and when, after many more things had been done to him, he looked in a mirror, he laughed aloud – the first time for many days.

'He joined the present of slaves, and very soon he found himself in the palace, where he passed the examination without question. For two days thereafter the eunuchs were shown their duties. By good fortune the Chief Eunuch took a liking to Mahsud and gave him a light post among those who served the more favoured of the women of the zenana.

'Now the Chief Eunuch had for many days caused Oneiza to be in those rooms in the women's apartment that the Moghul passed through most often, in the hope that he might notice her. In spite of her grief she was surpassingly beautiful; indeed, her sorrow served rather to augment her fragile charm than to destroy it, as is usually the case, for there are but few women who can weep and yet appear attractive.

'It chanced that the day after Mahsud had entered the palace, Shah Jehan was walking through the orange garden when he heard a sound as of bitter grief barely repressed. He pushed through the bushes and found

Oneiza sitting on the ground, rocking to and fro in the extremity of her sorrow. She frequently escaped into the orange garden, for she had no wish to inflame the desire of the Emperor.

'She did not hear him until he asked her why she wept: then she started up in alarm, and the Moghul, seeing her face, was instantly struck with a deep pity, for she seemed so utterly miserable that his own racked heart drew towards her. He sat on the ground beside her, and having comforted her a little, he commanded her to disclose the entire cause of her sorrow.

'Now Oneiza had been wholly without friends among the women, and her secret grief nearly choked her, so she poured out all her trouble to the Moghul.

'The Emperor and she found great sympathy one with the other on account of their respective bereavements, and Shah Jehan said, when Oneiza had done, "My grief is past all curing, but yours is not so. My Wazir may have been a wicked man – they told me that he was – but by the mercy of Allah his brother may well be a good and upright man. Rest in peace: we will instantly command letters to be written to the Shereef of Mecca, the Shadow of the Prophet on Earth, bidding him to cause Mahsud to return straightway to us. Meanwhile you will remain with my mother until he comes."

'With this the great-hearted Moghul raised Oneiza, and clapped his hands: eunuchs came running, and she was taken away to the apartments of the Queen-Mother.

'That same evening the gossip went through the palace and it came to the ears of Mahsud, whose heart first leapt with joy, and then fell heavily into the pit of his belly, for he could not reveal himself without betraying the fact that he had come into the women's apartments, and not even the magnanimity of the Emperor would save him from the death: also he would thus betray his friend Ismail.

'However, he formed a plan, and going to the Chief Eunuch he asked whether he might join the servants in the Queen-Mother's rooms, saying frankly that he was curious to see Oneiza. The Chief Eunuch, a genial man – which is rare among his kind – agreed, for he had taken a liking to Mahsud. So the next evening Mahsud carried dishes, among a train of other servants, and he saw Oneiza talking with the Emperor: his heart almost cracked in his breast, for she seemed happy, and for a second he doubted her.

'Their eyes met; for a moment he saw nothing but indifference in them; then Oneiza looked again and her mouth opened.

'He smiled, and she ran straight to him without a word, leaving the Emperor wondering. Instantly there was a great uproar, and armed men threw themselves upon Mahsud, who would have been killed had not the Emperor shouted to them to leave him.

'Oneiza ran to Shah Jehan and said, "It is he."

'And Shah Jehan replied, saying, "But how is he here, in the name of Allah?"

'"I do not know at all. But let him tell us everything."

'The Moghul agreed; all the people were sent away, and Mahsud, having prostrated himself, unfolded his whole tale.

'"Now verily, this tale is worthy of being written in gold letters!" cried the Moghul; and forthwith he caused the Court to assemble, and he raised Mahsud to be his Wazir, giving him great gifts of gold and lands.

———

'Later, there was born to the Wazir and Oneiza a son, who came to great honours, and he was the prop of his parents' declining years. Now all this great good fortune was directly attributable to the kindness of Mahsud to the story-teller who gave him news of Agra: therefore, if you wish to enjoy great prosperity, fill the small bowl that will now be passed round; in the name of Allah, the Merciful, the Compassionate, bestow alms freely and reap the reward in Paradise!'

The bowl went round again, and again Hussein gathered many coppers. The crowd dispersed and Feroze Khan swept the money into a bag.

'Am I not a prince of story-tellers?' he asked complacently, when he had counted it.

'Without doubt,' replied Hussein absently, for he was thinking of Sashiya.

They went to the house of a friend of Feroze Khan's — he seemed to have friends in every town and village they visited — and there Hussein spent a great deal of time writing to Sashiya. His letter was neither particularly original nor well-written; in fact, it was of the familiar type of love-letter written by young men all over the world. It dealt exhaustively with his own feelings and other such matters, of very small interest to anybody but Sashiya.

While Hussein was so engaged, a number of furtive-looking men came to see the story-teller in another room. Some gave messages, some received them, and to others Feroze Khan gave money.

The next day they went at daybreak to join the baggage-train of a regiment that was marching to Peshawar.

At noon Feroze Khan told a tale to the native followers:

———

they were mostly very poor, so some of them put a handful of rice into the bowl when it came round, and others a chupatti or some millet; only a few had money to spare. One woman — a remarkably good-looking one, too — threw a scarlet flower into the bowl and smiled at Hussein.

In the evening they went round the encampment to the place where the English officers were digesting their dinners. Various servants had to be bribed, and a good deal of haggling went on in undertones, but at last the baskets were set down before the white men and Feroze Khan began his performances.

He blew into a globular sort of flute and produced a reedy monotonous melody: the lid of the basket, which Hussein had brought, shifted: then it fell off sideways, and a cobra's head shot up. For some time it swayed to the time of the tune and then it slithered out on to the ground.

It was followed by two more, and together they moved intricately in a little space, tracing curious patterns in the dust.

Feroze Khan quickened the music, and the cobras moved more swiftly: their hoods swelled and they hissed. Their smoothly gliding coils had a strangely hypnotic effect, and Hussein had to make an effort to shift his eyes from them.

At first the dancing snakes seemed ordinary enough — the common performance of a thousand snake-charmers; but after a little there was something very unusual about it all; rather horrible and sinister. It was in the concentric dancing of the cobras that the strangeness lay: one lay coiled tightly, only moving its head; the second was coiled about the first, and it was writhed smoothly round and round in one direction, while the third revolved the other way.

Suddenly Feroze Khan stopped, seized the snakes by the necks, and dropped them one after another back into the basket.

'Shabash!' cried the audience.

From his voluminous robes Feroze Khan drew another snake: it was a white cobra; pure white, with no markings but its spectacles of Shiv on its hood. Its eyes were red; they shone.

The old man set it on his shoulder, where it lay quietly flicking its tongue in and out, while Feroze Khan smoothed out the dust where the other cobras had been dancing. Then from a bag he sprinkled red sand on the ground and set the white cobra upon it.

He began a slow tune on his pipe: the cobra looked up, but it did not move. Feroze Khan spoke gently to it, and went on with his tune. Slowly the snake poured its coils out over the sand, and then it began to move rhythmically in a set pattern. It moved swiftly and more swiftly, then it stopped, looking at Feroze Khan, who picked it up carefully.

He pointed to the sand: there was the lignam-yoni, the most sacred symbol in India, perfectly traced in the red sand.

When they had gone back to the place where they slept, having collected no less than seven rupees, Hussein asked Feroze Khan about the white cobra.

'Yes. Vakrishna always stays coiled round my waist,' replied the old man, ringing the coins against the brass bowl. 'He loves me more than his food.'

'May I see him again?'

'By all means' — the cobra slid out from the folds of his clothes. 'Do not touch his head, he dislikes it. I will tell you how I got him. Pass me that rice. It was long ago, probably before you were born, for Vakrishna is older than I am, and I was but a youth then . . . long ago. I was in Peshawar, and I heard a tale among the sanyassis about a white cobra that was the god of a village in Gujarat. They said it was a pure white cobra, an incarnation of Krishna, one of the gods of the unbelievers. Strange tales were told of the luck it brought, and stranger tales of the sacrifices these ungodly people made to it. Hearing of it, I desired it, for I charmed snakes even then.

'Now, it happened that I was in Gujarat some time later, and I remembered the tales of the sanyassis. The village itself lay in the path of my journey — mark the working of the Omnipotent! At nightfall I arrived there, and I told tales to the simple villagers until the rising of the moon. They would not speak of their god, although I professed their own belief, to the great danger of my soul. I stayed there three days before I even learnt where it was . . . Who is that outside?'

Hussein went to the door: it was the woman who had just given him a flower. She had a steaming dish of curry, very fragrant with spices.

'My father hopes that your master will come and tell a tale to-night at his tent,' she said, setting down the curry.

Hussein picked it up. 'It is possible,' he said. 'But we tellers of tales are very busy men.' He sniffed the curry. 'It is quite possible,' he added.

'These women . . .' said Feroze Khan, 'they would break

in upon the inspiration of the Prophet himself. Set the dish between us. It is quite edible. Now where was I? Oh, yes – I found where the snake lived by making very active love to the wife of the priest. I was a lusty youth,' the old man chuckled. 'I remember her well; she is surely in her grave by now, but she was well-favoured – a little fat, but as jocund as a negress . . . ah, yes. The snake lived in a great tree whose roots were twisted strangely: it lived in a hole in the roots. There was a shrine before it.

'Every evening the priest put a saucer of milk there, and the snake came out to drink it. I was staying with the priest, so it was easy for me to put a little opium in the milk one evening.

'I had one of my own snakes with me, although I had said nothing about it, and this snake, a worthless young hamadryad without brain – I painted it white. It was extremely difficult, but I managed it.

'Then, when I thought that the opium would have had its effect, I left the priest's wife and crept to the shrine. With a hooked stick I drew forth the white cobra, and put my own in its place.

'The painted snake was a poor imitation, but I hoped that it would not be suspected until I could get safely away.

'The next day I said that I must be going on my way: the white cobra was in a bag beneath my clothes.

'I gave out that I was going towards the next village towards the south, but secretly I told the priest's wife that I was going north. I had my own idea of what would happen, so I went south.

'A day's journey away I heard that the villagers had lost their white cobra, and that they were pursuing the thief with all speed towards the north. Hai! but I knew the ways of women even then!'

They finished the curry, and went to the tent of Dhossib-hoy the sutler, who had sent it to them.

His daughter, Parvathi, smiled repeatedly upon Hussein, but he missed it, as he was deep in a reverie that took him to the roof garden of a certain house in Haiderabad. At length she came and sat beside him — camp manners are free — and talked about this and that until his dream was shattered. He made some effort to please her, because he hoped for more curry, but his heart was not in it. Nevertheless he had his reward in the shape of kabobs on a skewer and a pomegranate that she put into his hand as they left.

Day after day the regiment marched: each succeeding day seemed exactly the same as the rest, for the routine was of an iron mould.

Parvathi smiled still more upon Hussein, for he was an extremely handsome youth. She was used to Bengalis, who run rather to flesh, and she admired the Mohamme-dan's clean-cut face with its high-bridged nose and new-tufted chin.

Hussein took but little notice of her, except now and then to drop a little praise of her cooking; but she was amorous and sent him a message in flowers which he could not fail to understand. He did not come, though; she sent him another message, accompanied by a most savoury dish, into which she had put a love potion. He came on account of the tahkian, for he had a proper respect for his stomach.

'But don't you care for me at all?' she asked at length.

'Surely you have a little heart? Or aren't you a man at all? Oh, don't tell me — it's another woman. I hate you — soor-ka-butcha-ka-soorneen!'

Hussein laughed — a most unwise thing to do — and she spat in his face.

The next day she sent a message with lambs' tail stew to say that she was very, very sorry, and that she hoped he was not angry. Hussein accepted the stew, but said that he was angry.

That night he was seized with horrible cramps in the stomach: the stew was poisoned. The story-teller heard him moaning, and found him doubled up. He sent for the soldiers' doctor, who used a stomach-pump with great effect. In the morning Hussein was out of danger, but for some days he was ill and weak. Parvathi came and wept by the wall of his tent in the night, for she was frightened of what she had done, and rather sorry when it was too late; but Hussein took no more notice of her.

In a few days a very ardent young soldier absorbed all her attention, and Hussein saw no more of her.

When the regiment they were following reached its destination, which was Lahore, Feroze Khan said that they must go at once to Peshawar. He gave no reason, and Hussein knew his ways too well to ask for any. They stayed in Peshawar for three weeks: throughout the whole time the old man did not stir from the house where they stayed, to tell any stories. Only in the evening did he sally forth, and then by himself. One evening Hussein, who was naturally curious, followed him at a distance. Feroze Khan went to the bazaar of the goldsmiths: he wandered down it, and looked sideways at one of the men, who glanced from his little furnace to give a shake of his head.

———

Feroze Khan wandered on, giving no sign, and saying no word. He went back to the house, where Hussein, coming in later, found him looking very worried. The old man seemed always to have enough money — Hussein had no idea where it came from.

Hussein was left very much to himself, and as he had quite a lot of money he used to go to one of those curious little houses that hang like swallows' nests on the ancient walls of the city. He only went to talk, and to smoke a scented huqa, for he was not interested in the charmingly frail inhabitants.

Nevertheless, he did not mention the House of Huneifa to Sashiya in his letters.

He also spent a good deal of his time in getting accustomed to the snakes, and in learning how to play the flute, so that they would dance for him. Sometimes Feroze Khan would lend him Vakrishna, and the more he saw of the white cobra the more he admired it. The snake seemed endowed with more than usual intelligence and Hussein soon began to feel a certain affection for it; for indeed it was an extremely beautiful creature, with its glowing eyes and its jade-like white body. In addition to drawing the lignam-yoni in the sand, Vakrishna could also trace the names of Allah.

One evening, as Hussein sat in the open lattice window of the House of Huneifa, pulling gently at the water-pipe and talking politics with a smooth babu, he saw a man come whom he knew that he had seen before.

The newcomer sat cross-legged on the cushions of a divan, and talked in undertones to Azzun, one of the dancing-girls.

For some time Hussein could not remember where he

had seen the man, and then suddenly it came to him: it was in Agra; the man had come in the night to see Feroze Khan. They were talking quietly in Hindi: Hussein paid scant attention to them until he caught the name of Feroze Khan, then he listened with all his ears.

He could hear very little of what they said, but more than once the girl mentioned the goldsmiths' bazaar.

Soon the man went out, and after a while Hussein left too. He was strangely intrigued by the mystery that surrounded Feroze Khan, and now he felt quite certain that the old man was something more than a story-teller.

He found Feroze Khan piping to the cobras, and he told him that there was a man looking for him. The old man's face looked drawn and grey. He pressed Hussein for every detail.

'What was he like?' he asked anxiously.

'Oh, quite unnoteworthy: he folded his turban like a Maratha, but from his speech he seemed to come from the south. I would know him again . . . shall I ask Azzun who he is?'

'By no means — these women . . . oh, Allah! Tell no one that you know me, and if the man comes again to that house, enter into conversation with him. Say that you are a snake-charmer — maybe he will ask if you know me. If he does, say that you met me here two days ago, but that I am gone to Umballa now; but in the name of Allah do not appear at all eager — it is horribly important. Go now, and stay at Huneifa's until late; here is some money, so that they shall not find you unwelcome.'

Hussein went back, and resumed his long, involved conversation with the babu. He stayed until all had gone except those who were not going at all, but the man did not come in.

Feroze Khan did not go out that night; he sent Hussein instead, telling him to look sideways at the seventh goldsmith on the left as he went down the bazaar, and to make a certain gesture with his hand: he was to mark closely whether the man nodded or shook his head.

Hussein did all these things, and he saw that the man shook his head. He went back to Feroze Khan, who was waiting impatiently.

'What did he do?' cried the old man.

'Before I tell you, you must tell me what the whole matter is about: I know more than you think, but I want to know everything.'

'Is this any way in which to speak to your master? Regard my white beard, and restrain your curiosity – tell me at once, or it will be the worse for you.'

Hussein said not a word, but began to write a letter. Feroze Khan watched him for a little while, and then said:

'It is a matter that cannot concern you; you will be far happier if you know nothing about it. Tell me, and I will give you a rupee.'

Still Hussein said nothing. For a long while he wrote his letter, and the teller of tales walked up and down plucking at his beard.

'Well,' said the old man at last, 'I suppose you would have found out in the end, so you may as well know now. Before I tell you anything you must swear by the Ninety-Nine Names that you will not betray anything that I say.'

Hussein swore, and Feroze Khan told him that he was in the employ of the Dewan of Waziristan, and that he was used to convey secret messages to the ministers of other native princes.

Hussein did not believe him, but it gave him more than an inkling of what the story-teller was really doing, so he feigned to believe it, and went to the house on the wall to watch for the man who had spoken to Azzun.

He had nothing much to do, so while one of the girls was singing and playing her guitar, he picked up an opium pipe, and looked round for someone to fill it for him.

Azzun came with a tray loaded with all the little instruments: she began filling the tiny bowl of the pipe, and then she exclaimed, 'But this is Ram Narain's special pipe – he will be very angry – here is another one for you, you don't mind?' And she smiled sweetly at him. Hussein grinned back, and said:

'Who is Ram Narain?'

'I don't know, but he always comes here when he is in Peshawar – he was here yesterday talking to me when you were here with that greasy old Chunderswami; he is—'

'Oh yes; I remember – a Maratha, isn't he?'

'I think so . . . but here he is: ohé, Ram Narain – here is a wretched man trying to steal your pipe.'

The Maratha and Hussein began talking about the recent falling-off in the quality of opium.

'Even my snakes have noticed it,' remarked Hussein. 'I give them a little, you know, before a long journey, so as to keep them quiet.'

'Indeed? Then you are a snake-charmer?'

'Just so.'

'Perhaps you may have met a friend of mine, one Feroze Khan, an old man?'

'Feroze Khan? He who has a white cobra?'

'The same.'

'Then I have met him: it was only a few days ago. I remember he told me that he was going to Umballa that evening.'

'A pity — I have some news for him: but it will wait, being quite unimportant.'

The talk drifted vaguely after that, and presently Hussein went back to Feroze Khan, to whom he recounted all that had happened. The old man rubbed his hands with glee.

'We will go back to Lahore now,' he said, and he began to tie up bundles at once.

They had a very long wait at the station, and after about an hour a man beckoned to the story-teller: it was the goldsmith from the bazaar.

Feroze Khan told Hussein that he would not be long and bade him wait with the baggage. After ten minutes had passed there was a great hubbub outside the station. At first Hussein took but little notice of it, but as the uproar increased he stood on top of the baskets to see, if peradventure he could, what was happening.

There was a milling crowd outside, and many of the people who were waiting left their bundles to go and gape. Hussein joined them. On the outskirts of the crowd, which was pushing its way into a narrow alley between the houses, he heard that someone had been murdered.

He shoved energetically and wormed his way into the heart of the crowd: in a little clear circle there was Feroze Khan lying on his face. A knife protruded from his back.

Hussein thrust his way forward and knelt by the body:

———

at that moment the police came, clearing a way with their lathis.

There was a storm of explanation from the crowd, and as the policemen turned the body over, Vakrishna glided out. Everyone pushed backwards, and a great outcry went up that someone was getting trampled underfoot. In the confusion Hussein caught up Vakrishna and slid him under his dhoti: then he wriggled back through the crowd. The few who had seen him could not pursue him because of the press of the people, so he got safely back to the station, where he unobtrusively slipped the white cobra into a basket.

For a long while he sat chewing pan and thinking hard. He had no wish to get mixed up with the police, for he was not certain what Feroze Khan had been doing; but he was fairly sure that it was nefarious, and he thought that he would find it difficult to prove that he was not an accomplice himself. Moreover he had no wish to be questioned on the cause of his presence in Peshawar as a snake-charmer.

The tickets for Lahore were already bought, and as the train came in he made up his mind and got into it.

On the way – it was a long journey – he read the book that Abd'Arahman had given him, and it occurred to him that he might be able to use some of the tales that he read, and to tell them as Feroze Khan had done.

He knew enough about the snakes by now to be able to give a creditable performance with them, so that even if his story-telling did not go well, he would have still something to do.

There was a Sikh soldier in the carriage, and he told Hussein that his regiment was about to march from

Lahore in a few days' time to relieve another regiment on the North-West Frontier garrisons.

Hussein decided to follow the regiment, travelling as he and his master had often done, in the baggage-train.

Nine

The road seemed endless: the regiment's band played in front, and behind, in a dense cloud of dust, tramped the native followers.

Hussein, luckier than most, sat in a bullock cart trying to piece together a tale in his own mind to tell in the evening.

He referred again and again to Abd'Arahman's book, but it consisted mostly of anecdotes and jests, none of them long enough for a story that was to earn him his bed and his supper, to say nothing of food for the cobras. If it came to the worst they would always be satisfied with a few mice, but he liked to give Vakrishna something better. Indeed, he had become quite attached to the snake, and he carried Vakrishna, as Feroze Khan had done, about his waist, or sometimes hanging limply round his neck, like a singular necklace.

Very slowly the sun sank from noon-height to the horizon: then quite suddenly it seemed it vanished and only the after-glow remained. As the sky darkened to purple, the tents of the regiment sprang up like mushrooms, and fires blazed.

Still the story refused to form itself in Hussein's mind, so he waited until the soldiers had fed, and then went round to the officers' quarters. He knew that he could only do this once in each march, for no one would pay to see the same thing twice in the course of a few weeks. Nevertheless the story refused to come, and he wanted some money; so having corrupted the colonel's khitmutgar in the usual way, he set down his baskets and began.

All went well, particularly the way in which Vakrishna cunningly writhed in the sand. At the end, one of the officers – a very young one – asked whether Hussein could do the rope trick.

'By all means, Sahib,' replied Hussein, with an eye to the main chance, 'but I should have to be provided with three chickens, a long rope made from swal, and a small basket with tobacco in it.'

'But why on earth the chickens and the tobacco?'

'Ah, Huzoor, that is a mystery that I may not reveal.'

'Are you sure you could do it if you had these things? And would you be photographed doing it?'

'Is there a moon in the sky, Sahib? I am the pupil of no less a one than Garwhal Ali, who could vanish at will. A paltry seven rupees would buy these things, and I would not ask any payment, trusting to your Honour's generosity alone.'

'Well, here are your seven rupees: come round to my tent at noon halt to-morrow.'

'The blessing of the Prophet on your house, Huzoor; may your wife bear you seven tall sons and seven daughters like peris.'

None of the other officers spoke: everyone has to learn

about the rope trick: no one will ever be persuaded that it does not exist.

Hussein salaamed to the ground, and gathered up his belongings: in the shade he met the khitmutgar again. This worthy man's hand was outstretched. Hussein sighed, and placed a rupee in it, then he vanished into the night. He got a lift in a peasant's cart and by morning he was in Agra again, a day's march from the regiment.

In Agra he found that there was a sort of union among the story-tellers. Feroze Khan had belonged to it, but Hussein did not, and when he had told a tale in the market-place, he found himself surrounded by about a dozen men, all demanding how he had dared to encroach upon their preserves. They were only pacified by the whole of the contents of Hussein's bowl, but then they told him that he could become a member of their guild.

He went with them to a house, where several other story-tellers and snake-charmers were gathered. He found that it was the custom of the guild that each member should tell his best tale and give it for the free use of the other members.

They fed — remarkably richly, too — and then two men who had just come from Mecca, where they had made the hadj, told two of the best stories that they had heard in their pilgrimage. After they had done, Hussein was told to tell his tale.

He knew that he could not use one of Feroze Khan's, as they would be sure to know it, and for a little time his invention quite left him. Suddenly he thought of Vakrishna, and the curious way in which he had been stolen, so he told it as a story, with a great deal of embroidery: sometimes he strayed into pure fiction, but on the whole he kept to the main facts that the old man had told him.

When he had done, he produced the white cobra, adding: 'And here is the proof.'

'Shabash!' cried the story-tellers, and they gave him mint tea.

He learnt a great deal about the ways in which the guild forced alien story-tellers out of their own territory, and how they spread their tales, of which there were a very great number, some of which had been in circulation since time immemorial.

From Agra Hussein went south again in the train of another regiment. He made his way quite well for a time by telling his stories and by snake-charming, and then he heard from Abd'Arahman, who wrote to tell him the news of Haiderabad. The letter, with which was enclosed one from Sashiya, filled him with a great longing for Haiderabad, and the familiar things which he missed.

Within a month he was in Haiderabad again, having walked nearly all the way. He found the old letter-writer in his accustomed place in the bazaar, and he sat before him. Until Hussein spoke, the old man did not recognise him, for wandering up and down had made him look considerably older; moreover, he was dressed as one from the north. Abd'Arahman was overjoyed to see him, and wept the easy tears of old age. When they had finished their greetings, Hussein asked whether the old man had seen Sashiya recently.

'Yes,' he replied. 'I saw her three days ago; she said that she had been dreaming of your return.'

Later Hussein sought out the old woman who sold herbs, and charged her with a message for Sashiya. Then he wandered out of the town towards the elephant lines; to his great surprise, Hussein found that there was no one left there whom he had known. New elephants and new mahouts had taken possession; one of the mahouts told him that they had replaced the previous occupants a few weeks ago, and that the other elephants had gone to Sivapore, where there was work for them. Hussein went disconsolately back to the town and killed time until sundown, when he could see Sashiya. As he was wandering through one of the bazaars, a small boy touched him on the arm. Hussein turned; it was the fakir's boy.

'What will you give me', said the boy, 'if I tell you something very important to you?'

'Tell me, and then I may reward you.'

'You must pay first. Let it be a rupee.'

'Here are two pice; what is it?'

'One more, and I will tell you.'

'Very well, shaitan-ka-butcha, but it will be an unfortunate day for you if it is not important.'

'It is. Three Pathans have been following you for the last hour. Do not look round, but pretend to abuse me, and walk on.'

Hussein felt a cold shiver go down his back; he cursed the boy exhaustively, and walked slowly on, keeping always among the crowded streets.

He made towards the Krishnavi bazaar, and he saw Abd'Arahman sitting at his desk. He made a sign to the old man to follow him, but the letter-writer did not grasp it at first. Hussein had to walk three times past him before the old man understood. They walked among the crowds together for some time, and then Hussein very quickly turned into an eating-house, where there were many

———

people. As they sat over their coffee Hussein told the old man what the boy had told him.

'You must not be in this town at night-fall,' said the old man, much perturbed. 'I myself will tell Sashiya what has happened, and you will go by a train to some other place, and wait until it is safe to return.'

Just then several men came in, and one of them stumbled over Hussein's foot; he fell, and arose full of oaths. He hit at Hussein, and tried to catch his turban. Two other men joined in the outcry, and closed round Hussein. There was a glint of steel, and Hussein fell to the ground with a scream. The three men ran from the eating-house, and were swallowed up in the crowd.

They picked up Hussein, and endeavoured to restore him. In a little while he opened his eyes and swore. The knife had not gone very deep; it had been partially checked by the coiled body of Vakrishna.

Hussein sat up, and felt for the cobra; it was limp, and when he pulled Vakrishna out from beneath the folds of his clothes, the snake was dead.

Abd'Arahman bound up Hussein's wound with a strip of his turban, and after a little while they were able to go on. The knife, after it had gone through the snake, had glanced against Hussein's shoulder-blade, and although it had made an ugly wound, it had not gone deep.

They went slowly towards the station, and sat among the crowds in the waiting-rooms for a long while. Then Hussein asked the old man to go to the fakir's hut and bring back the boy. When the boy arrived, Hussein gave him the limp body of Vakrishna, and told him that if it were discovered in the bed of the head of the family of the late Kadir Baksh, Abd'Arahman would give him a rupee. This would be a very fine counter-attack, as a dead snake in one's bed is an incredibly unlucky thing.

The boy went, and they discussed where Hussein should go. 'If I go to Sivapore I shall find many of the mahouts who know me,' said Hussein, 'and perhaps they will help me until I am able to go about my ways again.'

Three days later Hussein was there, and in the elephant lines he found many of his old friends, and they, for the sake of their craft, kept him for that length of time that his wound took to heal. To his great disappointment Hussein did not find Jehangir among the elephants for three of them had been drafted away to the north, and Jehangir was among them. The talk ran that they were joining the baggage-train of the Sixth Dogras at Panilat, so Hussein, with what little money he had left, and with that which his friends gave him, journeyed thither.

In the train, however, Hussein became very ill, and they carried him off the train at a small village, where he lay in the waiting-room for some time. A wandering sanyassi chanced to be there also; he was a man whom Hussein had encountered when he had been with Feroze Khan in Peshawar. This man was also a snake-charmer, or rather, he added snake-charming to his general equipment as a jadoo-wallah. Finding that Hussein's impedimenta consisted largely of a snake-basket, he became interested, and stayed by him until he was well. Hussein was very hardy, and he threw off the fever in about six hours, and the sanyassi applied certain herbs to his wound that did it a great deal of good, more especially as they were accompanied by various charms.

For a week Hussein was fairly ill, but the sanyassi and he managed to acquire a good deal of nourishment at the expense of the faithful and devout, so at the end of that time they were able to take the road again. Hussein had lost track of the Dogra regiment in whose train were the elephants, so he went on with the sanyassi towards the hills. They parted at Sihkri, because the sanyassi encountered a band of holy men who were going to Benares, and he wished to go with them, but Hussein did not. Hussein bought a number of trained snakes and a mongoose from the sanyassi, and went on his way towards the hills.

The mongoose was called Jellaludin, on account of his whiskers; he was both fat and lazy, but he was an amiable beast, and Hussein became quite attached to him. The mongoose was quite accustomed to Hussein's three tame cobras, all of whom had their fangs drawn, but the sight of a strange snake made the hair rise all along his back.

At length Hussein arrived among the hills; there he picked up another acquaintance whom he had known when he was with Feroze Khan, and from this man he learnt an admirable way of using his snakes. Hussein put it into practice; this was the manner of it: first he would make the acquaintance of some tradesmen who knew all about the white people, and from them Hussein would learn which of the sahibs had wives; then he would go to the houses of those sahibs and bribe the khansamah to let him give a performance in the compound. After the performance he would announce that he felt the presence of snakes in the house itself, and if this made a suitable impression upon the white people, he would offer to come back in the evening to catch the snakes – for a modest fee, of course. Then he would go round to the servants' quarters, and get them, with a promise of commission, to secrete his tame snakes in the house. One – the largest – he would always have put in the bedroom, another in the bathroom, and the third in any conveniently dramatic place. Towards sundown he would return, looking important, with a sack for the snakes, his flute, and Jellaludin.

In the house he would go from room to room, sniffing; when he came to the bedroom he would assure the memsahib that there was a cobra in the room, and, having produced Jellaludin from a fold in his clothes, he would play on his squeaky, globular flute, while the mongoose ranged round the room. When he felt that the tension had reached its climax, Hussein would change his tune, and the well-trained cobra would glide out from beneath the pillow and swell out its hood, hissing furiously. Then Jellaludin, who knew his part quite well, would dart at the snake and leap at its head; before any harm could be done, however, Hussein would rush at the cobra, and bundle it into his sack.

After he had gone from room to room, and collected his snakes, he could be practically sure of about four rupees from the grateful white people, and more if they were newcomers, but at least half of his reward had to go to the servants as commission.

When there was a child in the house he could be certain of at least ten rupees, for if he had heard that there was a child, he would borrow trained snakes from any fakirs he knew who possessed them, so that he could produce as many as ten of them from all around the child's cot before its mother's horrified eyes. This was particularly well paid, though of course the commission to the servants and the fakirs was higher.

Sometimes Hussein was rather put off his stroke by Jellaludin, who could not always distinguish between the strange tame snakes and the snakes that he was really supposed to kill: also, towards the end of a long performance, when he had apparently slain as many as a dozen snakes to the accompaniment of furious leaping in the air, he became rather tired, owing to his fatness, and was not quite as spectacular as Hussein could have wished; but on the whole things went off very satisfactorily.

Now it came to Hussein's ears when he was in Simla that the wife of the District Magistrate of Jullundur was known to be extremely fearful of snakes, and that her husband was very wealthy. This he heard from a sanyassi who had borrowed Jellaludin for a day; the mendicant had also remarked that the magistrate had two children. So Hussein, who had got all that he could reasonably hope for from the white people in Simla, packed up his flute, his snakes and his few other belongings in an old piece of cloth, and calling Jellaludin from the thatch of his hut, he set off south. After a certain time had passed he arrived at Jullundur, and there he sought out a friend of his, a sadhu who dealt in curses of all kinds. From the sadhu Hussein borrowed no fewer than nine several serpents, ranging from a small but venomous krait to an immense hamadryad cobra. They were all well trained, and Hussein spent a whole day in getting Jellaludin used to them. All his usual preliminaries went well, and one evening four days after his arrival in Jullundur he began to extract snakes from the magistrate's house.

He had various less spectacular snakes scattered in the usual places, and he had at least six in the nursery of the magistrate's children. He came to this room last of all, and when he had played his flute for a little the snakes began to come out into the open. One flopped from a tear in the ceiling-cloth, two more came from a rat hole in a corner, and the great hamadryad came from under one of the cots. At first everything went well, and Hussein had most of the snakes in his sack before he noticed that Jellaludin was not doing his part very well; indeed, he looked quite languid. The mongoose was so slow in dealing with the big cobra that before Hussein could very well say that Jellaludin had finished with it, another snake came out, and the white people, who were watching, became most uneasy.

Then another snake came out from the hole in the wall where the punkah came through, and the white man swiped at it with his riding-crop, killing the unfortunate snake by breaking its back. Hurriedly bundling the other two into his sack, Hussein cursed the magistrate bitterly in Urdu. Unhappily the magistrate knew the tongue perfectly, and replied in the same language; then he clapped his hands to call the servants, whom he told to throw Hussein out of the house.

This was done, and in the doing two of the snakes were hurt. The dead snake was the small blue krait belonging to the sadhu; it was said to be very valuable on account of the tricks it could perform. When the sadhu heard of its death he cursed Hussein root and branch; he also exacted ten rupees by way of compensation.

Hussein blamed Jellaludin bitterly, for if he had done what he had to do quickly, instead of being lazy, everything would have been well, and the sahib would have given him at least fifteen rupees; saying this, Hussein cuffed the mongoose repeatedly, and threatened to throw him down a well. Jellaludin felt the disgrace most keenly, and went off his feed, with the result that he became quite thin.

Fortunately Hussein had saved his own three cobras, so he was able to keep going by performing with them, although the sadhu had taken all his resources.

Ten

He left Jullundur as soon as possible. He was not at all alarmed by the sadhu's curses, for the red-bearded fakir of Haiderabad had given him an amulet against all curses, and he was supremely confident in its power. Some time later he turned up at Benares, where he hoped to pick up some information from the hosts of mendicants and priests who thronged the holy city.

For two days he sat before the great temple of Kali: he was dressed neither as a Mohammedan nor as a Hindu, but as a sort of indeterminate holy man who might be a Jain or something rather vague. In this guise he was able to appeal successfully to the devout of all sects, and his begging bowl was rarely empty for long. But Hussein did not wish to live like this for long, so when he met a sanyassi who cast horoscopes he set off for Kapilavatthu, for the sanyassi had told him that the rajah in whose state the town lay was entertaining a group of distinguished politicians, and that he was going to give them a great feast. On the way Hussein encountered a company of dancers, with whom he travelled, arriving in Kapilavatthu in a week. After the feast Hussein gave a remarkably successful performance with his snakes, and amassed no less than seventeen rupees. On the next day he presented himself at the political officer's house, and obtained permission to rid the house of snakes. He borrowed ten snakes, and had them concealed in strategic points. He resumed in the evening with all his paraphernalia. The Resident had seen it done before, and he had a shrewd idea of how it was worked, but he thought that it might entertain his guests, and he hoped that it might even stop the distinguished politicians from talking for a while.

First Hussein produced snakes from the ceiling-cloth — it was very striking to see a fat, writhing cobra wriggling out of the ceiling — and then he piped them out from under the beds of the white people. After that he went to the large, white-tiled bathroom that was the joy of the Resident's heart, where he had his last two snakes concealed. He had put them back into his sack, and was making preparations for his departure, when he saw, to his horror, another snake creeping out of the waste pipe.

It was a very large hamadryad cobra, the most venomous of snakes. In the hope that it would go back when it saw the people, Hussein kept on piping with his flute; but the cobra came on, and by the time it was half out, Jellaludin, who had been sniffing about on the other side of the room, saw it, and darted forward. Hussein was very much afraid lest the mongoose should take it for one of the training snakes, and only nip it gently in the neck, for if he did, he would be bitten, and if he did not find a certain herb to counteract the poison within a few minutes, he would undoubtedly die. This herb is known only to the mongooses, who run to find it if ever they have been bitten in a fight with a snake, and when they eat it, it nullifies the poison, and they take no harm. As soon as Jellaludin got near the snake, he realised that something was wrong, and he danced round on his toes, keeping at a safe distance. The cobra had no smell of man about it, so Jellaludin sensed that it was not one that Hussein had put there.

The hamadryad came fully out of the drain pipe, and coiled itself ready to strike. The mongoose darted round and round it, drawing slightly nearer. Suddenly the cobra struck, missing Jellaludin by an inch. It smacked against the white tiles with a sound like that of a cracked whip, and the mongoose sprang back out of reach. Hussein could not go to his help, as the cobra would have bitten him, and he would have died within a quarter of an hour, in great agony.

The snake recoiled itself, and Jellaludin began going round and round again. It turned steadily, watching for a chance to strike. It thought it saw its opportunity, but the mongoose was just out of reach, and as the snake faltered for a split second, Jellaludin leapt at its head. He got a grip on its neck just below the hood — too low down — and the cobra, twisting its head, managed to bite him twice before its spine was broken.

Without pausing for a second, Jellaludin dropped the dead snake, and leapt out of the open window into the garden; he had no time to waste if he was to save his life. He saw a patch of neglected grass, and ran to it, sniffing eagerly. Soon he found that which he sought, and having eaten the bitter herb, he looked for water.

In the house the Resident crushed the cobra's head beneath his heel, and Hussein put the body into his bag, for if Jellaludin were still alive, he would love the cobra as a meal.

The guests all chipped in with a couple of rupees or so, for they had been thrilled through and through, and what is more, they would have something to talk about besides politics, which was a boon; altogether Hussein got thirty-four rupees – quite a fortune for him. But he hardly waited for his reward: he was desperately anxious for Jellaludin. He got away as soon as possible, and ran out to the garden. He found the mongoose sitting on the gravel drive, licking his bites. Seeing Hussein, he trotted up and jumped on to his shoulder, whence he crept into the inside pocket in which he always travelled.

Then Hussein knew that all was well, for if the mongoose had been going to die, he would have known it, and crept away into some dark, quiet place to die in peace.

When they reached the house where they stayed, Hussein produced the dead cobra from his bag, and laid it in a quiet corner. Jellaludin took it away into a thick patch of grass; he did not reappear for two days, and then he crawled back, almost too fat to walk.

For some time after that Hussein travelled with the company of dancers as they went from place to place, for wherever they were in demand, he could be sure that he could pick up a living. They went mostly to feasts given by the rajahs of native states, for there the old ways are kept, and the traditional entertainments are appreciated. At the beginning of the rains, however, the dancers went to Haiderabad, and thither Hussein could not follow them, so he struck out on his own once more.

The rains had come very early that year, and he came

across a regiment who were still out on a route march, and who had not yet reached their station. They were a week's journey from their destination, and as they marched, the roads were swept away by the torrents of water that poured from the sky, and they had a most wretched time of it. At one place their guns sank deep into the mud overnight, in spite of all their precautions, and they sent for elephants to get them out.

It happened that they were near a place where some works were being done, in which twenty elephants of the PWD were employed, so these elephants were sent.

That night the rain ceased for a while, and certain of the camp-followers took the opportunity of building a few temporary huts, for the regiment would not move on for some days at least. Among them was Hussein, who built a little hut for himself near the elephants, so that he should smell them in the night, and dream of his former life, for which he frequently longed with a great longing. One thing he lacked, however, in his hut, and that was something dry to sleep on, so he went out to where the elephants were tethered, and he encountered the chief of the mahouts, who gave him an armful of straw.

When he had secured his bed with a piece of rope he turned to go, but the chief of the mahouts cried out, saying, 'The price, O son of Eblis.'

'Old man,' replied Hussein, 'who gave thee leave to sell the Government's straw, expressly provided for the greater comfort of my lords the elephants?' and with this he went away.

'Now,' said the chief of the mahouts, 'I clearly perceive that this man is fundamentally evil, and that this is an unfortunate day for me.' But he did not pursue Hussein, for he was an old man, and disliked tumult.

Hussein made a sort of nest out of his straw and burrowed into it. His hut was little more than a large umbrella made of thatch — it had no walls; nevertheless he slept very soundly until a little before dawn, when he was awakened by the trumpeting of an elephant, and the voice of a mahout abusing it. The trumpeting elephant was one that had just arrived, having been at a place more distant than the others. Hussein stirred, and rolled over in his straw; then he went to sleep again: he was dreaming a most curious dream when he was awakened again, this time by an elephant actually plucking the straw off him, and making a gurgling noise.

Hussein sprang up, abusing the elephant in the tongue of the mahouts. Nevertheless, it did not draw back, but touched Hussein gently with its trunk.

All at once Hussein perceived that it was Jehangir, his own very greatly beloved elephant. Then there was a scene that could not have been surpassed if the elephant had been a bride and Hussein a delayed bridegroom, just arrived in safety from the wars. When the camp was awake Hussein told Jehangir that he would go away for a little while, and that he would return almost at once. He came across one selling sugar-cane, and he bought several of the long, sweet sticks; then he borrowed some boiled rice from an acquaintance to break his fast, and went back to his hut. There he found a man endeavouring to lead the elephant away, and he ran up, and gave Jehangir one of the sugar-canes.

The man, seeing Hussein, cried, 'Stand afar off, thou, for this is a lordly elephant, and by no means one to be fed by lowly people.'

———

And Hussein answered, saying, 'O bahinchute, since when have the drovers of cattle called themselves mahouts?' for he saw by the man's caste mark that he was no true mahout, but a mere herder of beasts.

'Nevertheless,' replied the man, somewhat abashed, 'I am the official attendant of the elephant lines.' And he drew himself up importantly.

'Where is his mahout?' asked Hussein.

'He has no regular mahout,' replied the man, 'for he will suffer none to remain with him for more than a few weeks: it is said that he seeks his first own mahout, and that he will not rest until he finds him.'

'These are true words,' replied Hussein. 'You may fetch me water, a brush, and some arrack. This is an honour, for I am he for whom Jehangir Bahadur has waited. Be very quick, or I will have you trampled by him.'

The man was very much abashed by Hussein's great air of authority, and saying, 'On my head and heart,' he went straightway to get those things which were ordered. The water and the stiff brush having been brought, and the arrack having been set aside in a pot, Hussein washed Jehangir all over very carefully, cleaning his great ears tenderly, and plucking the small stones and thorns from his feet. All the time Jehangir made a continuous bubbling noise of happiness, and caressed Hussein with his trunk.

Then Hussein gave him the arrack to drink; by this time the other mahouts had come, and they said, 'What is this?' Hussein told them the whole case, and they, who had spent their lives among the elephants as Hussein had done, said, 'The matter is solved in a fitting matter; you will enter the service again, and they will make you the mahout of Jehangir.'

But some among them, the older men, said that it was hard to get back again once one had left, and this depressed Hussein, who knew it to be true.

'But this is an exceptional case,' said an old mahout, 'and Jehangir will undoubtedly pine to death if you leave him again; I will speak to the chief of the mahouts myself, for he has the say in these matters.'

And all the mahouts said, 'This is just.' But when the chief was brought, he looked sourly upon Hussein, for he recognised in him the man who had tricked him out of two pice the evening before over a matter concerning the payment for straw, and he said, 'Now this is without doubt an evil man, a but-pârast, and one whose female relations have no noses; who is he to consort with us?'

'But Jehangir will perish if he goes,' said one of the mahouts.

'That is not so,' replied the cantankerous old man, 'for I shall make him my own especial charge.' And then the chief of the mahouts, whose bile was enlarged by the frost of the morning, and whose temper was therefore more bellicose, caused Hussein to be ejected from the elephant lines. Then he shackled Jehangir with chains to prevent him from wandering again. When the elephant saw that Hussein was no longer among the mahouts, he raged and trumpeted, but he was impotent, on account of the chains.

Hussein dared not return to the camp, for fear of the enmity of the old man; but when the regiment moved on, he followed it, and saw Jehangir pulling the guns with the other elephants. He was very troublesome, however, and constantly stopped among crowds to look for Hussein.

———

The chief of the mahouts rode him, and wielded the iron ankus unmercifully, so that Hussein, watching from afar, raged furiously.

When it came to the place appointed, the regiment was split up, certain of the elephants being sent north with the guns, and the others to the south with various burdens. Among those who were sent back was Jehangir, for it was feared that he would go mûsth and run amok. The chief of the mahouts went north with the other elephants, and there he was killed by a certain stone that fell upon his head as he passed beneath a bridge. Hussein was able to see more of Jehangir as they travelled southwards, as he followed the returning detachment, giving performances with his snakes whenever he could. In a few days he approached the man who commanded the mahouts, and asked to be taken on, but the man refused, saying that he had been warned against Hussein as a wicked man who sought an opportunity to do evil. Hussein had no money wherewith to bribe the man, so he cried out to Heaven that this was an injustice, hoping to catch the ear of a white man; but the other man shouted louder, and men came running who beat Hussein with their lathis, and throwing him into a dry ditch forbade him to come near the elephants again. That night he stole into the lines and lay at the feet of Jehangir; the elephant lifted him up on to his back, and Hussein whispered his troubles into the broad, waving ears. Then he slept from weariness, stretched on the elephant's back, and Jehangir shuffled to the limit of his chains; he strained for some time against them, and presently Hussein was awakened by the sharp, clear sound of snapping iron. The noise was not enough to alarm anybody, so none saw the elephant slip away from the lines like a grey shadow, moving without a sound.

Hussein lay still for a moment, somewhat confused.

Then he felt Jehangir moving under him, and he sat up. The elephant had come out on to the road, and was moving rapidly towards the south, where the deep forests came close down to the road. After a little time, while Hussein was still collecting his scattered wits, Jehangir left the road, and turned into the thick elephant grass that bordered it; there he stopped, and stuffed a bunch of tender leaves into his mouth.

'Turn, Light of my soul,' said Hussein, very frightened; 'turn and go back before they find that you are gone. They will say that I have stolen you.' Jehangir remained motionless. Hussein slipped to the ground and argued with the elephant. 'If they catch me now, they will send me to the jail for many years, and I shall die,' he said. But Jehangir only gurgled in his throat, and his eye took on an obstinate gleam. 'Turn back before it is too late,' repeated Hussein; 'I cannot hide you, and they will catch us and put heavy irons on you.'

He stormed, but Jehangir only ate leaves, and rolled his head: he pleaded with the elephant, and wept at his feet, but Jehangir only ate wild sugar-cane and stood upon three legs to rest the fourth.

At length Hussein stood speechless, and Jehangir picked him up with his trunk; putting him on his back, the elephant set off towards the forest. Then Hussein gave in, and guided Jehangir on to a path which led more straightly into the deep woods. He urged Jehangir to his full speed, a peculiar loping shuffle that took them at a great pace; for, as he told the elephant, they would have to go far before dawn in order to have a chance of getting clear away. With his tireless gait the elephant gained the virgin forest before the moon had set, and by dawn they were so far away from the camp that Hussein felt safe; nevertheless, they kept on until noon, when they rested by a river.

Hussein lay on the warm sand and thought out a plan. He decided to lie hid until the hue and cry had died down, and then to go as far south as possible, keeping away from the towns; then he thought he would travel slowly about the country, hiring Jehangir and himself to clear away trees and to do work for which a well-guided elephant is essential. He had encountered men who owned an elephant and who travelled like this, so his appearance would give rise to no suspicion.

He decided that he would do this until he had amassed sufficient money to buy land and to settle down with Jehangir and Sashiya. Then he would have seven sons and a daughter, and the crops would be exceedingly good, and he would buy more land, and employ several men, and his sons would beget sons, and he would see great-grandchildren in his own lifetime, and many of his descendants would be mahouts of great fame, and some would be scholars, and some would be landowners, and he would have a funeral, when he died, that would be remembered for fifty years, and Jehangir would live to a great age with his eldest son.

Eleven

Hussein made a hut in a mango grove; there was a stream near-by, and close to it, on the other side, a deserted Ghond village. There seemed to be no particular reason why it should have been deserted, but Hussein disliked the look of it. There were plenty of ripe mangoes, and the jungle fowl laid their eggs in the grass, so Hussein did not do so badly. After a while he took to trapping small animals; as time went on he became quite adept at this, so he fed well.

The days passed very quickly; each one seemed quite long, but they slipped into the past one after another until a considerable period had elapsed.

Had it not been for Jehangir, Hussein would have perished in the jungle long before, but as it was he was quite safe from anything — or almost anything. One day, however, as he sat among the stones by the stream, watching Jehangir squirting himself, he felt something move beneath him, and as he got up, he felt an agonising pain, as if a red-hot wire had been thrust into him. He had sat on a scorpion.

The pain was excruciating, and he leapt high in the air. It was not very serious as scorpion stings go, for it was only a small one, and the sting had not been thrust right home. Nevertheless, he was intensely uncomfortable for a week. When he had recovered from the sting, he was forced to leave his hut by a host of soldier ants, who came marching through the trees early one morning, and decided to settle in the mango grove.

Hussein and Jehangir moved along the stream for half a day until they found another place, more pleasant than the mango grove, for their habitation.

It was near here that Hussein found a yogi in a small cave. He made the discovery quite by chance; it was at a place where the stream ran deep between fern-covered rocks. A huge frond covered the entrance to the cave; it moved in the breeze as Hussein passed, and revealed the yogi squatting on the ground. He was a very old man, bald and beardless. He had a face rather like that of a tortoise, and a remarkably benign expression. Hussein greeted him, and squatted before him, but the old man took no notice; he was deep in a contemplative trance; his eyes were focussed on a pebble. From time to time his lips moved, and a little whisper came from him; his hands occasionally half-spread themselves, as if he were arguing with someone, and emphasising a point. Hussein waited a long while, but the yogi did not come back to earth, so he left the cave quietly, since he was unwilling to break in on the old man's contemplation.

As he went out of the cave, Hussein noticed a track that led down to the stream; it was obviously used by a good number of animals. In one place, where it was muddy, there were the pug-marks of a tiger. They seemed very new, and Hussein felt rather uneasy. He shouted for Jehangir, and after a moment or two he heard the answering trumpet. He made towards the sound, hurrying along the little game tracks that wound through the jungle. He had an unpleasant feeling of being watched by something. Usually he rather liked the solitude of the jungle, and he seldom felt particularly afraid of anything; at this time, however, he felt that the jungle was unfriendly, and he was very much afraid. There were unaccountable little noises and movements that he would not ordinarily have noticed, but now they grated on his nerves. This feeling increased as he went on. He felt almost panic-stricken as he passed through a dark grove, and he started to run. The tiger that had been following him slid effortlessly through the undergrowth parallel with Hussein's path: it was not quite sure of itself, as it had not come into contact with men before, and although there was something about the scent that warned the tiger against following it, Hussein's feeling of terror reacted on it, and made it feel more confident. When Hussein began to run the tiger was almost ready to spring, but Hussein shouted for Jehangir again, and the sound disconcerted the tiger some what. Jehangir, very fortunately, was quite close at hand, and as the elephant came through the trees the tiger stopped, paused for a few moments, and slunk away. Jehangir caught its scent, and stood with his trunk outstretched, trying to locate it; he rumbled angrily in his throat, and sniffed Hussein all over, to see whether he had come to any harm.

They went back to the place Hussein had chosen; it was a small island in the stream with about a dozen large trees on it. The stream was fairly wide at this point, but not very deep; Jehangir could ford it easily. One end of the island, the end that met the run of the water, was piled high with driftwood and debris left there when the stream was in flood, but the other end tailed off in a long spit of sand. There was a good deal of bamboo among the trees, but the undergrowth was not at all thick, and one could walk about easily. In the middle of the lozenge-shaped island there was a triangle of three magnificent dak trees — some call them the flame of the forest — and these were in full bloom; one could hardly see the leaves for the great blaze of scarlet that flowered from the very top to the lowest branches. Hussein made his hut in the space between them, gathering a great heap of the fallen petals for his bed. A day or two later he went to see the yogi again, but the old man was not in the cave, so Hussein left a few mangoes on the floor and went back to his island.

That night there was a storm: for three hours the lightning hissed up and down the stream, and the thunder roared incessantly. Hussein sat on the sand-bank in the warm downpour, watching the lightning; seven times it struck trees on the banks, and twice it flickered low along the water by the sandbank, but it spared the trees on the island.

Jehangir welcomed the rain, but he did not like the thunder at all; he gave little squeals and started like a frightened woman at each great peal, so after a while Hussein left the sand-bank and came to comfort him where he stood, black and glistening, under the dak trees.

When the sun came up again, everything began to steam, and a very clean, sweet smell rose from the ground.

The dak trees were half stripped of their bloom, which lay sodden on the ground; but the new washed green of the exposed leaves against the remaining flowers made them more beautiful than before.

The stream had risen considerably and the island had shrunk correspondingly when Hussein went round on a tour of inspection. There was quite a number of leafy branches and pieces of creeper washed up on the top end of the island, and Hussein scrambled over the driftwood to investigate. He slipped on a wet trunk and fell forwards; before he could get up a python had flung a coil round his legs. The snake had been washed down-stream by the flood. The tree in which it had been sleeping had been pushed into the stream by one that had been struck by lightning. The python had only newly changed its skin, so it was very irritable; moreover, Hussein had startled it, otherwise it would not have attacked him, for it was not very large as pythons go; nevertheless, its strength was very considerable. Hussein tried to get up, but the snake threw two more coils around his thighs, and whipped its tail about a branch coming from a fallen trunk; this gave it something to pull against, and it tightened the coils, hissing furiously. Hussein fell flat again; he shouted once for Jehangir, and then the python shifted one of the coils with lightning rapidity round his neck; Hussein had time to get one hand in front of his throat before the coils tightened, and with his other hand he grasped the snake's neck. When the coil tightened he could hardly breathe, much less shout, so he struggled silently. The python was not long enough to put another coil around him, so it just tightened its hold on the branch, and squeezed. Hussein was lying on his back in the driftwood; his legs were clamped together by two coils like steel bands; his neck and one hand were held by the third, and with his other hand he held the python's head away from him: its tongue flicked in and out, and the transparent shutters on its eyes slid across and back.

For a time they remained immobile; the python looked expressionlessly at Hussein, and kept up a steadily increasing pressure.

Hussein's nose began to bleed; there was a drumming in his ears, and black dots shifted before his eyes. Then the dead branch about which the python had lashed its tail broke with a loud snap, and the coils loosened. With all his remaining strength Hussein thrust the coil away from his neck, and writhed away from the driftwood. So long as the python could get no hold for its tail he had a chance.

He rolled into a patch of grass; the python lashed its tail furiously, seeking something firm; it seized a clump of bamboos, but they pulled out of the ground. As it threshed about, it jerked Hussein up and down, bruising him very painfully, but he had time to draw a full breath and shout for Jehangir. The elephant, however, was not on the island; he had gone down the stream to a patch of wild sugar-cane.

The coil about Hussein's neck slipped down, seeking to pin his arms, but the python had nothing to pull against, and Hussein forced the coil away from him. He gripped its neck with both hands, and tried to twist it, but the snake was too strong. He managed to get to his feet, but just as he did so, the python's tail found a sapling, and Hussein was jerked to the ground again. As he fell he saw a stone on the ground; he snatched it up with one hand, and rolled over so that he held the python's head against the ground: then he hit it as hard as he could with the stone.

The python crushed him convulsively, nearly breaking his thighs: the pain was agonising, and he hammered the snake's head furiously, smashing it horribly. But the python still held him, and it was some time before he could get it away. Even then it writhed.

Hussein limped away towards his hut; half-way there he fell down, and fainted. When he came to about half an hour later, he found that his legs were excessively painful, and that he could hardly move them.

He crawled the rest of the way to his hut, and there the yogi found him.

The old man had had a difficult time getting across the stream, but he had seen Hussein on the island, and he was still sufficiently human to be curious. He was an ascetic, this old yogi, and he had spent five years in the depths of the jungle by himself, endeavouring to perfect himself as a yogi. He said very little to Hussein: he sat down and meditated for nearly an hour, and then he began to massage Hussein very carefully. The yogi seemed immune to fatigue; he kept on and on for a long while, chanting in an undertone. The pain decreased steadily, and after a while Hussein slept, for he was quite exhausted.

Suddenly the yogi was grasped firmly about the waist and lifted about six feet into the air. Jehangir had come up silently behind him. The yogi was perfectly calm; he did not move; he only coughed to awake Hussein, who saw what was the matter, and told Jehangir, in a peevish tone, to let the old man alone. The elephant did so, rather unwillingly, and felt Hussein all over very gently with his trunk. The yogi continued his massage until Hussein was asleep again.

Hussein did not wake until noon the next day: the yogi was squatting before him, brewing a decoction over a small fire. Jehangir stood behind the yogi, quite near to him. The elephant had been wondering all night whether to trample on the old man or not. The yogi had taken no notice of Jehangir at all, and this had rather worried him, because he was used to feeling some sort of response from people, either a friendly one, or one of fear, and to receive none at all was quite outside his experience.

As soon as Hussein opened his eyes the old man made him swallow the vile brew that he had been preparing: it tasted very curious indeed, and almost immediately after it Hussein went to sleep again, and did not wake up again until the evening of the following day. By this time Jehangir had taken the yogi well into his consideration, and had decided that on the whole he was a good thing.

Hussein felt very much better, and he thanked the old man, who pooh-poohed his thanks, saying that he had erred from his true course of contemplation in coming to see Hussein at all, and that he had gone even more astray by recognising the existence of physical ill-being. In fact the yogi became so morose at the idea of having descended from his sorely attained heights of contemplation that he moved to another part of the jungle when Hussein was whole again, and after that they never saw each other. But Hussein always kept an affectionate memory of the old man, who was a true yogi, very different from the average sadhu or sanyassi; he was, indeed, a man of very great psychic attainments, and it was only his complete disregard of the dangers that beset the ordinary man in the jungle that kept him safe. There were very few animals who could not feel that he did not fear them at all, and who were not very much taken aback when they felt this reaction; that is, of course, all those animals who were attuned to a reaction of fear in other beasts; the more timid deer and the myriad birds were rather attracted than repelled when they encountered the yogi, and they did not fear him in the least.

Twelve

Hussein grew better quite quickly, and after the yogi had left him, he decided that he had stayed in the jungle long enough, so he carefully pared the Government number from the nail of Jehangir's off forefoot; he also took the silver bands from his tusks, putting them on his arms as bracelets, that he might look the more respectable, as one would who owned an elephant. Then one morning they started off up the stream, for Hussein knew that the Grand Trunk Road crossed it on a bridge quite near its source.

Hussein wanted to keep to the little villages until he had gained confidence, and had perfected his story by hearing it questioned, so he desired to cross the great road unobserved. But as Fate would have it, the third man they encountered on the Grand Trunk Road was a man on a Government elephant. This was the same man who had caused Hussein to be beaten some time previously. They recognised each other immediately, and the man bawled 'Stop thief,' and urged his elephant forward, beating him with his heavy ankus.

Hussein leant forward and spoke to Jehangir, who burst into a tremendous gallop. There was open country on the other side of the road, thinly interspersed with trees. Jehangir charged across the road and thundered away over the plain. The man set his elephant in pursuit, and the two rushed furiously away towards the west. Quite soon Hussein saw that Jehangir was losing ground, so he pulled up, and the two elephants faced each other.

Suddenly they both charged, and met head-on with a thud that shook the ground. Forehead to forehead they pushed furiously, each trying to force the other backwards. The two mahouts hurled abuse at each other as their mounts strove together with all their giant strength. His opponent was gaining a little, being somewhat heavier, so Jehangir, getting a foothold in the loose soil, made an immense effort, so great that his fore-feet left the ground, and he leaned with all his weight on his enemy, who began sliding slowly backwards, his feet slipping in the dust. At the same moment Hussein leapt across on to the other elephant's neck, and seizing the mahout, he cast him down. In another second Jehangir had defeated his opponent, thrusting him backwards and sideways; very quickly Jehangir backed, and then charged, ramming the other in the side. He went over with a crash right on top of his mahout, who was struggling on the ground. Hussein had time to leap clear, and immediately he ran to Jehangir to stop him battering the other elephant to death. Jehangir obeyed at once, and Hussein, mounting on his neck, guided him back into the forest.

Having concealed him in a clump of bamboos and forbidden him to move, Hussein went back to the dead mahout. There was nothing to be done for him; the falling elephant had killed him instantly, and in a panic had run back to his elephant lines.

Presently the people who saw him return without his mahout sent out a search party, who found the body, and Hussein, coming up as if he knew nothing about it, learnt that the man had been trampled to death by his own elephant, which he was known to have treated very harshly.

Nobody recognised Hussein or suspected him even when he appeared riding on Jehangir; it was a district in which he had never been before, and his story was accepted without question.

After that Hussein moved towards the south, finding a good deal of work on the way. As soon as he could he wrote a long letter to Sashiya, telling her all that had occurred.

It was five months later, in a little village called Laghat, that Hussein found that which he sought.

A childless man had died, and his heir, a distant cousin in Bombay, wished to sell the land that he had inherited. There was a little house, and four fields, but the house was rather tumble-down, and the fields were untilled, so the man did not ask a large price; even so, it would cost more than Hussein had saved, but after a great deal of bargaining with the man's agent, it was arranged that a lump sum should be paid, and the rest in the form of instalments, payable when the crops were sold.

Hussein was overjoyed when he stood for the first time in his own fields: there was something so solid and real about them. He felt a curious love for the brown earth.

His little farm lay between two others, with the village behind it, and the jungle before it. His house stood near the others in the village, and the fields stretched away, one after the other, almost to the green edge of the jungle. They were not separated by hedges, but by little irrigation ditches which led water to the crops. With his four fields, Hussein was quite a considerable man in the village, and his elephant gave him a great advantage, for Jehangir had more strength than six bullocks, and many times their sense. Although many of the villagers were Hindus, Hussein soon became popular, for he told his tales in the open space where the men of the village sat after sundown, talking of this and that; he asked no recompense other than part of the knowledge that the villagers had of the land, and this they gave him willingly, and with good will, for there are few things more pleasant to give than advice. Indeed, their ardour could hardly be restrained, and many of his neighbours would come and work in his fields to show him how a thing should be done, so as to prove that their advice was of more avail than another's.

He made real friends, however, of his immediate neighbours, for they were fine men, both Sikhs of the Khalsa. The one was called Rustum Singh, and the other Hurri Singh; they were cousins, and they were both ex-army men, fine, tall, upstanding men with large black beards; they both had sons in their old regiment. On high days and feasts Rustum Singh and Hurri Singh would array themselves in fine attire, and they would don their medals, acquired in Mesopotamia and on the Frontier. They both liked Hussein, and Hussein liked them. They did more for him than all the rest of Laghat put together.

Sometimes, when they needed great power, Hussein would come and help them with Jehangir, and they helped him to plant millet in the two fields nearest his house, and sugar-cane in the other two. This sugar-cane crop, if it were successful, would enable Hussein to buy a plough — a great thing for him, as he had to hire one, which was expensive. He had, therefore, taken much trouble over the sugar-cane, spending long hours in the sun preparing the earth for it, and doing similar things that were essential for its well-being.

On the advice of his neighbours he built a thorn hedge at the end of the field that lay next to the jungle, in order to keep the deer out of his crops.

Hussein had never worked so hard in all his days, but he liked it, for it was his own land, or would be, and he wished to have it perfect so that he could bring Sashiya to it, and say, 'I did all this by myself.'

Sashiya, by her letters, seemed delighted with everything, only she wished the crops would hurry, so that he could return to Haiderabad and take her away, for the man to whom she had been betrothed was anxious to have her.

When Hussein read this he cursed aloud, and straightway he took paper and pen, and wrote a letter to Abd'Arahman, the old letter-writer of Haiderabad, with whom he had been in communication since he left, charging him to go at once to the red-bearded fakir, and to request him to terrify Nurredin Shah that he might renounce the idea of marrying Sashiya. He enclosed all the money he could spare, and then waited impatiently for an answer.

Two weeks went by, and then a third, before the old man replied; he said that the business had been performed, and that Sashiya was unbetrothed, but that the fakir had demanded a greater sum than Hussein had been able to send, and he (the fakir) had said that if Hussein did not send it before a certain date, his crops would be withered. Hussein felt intensely relieved, and he borrowed the extra eleven rupees from Rustum Singh, sending them off at once, for he had a great respect for the fakir's curses.

One morning, when the canes were springing up fresh and green, he found that wild pigs from the jungle had broken in and eaten nearly a quarter of his crop in spite of the thorn hedge.

He strengthened the hedge with some more thorns, and in the evening he sat in the branches of a tall tree which marked the boundary of his land, to watch for the pigs. A little after sundown he saw a sounder of pigs, headed by a big, dangerous-looking boar, come out of the jungle, and after pushing in vain for some time against his hedge, break through into his neighbour's field. Hussein shouted, and threw the stones which he had carried up with him; then he leapt down from the tree and ran to Rustum Singh's house, where he told the old Sikh what had happened. They roused Hurri Singh, and ran down to the edge of the jungle with lathis in their hands; the old boar was still there, and seemed disinclined to move for anyone. Hussein threw a stone at him, hitting him in the side, and he trotted out of the sugar-cane to have a look at them. For some time he seemed in two minds whether to attack them or not. The boar would have been a very ugly customer to deal with had he charged, but he did not; he just grunted once or twice, and rooted at a particularly succulent sugar-cane. Rustum Singh trembled with rage; his beard seemed to bristle, but still caution held him back; then the boar scratched up two or three roots quite wantonly. With a shout of 'Khalsa ki jai' Rustum Singh whirled up his lathi and rushed at the boar; he hit it very hard on the head, and it turned and ran.

It was a long time since wild pigs had troubled the village, for there were many leopards in the jungle. The next evening Hussein, Rustum Singh and Hurri Singh all watched for the pigs, but they went to bed when the moon set without having seen any.

In the morning, however, they found that the pigs had broken through after they had left, and had ruined much of the young sugar-cane. The next night the same thing happened in fields some distance from Hussein's; these fields were held communally by the whole village, and everyone did a share of the work on them. In the open space where they met in the evening the men of Laghat discussed the matter. At length it was decided that the pigs should all be allowed to get into one field, where they could be surrounded by the villagers armed with sticks and ancient swords, for there were no firearms in the village. Then there arose a great discussion as to whose field should be used for the purpose. No one would willingly allow his crops to be trampled, either by pigs or men, much less by both.

The argument grew very hot, and Rustum Singh plucked several hairs from the beard of a man who opposed him. For several days no solution could be reached, and everyone guarded his own crops with rattles and stones as well as he could. Hussein, Rustum Singh and Hurri Singh, however, took it in turns to keep the pigs out.

At length the problem solved itself, for a tiger made

its appearance, and it carried off the pigs at the rate of one every other day.

Within a month the raids on the crops had practically ceased.

One night, however, there was a terrific bellowing in the place where the village buffaloes were kept, and in the morning it was found that the tiger had carried off a calf. All the villagers, with the exception of the owner of the calf, agreed that this was only a fair exchange for the tiger's removal of the pigs. They even smiled tolerantly when the tiger took a goat, but when another young buffalo disappeared it seemed to everyone that the tiger was getting the best of the bargain.

One evening, as the buffaloes were being led back from their grazing, the tiger tried to take another calf, but its mother charged the tiger, and wounded it severely. The tiger lay up in a dense bamboo grove for some time, recovering from its wounds. When it was whole again it changed its hunting ground for a time, and harried the deer in the jungle. But very soon it perceived that its spring was not so quick, nor was its strength so great. The tiger was getting old. Its beautiful coat grew matted, and lost its sheen.

For two days, some time after this, the tiger felt very sick, and it lay up, but on the third day its appetite returned, and it went out on the trail of a sambhur. For three hours the tiger hunted the deer, until at last it brought its quarry to bay; twice the tiger circled round the sambhur, and then it leapt, but its spring was a little too short, and its hold broke. The great deer lashed out with its hind feet, breaking two of the tiger's long canine teeth.

———

One evening, as he was talking with Rustum Singh in his fields, Hussein heard the tiger roar in the jungle, and he knew that it was back again.

The tiger was still an immensely powerful brute, and very dangerous, although it no longer felt equal to tackling a buffalo.

That same evening it took a child who had wandered to the edge of the jungle. None dared follow the tiger in the darkness. It would have been almost certain death to have attacked it without a rifle, and there was nothing of the kind in the village.

The tiger did not particularly like human flesh; it was somewhat too coarse and ape-like; but the extreme ease with which the meal had been obtained made it disinclined to take the greater trouble that was necessary to stalk down a deer, so three days later the tiger took a woman who had stayed behind the others at the stream where the pitchers were filled, which was a little way out of the village.

The panic-stricken villagers no longer left their houses after sun-down, and the women kept the children within doors all day.

Now it happened that Hurri Singh, who had been a widower for five years, had been negotiating for some time with one Ram Das of Surendranath for his daughter, whom he wished to take to wife. Her name was Diwana, and she was surpassingly beautiful.

As the villagers did not come out of the safety of their houses in the dark now that the tiger was about, it became increasingly bold, and in the full light of the day it took Diwana at the stream, and carried her into the jungle. There had been about twenty women filling their pitchers at the same time, but it had all happened so quickly that they had not been able to help, even if they had not been so frightened.

When Hurri Singh heard the news his heart was black, and he rent his clothes. Then he called Hussein and Rustum Singh and said that he was going out into the jungle to see whether by chance he might catch up with the tiger before it had killed the girl. They sought to dissuade him at first, but seeing that it was useless, Hussein called Jehangir to him, and they set off as fast as they could. They carried lathis and two old tulwars. They found the tiger's trail easily enough near the stream, but after a while it became very slight, for the animal had gone over stony ground and had then crossed the stream. For the whole of the rest of the day they searched, and a little before sunset they found the remains of the tiger's meal. The remains were very dreadful to see, and they went back to Laghat sick at heart.

The next day a deputation from the village went to the District Magistrate, one Chetwynd, and they asked him to come and shoot the tiger. Chetwynd came as soon as he was able, but not before the tiger had taken a travelling pedlar who was passing through the jungle.

Chetwynd stayed in Rustum Singh's house, which was the largest in the village. In the evening he discussed the plan of campaign with the villagers in the open space where they usually congregated. Most of the villagers were in favour of digging a pit which would be lightly covered over, and into which the tiger would, if all went well, fall, and be impaled on concealed spikes.

But the Englishman, the Sikhs, and Hussein agreed that there would be no honour in hunting that way. Hussein suggested sitting in a machan over some kill of the tiger's, and shooting it when it came to eat again. But Rustum Singh said that there would be more izzat to be gained by going to the tiger than by waiting for it. So it was decided that the whole village would turn out as beaters, while the sahib rode on Jehangir to shoot the tiger. In this way it would be more like a rajah's tiger hunt than anything else.

Next day it was ascertained that the tiger was lying up in a thick patch of elephant grass, so the villagers, armed with sticks and drums, with which to make a noise, formed up in a line behind the elephant grass, and, at a given signal, moved forward; they hoped to drive the tiger along to the clear place where Chetwynd was waiting on Jehangir. If Chetwynd had had more experience he would have known that a thin line of inexperienced beaters is worse than none at all, but this was his first tiger.

They started the tiger from his deep grass with some Chinese crackers, and in time it came bounding out into the clearing where Chetwynd was waiting on Jehangir. His heart was thumping almost audibly with excitement as he raised his rifle. The tiger paused at the edge of the clearing: Chetwynd fired, scratching the tiger's ribs. Turning, the tiger dashed through the advancing line of beaters. Two old men were in its way; it knocked them flat, wounding one seriously. In a few moments it was out of sight, and Chetwynd was left cursing his own stupidity.

They went back to Laghat, carrying the injured beater.

The same night the tiger broke through the mud wall of an outlying hut and took a boy. Chetwynd, in the morning, decided to follow up the tiger on foot, tracking it as best he could. Hussein was the best shikar in the village, so he went as gun-bearer.

At dawn they set out on Jehangir, whom they were going to leave as soon as the trail grew so slight as to have to be followed on foot. A boy went with them to take the elephant back. At first the tiger's path was clearly visible; a broad swathe of grass showed where it had rushed through without a thought of picking its way. Soon it was obvious that the tiger had slackened its pace, and although at intervals the broad pug-marks were visible in the mud, the track became harder to follow. Suddenly they came upon a place where the undergrowth was all trampled, and where there were splashes of dried blood. Hussein tapped Jehangir's head and whispered to him, the elephant knelt down, and the two men dismounted.

A faint cry from a tree made them look up. Wedged between the bole of a tree and a branch some fifty feet up was the boy whom the tiger had carried off. As soon as it had broken through the mud wall of the hut the tiger had seized him by the arm, flung him on its back, and made off into the jungle. The boy had been paralysed with terror at first, but when the tiger had paused to change its grip, he had snatched at a hanging branch. The tiger had been too surprised to leap up at him for a moment, and he had been able to scramble to safety in spite of his badly lacerated arm. For some time the tiger had stayed at the bottom of the tree, but it went away a little before dawn. They sent the boy back on Jehangir to Laghat, and set out again.

They were able to follow the trail quite easily for a good way beyond the tree, but at length they came to a place where it became slighter and more confused. For some time it was possible to see the tiger's pug-marks here and there in the mud left by the rain which had fallen in the night, but soon the sun rose higher, and its heat began to pour through the thick greenery of the jungle, so that although it grew much lighter, the steam which arose from the ground made it much more difficult to see.

While they followed up the tiger's trail, Jehangir took the injured boy to Laghat. When he saw Hussein's elephant, Rustum Singh thought that he had better take him to Hussein's house, but the elephant thought otherwise, and gently pushing Rustum Singh aside, he went back into the jungle.

The elephant's swinging pace took him quickly along the path to the tree where Hussein had left him. Here he picked up the scent of the men, and followed it. On his padded feet the elephant moved silently, and soon he came within sight of the men. He followed them slowly, moving so quietly that they had no suspicion that he was near. He did not want to show himself, for Hussein had told him to go home, and he knew perfectly well that he should have stayed in the village. Soon the men came to a thick patch of tall grass where the tiger was resting. Before it had pushed its way into the elephant grass, the tiger had gone round it, so its tracks ran on for some way past the place where it was lying. It was obvious to Chetwynd from the freshness of the pug-marks that they were quite near the tiger now, but he did not think that they were quite so near as they were. A jungle fowl which started up from under Hussein's feet awoke the tiger. It crept to the edge of the elephant grass, and crouched there, watching the men intently. It was intensely still;

only the tip of its tail moved, twitching nervously from side to side. The men were walking slowly up a broad path: the tiger watched them on the one side, and Jehangir on the other.

Very quietly the elephant raised his trunk and sniffed the still air. He caught the heavy musty scent of the tiger: by the strength of it he knew that the tiger must be very near, and he looked anxiously about with his little eyes. The tiger's stripes blended perfectly with the elephant grass. It was practically invisible, but Jehangir caught the movement of the tip of its tail.

When they were almost opposite the tiger the men stopped, and Hussein ran back to pick up something that Chetwynd had dropped. Chetwynd stooped to brush a mosquito from his knee, and at the same moment Jehangir saw the great muscles in the tiger's back rise and tense themselves as the tiger prepared to charge. The next second the tiger shot out of its hiding-place: Chetwynd was knocked flat, and the tiger stood over him, roaring very deeply. At once the elephant stepped from his side of the path, and stood for a moment with his broad ears standing out stiffly; the tiger looked at the elephant; its attention was distracted from Chetwynd, who lay quite still. All this happened in a few seconds, and Hussein, who was carrying the rifle, ran up without any hesitation, seized the tiger's tail with one hand, while with the other he hit it with the clubbed rifle. In his excitement he had quite forgotten how to fire it. The tiger, amazed, leapt round to meet this new enemy, and then Jehangir charged. With incredible nimbleness the elephant avoided the men, and threw the tiger about ten feet, where it lay for a second, sprawling on its back. Hussein dragged

Chetwynd out of the way. Jehangir darted forward before the tiger had time to recover, and knelt on it, driving his blunted tusks through and through the striped body, quite pinning it to the earth, so great was the force of his charge. The tiger died with a roar that ended in a scream as the elephant's weight crushed in its ribs. Then Jehangir twitched it up into the air with his trunk, and flung it into the grass, following it with the intention of trampling it into a thin paste, but Hussein ran to call him off, for he did not want the skin spoiled. Then he turned to Chetwynd, who had scrambled to his feet. He was not even scratched, for he had instinctively dodged as the tiger sprang, and he had only been knocked down by the tiger's body – the terrible claws had missed him altogether. Hussein pushed into the grass and cut the tiger's whiskers off – they are a very potent charm – for that was his due as a shikari. Chetwynd came over to the tiger's body with his hand stretched out, and they shook over it: a trifle melodramatically perhaps, but perfectly sincerely. Then they mounted on Jehangir again, and went back to Laghat, whence half the village turned out to bring in the skin.

There was a tremendous feast that night, at which Hussein told the whole episode in the form of a tale, most wondrous to hear – the same tale that one may hear to this day – with variations – in all the villages for fifty miles round Laghat.

Then the District Magistrate went his way rejoicing, for he, too, had a tale to tell in his old age, and life resumed its even tenor.

———

Thirteen

After the tiger had gone the pigs did not come back; a blessing for which the priest at the village temple grew fat and oily.

However, as time went on, another misfortune befell Laghat: a great drought began, and the early crops shrivelled in the iron-hard ground. At first they were able to preserve them with the water from the primitive irrigation system, but presently water became too precious for that, as the stream shrank to a mere trickle flowing between great cracking spaces of dried yellow mud. There was not enough for the people, let alone the crops. They were reaped early, and they were poorer than the gloomiest prophets had foretold. Hussein saw the prospect of Sashiya coming to his house that year fading.

The whole village, after the failure of the early crops, planted their faith firmly in the success of the later harvest, which was to get the benefit of the tremendous rains of the monsoon.

The time for the breaking of the monsoon came, but although the whole land prayed for it, the rains did not come. Day after day the great cloud-banks swept northwards across the sky, and day after day the villagers did poojah in the temple of the Hindu gods; even the Sikhs and Hussein sent gifts to the gods so that the rain might come.

But the clouds swept on over the parched earth, and let loose not a drop of their burden.

At length, as if in answer to the innumerable prayers, the stream waxed a little, and thin trickles ran through the irrigation ditches: none knew why the stream increased, for no rain fell, but they were content with the miracle. But it did not last long, although the water was strictly rationed, and men fought furiously in the fields, each saying that the other took more than his share. Weeks passed, and the stream shrank again, but still the monsoon did not break. There was no water for the buffaloes to wallow in. Their hides became hard, and they could not work. Every day seemed full of the promise of rain: thunder rumbled about the hills, and lightning flickered across the sky, but always the rain held off. Hussein found himself dreaming of rain — warm sheets of rain, soaking the whole earth.

The crops waited as long as they could for the rain, but as it did not come, they withered where they stood.

Then Purun Dass, the Brahmin and priest of the temple, took out his fat, brass-bound account book, and lent a rupee here and a rupee there, sometimes more, sometimes less, but always he made a bond on a little piece of land, or a bedstead, or the produce of next year's crops. His rate of interest was 60 per cent, but that is quite moderate for India, and the villagers had to borrow or starve.

At last the rains came, just as Hussein had dreamt of

them, and Jehangir and the buffaloes stood out in it, absorbing it through their skins. But it was too late: nearly everything was dead.

The stream rose several feet in the night, and the irrigation ditches overflowed, but it was too late. Several of the water-buffaloes had died, and the whole village, with one or two exceptions, was in debt to the full extent of its pledgeable value.

Hussein sat in Jehangir's shelter, between the elephant's great feet, watching the tremendous rain falling. The dry earth drank it in with a strange sucking noise that seemed to come from everywhere, yet from no one place in particular.

Hussein looked out over his fields, and he said, with a bitter smile, 'What is written is written. Inshallah!' for he was well-nigh ruined. But he sighed, for he had worked on his own land as he had never worked before, and he loved every inch of it.

The rain poured on, beating down with a loud roar, and Jehangir stepped delicately out over Hussein to stand in it. His wrinkled skin shone with the wetness, and he was happy. He was only happy with his body, however, for he felt in his mind that Hussein was miserable, so he was miserable in sympathy.

Before long Hussein had to go to Purun Dass like the rest of the villagers, and he borrowed money on the field next to the jungle.

One day Rustum Singh had a letter. His son had been killed on the Border. The old man no longer cared to live, and he fell sick of a palsy. Hussein and Hurri Singh fed him with a spoon, and tended him night and day, but it was of no avail. He died within a week. Purun Dass, the bunnia, seized all his land, showing bonds to justify himself. Hurri Singh protested, for he was sure that his cousin had not borrowed so much, but the bunnia showed the bonds. They were all signed with Rustum Singh's mark.

Hurri Singh would have yielded, but Hussein said, 'Have you read the bonds?'

'No, for I am a plain man, as you know, and unable to read.'

'Then show them to me, for I am surpassingly learned, and I can read all manner of tongues.'

The bunnia looked uneasy, but he could not refuse. He passed the bonds to Hussein, and as he put them into his hands, he cunningly shuffled three rupees in among them, and winked at Hussein, who slid the money into his waistband. But in spite of the bribe Hussein read the bonds aloud as they were written.

The bunnia had no right whatsoever to the whole of the land. The first bond was on half the next year's produce of two of the fields, the second was on a charpoy and two buffaloes, and the third was on a spade, an axe, and some furniture. When he heard these things Hurri Singh cried out in anger, and fell upon Purun Dass, threatening him with his lath, but the Hindus of the village, who were sitting around – they were all in the open space in the evening – dragged him off, and the bunnia, who was a Brahmin, and therefore holy, escaped to his temple. The Sikh sent after him those things to which he was entitled: then he regaled Hussein with a great feast in spite of his poverty, for he held gratitude in high esteem.

The bunnia cherished a great hatred against Hussein

———

after this: he hated him anyhow for a Muslim, but now he hated him as a personal enemy as well, but he dissimulated it well.

As time went on Hussein's small stock of money dwindled away. He sold various things, but he could not scrape together nearly enough to be able to sow his fields again for the next crop. At length, having sent out feelers through various friends to ascertain whether the bunnia would entertain the idea of another loan, he went to the Brahmin, who received him pleasantly, but with black hate well hidden.

Hussein borrowed a good sum, and for security he gave a bond on the rest of his land. With this he was able to buy enough seed to plant his fields well.

In his letters to Sashiya and to old Abd'Arahman he did not say that he was doing so badly, for he wanted Sashiya always to think of him as one who did not make mistakes, so he merely said that the price of millet had gone down, so that he had got a relatively poor sum for his harvest, and that what with one thing and another, she would have to wait just a little longer before he could come to Haiderabad and take her away in the splendour which she deserved. He wrote his fiction well, so well, indeed, that he even managed to deceive her, which was a remarkably difficult thing to do, because she loved him very deeply, and nearly always she could tell when a note of insincerity crept into his letters.

But the price that he had to pay for replanting his land was a stiff one, and it left him with practically nothing to live on, and presently he had to go to the bunnia again, and he pledged his house.

The interest was 60 per cent, not too exorbitant for the

average bunnia: the loan was to be repaid when Hussein's next crop was sold, or else, by the bond, the bunnia could seize the house and the land. Hussein could read, and he scanned the documents carefully for any trickery, but he signed them when he was satisfied that there was none. But the bunnia, educated at a secondary school, was more cunning than Hussein, and after the 60 per cent he had written in, 'per mensem' instead of 'per annum', which made the interest 720 per cent, so that Hussein, who could not read the English characters, and who had not suspected the trickery to lie there, was hopelessly in the Brahmin's power.

Time passed, and the money went while the crops were ripening, but it had all gone before the harvest was ready to be reaped, for it had been planted late: nevertheless, it was a magnificent crop, and as Hussein looked out across his fields, waving thick and green down to the jungle, his heart filled with pride. His pride echoed to Haiderabad, and Sashiya dreamt of the wind in the fields, rippling the high crops like water.

But while they ripened, there was the problem of existence to be faced, and Hussein had to go to Purun Dass again: this time Hussein had no more land to pledge, so he offered to give a bond on the produce of his fields for the following year, but the bunnia refused, saying that anything might happen to the crops, whereas a bond on Jehangir would be as good as the security of land. Hussein refused indignantly, and went home.

The bunnia had not disclosed the trick in the bond yet, for he wished to get everything possible out of his enemy, and he would wait until the sugar-cane and the millet were reaped and sold, so that he would get the utmost in money as well as land. But above all things, even above money, the bunnia desired to get possession of Jehangir, for he knew that Hussein loved the elephant.

The next day Hussein came back and offered to give a bond on his produce over the next two years, and he said that he would even pay a higher rate of interest, but the priest laughed pleasantly, and said that he would rather have a bond on the elephant, and Hussein could not shake him from that decision. Hussein refused again, but that night he went and drank arrack with Hurri Singh, who was as poverty-stricken as himself, but who also had a fine crop standing in his fields, and they felt justified in celebrating. They both had considerably more than they could stand. Towards the setting of the moon Purun Dass appeared, and they received him cordially, for their hearts were warmed towards all men.

Presently Hurri Singh fell asleep, and Purun Dass urged Hussein to sign the bond on Jehangir that he had prepared. As his usual caution was gone, and as he felt very optimistic about his crops, Hussein signed, took the money, and fell asleep counting it.

The crops ripened daily, and it was obvious to all Laghat that it was to be a very fortunate year. The time of reaping came, and Hussein sold his produce well to the travelling merchants who came round from village to village with their train of bullock carts, and their great scales with shining brass pans.

He came back to his house from the place where the merchants stood with a great bag of silver rupees on his head, for he distrusted notes. In the doorway of his house Purun Dass was waiting for him, with papers in his hand. Hussein greeted the moneylender cheerfully, for he had easily enough to pay off the debt, principal and interest, and still leave him sufficient to live on until the next harvest. First he put down the sums that he had borrowed and then he said, 'Let us work out the interest.'

'Here are the bonds,' replied the bunnia. 'You will see that the interest is 60 per cent per month – quite a usual rate for a short-term loan.'

Hussein protested, thinking that the bunnia was jesting, but Purun Dass explained the meaning of 'per mensem', and he kept stressing the point that the bonds were quite legal, because they were bonds that made it appear as though the loan were to be repaid in a short time. He smirked as he computed the huge amount due to him, and tittered nervously as he noted it down on a sheet of paper. Hussein was overwhelmed: he could never amass such an amount, and he saw everything that he had going from him, even Jehangir. He had the poor man's innate distrust of the law, and it never entered his head that he should employ a lawyer to adjust the matter in court.

The bunnia began a remark about the exceeding unwisdom of infidels interfering with Brahmins, but when he looked at Hussein's face, he snatched up his bonds and ran to his own house.

Hussein sat in his doorway, quite still, until it became dark. His usually quick mind seemed numbed. Then he arose and fetched a jar of arrack. He pulled fiercely at a bowlful of the fierce spirit: he had drunk a good deal before he felt his mind working as usual. Then he emptied the jar and opened another. When he was half-way through the second he thought of a plan: he would take his money – the bunnia had not touched it, he had thought it wiser to wait until Hussein was numbed with despair – and Jehangir and go as fast as he could into the jungle, but first he would visit the bunnia. He sprang to his feet; he was rather unsteady, but he could walk perfectly well. He took the broken handle off a hoe from the corner of the room and went out.

Passing Hurri Singh's house, he saw the burly Sikh standing in his doorway. He said nothing, but went on; presently he came to the small temple in which Purun Dass and two other Brahmins lived. Hussein went in through the open courtyard. Before the gate of the temple he paused, and took off his turban, which he wound round his face and head with a vague idea of disguising himself. Then he pushed at the door; it gave with a squeak, for it was not locked. Hussein went in: he walked past two great images of Krishna and Siva, and he spat contemptuously. From beneath the door of a little room behind the images a beam of light showed clearly. Hussein, leaning on his stick to steady himself, crept to the door, and opened it softly. The Hindu did not hear him at first; he was adding up a row of figures, and muttering to himself; sometimes he tittered in a peculiarly revolting way. Suddenly the Brahmin looked up and saw Hussein standing in the doorway. They looked at each other: neither said anything, Hussein because the words seemed confused as they came to his mouth, owing to the arrack, and Purun Dass because he was stiff with fright.

Suddenly the Hindu flung a small brass kali at Hussein, hitting him on the chest. Hussein grunted, and leapt upon Purun Dass; he hit him on the head, knocking him out of his seat. Then he put his foot on the Brahmin's back as he sprawled on the ground, holding him down firmly, and he thrashed the squirming body all over, wherever he could for its wriggling. Purun Dass screamed in a high falsetto that broke ludicrously; he had not even the spirit to try to drag Hussein down on to the ground, but flung his hands about in a wild endeavour to protect himself from the rain of blows. To stop the foolish, piglike screaming, Hussein hit him very hard two or three times on the head, and after that he lay still, only squirming a little. Presently he stopped squirming, and the hoe handle broke over his head: Hussein threw the end away, and rolled the bunnia over with his foot. Purun Dass was bleeding all over, particularly from his head, for the stick had been tipped with iron. Hussein sobered quickly when he saw what he had done: he knelt, and tried to see whether the Hindu was still breathing, but Purun Dass was quite still, and Hussein could detect no pulse.

Hussein straightened, and ran from the room: he was not particularly frightened or sorry, but he knew that the sooner he was out of Laghat the greater would be his chance of escape. At the gate of the temple he paused, and went back. The big red account book and a dozen bundles of bonds lay on the table; he took them, and ran out again. In the courtyard he ran into the arms of the two other Brahmins, but they were slight men, and he knocked them aside: they did not follow, for he was stained with blood, and looked very grim.

He came on to the road, and from behind some trees Hurri Singh ran out to him.

'Come quickly; the other priests heard you, and they have raised all the Hindus, crying sacrilege. I have Jehangir waiting for you.'

They darted behind the trees. A loud shouting came from the village: the priests had said that the temple was being desecrated, and it had taken little time for the news to spread. Hussein started at the waving torches; he was still not quite himself.

Hurri Singh tugged at his sleeve. 'Quick,' he said, 'I have put food and money in this bag. But why did you use a stick and not a knife? So much less noise.'

'I never meant to kill him. Take these books and burn them; they are the accounts of all the debts. Allah's blessing on your head and house.'

Hussein gave Hurri Singh the papers, and mounted Jehangir; then he leant down, and whispered — all their talk had been in whispers — 'There is a great bag of rupees in my house. Put them in a safe place for me.' In another moment the elephant had disappeared among the trees.

Fourteen

Hussein travelled all through the night. The next day he was fifty miles away, in the heart of the jungle. Until his food gave out he pushed on, and then he came into a village to buy provisions. He had left Jehangir in the jungle a mile from the village, and he answered vaguely to the questions put to him by the shopkeepers; it was a fairly large village, and that day there were a number of merchants gathered there, so all might have passed off well, for he walked about with a nonchalant air, as if his business took him into strange villages every day. But one of the merchants spoke to him and said, 'Are you not the same man whom I saw, long ago, telling tales in the city of Agra?'

'No,' replied Hussein, 'I have never been there.'

'That is strange; I could have sworn that you were the same man. Pray, what do you do here?'

'I am merely passing through this village on my way to the shrine of Pir Jafer, which is in Minapur.'

'That is odd – I was there last year ... come and partake of some cous-cous with us.' Hussein did not like to refuse, so he went with the merchant to the place where the company lodged, and he fed with them. When they had wiped the grease from their hands and from their beards, the man who had first spoken to Hussein began speaking of all the cities he had visited, and of the strange sights that he had seen. 'Once,' he said, 'I was in Peshawar . . . there I saw an old man killed, I know not for what reason . . . it was a curious thing, for the people who stood around said that a cobra came from beneath his clothes . . . a white cobra.' Hussein felt a curious cold shiver run down his back; he looked attentively at the man. He felt almost sure that he had seen him somewhere, but where he could not remember. Then the man lit a pipe, and in the flare that shot up from the bowl – for it was twilight – Hussein recognised him; it was the same man whom he had seen long ago, in Peshawar, at the house of Huneifa, a little while before old Feroze Khan had been killed. He strove to recall the name that he had heard, and then, quite suddenly, a little bit of conversation came back to him. There was the dancing girl Azizun, filling him a pipe. 'But this is Ram Narain's special pipe – he will be very angry – here is another one for you . . .'

The man was looking at Hussein in a singular way all the time he told this tale, but Hussein set his face in an expressionless mask, and said composedly, 'Very curious; I heard of a similar instance once in Poonch.'

After a little more speech, Hussein rose to take his departure. After he had gone a little way, he was aware of Ram Narain following close behind him.

'This is my way also,' said Ram Narain. 'We will walk together for a little way.' There was a pause; each was trying to guess if the other was sure of his ground; then

Ram Narain said, 'I think the name of the old man whom I saw killed was Feroze Khan; perchance you may have heard of him? He was a notable teller of tales.'

'Feroze Khan is quite a common name: I remember one called by that name who was a dealer in grain at Jubbulpore, but he was a youngish man, with a wen on his neck.'

'No, this was an old man: in Peshawar he had, I remember, a young man with him, for whom, so they say, the police have been searching for some time, for it is said that he was a seditious man, one who carried messages from certain princes to an emir of Waziristan.'

Hussein did not reply, but yawned elaborately. They came to a place where the path forked: 'Which is your road?' asked Hussein.

'The left,' replied Ram Narain.

'Mine, unfortunately, is the right,' said Hussein.

It was many days before Hussein went to another village, for he was very much exercised in his mind as to the significance of Ram Narain and his curious speech. He knew that there was something very odd about Feroze Khan's death in Peshawar, and the old man had told him that he was in the service of the Dewan of Waziristan. He thought for several days about the matter, but he could arrive at no conclusion, so eventually he dismissed it from his mind.

At length his money ran out, and he had to live in the jungle. At first he did not do so badly; his old skill in snaring small beasts returned to him, but one day he was afflicted with the most grievous fever, so that for a while he was out of his wits. That did not endure long, however, but when he recovered he was very weak, so he made his way to a small town, and, having left Jehangir in a safe place, he sat in the market-place, and told several tales. His recompense was meagre, but it brought him food, and the next day he did the same thing in a village some distance away. For several weeks he travelled like this, until one day, when he had become sufficiently confident to hire himself and Jehangir as he had done before he came to Laghat, a policeman questioned him, saying that an elephant had been stolen from the palace of a local rajah. Hussein was taken to the village police-thana, and kept there until the rajah's mahout came, and said that it was not the same elephant. The incident shook Hussein considerably, for he thought that if a report had been circulated that a man with an elephant had murdered a bunnia, the police of that village might remember it, and report that he had been seen. For a considerable period after this he kept to the very small villages, and made himself as inconspicuous as possible. He had thought of sending to Hurri Singh to ask him to send him his money, but then he remembered that Hurri Singh could not read, and that the only men in the village who could were the Brahmins.

Hussein had wandered a great distance from Laghat by this time, and he had come to the hills of Assam. He was going through a wide plain, thinly wooded and very far from anywhere in particular, when he heard a noise rather like the whistle of a train, and he saw a great grey shape coming at him in a cloud of dust.

It was a rhinoceros; a huge, savage brute. It had been looking for something to vent its anger on all day, but hitherto it had only been able to plough up shrubs and bushes. Hussein, walking a good way ahead of Jehangir, had awakened it from a half-doze, and the wind had taken his scent right to the rhinoceros, who had charged without another thought. Hussein did not pause to look at it; he ran as hard as he could for a tree, and shot up into its branches. Jehangir was too far away to be reached in time, and even the short distance between him and the tree took enough time for the rhino to be practically upon him before he reached it.

Hussein shouted for Jehangir, and the elephant came slowly towards him, picking a branch here and a branch there as he came. He had not caught the scent of the rhino, who was backing to charge the tree, but in a moment he heard the crash as the great beast hurtled against the trunk, almost uprooting it. Jehangir broke into a rapid shuffle, and the rhino turned to face him. The rhino's little eyes were red with rage, and it pawed impatiently at the ground. Suddenly it gave a great whistling snort, and charged at the elephant; it travelled, for all its vast bulk, like a galloping horse, and the ground shook beneath it.

Jehangir met it half-way, and there was a great thud as they met; a cloud of dust flew up. When the dust cleared away Hussein saw the rhino scrambling unwieldily to its feet; it had been knocked flying. Jehangir had cunningly avoided the great horn, and had sidestepped, ramming the rhinoceros in the side as it shot past.

The rhino peered uncertainly at its adversary; its eyes were very poor, and it was the wrong side of the wind. Twice it scraped up the ground with its single horn, and then it charged again. Jehangir stooped, and met it shoulder-on. The elephant was thrust back nearly a yard, and the rhino stopped dead.

———

Instantly Jehangir whipped his trunk round its leg, and jerked with all his might; the rhino crashed over with a bellow of rage, and Jehangir heaved himself up to kneel on it. He was very much hampered by his blunted tusks, for he could not thrust them through the rhino's hide, but he crushed all the breath out of it. The rhino, however, was a beast of enormous strength, and it heaved up under Jehangir, and cast him off, gashing furiously at him as he did so. The sharp horn scored a deep furrow in the elephant's side, and Jehangir backed away for a moment, discomfited. The rhino dashed forward, striving to get beneath the elephant so as to disembowel him, but Jehangir knelt on his fore-knees and received the charge on his shoulder; the horn wounded him deeply again, and blood poured from him.

Then, spreading his ears, Jehangir gave a great trumpeting bellow, and charged at the rhino, who stood to meet him. At the impact the rhino was knocked over and over, for Jehangir, with incredible nimbleness, jigged to the side immediately before striking, in order to avoid the horn. At once Jehangir bore down on the rhino again, and dashed his whole weight on it. Twice the rhino tried to heave from beneath him to get its horn into play, but Jehangir was immovable, and he thrust and thrust until the rhino's bellowings died down; then he backed for a moment, and rearing up, he stamped on the rhino with both forefeet. With a last effort the rhinoceros scrambled up before Jehangir could stamp again, and it staggered away. The elephant charged again, and again the rhino went down. Jehangir crushed it until its very armour seemed to flatten, and blood came from its nose; he tried, unsuccessfully, to gore it for a few moments, and then stood away. The rhino lay still, breathing heavily. Its eyes were closed. It seemed almost dead. But a rhino is a very difficult beast to kill, and after a little while it got to its feet and shook itself. The elephant and the rhinoceros looked at one another; Jehangir's ears flapped out, and he raised his trunk: the rhino wheeled and trotted away. At a couple of hundred yards it turned, snorted fiercely, and then made off at a good speed into the bushes.

Jehangir came to the tree where Hussein had taken shelter, and they continued their journey until they came to a river, where Hussein bathed Jehangir's wounds. Twice on the way Hussein saw the rhinoceros looking at them, but each time it only scraped the earth and charged away.

By the time Jehangir's wounds had healed they had come to a small town, where Hussein told various tales in the evening. He stayed there two days, and on the evening of the second day he saw Ram Narain in his audience. Hussein gave no sign that he had seen the man, and he finished his tale, but inside he felt a curious misgiving, as if something unfortunate were going to happen.

When he went away from the market-place, Ram Narain followed him, and greeted him, saying, 'This is a singular coincidence. What are you doing here?'

'I was obliged to give up my pilgrimage,' replied Hussein, 'because various misfortunes befell me.'

They talked for some time about indifferent subjects, and then Ram Narain invited Hussein to come and have food with him. Hussein refused, saying that he must go on his way, but Ram Narain insisted, saying that he had one or two things to discuss that he thought might interest one who was a teller of tales. So Hussein consented, and when they had done with their meat, Ram Narain said openly, 'I know that you remember seeing me in the house of Huneifa at Peshawar, when I asked you whether Feroze Khan was in the city, and you replied that he was at Umballa. I also know that you are the same man as he who was mixed up in a curious affair at Haiderabad.' Hussein did not reply, but smoked his pipe with the utmost composure.

'It is because I know that you know what Feroze Khan was doing that I have sought you out, and now that I have disclosed myself, I want you to tell me something, and for this information I will give you fifty rupees. Where did Feroze Khan go from Haiderabad, and when he came to Peshawar, did he have dealings with any man in the goldsmiths' bazaar? and, most important of all, what did the Dewan tell him about the Rajah of Kappilavatthu?'

Still Hussein did not reply. Ram Narain went on, quite amiably, and in the same quiet monotone that he had always employed, 'If you tell me these things I will give you fifty rupees; I have them here. If you do not, I will tell Lutuf Khan, the cousin of Kadir Baksh, who has his string of horses quite near here just now, where you are.'

Hussein smoked in silence for some time; then he said, 'First we went to Jubbulpore, and then we followed a regiment whose name I have forgotten until we came to Peshawar. There was a man in the goldsmiths' bazaar who nodded at me, and I told Feroze Khan. I do not know anything about the Dewan; in fact, I thought the old man was lying when he told me about it.'

There was a short silence; Hussein saw that Ram Narain believed him.

'That is what I wanted to know: here are the fifty

---

rupees. Will you come and see me here to-morrow night? I may be able to give you a commission that will earn you some more money.'

'I will be here,' said Hussein.

The next night Hussein came to the house where Ram Narain was staying, and they fed together.

Ram Narain talked for a long while, asking Hussein innumerable questions. Hussein answered them all quite freely, and he told practically the whole story of his life, with the exception of that concerning the time during which he stayed at Laghat: he left that out, and said that he had wandered about with Jehangir. Ram Narain let fall one or two remarks that showed that he did not believe this, but he did not press the point, seeing that Hussein wished to hide something. Then he unfolded his proposition; Hussein was to go to Kappilavatthu, a small native state in Rajputana, and obtain employment in the Rajah's household. When this was done he would be told what to do next. Ram Narain warned him repeatedly that any mention of his being employed to do this would endanger his life. He said that Hussein's employment in the Rajah's household would be arranged, and that he would be supplied with money for his journey, and after that, with a sum varying with his success in performing whatever he was told to undertake. Ram Narain stressed the point that it would be nothing dangerous, but requiring the exercise, possibly, of cunning.

Hussein raised several objections, and pointed out that he had to think of Jehangir; but Ram Narain smoothed them all out, and said that it would be easier with the elephant than without, and that Jehangir would have a very fine home with the rest of the rajah's elephants, for it would be arranged that the rajah's chief mahout should hire him.

By dawn Hussein had agreed, for the whole plan fitted in very well with his own desires; his only objection to it was that he did not know what they were going to ask him to do, and his memory of seeing Feroze Khan lying dead in the street — for the old man had, presumably, been in the same employ.

'Then that is all settled,' said Ram Narain at last. 'There is one thing more; remember always that it is best for you not to know whom you are working for, and that it would be very unwise for you to attempt to find out: you may be sure that we are on the right side, and you may interpret that however you like. Also, if anyone mentions the incident of Feroze Khan casually, in speaking to you, you are to know that he comes from me.'

Fifteen

Behind the great stables of the Royal Palace at Kappilavatthu there lay the quarters where lived the hawks, hounds, cheetahs, and other animals used for hunting. The men who looked after them lived in little huts round about, or in lofts over them: of these men the only one who had not inherited his office from his father and grand-father was Hussein, who was therefore despised.

Hussein had been given charge of a young hunting-leopard called Shaitan. The cheetah was a very highly strung beast, and nervous; in the beginning it did not like Hussein at all, but he soon made friends with it, for he had a way with animals.

At first all the other men regarded Hussein with enmity, for they looked upon him as an interloper: more-over, they were all Hindus, with the exception of one man. Hussein would have been very lonely at first had it not been for Jehangir.

The one other Mohammedan was a very old man called Yussuf; he also looked after one of the cheetahs. This old man had four wives, the youngest of whom was called

Fatima. She was the daughter of a Bikaneeri camelman, who had given her to Yussuf as part payment of a debt. One day she called to Hussein as he passed by the balcony that ran along the side of Yussuf's zenana, and asked him to give her husband a message. She stayed talking with him a while, until a voice from inside called to her. As she turned to go, her light chudder dropped — whether it was done on purpose or by accident Hussein could not tell, but he saw a remarkably pretty face beneath it.

A day or two later the same thing happened again, and they stayed talking for nearly half an hour. That night Hussein received a flower message telling him to return at moon-rise.

Hussein was always faithful to Sashiya, for she was more important to him than anything else, and he always guarded her memory very close to his heart; but he was, like most men, faithful in his own way. So moon-rise saw him by the balcony.

They talked about many things, and Hussein learnt that old Yussuf was completely under the domination of his third wife, a very strict woman who would not let him take the opium to which he was addicted. She was furious if he took any notice of his other wives, and frequently threatened to poison them. Moreover, she controlled her husband's money, and only allowed him a very little of it. The old man was curiously terrified of his wife's displeasure, and although he hated her for her strong will, yet he loved her as well.

After they had spoken for some time about Yussuf, Fatima told Hussein how unhappy she was: she said that no one understood her. Then there was a long silence. The girl swayed yieldingly against him; and Hussein, more

---

from a feeling that it was expected of him than from any powerful inclination, held her to him.

He was a little dismayed when she proved to be exceedingly amorous, but he closed his eyes, and saw Sashiya in her place.

Now Hussein had, for some time, desired to learn more about the proper training of hunting leopards, and of their care, but none of the other men were at all friendly to him. He thought about that which Fatima had told him concerning Yussuf's frustrated desire for opium, and the next morning, when the cheetahs were being exercised, he walked in front of the old man, and ostentatiously dropped one of those little heart shaped brass boxes with various compartments in which one carries hashish, bhang, betel-nut, or opium, according to one's taste. As he picked it up he let fall a few opium pills. Yussuf said nothing at the time, but in the evening he came to Hussein, and said, 'I have a cheetah collar for which I have no further need: it would fit your Shaitan perfectly,' and with this he scratched himself with an embarrassed air.

'Alas,' replied Hussein, squatting down before the cages, 'I am a poor man, and although I know that Shaitan needs a new collar, I am too needy to buy him one befitting a cheetah of his quality: also, I dare not apply to the chief hunter for the money, for he is said to be both parsimonious to a degree, and excessively prone to wrath.'

'Now I see that you are a deserving man, and modest,' said Yussuf, 'so I shall give you this collar. It is a poor gift, although a discerning eye might find some small merit in the chasing of the brass ring that encircles it.

Indeed, now that I compare the unworthiness of this collar with the manifest excellence of the one to whom I address myself, I am overcome with shame, to such an extent that I can no longer think of giving you this bauble – although it has, undoubtedly, a certain merely commercial value – as a gift.'

'Assuredly it would be a royal gift,' said Hussein uneasily.

'Even so,' replied the old man, 'but it is unworthy of you: however, I see a way out of the difficulty; in order to show the lack of worth of this collar, I will exchange it with you for a certain trumpery brass box that I saw you drop this morning.'

Without more words Hussein produced the box; Yussuf's eyes glistened, and he stretched out his hand.

'But I forgot,' said Hussein, as if moved by an afterthought, 'I have foolishly left certain pills in this box; I will remove them.'

'Pray do not trouble yourself,' stammered the old man eagerly; 'they may assuage various pangs that I feel after having partaken too freely of dates.'

'But these pills are of no value for such pangs: they are more concerned with giving ease to the mind, being made from the best opium.'

There was a pause while Hussein transferred them to another box. Yussuf's face fell as he saw the last pill go, and he said, with a melancholy air, 'The Prophet never forbade its use; he only referred to intoxicating liquors . . . only the most bigoted and stiff-necked would twist the holy words . . . women, camels, and goats . . . all very much the same . . .' The old man fell to muttering in his beard until Hussein invited him to drink coffee with him.

———

When they had drunk their coffee, Yussuf returned to the subject of opium. 'Perhaps one of those pills might help a peculiarly heavy feeling that I can discern in my head,' he said.

'It is possible,' replied Hussein, handing him one; 'yet it may have strange effects, such as producing hallucinations, or even boils.'

'Nevertheless,' said Yussuf, swallowing the pill contentedly, 'it is good to mortify the flesh. My father told me that in Uidapur he once saw a remarkably holy dervish completely covered with boils. This holy man, dying, became a famous pir, and the devout still flock in great numbers to his tomb.'

'Allahu akbar,' replied Hussein, and unrolled his rug towards Mecca, for the sun was setting, and the hour of the evening prayer was at hand.

After they had prayed, Hussein blew gently upon the smouldering embers of his fire, and fanned it into a blaze, for the nights were cold at that time. They made themselves comfortable about the fire, and Hussein led the conversation to the subject of cheetahs. Long into the night the old man spoke of their correct training, and the way in which they should be caused to hunt. The one pill that Hussein had given him was not sufficient to send him off into a coma, for he had a strong head, but it was enough to loosen his tongue, and Hussein, listening eagerly, learnt a great deal.

The next evening Yussuf came again: Hussein gave him another pill, and they talked until the moon set, when the old man, having taken a second pill when Hussein's back was turned, went to sleep. Hussein had to carry him back to his house; he was pushing him gently through an open window when there was a sound of someone moving within; Hussein left the old man propped against the window and faded rapidly away in the darkness towards his own place. As he went he heard footsteps following him, and then came Fatima's voice, saying, 'Stop', in a loud whisper.

Hussein did not feel like dallying with her then, so he ran on, and presently her footsteps ceased.

As time went on, it became the accepted thing for Yussuf to spend his evenings with Hussein. To the questions of his third wife the old man replied that he and Hussein discussed grave matters of the law of Islam, and that it was only correct that the only two Mohammedans among the Rajah's hunters should help one another as much as possible. In this way Hussein learnt a great many things about his new craft, and by the time the season for hunting antelope and gazelle came round, he felt confident that both he and Shaitan would do as well as most. Shaitan was a good-looking young cheetah with a very affectionate way about him: indeed, he was more like a great dog than a cat. When he was still he looked a gawky beast, but potentially beautiful; it was only when he got into action that one realised his surpassing perfection: all his clumsiness disappeared: his legs, which, when he was still, seemed too long for his slender body, were hardly visible when he was at the height of his speed. During the brief space of his utmost endeavour, there was nothing on four legs that Shaitan could not catch.

But neither Shaitan nor any other cheetah could keep up a great speed for more than a few minutes at the uttermost, so it was necessary that the hunting-leopard should be brought up as close as possible to his quarry

———

before being unleashed. The common way of hunting with a cheetah is to bring it to the field of action on a cart, and then to leave it to stalk its own quarry; but this is by no means as sensational as the method that obtained in Kappilavatthu, where they were usually used to hunt gazelle and bustards. The hunters of the Rajah were accustomed to stalk their own quarry, leading the hooded cheetah until they were near enough to unleash the animal, and let it run the gazelle down in full view of the hidden spectators. Very considerable skill was necessary in doing this, for one false move by a clumsy hunter might easily startle a whole herd of gazelle, and a day's sport might be lost. Perhaps the most difficult thing for the men who led the cheetahs was getting their quarry between them and the spectators, for this was the only way in which the whole of the chase could be watched. Sometimes, particularly at the beginning of the season, when the gazelle were less wary, a very big hunt would be arranged, and then the little deer would be driven slowly between the cheetahs and the spectators.

There was an immense plain near the Rajah's summer palace which was one of the largest preserves of antelope and gazelle for a hundred miles round. One day at the beginning of the season, all the court moved out to the summer palace, and towards the end of the baggage-train the cheetahs with their keepers travelled in bullock carts.

Hussein left Shaitan in charge of Yussuf, and walked by the side of Jehangir, who might otherwise have been worried by the tumult and the noise. He spent a good deal of time every day with Jehangir, for neither of them had very much to do.

When everything had arrived at the great white

summer palace, and Hussein had seen that both Jehangir and Shaitan were comfortable, he joined Yussuf, and they went with the rest of the hunters to the great plains where the gazelles were to be found, for there was to be a hunt the next day, and it was necessary for each man to know the place where he should hide, as it was going to be a hunt in which the gazelle were to be driven.

The men disposed themselves cunningly among the bushes so as not to disturb the feeding deer, and they whispered together.

'It seems to me,' said Yussuf, 'that the gazelle are more timorous than formerly, and more watchful.'

'Perhaps the villagers have been harrying them.'

'After what happened last year they would never dare to come within miles of the preserves.'

'That is true: it is more probable that the leopards have increased. I saw three half-grown cubs last year, but Khem Singh would not let me shoot them, saying that they would provide sport for the Rajah when they grew up.'

'Khem Singh is the son of a noseless mother: he thinks of nothing but the honour that he will obtain by driving his leopards out to be shot — he never considers us.'

'Inshallah: but did you hear the tale which is told of his wife's cousin?'

'A jocose tale, but I heard a better concerning his second son's third wife . . .'

At length the plans for the hunt were completed, and it was decided that some picked deer should quietly be separated from the herd, and driven across the plain towards the Rajah's stand. At various points the cheetahs would be concealed, one for each gazelle.

———

The next day Hussein arose early with the rest of the hunters and went to his appointed place. He led Shaitan, hooded, by a leash. From his place Hussein could see down the bush-covered slope to the sandy plain, and over it to the belt of trees where the spectators were.

He squatted down behind a bush. Shaitan sat beside him, sniffing the air eagerly. He slipped the cheetah's hood off, and Shaitan looked round, taking his bearings. They could not see a sign of the other hunters, but Hussein knew that old Yussuf was a little way to the right, and another man to the left.

They waited nearly two hours for the Rajah and his party to arrive before anything began to happen. Hussein and Shaitan had settled down into a waking doze. After the Rajah had arrived the gazelle were driven slowly towards the belt of trees.

Hussein was staring vaguely out over the bushes, tickling Shaitan's ears. All at once something in the bushes lower down the slope caught his eye. He looked more closely, and saw a tawny beast creeping flat on its belly between the bushes. At first he thought that it must be one of the cheetahs, but soon he saw that it was larger, more thick-set, and without a cheetah's long neck: he realised that it must be a wild leopard. He watched it for some time before he was convinced; then, when he was sure that he was not mistaken, he decided to creep along to Yussuf, who would know what to do.

If the leopard were left undisturbed it might spoil the whole hunt by taking one of the gazelle, and heading the rest. Hussein put the hood on his cheetah's head and tied the leash to a sapling. Then he began to crawl quietly towards Yussuf. But by the time he was half-way there the gazelle had come into that part of the plain which lay between the slope and the trees. Hussein was in a particularly exposed position; there was no good cover for yards, and if he moved or made a noise the gazelle would certainly be headed back. He crouched quite still, pressed against the ground: the little deer were uneasy, but not panicking; they were trotting in fairly close formation towards a patch of tall grass some way to Hussein's right. From the corner of his eye Hussein could see that Yussuf had unleashed his cheetah, which was creeping down the slope towards the deer. Suddenly he saw three of the cheetahs break cover and dash into the open. The gazelle were flying before them right past the leopard. They were all going at a tremendous speed, with the cheetahs gaining a little. They were all quite close together. All at once the leopard gave a loud, hoarse scream and leapt into the midst of them. At first nothing could be seen for dust, and then Yussuf's cheetah shot away from the bushes and charged into the cloud of dust. At its first leap the leopard had knocked one of the long-legged cheetahs over, and had cannoned into another. Instantly they all set upon the larger leopard, who disabled two so quickly that Hussein could hardly see what had happened before they fell. Yussuf had not seen the leopard, and could not see it for the dust; he thought that the cheetahs were fighting amongst themselves, so he caught up his staff and ran down to separate them.

The leopard had dealt with three of his slighter adversaries before Yussuf reached them, so he was free to spring at the man. Hussein snatched up a stone and ran down the slope; he flung the stone, and hit the leopard in the side. At the same time Yussuf hit it on the head with his stick, which broke in his hand; the leopard sprang at him, and knocked him down. The old man fell heavily, striking his head against a stone. Hussein tripped over a root, and his speed carried him sprawling full on to the leopard, which turned under him. For a second both were too stunned to do anything; then Hussein seized the leopard's throat, and squeezed it with all his strength. The leopard grunted, and jerked convulsively to free its legs, which were under Hussein's body. At first they were entangled in the clothes, and Hussein pressed himself as hard as he could on to the leopard to keep him there. But there was a rending sound as its hind feet kicked clear: Hussein felt the claws tearing into the flesh of his thighs, and he crushed the throat between his hands furiously. He glared fixedly into the yellow eyes a few inches in front of his, and ground his teeth with rage: he dashed the spotted head up and down for a moment, and then put all the strength of his body into crushing the leopard's throat. For a moment he could hear the choked sounds of the leopard's breath hissing in and out, and the ripping of its claws. The pain was appalling, and there was a redness before his eyes: sweat dropped from him on to the leopard. The sinewy body beneath him writhed and jerked power- fully: the forefeet came into play. Once more Hussein clenched his hands; the leopard's tongue was protruding stiffly, its breath was hissing more thinly; it was half-dead. It clawed madly in a last effort, and for the first time Hussein cried aloud. He did not shriek from the pain, but shouted in his fury.

Then everybody ran up: the Rajah himself shot the leopard through the head, and someone pulled Yussuf from beneath the two. He was half-stunned, but not seriously hurt. Hussein was in a worse way; he was carried home on a litter.

By the time he reached his quarters Yussuf was quite recovered, and he swore that Hussein had saved his life, saying, 'See what men are the Faithful, what lions of the desert. Allah's curse on all unbelievers. By my father's beard we will be blood brothers, and my women shall nurse him. Inshallah.'

And although he was old enough to be Hussein's father, he performed the ceremony that made them blood brothers, and took him into his own house, where his women, especially his third wife, who was grateful – for she loved Yussuf – and his fourth wife, Fatima – for she loved Hussein – nursed him most tenderly.

They sent for a famous hakim from Dacca, who gave Hussein a stewed leopard's heart garnished with texts from the Q'ran, and the Rajah sent his own doctor, a Scotsman, who applied antiseptics, which were, however, carefully wiped off as soon as he departed.

Sixteen

But in spite of his doctors Hussein recovered, although at one time it had been a very near thing. For the whole time of his illness, Jehangir had stood, almost without cease, before the door of Yussuf's dwelling, and he became extremely thin; he hardly fed at all until they brought Hussein out on to the verandah.

It was the same, to a lesser degree, with Shaitan, who also became thin, and pined visibly, so that his beautiful coat became matted. Because of this, and because of his deed — but principally because his cheetah pined for him — Hussein gained great izzat in the eyes of the other hunters.

When he was walking about again he was sent for by the Rajah, who had been greatly impressed by the incident — especially by his own part in it. At this time there were a number of Englishmen visiting the state, and the Rajah wished to demonstrate his own magnanimity, kindness, and other virtues, so Hussein was brought in, dressed magnificently in a gold-embroidered robe lent for the occasion. He knelt before the throne — the Englishmen and the rest of the court were on either side of it – and the court poet recited a long poem in Persian describing the deed, particularly the Rajah's part in it. Then the prince drew a ring from his finger and threw it to Hussein, who called a long blessing on the Royal House and its heroic head, giving all the credit for the slaying of the leopard to the Rajah. The Rajah, who was in a good temper that day, was delighted when he saw that his visitors were impressed, and he said to his treasurer, who stood behind the throne, 'Fill this good man's mouth with gold.'

The treasurer looked rather sour at this, for finances were low as usual, but he pulled a fat purse from his waist and came to Hussein.

Hussein opened his mouth as wide as possible, and pressed his tongue down to make more room. The treasurer, a Bengali Brahmin, drew some coins from his purse and put them in; Hussein tasted that they were copper at once, but he dared not say anything; he had to content himself with glaring reproachfully at the Brahmin. The treasurer, looking distinctly less sour, filled the open mouth and retired. Hussein closed his mouth with some difficulty, and struck his head on the ground three times before shuffling out backwards on his knees, according to the custom of the court. However, he was consoled by the fact that the treasurer had accidentally slipped in a gold mohur among the rest, and that the Rajah's ring was of good red gold, with a small, but sound, ruby in it.

While he was convalescent, Hussein had great difficulty with Fatima. She had believed that he had given Yussuf opium simply to the end that he might come to her with more safety, but when she had found that she was mistaken in this, she began to wonder whether she was not also mistaken in Hussein. She had persuaded herself that he was passionately in love with her, whereas it was she who did all the loving. It was a God-send to her when he was brought helpless to Yussuf's house, for she was able, whenever she was alone with him, to ask him whether he thought that she was peerlessly beautiful, excessively intelligent, and infinitely too good for her surroundings, and Hussein was constrained to answer, 'Yes', for he liked his wounds to be dressed tenderly, and he had a wholehearted dislike for poison in his food. She was a pleasant enough woman if one stroked her the right way – perhaps a little too passionate, but then, a woman with only one major defect is as rare as a two-legged ass with only one eye – but if, on the other hand, one were to thwart her powerfully, or to wound her vanity deeply, she was of the type that would busily grind up a glass bottle into a fine powder, and put it into one's food. But she had to be content with Hussein's almost monosyllabic love-making, for no other token of affection passed between them.

'There was once a man called Ismail Dinn,' said Fatima, 'who was very much in love with me, although I could not care for him at all: he used to say that I was like Balkis of Sheba, only she had hairy legs, and I have not. He also used to say that my beauty was such that when he first saw me, he said to a friend of his that he would rather possess me than the whole of the harem of the Amir of Kabul; was he not a foolish man? Would you say in your heart that he was a flatterer?'

'Oh no,' replied Hussein, rather wearily. For many days the opinions of this abominable Ismail Dinn, and several others, had been put into his mouth in this way, and he was heartily sick of it, and of the vain, foolish woman, who talked ceaselessly. He sometimes wondered where she got all her wind from, for when she was talking about herself, and she rarely spoke of anything else, she never seemed to pause for breath, but went on and on and on, quite remorselessly.

Frequently he cursed the day on which he had first seen her, and often he had cursed the eyelid that had automatically dropped over his left eye when her pretty face had been revealed by the dropping of her veil. He had ample time to think about the best way of breaking with her as he lay, day after day, on his spring bed, but think as he might, he could not devise a plan which would rid him of her clacking tongue while he was in Yussuf's house. As soon as he was well, he would be free of it, but he did not wish to incur a feud with a woman — he had had experience of one — and he could not think of any other feasible way of getting out of the entanglement into which his misguided desire for amusement had got him, except by alienating her somehow, and that was not at all desirable while he was still ill, and not so very desirable afterwards.

Hussein's code was an elastic one, and it would stretch surprisingly on occasion; but he did not like making a cuckold of a man whose salt he had eaten, when he was not in love with the woman.

As he became convalescent, the situation became more and more trying: Fatima progressed from delicate hints that indicated her desire for a more robust type of love-making, to broader hints, and from broad hints to positively improper suggestions.

———

She was curiously obtuse in some ways, and although Hussein was consistently unenthusiastic, she put his attitude down to his sickness, and to the diet that the hakim had ordered for him. After she had come to that conclusion, she fed him almost exclusively upon meat and violent curries, but they only made him very liverish and irritable.

The situation was rapidly nearing a crisis, and Fatima had begun to punctuate her kisses with long, meditative stares that made Hussein most uneasy, when Ram Narain came to Yussuf's house. He came with the old man, dressed as a Mohammedan; Hussein hardly recognised him at first, and he looked at Hussein as if he did not know him at all.

'This is Ibrahim Khan,' said Yussuf, introducing him to Hussein. 'He is of the Faithful, and he has the care of three of the hawks — he is newly come into the service of the Rajah.'

Hussein saw that they were supposed to be strangers, so he made no sign of recognition.

Yussuf related the whole of Hussein's adventure with the leopard, and then he called for food. It was Fatima who served them; she attended to Hussein's wants with such care that Ram Narain looked at her twice. Only Yussuf noticed nothing: he was an old man.

After they had fed and talked for some time, Yussuf went out, and they were left alone.

'Did you get my message?' asked Ram Narain, speaking in Pushtu.

'I have had no message since I have been here,' replied Hussein in the same tongue.

'Did no sanyassi carrying a bundle wrapped in blue cloth ask you for alms?'

'No. No such man came near me.'

'He was an old man, with a long white beard.'

'An old man? Now I heard gossip of an old man being found dead on the road near here: they said that he had a white beard.'

'That was probably he; I heard nothing from him or from you, so I came here to find out what was happening. He was to have told you that you were to ascertain the names of the sahibs who were here not long ago – it was a small thing, and not very important – he was doing something else as well.'

'I saw those sahibs when the Rajah gave me this ring; there were seven of them.'

'Seven? What were they like?'

'Two were tall, proper men, soldiers, I thought, although they were not in uniform; then there was a dark one, with a beard, and one short sahib, very fat and red: the rest I forget.'

Ram Narain thought in silence for some time, then he chuckled to himself, and asked after Hussein's health.

'I am getting well rapidly in my body,' replied Hussein, 'but in a little while I may be poisoned, and even if I am not, it seems to me that before I can walk again I shall be driven out of my mind.'

'But how is this?'

'Well, there is a certain woman in this house who talks to me without cease about love.'

'But is that so deadly?'

'Without doubt: it is of my love for her that she talks so endlessly. I may have passed some few light words with her, or even more; do not take me for a lecher, but what is a man to do in a dismal place like this? If it were an ordinary affair all would be easy enough, but with me it is different . . .' Hussein unfolded his whole tale concerning Sashiya, and concerning Yussuf and their blood-brotherhood. It was an unusual thing for a man of his race and type to speak thus to another about these matters, and Hussein would never have done it but for the fact that he was somewhat feverish and overwrought; moreover, there was something about Ram Narain that made him think that his confidence might be fruitful. He wound up by saying: '. . . she is extremely passionate, and I feel sure that she might be very dangerous.'

'It was she who served our meat?'

'The same.'

'You are right; she would be a bad enemy. I have had to do with those Bikaneeri women before. However, it all sprang up very quickly, and perhaps it may be induced to perish in the same way. I will do my best.'

Hussein began to thank him most profusely, but Ram Narain cut him short. 'You would be of very little use to us', he said, 'with your belly full of various poisons.'

Ram Narain started his campaign that very night, and Hussein heard him softly strumming a zitar outside the verandah at about midnight, and singing a song that the love-sick youths of the Bikaneer sing.

His efforts were remarkably successful; within three days Fatima had become distinctly more cool towards Hussein, and as he, being led thereto by Ram Narain, became for a while more ardent towards her, the affair died naturally, and she bore him no grudge, for she judged that he should be almost heartbroken.

*

Time passed, and Hussein became well enough to return to his own place. One evening the chief of the Rajah's mahouts came to him, and said that one Ibrahim Khan had told him that Hussein was a mahout of great note, and as the mahout who sometimes rode Jehangir had disappeared, he thought that Hussein might do for the post. The man did not seem at all overbearing, and he did not even hint at a commission, so Hussein put two and two together, and decided that Ram Narain was behind the whole thing, and accepted the post. He wondered what had happened to the mahout who had disappeared, and he spent rather an uneasy night pondering on the great mortality of Ram Narain's acquaintances.

The next day he sought out Ram Narain, and thanked him, but Ram Narain replied, 'You will probably be more useful in this way: do not forget that we must be strangers here.' Then he suddenly hit Hussein, and let flow a scream of the vilest abuse. Hussein saw, out of the corner of his eye, a number of men approaching, so he plucked at Ram Narain's beard, shouting and gesticulating in a magnificent rage.

After they had been separated by the alarmed men, who came running from all parts, they treated one another coldly and with contempt in public. Fatima heard of this: she was delighted, for she thought that they fought over her.

It was very fine to be with Jehangir again, and in the company of mahouts.

If he had had Sashiya with him, Hussein would have been in Paradise, as he told her when he sent her the Rajah's ring, by way of Abd'Arahman. He had consulted with Ram Narain as to the advisability of writing to

Haiderabad, and he had said that it would be quite safe, as it would be addressed to the old letter-writer.

It was a long while before Ram Narain asked Hussein to do anything for him, and Hussein had almost forgotten that he was there for some unknown purpose.

Seventeen

There was to be a tiger shoot, and Ram Narain had arranged that the Rajah's howdah should be on Jehangir. Hussein knew of this for several days before the hunt, but it was not until the evening before it that Ram Narain came tapping softly at his window.

'To-morrow is the day,' he said, when Hussein had let him in, 'for which we have been waiting.' He paused, listening intently for a moment, and then he went on, rather more loudly, '. . . to-morrow Hussein will be away with the elephants, Ramendranath, and we shall have the whole day to search this place – we have no time to-night; he is coming back earlier than I had thought. I know he is only a tool, and he does not know what he is doing, but there might be something in what you say.'

As he spoke Ram Narain knocked a small table over, and, in picking it up, he pushed Hussein away from the door into the shadow. Hussein had his wits about him, and he stayed in the shadow; Ram Narain went on, 'But he may be back any minute now. We will meet to-morrow at noon. It would be wiser for us to go now, I think.' He went towards the door; Hussein, straining his ears, caught a little creaking sound outside the door. On the threshold Ram Narain paused, and pointed to the window; Hussein understood, and he nodded.

Ram Narain smiled, and the next moment he was gone, walking on his toes, and whispering as if he were with someone.

Hussein put out the lamp and slipped silently out of the window. Then he went round to his own door. As he passed the door next to his — there were several rooms in a row on top of the stables — he saw that it was ajar; the beam of light that came from it narrowed as he passed by into his own room.

The next day Ram Narain was gone, and there was a rumour in the palace that one of the Rajah's bodyguard had been killed, while another had been half-strangled in the night.

Hussein was keyed up inside to an extraordinary degree: he took a little opium to keep himself steady, and to the outside world he presented a perfectly normal appearance.

He was wondering what Ram Narain had meant by saying that 'to-morrow is the day for which we have been waiting'. He also wondered what had happened to him; he had grown to like Ram Narain very much in the last few weeks, and he felt certain, in his own mind, that he was working for the Sirkar. Hussein was no fool, and he had gathered quite a lot from Ram Narain's conversation, guarded though it always was.

He felt fairly sure that what he had been meant to do was connected with his driving the Rajah during the hunt, but he could not reconcile a plot for kidnapping or doing away with the prince with what he felt sure was Ram

Narain's aim. He felt a certain amount of loyalty to the Sirkar; he had been in Government service, and those sahibs whom he had encountered had been fine men, and he had more respect for them, as rulers, than he had for the men of any other race. He knew that there was izzat to be gained serving them, for they had roughly the same ideas of honour as the men of the Faithful, as well as material recompense, so he entered more whole-heartedly into Ram Narain's schemes, although he had little more than a vague idea of those against whom they were directed.

He was turning all these things over in his mind as he slowly scrubbed Jehangir's feet early in the morning. As he scrubbed, a shadow fell between him and his pot of water; he looked up, and saw a man whom he did not know. The man bent down and whispered, 'Ibrahim Khan says "Kill to-day": you understand?'

Hussein started to his feet and overturned his pot of water: he thought very rapidly; a doubt flashed through his mind. The man had called Ram Narain 'Ibrahim Khan'. With hardly a pause he answered, 'That soor,' and spat; 'I am a match for him any day, if that is what he means.'

The man looked at him piercingly for a moment, but Hussein bore the scrutiny without flinching, and the man said, with the lie plain in his voice, 'But you are Wali Dad, are you not?'

'Bismillah, no. I am of the true faith, unlike that pig-eating Ibrahim Khan, the Sunni,' and Hussein scrubbed Jehangir vehemently, muttering the while.

It was really convincing, and the man left him without more words.

An hour later three elephants with howdahs left the

summer palace. In the foremost was the Rajah; his treasurer and one or two other officials were in the other two.

The hunt itself was fairly good; a place was known where a pair of very fine tigers lay up during the day. The Rajah's head shikari made sure that they were in one particular patch of elephant grass, and then Hussein rode Jehangir in until they came upon them. One sprang straight at the elephant's shoulder, but the Rajah, who was a very fine shot, put a bullet through its head as it leapt: the second turned tail, and the Rajah was only able to wound it in the hindquarters as it ran. They followed it up for some time, until it turned upon them in a deep nullah.

The behaviour of the treasurer on this occasion was a little odd: the Rajah had insisted upon his coming, and when the second tiger turned at bay, the unhappy Bengali was on an elephant only a few feet from Jehangir: the tiger, looking extraordinarily large and savage, suddenly burst from the dense undergrowth, giving vent to a nerve-shattering roar as it did so. In two bounds the great striped beast was clawing its way up on to the neck of the treasurer's elephant. The mahout slipped off as the tiger came up, and the gun-bearer behind the howdah thrust a rifle into the Bengali's hands, but the treasurer, who had turned a curious putty colour, dropped it, and gave a very high, shrill scream, almost a squeak.

Hussein had been manoeuvring Jehangir so that the Rajah could get a safe shot at the tiger, and just as it reached the edge of the howdah, the Rajah drilled it from ear to ear. It gave one convulsive spring, and knocked the treasurer out of the howdah, so that he fell to the ground with the dead tiger on top of him. Men came running, and they dragged the treasurer from beneath the tiger; he was unscathed, but it was nearly an hour before he came to himself, for he had really believed that he had been killed.

Then they went to a small hunting lodge, where the Rajah was going to spend the night; there were stables behind it, and the followers were to sleep there.

When Hussein had seen that Jehangir was comfortable, he wandered around and about, for he felt sure that Ram Narain, if he were alive, would be somewhere near by. But he heard nothing, and saw nobody, so he returned, feeling rather gloomy, to the place where they were preparing the evening meal. A little after nightfall half a dozen troopers of the Rajah's bodyguard came, and demanded food. Then there arose a most bitter controversy, as there was not a great deal to eat, and the soldiers had brought nothing with them but empty bellies: the argument, however, was settled by one of the troopers skewering a large piece of meat on his sword, and asking the world at large whether any man wished to take it away from him. Nobody replied, and the soldiers ate their fill, but the mahouts and the beaters muttered continually, and a fight might easily have been started if their attention had not been diverted by the sudden appearance of a sadhu, who wandered into the circle of light, and squatted before the fire without a word. He was an oldish man, smooth-faced, and his eyes gleamed red with bhang beneath his scarlet caste-mark: his matted hair hung to his shoulders, and his body, naked but for a dhoti and a withered marigold wreath, was indescribably filthy. He leaned forward on the black-buck horns that he carried, and spat left and right. No one spoke a word, for he was evidently a very holy man. He pointed to some chupatties on a leaf, and someone brought them to him. When he had eaten, he snorted, and spat again; then he began a querulous complaint against the modern generation, comparing them most unfavourably with those who had lived in the time of his youth. He was particularly bitter about railways, which, he said, caused pestilences, and were offensive to the gods, being presumptuous. Then he meandered off on to another subject — the impiety of those of other beliefs. '. . . there was a man of Peshawar', he said, 'called Feroze Khan, a flesh-eating Mohammedan; he mocked me in the gate, and I cursed him — he was dead within the week, and a white cobra crept from his body . . .'

He went on to deliver a homily on the virtues of the free-handed and reverent, describing with a wealth of detail the ultimate fate of those who mocked at holy men.

Hussein's heart had leapt to his throat when he heard the sadhu speak of Feroze Khan; he looked intently at the man for some time, but he could not recall ever having seen him. Then the leaping flames cast a shadow on the lower part of his face, and Hussein recognised Ram Narain. The loss of his beard, which had been a magnificent bushy one, had completely changed the balance of his face, and the rest of his disguise was as perfect as it could well be. Only the chance-thrown shadow, which for a moment had put darkness where the beard had been, made him at all recognisable, even to one who knew his face well. Even his voice was different — he had captured, even to a half-tone, that unpleasant, harsh whine that so many sadhus and sanyassis of the baser sort have.

As the sadhu rambled on, Hussein rose to his feet, snorted, and said, 'Venomous old dodderer.' He strolled away, and stood yawning at the edge of the circle of men. They looked at him fearfully, and some murmured angrily, for so ill-placed a remark might easily call down a curse upon all of them. Several spoke placatingly to the sadhu, who was champing his jaws menacingly, and glaring at Hussein. The holy man brushed them aside with a wave of his hand, and said, 'For that you will be afflicted with a most grievous agony at midnight, and you shall not sleep for eight nights, but only walk to and fro desiring sleep. Were it not for the excellence of the chupatties that I have eaten here, I should have withered the flesh from your bones, but I am a forbearing man.' He arose, bade good fortune attend the rest for eight days, and departed into the night, disregarding those who asked him to stay until the morning, and sleep comfortably.

Hussein laughed contemptuously, and stretched himself, but the men drew away from him, as from a leper, and regarded him from a little distance, with a boding watchfulness, as they made their beds in the straw.

Hussein lay awake hour after hour, until he judged that it was about midnight; then he began to moan, and the men awoke, saying one to another, 'He is seized with the sadhu's anguish.'

After he had moaned for a little while, he arose from his straw, and walked restlessly up and down; then he wandered away from where the men lay, and waited. He wandered about for some time before he met with Ram Narain, who was sitting in some bushes by a bundle, and eating cold boiled rice.

'I thought you would come,' said Ram Narain, handing him some of the rice, 'but it is too early yet.' They sat eating for some time, and then Hussein said, without any preamble, 'Are you working for the Sirkar?'

Ram Narain did not answer for some time, then he said, 'You remember what I told you before you came to Kappilavatthu?'

'Yes.'

'Nevertheless,' said Ram Narain, musingly, half to himself, 'things are different now. I need a man who will fight with me now, and Dost Mahommed has not come in time. I know you far better now, and I feel fairly certain that I can trust you, although that is a feeling by which one should rarely be guided until a man is well tried, particularly by money. However, I will tell you; we are employed by a Prince who is wholly for the Sirkar. With this you must be content.'

'I am content.'

They sat in silence for a long while, each deep in his thoughts. They could see the lodge from where they were, and they watched the lights go out and the fires die down. Three men of the Rajah's bodyguard squatted before the lodge, and one marched up and down.

Suddenly the three soldiers jumped to their feet as a man came out of the lodge; he was followed by two others, one of whom carried a lantern.

They went out along a little path into the jungle. Ram Narain touched Hussein's elbow, and they followed the three men. Hussein was surprised at Ram Narain's exceeding skill in moving silently; he slipped along like a shadow, picking his way cunningly between the trees, and avoiding the thick undergrowth. He went after the men at their own speed, keeping always away from them. Hussein had his work cut out to follow; once he stumbled, making a slight noise, and Ram Narain shot a furious glance back at him. Often the three men were lost from sight, but they could be heard in the silence of the night, and always Ram Narain kept closely to them.

For half an hour they travelled, or perhaps more; it seemed like an eternity to Hussein, who, towards the end, became increasingly aware of the strain of following so silently. At length the three men came to an old temple half overrun by the jungle. There was a light in it, and Hussein heard the sound of voices. The lantern made its way towards the temple, and disappeared inside it. Ram Narain went on with more caution than before, creeping like a wraith towards the bamboo brake that had grown over the fallen wall of the temple courtyard. In the courtyard itself was a tree whose roots had upturned the green paving stones; they crawled towards it. Across the courtyard the light came out of a small room in the temple; they could not see into it, and they could not distinguish the words of the talk that murmured inside.

Ram Narain took off his loin cloth; Hussein stripped also. Together they crawled again until they came to the window of the room. By very slow degrees Ram Narain got up; Hussein imitated him. They peered in. There were seven men in the room. Hussein recognised the Rajah and the treasurer; the other men he did not know, but it seemed that Ram Narain did, for he caught his breath as he looked into the far corner of the room, where there was an old man who sat apart from the rest.

Hussein's attention was riveted to the middle of the floor, for there was a great sack of the kind that is laid

---

across the back of an elephant lying open there, and it had so great a store of gold coins showing in its mouth that a fierce emotion seized him by the throat as he looked on them, and he was hardly able to contain himself. The Rajah and the treasurer were arguing about some matter with four of the other men; the old man sat remote. There was a paper on the floor between them, and the treasurer kept tapping it with a pen, saying, '. . . but the expense is too great . . . too great . . . even with such a consideration . . .'

Hussein could not pick up the whole thread of their discourse at first, and just when he was grasping it, the old man came over from the corner, and standing before the Rajah, spoke to him in a tongue that Hussein had never heard. The Rajah nodded again and again; the treasurer shook his head and spread his palms.

Hussein looked across the window at Ram Narain: the other's face was lit with such a triumph as Hussein had never seen before on any face but that of a carved god. The old man finished speaking and then threw out his hand, palm upwards, fingers spread. The Rajah smiled and squared his shoulders, then he took the pen from the treasurer and wrote on the paper, at the bottom beneath all the writing that covered it. All the others did the same, the treasurer much against his will — he shrugged and sighed as he signed. Then three other papers were signed; two were given to the treasurer, and two to the old man. Suddenly Hussein felt his arm grasped with great force; Ram Narain jerked him to the ground. They lay flat while long minutes passed; they could no longer hear the talk, for it seemed to go out of the window and beyond them. Presently the third man of the Rajah's party came out, carrying the lantern. He ran back in the way that he had come. Hussein heard Ram Narain grind his teeth together with a little grating noise; then he felt his breath in his ear as Ram Narain whispered, 'Go before him with all your speed, but silently; if he orders a mahout and an elephant, see that it is yourself and Jehangir. I will tell you what to do in whatever way I can find. If he does not, return with all the haste you may, and seek me here.'

Hussein nodded, and crept away to the tree where his clothes were. Inside the temple the talk went on.

Eighteen

Hussein gathered his clothes with infinite caution; when he was out of range of the voices he put them on and sped along the path back to the lodge. It was little more than a deer track, and at one place he paused, straining his eyes in the darkness to find where it lay: he felt himself trembling all over — not from the cold, for it was not cold, and warmth still came upwards from the earth. The lantern had disappeared. He felt strangely disinclined to move. As he stood, quite motionless, he knew that he could not look back over his shoulder into the darkness. For timeless seconds he stood there, sweating, so that it ran down in drops from his armpits. More and more his neck grew wooden, and his hands, half-clasped, rigid. For this strange time he stood as a stone stands; then he must have swayed on his stance, for he moved his foot involuntarily to preserve his balance. That broke the continuity of the sensation, and Hussein ran from nothing as if Kali were breathing on his neck; it hunted him until he was in sight of the lantern, and he composed himself with a fierce effort.

Stealthily he skirted round the bobbing light through the jungle, and came again on to the path. He still ran very swiftly, but he knew himself again, and the running was but part of his plan. He came to the lodge well before the man with the lantern, and walked casually back to where Jehangir stood.

Jehangir swung him up, and he lay a-sprawl on the elephant's neck, thinking. He was but little given to introspection, and his essay into it caused him unhappiness. He could by no means explain to himself his extraordinary feeling at the break in his running. Ordinarily he would have dismissed it with the easy explanation of a curse, or of a devil, but somehow he knew that it was something wholly of himself. For the first time in his life he felt his own self as something to be reckoned with: ever before he had taken himself for granted. Jehangir felt the trouble of his soul, and reached up with his trunk. Hussein stroked him; he was vastly comforted, for Jehangir was so essentially material, and he was still terrified of that which he knew not at all.

The coming of the man with the lantern broke his laboured train of thought. He slipped down as he heard the man speak to the guards, and went to where the soldiers lay. In action his thought and his deed were never consciously apart; his plans, strategy, and execution just happened because he was Hussein, and that was how he was made.

He stumbled purposely over the legs of one of the sleeping men, kicking him hard. The soldier started up, cursing him most foully. Hussein answered him with a more vile tongue, and loudly; men awoke all about and joined in.

———

Almost at once there was a great noise, and as the man with the lantern, whom Hussein recognised for the first time as the Rajah's master of horse, came with the guards, Hussein spat in the other's face, crying, 'Soor! I am the mahout of the Rajah's own elephant, a man immeasurably—'

'Come here, mahout,' said the master of horse. Hussein went to him and salaamed. The man bade him bring Jehangir round to the lodge, and commanded silence.

Jehangir knelt; the officer mounted and pointed out the way. As they went back along the path to the temple, Hussein glanced at the place where he had stopped, but he was not moved.

They came to the temple, and the master of horse, whose name was Mirza Shah, caused Hussein to bring Jehangir to the front of the temple, where there was a great gateway.

'Stay there,' he said, and went into the temple. After a few moments Hussein followed him to the wall of the room where the others were. He knelt and listened.

'We must get rid of him while we arrange everything,' said the treasurer.

There followed some talk that was indistinct, then the Rajah said in a mellow, jocose voice, 'He had better die in a quarrel to-night or to-morrow.'

'It will fit,' replied Mirza Shah, laughing.

Footsteps came towards him, and Hussein darted back to Jehangir. Almost at once Mirza Shah came out with a note in his hand.

'Run back and give this to the captain of the guard,' he said, 'and return straightway.'

'On my head and heart,' replied Hussein.

———

He ran back a little way and then returned silently, looking about him for a sign from Ram Narain. He stood very still beneath the tree where he had left his clothes before, and he opened the note; in the darkness he could see no writing on it, so he returned it to his dhoti.

After a little while he became aware of an uneasiness, and, turning, he found Ram Narain just behind him. The other drew him some distance from the temple before speaking. Then he said, 'You heard what they planned for you?'

'Yes.'

'Well, now there is only one way for you, and it is that you and I shall do all that we may now. It is necessary that we obtain those papers that they signed and depart very quickly on Jehangir. There is no time left to us for anything but force. Have you a knife?'

'No, but I have my ankus,' answered Hussein, showing the heavy iron spike: he only carried it for glory, it being the mark of a mahout, but he never used it.

'It will do at a pinch,' said Ram Narain, examining it. 'Remember to strike hard when you use it.'

They slowly worked round to a place from where they could see Jehangir, and squatting there they finished the chupatties that Ram Narain had brought. Presently all the men came from the temple in a confused group, drawing with them the great pad-bag of gold. Jehangir was kneeling, as Hussein had told him to do, and together the men hauled and pushed the bag on to his back.

'Now, in a few minutes', said Ram Narain, 'you must go back to them, running. You will be told to take Jehangir back to the lodge. Probably the Rajah will ride and the other two will walk. About half-way between here

———

and the lodge I will leap out on Mirza Shah without any warning, and at that moment you must strike the Rajah. We can leave the treasurer until afterwards. I shall come without any warning, therefore be exceedingly alert, for we must both act at once.'

He paused for a few moments. Hussein was conscious of the dryness of his mouth, and of the trembling of his hands. His nerves were at concert pitch.

Ram Narain leant forward and touched Hussein. 'I am glad you are not trembling,' he said. 'I could not do this great thing with a coward.'

This heartened Hussein curiously; he said, 'I will go now.'

As he went down towards the place where he would come to the path, he was filled with a great complexity of feelings; he wondered vaguely whether he was afraid, but as soon as he began running back to the temple all these thoughts left him. As he came again to where Jehangir knelt he saw that the other men had gone away, and only the Rajah, the treasurer, and Mirza Shah were there. He was glad of this, because he had feared that the others might possibly return to the lodge with them, and thus disconcert Ram Narain's plan, and encompass his own death. The great bag was on Jehangir's back, and the Rajah sat, most uncomfortably, upon it; he bade Hussein return to the lodge.

They went along with the two men riding and the other two walking, as Ram Narain had predicted. Jehangir grumbled a little in his throat at the weight, but Hussein whispered to him, bending low to his ear. As they journeyed along the dark way, Hussein looked incessantly from left to right, and grasped his ankus firmly. Suddenly the Rajah broke the silence, and said that he would walk also. Hussein could think of no means to prevent him, so he inclined his head and caused Jehangir to kneel again. He felt fearful lest this unexpected move should frustrate them, for he did not know whether Ram Narain was creeping along near-by or whether he had gone on ahead to a place from which he could leap out to the best advantage. It was worse because the Rajah walked a little behind the elephant, talking in an undertone with the treasurer, who kept darting apprehensive glances about him, and clasping his hands nervously.

The darkness seemed to press in on them; when they entered a great mango-grove it seemed almost palpable. The Rajah called a halt, and told Mirza Shah to light the lantern. There was a light breeze, and they stood about the flame to shield it. Hussein poised himself on Jehangir's neck so that he might easily leap down. He felt sure that Ram Narain would attack now if he were following them, and he was right. As the flame flickered something which had been a shadow sprang into life, and at that moment Hussein launched himself at the Rajah.

In a moment all four were writhing on the ground. Hussein was on top of the Rajah, pressing his face into the earth. Ram Narain and Mirza Shah rolled over and over, grunting loudly. Hussein's ankus had jerked out of his hand, and he was only just able to keep his man down, for the Rajah was a powerfully built man, and he threshed about like a great fish.

For some time the treasurer stood petrified, then he screamed and ran for about twenty yards; he tripped, and lay where he fell, quite paralysed with fear.

Hussein heard a shuddering gasp behind him, and he

———

saw Ram Narain get up. Mirza Shah lay still. At that moment the Rajah flung up his legs and caught Hussein's neck with his feet. There was a swift, confused writhing, and Hussein lay flat, half unconscious from a kick in the groin. The Rajah leapt away into the jungle, and Ram Narain, confused in the darkness, pinned Hussein to the ground. Hussein could hardly speak by reason of the extremity of his pain, and Ram Narain's fingers pressed into his throat so that there was a hammering behind his eyes, and a swelling of his tongue.

Suddenly Ram Narain sprang up with a most appalling oath; he glared round, and saw nothing, but he heard the Rajah pushing his way through the undergrowth. He hauled Hussein to his feet, where he stood, half doubled up.

'Get on the elephant; we must catch him,' he said. Hussein groaned feebly, and Ram Narain pinched his arm fiercely, so that the blood came. This fresh pain brought him to somewhat. All this time Jehangir had stood stock still, uncertain what to do. Hussein spoke to him; he knelt, and in a moment they moved rapidly towards the sound of the Rajah's running. The wretched man concealed himself in the roots of a mangrove, but Jehangir followed his scent, and he broke away, dashing madly through the thick undergrowth. He tore through, ripping his clothes and cursing until Jehangir came up with him. Ram Narain leapt down. They swayed and stamped, locked together: Hussein could only see them vaguely. Suddenly they fell; Ram Narain twisted about so that he knelt on the Rajah's back, then he hit him hard with the edge of his palm on the neck. They went back, carrying the prince, to where Mirza Shah lay. There they collected the treasurer, who was almost unconscious from terror.

They searched about for the lantern, which they found under a bush; when it was lit Ram Narain went through their clothes, and in the treasurer's belt he found the papers that he sought.

Then they bound the men with their own turbans.

Ram Narain pondered for some time the advisability of killing them, but he decided against it, so they left them tied in a heap with the lantern burning beside them. Hussein was still in considerable pain, but he had recovered a little. Ram Narain stood silent for a long while, thinking: they were in the middle of the native states; it would be a long journey to reach British India.

'It is a great way from here to Ghondal,' he said, 'but we must be there before daylight; it is essential that we leave the gold there.'

Hussein's heart sank when he heard this; he had not had time to think that they had won a great sum, but this called it to him. He answered, speaking low and slowly, 'I say, on my honour, that Jehangir can carry both of us and the gold to Ghondal by dawn.'

As he spoke he extracted sixteen gold coins from the pad through a little hole, and hid them in his dhoti. He did not know how far it was to Ghondal, and Jehangir had already grumbled about the weight, but Hussein was ready to do anything in the world to get this great fortune; the thought of killing Ram Narain arose in his mind, but he repelled it. Ram Narain did not answer for some time.

Hussein thought furiously; he was very willing indeed to share with Ram Narain, for he loved the man, but to give up the gold altogether, just as he was beginning to realise it – that was more than he could stomach, even for twenty treasonable treaties. The gold would give him Sashiya, and he loved her very dearly with a strangely constant love and a most rare affection. At one word from him Jehangir would trample Ram Narain into a mess. It would be so easy.

Ram Narain divined Hussein's thoughts, and he revolved in his mind the idea of killing Hussein, for he knew well how men break under the strain when money is concerned. He, too, was desirous of the hoard, but first in his mind was his safety, and the getting of the treaty into the right hands: he was not subjected to the great motive for the gaining of the money that Hussein was.

The atmosphere was tense; both men were on edge from what they had done.

Then Ram Narain spoke. 'Well, we must waste no time,' he said.

'First we must arrange the pad properly,' replied Hussein firmly, 'or Jehangir will be galled.' Ram Narain chafed at the delay, but he helped as well as he was able. In a little while the pad was comfortable and they went away towards the east as fast as they might.

For a long while they travelled in silence, each enwrapt in his own thoughts. From time to time Hussein would whisper to Jehangir, who was not a little ill-tempered, because of his load. Ram Narain seemed to know the country intimately, for, although it was still dark, he would, ever and again, point the way. When the false dawn came they were in a bare bushy country; in a little time they came to a river, a small river with muddy banks.

'On the other side', said Ram Narain, 'we shall be in Ghondal – not that we shall be much safer there.' But when Jehangir came to the river and felt the mud, he stopped, and would not go on. Hussein turned him up the river, and they sought a dry ford.

'The banks of this river are always mud banks,' said Ram Narain lugubriously. 'We must throw away the gold.'

'It would make no difference,' replied Hussein; 'if he could get through the mud unladen he could do so with all this and more; moreover, he desires the water, so the mud must be very bad if he will not cross to it.'

'I am very hungry,' said Ram Narain inconsequentially. After some time they came to a place where there was mud and shingle going down to the water. Hussein slipped down, and went slowly to the edge.

'It will probably be just as bad the other side,' observed Ram Narain. Hussein did not reply. He stripped, and swam. When he was half-way over there was a swirl in the water, and a long snout appeared. His heart beat fast, and then it seemed to stop for a long time. He dived, and swam under the water, expecting the grip of teeth at every moment. The crocodile, a small, inoffensive fish-hunting gharial, swam even faster in the opposite direction. Suddenly his hands were scrabbling in the sand; he had reached the other side far sooner than he had expected. Ram Narain was wrong; the other bank was grassy down to the verge. Hussein waded out, shivering. He called to Jehangir, who spread his ears, but did not move.

'Walk slowly before him,' he shouted to Ram Narain. Ram Narain leapt down, and stepped gently towards the water. Jehangir moved forward very slowly: he felt his foot sink a little in the mud. Instantly he shot out his trunk, seized Ram Narain about the waist, and threw him down to provide a firm foothold. Hussein bellowed so that his voice cracked, and he felt a sharp pain where he had been kicked. Jehangir stood still for a moment, and then scrambled backwards to the firm land. Hussein swam over again, and picked up Ram Narain, whose head had struck against a stone so that he was stunned. When he had laid him in the grass he stood before Jehangir, and reviled him most bitterly.

'Pig-spawn, you have shamed me beyond all measure: my izzat is black before this honourable man. I have no further use for you at all.'

Jehangir rumbled in his throat, shifted his feet uncomfortably, and put out his trunk to touch Hussein. Hussein slapped it hard. 'Bahinchute!' he shouted, 'afraid of the slime you came from! Get across that river. Get across that piddling stream. Shame on your gross hulking belly that weighs you down! I would have bought you six gold tusk-rings. Now you shall have none, but a very great beating. Gold on a boar-pig!'

Jehangir rolled his eyes, and grunted softly.

'Afraid of a shadow! Afraid of a muddy puddle! Afraid of a little calf without tusks! Shaitan ka butcha, soorneen, get your pig's belly across that brook. Get your bunnia's heart to the other side. Camel! A jackal has more courage. Shuddering, stinking hulk, get in!' He pointed at the water; Jehangir looked on the ground and moved forwards. He came to a muddy patch and scuttled, squealing, into the water. He was across in a few minutes.

Ram Narain stood up and shook his head. 'I thought I was gone that time,' he said, smiling at Hussein; he very rarely smiled.

'I am ashamed for Jehangir,' said Hussein unhappily.

———

Ram Narain smote him on the shoulder, and said, 'He is the noblest elephant I have ever seen.'

They swam across and rested on the other side. They were utterly weary, and very cold; Hussein was past hunger.

'I believe there is a village about two hours east from here,' said Ram Narain, breaking a long silence; 'we will go near to it, and I will go in and get food.' They did not speak again until they were in sight of the fields.

Hussein waited a long time among the trees; a man passed along a path fairly near. The sun came up, and with it a white mist that shook every joint in Hussein's body. When the mist was going away and the sun was warm again Ram Narain came back. He bore food and some old clothes. They ate their fill in the sun, and their hearts expanded; they talked, and there was no tension between them. Jehangir fed with a continuous crunching noise as he tore up tender green shoots. When they had wiped their lips, Ram Narain said, 'We must go on as quickly as possible to Punait, which is in the Sirkar's country; there I can telegraph, and all will be well: we should be able to do it in three days. I think it would be unwise to travel by night, as we must go through the jungle, and I do not know this country very well.'

They slept for a few hours in a hidden spot, and then pushed on, keeping always away from the villages.

They had again enough food to eat, but by the evening they were hungry. They skirted about the fields of a village, and smelt the cooking of food on the wind. Ram Narain sniffed longingly, and said, 'If we were to leave the elephant, do you think that we should find him again – you have no chains here?'

Hussein laughed. 'If I told Jehangir to stay here until I came back, he would stay quite still, and if I could not return for many days, we should find him dead exactly where he was told to stay. But I shall bid him remain about here, so that he can feed while we are gone.'

'It is undoubtedly a fine thing to hear that,' said Ram Narain; 'we must alter our appearances, however, and go into the village as travelling soothsayers, or some such thing. I have it — you can relate a tale; that will be most convincing.'

It was dusk when they walked into the village. They were dressed in other clothes, and they looked exactly like travelling story-tellers. The men of the village were squatting in a group about a fire, discussing some matter. Hussein hailed the headman and the priest, giving an account of himself and of his companion, as the custom is. The headman greeted them in return, and the people made room about the fire.

'What is the truth of this tale concerning the Rajah of Kappilavatthu?' asked the headman of Hussein. 'You have come from those parts, I believe you said.'

News travels with extraordinary rapidity in India, and although they had journeyed as quickly as men might, it had gone before them. Hussein was seized with a fit of coughing before he answered.

'We heard something of it, but I do not know how much truth there is in it — how was it told here?'

'Oh, they say that the Rajah was attacked by a band of dacoits as he walked in the night, and his great ruby was taken from his finger, and an old councillor who was with him was found dead from no other cause but dread, so it may be that they were ghouls and not common badmashes.'

'Is the prince dead?'

'By no means; his ring finger is cut off, but he was found alive by his guards — or so it is said.'

'We heard much the same tale, only they told us that he was dead, and that there was disruption in the state: however, if you permit, I will tell for your delectation the tale of the Maharajah of Oudh, and of the Maharani, who was a ghoul —'

The tale was very well received, and they filled a great dish with the most noble cous-cous for the wayfarers, pressing them to remain the night. Hussein felt his heart swell with the joy of a teller of tales whose story is well rounded, exactly delivered, and fully appreciated, but looking at Ram Narain he refused, saying that they were to meet some people at a certain place a few miles away.

'Mirza Shah must have taken the ruby,' said Ram Narain as they went away, 'if it is true that it is gone — yet I could have sworn that I killed him.'

They went on until the moon rose, and then they rested. They slept rather far into the next day, for they were very weary. Ram Narain was furious when they awoke. By the evening they were near a small town where there was a market. Leaving Jehangir about five miles away, they went into the town, and there they fed at a small eating house. After they had filled themselves they walked out into the open market. Two men followed them. One of them asked the distance to a village in Kappilavatthu. Ram Narain gave a vague answer, but the strangers walked along with them, conversing about this and that, frequently questioning Ram Narain and Hussein about themselves and about their movements; they returned smooth indefinite answers for the most part, saying that they were story-tellers. One of the men asked several shrewd questions about the people of various districts, asking what kind of tales they desired, and to what extent they gave to the teller. Hussein was able to answer them aptly.

'You have not been here long?' asked the stranger. 'No, we came within the hour.'

'Then doubtless you will tell a tale this evening, while all the people are here for the market?'

'By all means,' replied Hussein, very much troubled within, but smooth and natural without. 'That is our purpose in coming here.'

'This is very pleasant; I am very much minded to hear a tale — one perhaps of the death of princes, or some such matter; it would blend with the talk concerning the Rajah of Kappilavatthu.'

The strangers looked very keenly upon Ram Narain and Hussein when this was said. Hussein noticed a little artery pulsing on Ram Narain's temple, but his face seemed perfectly calm, and rather bored. With hardly a pause Hussein assented. 'Yes, yes; such a tale would be most fitting,' he said.

The two men drew away to the other side of the market square. As they stood by some horses they continued to watch, appearing to be engaged in casual converse with a syce. Two of the horses were fine blood stallions; they seemed almost ridden to death.

'They suspect us fairly strongly,' said Ram Narain, speaking softly in Pushtu, and laughing as if he recounted a jest. 'It is possible that they may have traced Jehangir;

our only chance is to carry this through. Can you tell some tale that will serve? Everything depends upon it.'

Hussein laughed, as though he savoured the jest; the laugh was a little false, because his throat seemed half choked with terror. He could hardly stop himself from looking over his shoulder. He twitched his eyes from the men by the horses.

'Do you mean that they may have found Jehangir?' he asked.

'No. But we may have been seen as we slept this morning. I had a half-fear that I saw a man as I awoke, or they may have sent out to every place within possible reach to watch for us; that is the more probable thing. He would give fifty elephant loads of gold for this little piece of paper. I feel practically certain that Jehangir is not found. See those horses, and how those men walk; they have been here less than an hour, and therefore they were here before we began walking, because we took well over an hour coming.'

This comforted Hussein very greatly. While there was still a chance of getting away with Jehangir and the gold, and thereby of gaining Sashiya, he was of high courage.

'Have you any opium pills?' he asked.

Ram Narain produced a little box, and they both swallowed some. There was a man near-by with a great huqa; they paid their pice and squatted, each with a mouthpiece. Ram Narain spoke to the man in Pushtu; he was deaf, and he did not understand the tongue, so Ram Narain continued talking to Hussein. In the box with the pills there was a little compartment with three or four pills of a slightly different size and colour.

'If they take us', said Ram Narain conversationally,

'swallow that. You will be dead within the minute.'

'Would there be no other hope if they did?'

'Practically none. There are seven of them here, of whom those two are the chief. Five are minor agents, having other avocations, living in the town, but they are all dangerous, and we are in their country. We might run for the horses – it would be a slight hope, but it would be worth trying. If you see me tap three times upon the ground, rush for them – if you cannot get there, well, the pill is better than what would happen otherwise.'

'That is true,' said Hussein, blowing out a cloud of smoke, 'but I may be able to manage.'

They took up a position quite near to the horses, spreading a cloak upon the ground. Hussein raised his professional cry, and presently there was a sufficient audience. The two men who had spoken to them squatted in the front of the crowd.

———

Nineteen

'When the Prince of Kathiawar was a young man,' he began, having got through the inevitable prelude of self-praise and exhortation to generosity — it was a long poem that came to his mind — 'he was much given to the reading of the works of poets, and to the hearing of tales; he was a high-minded youth with innumerable merits, not the least among which was his amiable habit of filling a story-teller's mouth with gold when the tale pleased him. He was also a youth of surpassing beauty; his eyes were large and black like black pearls on the finest porcelain; they lay beneath exquisitely arched brows, which rose a little at the ends in the form of a bat's wing; his lips, large and full, but by no means sensuous, were of the texture of jade and of the colour of rubies; his cheeks were fairer and more delicate than those of a Circassian virgin; his neck slender and rounded, but firm; his fingers tapered long and smooth, they were tipped with nails like the finest slips of agate; his feet were high-arched and in every way perfect. Indeed, his whole body was of an indescribable excellence, and his skin gleamed as though it were powdered with the dust of pure gold.

'His mind, too, was of the loftiest mould, wholly befitting such an habitation; a mark of his surpassing excellence was his munificence towards those most deserving of all the humble people, the tellers of tales.

'Now by reason of his perfection, the Prince was much desired by many of the most exalted of his father's court, particularly by the wazir, who was a wicked man, and by the Maharajah's third concubine, a woman of great power, who had been a dancer.

'But the Prince joyed in none of these delights, applying himself both day and night to reading in all the tongues of the world, in hearing tales, and in playing chess.

'The wazir endeavoured to corrupt the youth with inconceivable guile. He hired base poets to recite works of the most dubious nature, and caused beautiful singing boys to act plays before him of a nature that was not even dubious in its depravity. But although the Prince sometimes admired the metre and the cadence of the poems, and although he admired, as an onlooker, the beauty of the singing boys, yet he was never moved in the least degree from his high-souled and distant attitude towards the bodily aspect of love.

'As time went on, the wazir's lechery and ambition, turning to nought in this instance, soured him against the Prince, so that from desiring him he turned to hating him.

'At the same time the delight of the Maharajah's life, his favourite concubine, endeavoured to seduce the Prince; at first by the usual devilish ways of women, with sighs, with complaints to him of the lack of understanding of those about her, with praise, with rollings of the eyes, giggles, and sensual movements of the body; then, these failing signally, by notes delivered in the night, by love philtres, by aphrodisiacs, privily administered by corrupt servants, and eventually by even more disgraceful methods. But the young man disregarded all these matters, and applied himself still more to literature in all its forms, and to chess.

'After the failure of one particularly seductive plan, the concubine had seven of the Prince's story-tellers poisoned, and within two days – the weather being hot – three of his poets were found in a well.

'Then, like the wazir, the concubine begat on her love a loathing for the Prince, and she worked to do him evil. The underground gossip of the palace had long acquainted each of the Prince's lovers with the desires of the other, so one day the concubine sent for the wazir, and being without shame, she came straight to the matter which was uppermost in their minds without preamble. The wazir, having ascertained that there were no witnesses other than a deaf-mute eunuch, opened his heart, and they spoke together for a long while.

'It was plain that the Prince could be dangerous to both of them; they were both afraid of his influence with the Maharajah, and, moreover, they hated him for his temperance, which, they concluded, was due to indulgence in some curious vice of which they did not know.

'Within a few days the Maharajah sent for the Prince, and, addressing him kindly, as was his wont, he enquired into the state of his studies. The Prince answered dutifully, and at considerable length, but his father interrupted him, saying that the time had come for him to thrust these pursuits into the background, and to learn statecraft.

'"I have been assured," said the Maharajah, "that your delight in these matters is very bad for you, and that it will unsuit you wholly for the task that will be yours. Now, tell me briefly, how would you govern an unruly, obstinate, and well-nigh untaxable people?"

'"By love," answered the Prince.

'His father directed an expressive glance at him, and made a singular noise with his lips. Then he dismissed him, bidding him bear in mind that which he had said. The Prince was much exercised in his mind by these things, but he escaped, by means of poetry and tales, into a world where all matters were translucent, and love a pure flame.

'The concubine knew that she was ageing, and in the bitterness of this knowledge, and her bitterness against the Prince, she had become filled with an insensate lust for power. Aided thereunto by the wazir, who had procured her for his master in the first place, she strove to isolate him from all other influences.

'With the passing of time another summons came to the Prince from the Maharajah. He was received in full audience: the councillors were ranged about the leopard throne, chief among them the wazir, whose eyes sought the ground; behind the throne a curtain moved.

'"My eldest son", said the Maharajah, "is now of a marriageable age: since the union which we had contemplated for him cannot take place now — (she to whom he had been betrothed when he was five had died early in that year) — we have contracted another, and even more politic, match. He will marry the eldest daughter of our cousin of Dharmapali . . ."

'His voice went on, but the Prince did not hear it. The Princess of Dharmapali was almost an idiot with a dribbling mouth and a body whose ugliness was almost legendary, but she would bring wealth beyond measure in dower. He returned inaudible answers to the congratulations of the wazir and the other councillors, and went away as soon as he could.

'Sitting by himself in deep thought, he resolved in his mind the ways in which the people of his other world would conduct themselves under similar circumstances. Eventually he roused himself, and collected a number of jewels and some money; then he put on his most ordinary clothes, and bade a horse be brought to a little courtyard by the peach garden. The concubine and the wazir were watching from a window as the Prince rode away; in their deep cunning they had foreseen all this, and evil men followed the Prince.

'But these men, as they followed him, disputed among themselves, saying, "If we kill him, then assuredly the wazir will kill us, for we should then hold his head in our hands: if we do not, then equally he will kill us for disobedience. Therefore, we must flee." So they ceased from following the Prince, and scattered to distant lands.

'He rode on for many days, until at length he came to the desert called Qarazim; he intended to travel to the court of the Shah of Persia, for he was an accomplished poet, and the Shah loved poets.

'But as he passed through the acrid desert, he came to a village, where the men dwelt in black tents, made from the hairs of camels, and the women walked with bare faces. As the Prince paused by the well, one came thereto, bearing a pitcher, and she was of so exquisite a beauty

---

that he blushed and cast down his eyes for fear that the desire that leapt naked from them should scorch her modesty. Her name was Sashiya, and she was as a gazelle in the moonlight, or a spotted sand quail in the shadow of a leafless bush. Her face gleamed with the splendour of the full moon; all words would sully her perfection. Her hands moved as golden grain flows from a full sack. She spoke in a voice like the ring of rubies upon hanging green jade, but the Prince could utter no word. His knees almost failed him, and his heart stopped his throat, such was his extremity.

'She turned with the laden pitcher, and the sun was gone from the sky.

'He stood in an amazement while a man might tell a thousand. Then he sighed profoundly, mounted his horse, and turned back into the desert.

'He rode with a slack rein, still in a dream, but he guided his horse away from the village, and his purpose was clear, for he was a poet, and he knew that he must not seek to prolong that fortuitous moment, but that he must keep it perfect, enshrined, if he could encompass it, in words, but never changed, for it was the absolute, and anything added to it would take away from it.

'For many hours he rode, seeking vainly the words of the poem that he felt, and presently he became aware of a great city gleaming among the dunes before him. He spurred his horse, which responded but feebly, and rode towards it. He rode along, yet it seemed always the same distance away; he could see the people moving to and fro therein. Suddenly the city vanished, and in its place there appeared a sandstorm; in the midst of the swirling dust there was a djinni of the most malevolent aspect, who, riding on a camel, waved a lance tipped with fire. The djinni was a considerable distance away, and the Prince was minded to escape by flight. But he reflected that if he were to fight only his body might come to harm, whereas if he fled and escaped his honour would undoubtedly be irreparably harmed. So he drew his sword and charged, proclaiming the unity of God.

'The camel came nearer and nearer, the djinni was upon him. The Prince rose in his stirrups, raised his sword, and lo, the djinni vanished. He struck hard at the flying sand, so hard that he cast himself to the earth, where he lay senseless, while his horse galloped back to the village of black tents.

'He came to himself when the first stars were pricking in the sky. About two miles away he could see the tents of the village, for he had ridden in a vast circle.

'Now the men of the desert are of a catholic hospitality, so when the Prince's horse came back some of the men went out on their camels to search for him. The sand-storm had obliterated his horse's tracks, so they were obliged to leave their search when the evening came.

'The poet in the Prince would not consider returning to the village, but the man in him was very hungry, and infinitely more thirsty. He sat on a stone for a long time, while the stars came out, and the lights appeared among the tents.

'In the end he compromised with himself, saying that if by chance he saw the girl, he would neither look at her nor speak. He came halting into the village, and the dogs barked. Men came out, and he was led to the chief's tent, where, after he had eaten and drunk, the men came in, and they spoke together. Sashiya brought coffee, for she was the daughter of the chief, and when men spoke to her she answered them, looking in their faces, as the custom is in those parts.

'The Prince thought very deeply for some time as he watched her, and looking into his thoughts he perceived that he had been wrong, for she was flawless, so she could not be idealised and spoilt by herself; she was perfect.

'The Prince, who gave his name as Ikbal Haider, remained several days in the black tents reciting poems and telling tales beyond compare, so that his hosts were filled with exceeding great joy.

'Now it is the custom in those parts that the women may not be betrothed until they consent thereunto, and up to that time Sashiya had not been pleased with any of the suitors who came to her father. After a little time the Prince, or Ikbal as he called himself, remarked that her father was a man of importance in the desert, for he owned more than a thousand camels, which is great wealth; and although he dwelt with all the simplicity of the nomads, yet he was a man of fierce pride and high lineage, being the chief of his tribe.

'The chief favoured a marriage between Sashiya and Sikander, the chief of a neighbouring tribe who was of equal lineage, and Sikander was ardent in his wooing. This caused Ikbal great unease, for he hesitated to declare his love, and concealed it under a lighthearted mien. But it did not deceive Sashiya at all; she had known of his state from the beginning, being a woman, and she was by no means displeased, for his beauty and his excellence had set a flame within her. Yet she, for her part, was afraid to declare herself, for fear that her father and Sikander would straightway kill Ikbal.

'So the days passed, and they abode in this perplexity. A man came bearing news through the desert on his way to the court of the Shah. He was a Persian, a servant of the Persian ambassador – Ikbal had seen him at his father's court. He paused at the well, where Ikbal spoke to him in his own tongue, asking news of Kathiawar.

'"The Maharajah is dead," said the man, remounting, "and the state is in turmoil, for the Prince is gone."

'He shouted the last words as he galloped away, and Ikbal sat suddenly on the kerb of the well. Until twilight he grieved for his father, and then Sashiya came to the well.

'They looked full into each other's eyes; and that, as one might say, was that. When they resumed to the village the moon was high and brilliant. Ikbal saddled his horse and rode furiously towards Kathiawar; Sashiya stood long at the well, watching him go in the moonlight. She saw three camels come from behind a sand dune and follow him; Sikander and two of his cousins were on them.

'The Prince rode for three hours before he was aware of the camels. He noticed them as he was walking his horse up a steep incline of loose sand, and he turned to look at them. He was troubled, not knowing their purpose, so he went up to the top of the dune and loosened his sword. As they came nearer he saw that they bore lances, and, his doubt resolved, he felt a strange joy that he had never known before. His sword blazed in the moon; it was an ancient blade of very notable steel; it had come out of the West when the Franks fought with S'allah ud Din.

'At the foot of the dune the men halted; one struck his lance into the sand and came forward unarmed; Ikbal

---

sheathed his sword. They greeted one another courteously, and after they had spoken of indifferent things a little, the man said, "By an unfortunate chance you have offended my cousin Sikander in a matter of which you know, and he will kill you now; in what way would you wish to encounter him?"

'"I shall be pleased to dispatch your cousin, for whom I have the greatest respect, with whatever arms he chooses — either mounted, armed as we are, or on foot, with swords."

'"Swords would, I think, be quickest. I wish you a speedy journey to Paradise, for you are a proper young man."

'They encountered half-way down the slope. Ikbal held his sword with both hands, for it was long-handled with a long straight blade, after the manner of foreign swords. They stood with their sword points touching for a moment, then Sikander's blade hissed forward and shot by Ikbal's neck, cutting it lightly; he sprang back, and they circled round warily, feinting for an advantage. With the sharp pain of the wound, Ikbal lost all fear; he gripped his sword firmly, and it quivered in his grasp. He felt imbued with a new virtue. Suddenly Sikander beat twice at his sword and cut again and again with great power and speed at his head. Ikbal laughed, and budged not an inch, but guarded himself perfectly, hardly knowing how he did it. Twice Sikander's sword cut into his shoulder, but he did not feel it: there was a pause, and Ikbal attacked with all his heart. The swords flashed and blazed in great sweeps, ringing together with a joyous sound; their feet stamped, and they breathed hard, gruntingly. All at once their swords were locked at the hilts, and they stood face to face, with their arms upstretched. Then, by tacit agreement, they stepped back and wiped the sweat from their eyes.

'They began again with the same furious onslaught; this time Ikbal struck Sikander under his left arm, so the blood flowed from them both. For nearly an hour they fought thus, pausing now and then, but continuing with renewed fury after every rest.

'Neither could gain any advantage until the very height of the onslaught, when they seemed ringed with the gleam of their swords, and the sound of their fighting was like the shoeing of seven horses; then it happened that each struck with great force so that their blades met edge to edge. Fire sprang therefrom, and Ikbal's sword bit clean through the opposing steel, leaving Sikander with six inches of blade. Sikander sprang back, and slipped on a blood-wet stone. Ikbal ran to raise him, and called for another sword. Sikander thanked him gravely; they refreshed themselves with a little water, and began again. But Ikbal had remarked the great virtue of his blade, and within five minutes Sikander was swordless again.

'He would not turn and run, but stood to await the blow; yet again Ikbal called for the third sword, but Sikander would not accept it.

'"I yield myself wholly," he said, "for you are the finest swordsman in the world."

'"By no means," replied Ikbal, "you are the better fighter, but I had the fortune of the blade."

'Then they attended to their wounds and ate food. They slept until the morning, and then Ikbal took Sikander aside and unfolded his whole case to him. It transpired that Sikander did not greatly desire Sashiya, for the standards of the desert were not those of Kathiawar, but he had desired to be her father's heir — the old chief had no son.

'Ikbal promised him this, and they swore brotherhood upon bread and salt.

'They returned to Sikander's tents, and he sent out a call to the men of his tribe. By evening a thousand armed horsemen were there, and at dawn the next day they rode for Kathiawar.

'They found that the wazir had already killed the concubine, and had seized the leopard throne by corrupting the palace guard. These put up something of a resistance, but Sikander's men went through them like fire through dried grass.

'Ikbal came to the wazir in the audience hall. The wazir faced him with a scimitar, but Ikbal forced him back and back until he was in a corner, and then Ikbal drove so furious a blow upon him that the sword bit him from his forehead to his loins, so that he fell in two pieces.

'Then Ikbal feasted Sikander and his followers with a feast that continued without break for three days and two nights, and he sent them away laden with royal gifts. As soon as his state was untroubled, he took ten noble stallions, and rode them without any pause at all until he came to the village of the black tents.

'Sashiya stood by the well. He leant from his saddle and plucked her from the ground.

'She was his maharani for thirty-eight years, and she bore him seven sons and some daughters. The tale is done!

'And mark that the greater part of the Maharajah's good fortune was attributable to his munificence to the tellers of tales.'

Twenty

The audience threw pice and annas on to the cloak that Hussein sat upon. The two men cast in a rupee, and walked away with the crowd, following a pair of new-comers. Hussein and Ram Narain waited until they were out of sight, and then they walked away slowly in the other direction, taking every conceivable precaution. When they were out of the town, and walking through the fields, Ram Narain said, 'I hardly think, with all my training, that I could have done that.'

'It was a poor tale, and badly mangled in my great desire to reach the end rapidly without entirely spoiling it, but it served.'

'That is true; from the beginning to the end they could not suspect anything, yet they were watching most keenly, for your faults were the faults of a true story-teller. I thought time and again that you would falter, but it was flawless for our purpose.'

'To tell you the truth, when I was once into the tale, I almost wholly forgot them, and at first the swing of the verse was a great help in keeping on; but towards the end

I was obliged to improvise a good deal, and I became nervous, so the tale suffered badly.'

When they approached the place where they had left Jehangir, they separated, and crept towards him with an infinity of care, but Jehangir caught the scent of them, and came slowly towards Hussein.

There were no signs of any man having been there, so they continued their journey after Hussein had rearranged the pad more comfortably. It was very hard work doing this, for when they got it off they had to take all the gold out before they could get it back again, and they took peculiar pains to pick up all the pieces again. However, it was a delightful task handling the great hoard. When it all lay on the ground Hussein rolled upon it with almost indecent joy. Ram Narain, too, poured it through his fingers with a gloating sound. The rest of their journey appeared flat and tame: they reached Puniat in two easy stages, and Ram Narain went to the station and sent a telegram; then he came back to await the arrival of the other men.

'Perhaps', he said, 'it would be as well not to mention the gold in my report. Its absence might lead to adverse comment.'

'Maybe you are right,' replied Hussein. 'After all, you know even better than I the inconceivable turpitude and unclean minds of officials.'

They had taken possession of a disused hut in the jungle outside the village, and the gold lay upon the floor. Ram Narain had bought some grain sacks in Puniat, and they filled these; when all was divided they leaned them against the wall of the hut, and tied their necks with grass. It was then that Ram Narain told Hussein that

Purun Dass had not died from his beating – he had known it for a long while.

The next two days passed in a happy daze for Hussein: they took turns in keeping guard, but nothing untoward happened. In the morning of the third day Ram Narain went into Puniat and returned with two Englishmen and an old wrinkled man, who might have been a sadhu had he not been dressed in ill-fitting European clothes. Ram Narain had hidden the paper, wrapped in cloth, in the branches of a high tree. He brought it down for them, and they read it in the hut. Hussein squatted before the sacks, so that no one might bump into them. When they had done the Englishmen shook hands with Ram Narain without a word, and the old man sat cackling upon the floor.

Then one of the sahibs bade Ram Narain relate the whole circumstances, which he did, enlightening Hussein upon many points of his earlier movements. When he had done, the larger Englishman, speaking perfect Urdu, said, 'But this excellent young man must be rewarded. Will he work with you in the future?'

'I think not, huzoor,' replied Ram Narain, 'for the present, at any rate, I know that he has other and pressing affairs to attend.'

'But some suitable reward . . .'

'Mam-bap,' said Hussein, 'any reward at your hands would be excessive, but if your servant might venture a suggestion, there was a certain trifling matter of one Purun Dass, a bunnia, who was beaten in his temple by a friend of mine who wishes to return to those parts – perhaps, possibly, some slight amelioration of the criminal proceedings . . . ?'

'It is, of course, quite impossible to corrupt British justice,' said the Englishman, 'a matter of assault . . . hm . . . and possibly sacrilege . . . hm. Did it all happen some time ago?'

'A long time ago, huzoor,' replied Hussein fervently.

'Well, it is conceivable that a fine might be held to cover the matter. Purun Dass was the bunnia's name? Where did this happen?'

'In Laghat, sahib: he is a notoriously evil man.'

'Who — your friend or the bunnia? In passing, what was the friend's name?'

'Assuredly the bunnia, huzoor; my friend is a benevolent man, mild, peaceable, well-disposed towards the Government, and an incomparable teller of tales; a most worthy man; one deserving of all possible clemency.'

'His name?'

Hussein gazed upon the ground, and began to cough. The sahib said, 'Well, perhaps that is not a vital point at the moment. I feel moderately certain that if your friend returns to Laghat, he will find that a fine will be all that he is faced with. Moreover, although I, of course, can make no promises, it is also possible that the fine will be paid for him by some benevolently disposed person. Your friend will naturally appreciate the value of discretion and silence.'

'Huzoor, I am your servant's servant.'

When the men had gone, Ram Narain said, 'Now we must go to Patalipore; we shall arrive there by noon, and if you are wise you will put the gold in the English bank there, as I shall. I understand these matters.' He explained it all to Hussein, who saw that it was a wise thing.

Jehangir lifted the long sacks up to Hussein and Ram

Narain on his back, and they arranged them there. It was strange that they were able to travel on the road through the village; at first Hussein had a crisis of nerves as each man passed them on the road, and he grasped the sacks convulsively, but by the time they were near Patalipore he was used to it. They stopped at a merchants' caravanserai, and Ram Narain went on to speak with the manager of the bank, where he had an account. He came back in a little while with the manager and a lorry. They loaded the sacks into the lorry, and drove to the bank; there the gold was weighed out before them, and a large number of papers were signed. Hussein thought it a little odd that no questions were asked, but he knew Ram Narain's surpassing skill in explaining matters.

Eventually they gave Hussein a book showing an enormous sum standing to his credit, and a cheque book. They each drew out a considerable sum in rupees, and left.

As they walked towards the caravanserai, Ram Narain said, 'I have other matters to pursue, and I must leave this afternoon by a train. You are safe now, for the Rajah will not do anything at all to annoy the Sirkar, but beware of appearing too rich; dress as a wealthy merchant, but be frugal in your expenditure, and haggle over an anna, otherwise you will be cheated. Again, remember that if anything untoward occur, you are to go straightway to one or another of those sahibs whose styles and whose dwellings I recited to you. Now we shall buy clothes.'

They turned in at one end of the cloth workers' bazaar itinerant story-tellers; they came out at the other, after the passage of time, rich merchants, proud bellied, and haughty-eyed. Then they returned to the caravanserai and commanded a most notable meal. After they had wiped their lips and washed their hands, Ram Narain said, 'Here are three maxims that have guided me always with women: employ them and be happy. The first is, "Women are fundamentally immoral, essentially possessive, and infinitely variable", the second is, "A woman who is kept busy bearing sons has no time for adultery", and the third was told to me by a sahib, who translated from his own tongue for me; it contains the wisdom of the West, "A woman, a bitch, and a tree that bears walnuts are the more fecund the more they are beaten". Bear these things in mind, eschew dangerous evil, and die young, then you will be happy.'

They took a very affectionate leave of each other, and Ram Narain departed.

Suddenly he heard running footsteps behind him; he stiffened, glided his hand to his knife, and slipped into a doorway.

It was Hussein. 'I had forgotten these,' he said, showing a handful of gold. 'I drew them from the pad when it seemed that we should have to leave the rest — eight fall to your share.'

'Thank you, Hussein,' said Ram Narain, with his rare smile; he sought for words, but none came: then he shook him by the hand in the English manner, and went away into the crowd.

Hussein walked slowly through the bazaars; at first he was somewhat downcast at his friend's going, for circumstances had brought them very close together. But his discovery of the power of money revived his heart as he wandered through the stalls of the goldsmiths, knowing that he could buy anything that he desired.

*

He pondered deeply as he walked; he was imbued with the spirit of tales through the telling of them, and he knew that now he could live in one. He seemed to sink into his thoughts, his golden thoughts, until he was aware that he was unalterably decided that he would live in an imagined tale until he had attained Sashiya, for he could shape his world with his riches. He found himself in the street of those who make all manner of harness, and there he saw a howdah that had been made for a Prince who had died without paying for it. It was superbly magnificent, befitting the most noble elephant.

He enquired the price of various other articles, rejecting them all on the ground of expense; as he walked away he glanced casually at the howdah, saying,

'This, undoubtedly, is very cheap, seeing that there is no market for such things in these times.'

The merchant's eye lightened, for he knew all the moves of the game, and perceived that it was the howdah that Hussein desired, so he praised it to the heavens, and, in verity, it was of notable craftsmanship. For three hours they bargained; twice Hussein began to walk away, and twice the merchant pursued him, abating the price. In the end the howdah changed hands for a little over half the opening price. Hussein paid for it straightway, and bought magnificent silk elephant cloths of the kind that the elephants of Maharajahs wear. From the merchants he extracted receipts showing greater sums than he had paid, after the custom of those who buy for Princes; this was to allay suspicion. Then he bade the merchants send him any mahouts whom they knew to be of great merit.

The next morning, after he had fed, washed and watered Jehangir in his old clothes, he changed again into a rich merchant, and interviewed the twenty-four mahouts who had sat before his door since the dawn. He questioned them severally, most pertinently, so that they were beyond all words surprised, and many of them were discovered in manifest falsehood. One, however, an ancient man, delighted Hussein; he was a mahout from his birth, and he was of the properest clay; he had not been able to find employment since the death of his master, by reason of his advanced age, and he starved for the company of elephants. Hussein took him to Jehangir, who approved of him, so he was engaged. The ancient fell on his face and wept with joy.

The next day Hussein became intoxicated with his power, and he bought twenty-three different gramophones, but no needles or records, a very large teapot, and a variety of magnificent shoes with curious toes. But it was a brief spell, and he came to his senses when he sat in his room gazing at the packing cases. He had so often had to look at both sides of an anna that he knew the value of money, and his natural level-headedness made him ashamed of waste.

Among the merchants there was talk of a great necklace of rubies that had vanished from the temple of Kali at Secunderabad. It was rumoured that it had come by devious ways to one Ditmars, a half-caste Frenchman from Pondicherry, a goldsmith.

Hussein went to him, and, having bought two thick broad gold rings for Jehangir's tusks at a fair price, he spoke about the rumours of the necklace. Ditmars replied vaguely, but Hussein felt something behind his reserve, and as he was going, Ditmars said, 'If the matter interests your excellence, I know of a man who is said to know the truth of the matter. He usually goes to the house of Miriam the Englishwoman, in the evenings. Probably he will be there this evening.'

He said this with a slight emphasis; Hussein followed the meaning. He went to the house of Miriam that evening; it was kept by an incredibly obese blonde woman, whose name had once been Mary Saunders. Ditmars was there with two non-descript, furtive little men. After a while they all went into an inner room: Hussein was not without suspicions of a trap, but he knew that he could deal with those three men. When the opium pipes were brought he took that which was offered to Ditmars by a subterfuge.

'It is a curious thing that there should be a tale concerning the disappearance of Kali's necklace,' reflected the half-caste, 'for there is a remarkably similar necklace on the market just now. I am told that it comes from an exalted house that is pressed financially — of course, the name of His Highness, of the house, that is to say, could not be revealed.'

The talk went on and on, drifting over a multitude of subjects, but coming nearer and nearer to the advisability of Princes investing in gems as security. It was fairly well established by Hussein's cunning in the bazaars that he was the agent of one of the minor princes.

At length the necklace came into the dim light. It was a great rope of seventy-three flawless gems, simply strung with no setting; they were graduated from one the size of a pea to one of the bigness of the body of a mouse that sleeps curled up.

No words could encompass their blazing splendour. For a little Hussein left speech to the others, he could not decry the perfection of the rubies. But he recovered himself, and appeared unimpressed.

'I had conceived them to be of finer colour, and of greater size and number; however, it has been most interesting to have seen them,' he said.

These words rather damped the men, but Ditmars forced the talk along, and presently Hussein asked what sort of price was put upon them. He knew that he would have the necklace if it took his whole fortune; he could see it blazing on Sashiya's honey skin, lighting her whole body, but he intended to fight for it with all his power. They mentioned a great sum, five lakhs of rupees. Hussein did not reply to this at all, but looked at them as if he suspected a jest. They continued until very late, pointing out the excellence of every gem, but of course not even the most tentative bargaining was begun that night.

Twenty-One

On the following day Hussein went to see the manager of his bank, and desired to be directed to an honest lawyer — an English one.

'An honest lawyer? Well, I know of several rich ones, who are therefore less likely than most to embezzle, and there is a very old firm in Bombay whose probity has never been questioned; but an honest lawyer . . . Nevertheless, here are the addresses of the two who most nearly approximate to the impossible.'

Hussein thanked him and went to one, to whom he confided the business of his land at Laghat, requesting him to regain it and to settle all legal disputes at any cost and with the greatest possible dispatch. This was a very wise move on his part, for Purun Dass, confronted with an English lawyer, was badly frightened; he was not so foolish as to offer a bribe, but he advanced the questions of sacrilege and incitement to riot. The lawyer instantly opposed him with innumerable precedents of the Government's singular attitude towards these matters.

Eventually the entirety was settled for little more than five times the amount of the original loan, and the suit which had previously been entered against Hussein was cleared by a fairly stiff fine, which was paid into court by an unnamed man on Hussein's behalf.

While all this was being arranged Ditmars visited Hussein, and, desiring to speak with him in the utmost privacy, he suggested by the most intangible circumlocution that if the necklace were bought at three and a half lakhs, one-third of the price would be given to Hussein. But Hussein would not see the implication: Ditmars advanced the suggestion in the form of an interesting experience at which he had assisted as go between, so he departed, believing Hussein to be unsatisfied with the amount of the bribe that he had offered.

By day and by night Hussein dreamed of the rubies; he meditated various ways of obtaining them by guile, and he wished that Ram Narain were with him.

Negotiations proceeded, however, on only a moderately dishonest basis, and on a day Ditmars and Hussein travelled to Madras, where an expert on gems gave his opinion on the rubies. In this course Hussein exercised the greatest precautions to avoid the bribing of the expert, to Ditmars' great discontent. After the expert had examined the stones, Hussein bade him seal them up in a packet, to guard against substitution, not, as he explained, that he was in any way suspicious of Ditmars' good faith, nor had he any fixed intention of buying them, but it was a wise thing to do as a general measure in case of unforeseen circumstance. Ditmars assented rather acidly; he saw fairly plainly that Hussein would buy, but at the lowest possible price, so he comforted himself somewhat.

Then Hussein took the expert aside to learn his unbiased opinion, in an inner office.

'The stones are all genuine,' he said, 'and as a collection they are very much more valuable than they would be singly, on account of their perfect graduation. If they are Kali's necklace, and I feel that forty-seven of the stones might be, although I could not swear to it, then they have been re-cut, and three of them not too well re-cut, which detracts from their value; the great pendant stone is certainly not from Kali's necklace, though; it bears a certain resemblance to a stone that was sold thirty-odd years ago to the Thakur of the Deccan' — it came to Hussein in a flash of memory that the Rajah of Kappilavatthu had taken a daughter of the Thakur to wife; Mirza Shah, if he had taken the stone, must have sold it quickly. 'A fair valuation of them in the open market at present would be one hundred and forty-three thousand rupees, roughly one and a half lakhs. Perhaps you intend to purchase them?'

'If I can name my price.'

'Then — quite confidentially, you understand — I should advise you to let me re-examine them immediately after their delivery: accidents frequently happen in this trade.'

'Without doubt I shall do that, although I doubt whether I shall buy them,' Hussein added in a louder tone, for he heard a slight movement at the door.

The bargaining continued day after day: when a considerable pause was politic, Hussein went to Laghat, whither he brought royal presents for Hurri Singh, who wept upon his neck. Purun Dass welcomed him with incredible unction as he rode in, seated in magnificence upon Jehangir, whose tusks burned with silver and gold.

Upon his land he bade to be built a house with great dispatch; by no means a fantastic house, but a sober and excellent one. He commissioned the Sikh, whose probity he knew, to oversee the construction of it, so that he might not be more cheated than necessary. He likewise caused notable craftsmen to assemble from all about; painters, carvers in wood and stone, and men greatly skilled in the juxtaposition of coloured stones upon the floor, for that his house might be of the greater excellence, although it would be moderate in size.

Now until the time that Hussein had gained his wealth he had written to Sashiya always at intervals of five days or so, frequently more often, through the medium of the old letter-writer, Abd'Arahman, but since he had reached Patalipore he had only sent a brief note, sending his heart in few words, and omitting all mention of the gold. This was part of his plan to live in his own tale.

He returned to Patalipore, and found Ditmars most agitated by his absence. The dealing went on steadily; in a little while Hussein knew that he could name a price, and then they could work up and down between the two figures.

He engaged three servants for his greater glory. Two of them were old soldiers, most proper men, and the third was a pleasant youth, versed in letters, and apt in affairs of money.

In order to press Hussein, Ditmars produced another man, who also negotiated for the rubies. At first this troubled him, but by watching the man closely, and by weighing his words, he perceived the stratagem, and he abruptly named a price, saying that he had to leave Patalipore that day.

———

He sent this message to Ditmars, who came at once to see him, expostulating about the meagre sum. He said that the other man had already offered a greater sum.

'Then let him have the necklace,' replied Hussein with perfect equanimity; 'there are other rubies in the world.'

As he said this his heart beat most violently, for he could not be certain that the other man was not genuine.

'Oh well, it is a pity, for I would rather you had it, being a lover of gems after my own heart.'

They dropped the subject, and drank coffee. Neither could tell for certain to what extent the other was sincere: it was most tormenting, but they kept up a perfect show of indifference. It was Ditmars who broke first.

'Perhaps even now we may come to some arrangement,' he said. 'I am not altogether satisfied with the honesty of the other agent. Now suppose two lakhs were to be paid for it, and out of my small share of the profit I were to allocate, let us say, perhaps 10,000 rupees to various charities of such a nature that you would be the most suitable person for the actual distribution of it . . .'

Hussein knew then that he had gained his will; they both knew it, but of course they could come to no definite agreement until late that night. When at last it had come to the actual naming of the final price, Hussein caused a contract to be drawn up describing all the things to be done and not to be done with the utmost nicety, and he obliged Ditmars to put to it his signature and his seal. He also sent a hasty message, by means of the telegraph, desiring the expert to come instantly. It was arranged that the deal should be completed the following evening.

Waiting for that time to come, he went forth in splendour upon Jehangir. The day seemed very long indeed to him; he wanted so very much to go straight to Sashiya, but his desire to pursue his tale was stronger. He longed to pay the money for the rubies, and have them at once, but his caution was greater. He had lived a very long while in a year or so.

After an extraordinarily long time had passed the evening came, and with it the jeweller from Madras. They met Ditmars at the appointed place, where they consumed an interminable meal. Then at last Hussein had the rubies in his hands; they were warm, because Ditmars had carried them about him for safety. The expert examined them, and passed them; he left, and Hussein paid the agreed sum. Ditmars gave him a receipt, and returned to him the agreed bribe.

They parted with many expressions of good will and respect, Ditmars leaving also a most artificially wrought gold betel-nut box as a present, for they had each conceived an admiration for the other's ability; it had been a notable and a satisfying bargaining.

Almost the whole night Hussein held them in his hands, savouring their perfection. He awoke to gaze at them in the new sun; they had in their splendour a hypnotic effect.

Then he went away to Laghat, wearing them beneath his clothes, feeling their weight and hardness. The house was taking shape rapidly, but there was great dissension among the craftsmen, who had fallen out upon various points of technique. Hussein pacified them with threats and with presents, and brought a horde of workmen to hasten the building; he also bade thither men to lay out gardens with all manner of flowering trees and plants. He worked himself, and made his attendants do likewise, to their immeasurable distaste; Jehangir lifted great blocks of stone, and hauled vast baulks of timber.

Hussein worked his men as they had never been worked before in their whole lives, but he paid them large wages, and admired their work, so they were content. He had built a notable place for Jehangir, of such a kind that he would have all that an elephant desires; this he did with the collaboration of his old mahout, who had a great store of knowledge.

At length it was done. The gardeners, by devious arts, had the peach trees flowering out of their season, and all their province seemed to have been established for many years.

In the courtyard — the whole house was surrounded by a high thick wall, and it lay about an internal square courtyard — there was a noble fountain. There were fair carpets on the walls, and the windows were closed by shutters of the most involute carving. On the floor of the house one might follow with a dagger's point the intricate weaving of the mosaics in divers strange stones; these were most excellent.

Then, on a day, Hussein gave all the men a feast, and he sat among them with a wreath about his neck after they could eat no more, telling them tales until the dawn broke green. When they had all gone, calling peace and happiness upon the house, he sat with the youth skilled in figures, and cast his accounts: he found that with the rubies, his land — he had bought a good deal about his house — the house itself, and all his other purchases, he had spent rather less than a third of his wealth, and that with the rest he could live in great ease and comfort for all his days, and then leave a rich fortune. This contented

Hussein so much that he decided to build a mosque.

After sleeping a little space, he dressed himself in his finest clothes, with the rubies about his neck and a considerable amount of money in his belt. He made Jehangir resplendent, and set out for Haiderabad. He travelled in very great haste, being in a state of exaltation, not unmixed with apprehension, for he knew that he was risking a great deal in following his tale so strictly, yet he had made an iron resolution in this matter.

He came to Haiderabad, and rode magnificently through the streets; this was very sweet. He did not fear the Pathans, his enemies, for he knew that they would never dream of looking for him in a Prince's howdah. He stayed in the finest place that there was in the city, and retired to a private room. There he undid a bundle that he had brought with him, and stripped himself. In the bundle were his old clothes, and some dust and ashes. These he put on, and sullied himself, that he might lose all appearance of wealth. He secured the rubies in his dhoti, and went to Jehangir; the old mahout gaped at him with open mouth for a little, but Hussein did not regard him; he bade him be at a certain place within a certain hour with Jehangir as beautiful as he might be. He also called his servants, and told them that it was his design to walk about in this guise upon certain errands, and that he feared the intentions of evilly disposed men and told them to follow him in a discreet manner to protect him.

'On my head and heart,' replied all the men, and Hussein went out into the bazaars. He came to the Vishnavi bazaar, and perceived the ancient letter-writer sitting in his accustomed place. He seemed a little older, but otherwise the whole bazaar was unchanged. Coming to the old man he salaamed, and greeted him. Abd'Arahman exclaimed aloud, and wept an old man's tears, but when their greetings were done, and Hussein had taken him to drink coffee, he expostulated with him on account of the danger that he incurred in being in Haiderabad.

But Hussein reassured him, secretly pointing out his men, who had followed him cunningly, and sat about the coffee house. The former soldiers were armed, and the youth was a subtle youth, so Hussein felt himself secure against mischance. Then Hussein, after he had answered a great many questions, asked the old man to get a message to Sashiya. He wrote it there, asking her to be on the roof garden that night.

Awaiting that time he went to see the red-bearded fakir. As he walked through Haiderabad he was conscious of a slight annoyance that it had not changed at all; it seemed that the city had not remarked his absence. He found the fakir sitting where he always sat, looking as unpleasant as ever.

'Well, mahout,' said the fakir, as Hussein sat before him, 'so you have come back.'

'That is plain,' replied Hussein, who no longer felt in such awe of the holy man — he had seen so many of them in his walking up and down.

'You have become rich,' said the fakir, after a pause. Hussein did not reply. He had come to make sure that there was no curse on the rubies, or to have one removed, if it existed, but he did not desire to pay a rich man's price for it.

'And you wish me to remove the potent curse upon Kali's necklace.'

———

The talk ceased for several minutes.

'It is of no use to endeavour to deceive me: I am aware of all things. Give me five hundred rupees. Come; hastily.'

Hussein hesitated. 'But surely the amulet you gave me will cover all curses?' he said.

'But if there were a certain curse on the rubies your woman would die in childbirth after she had put them on.'

'Here are a hundred and fifty.'

The fakir gazed at Hussein steadily, but did not speak.

'Now see, here are two hundred and fifteen — a lordly sum, is it not?'

There was no reply. Hussein got up to go, and the fakir laughed. Hussein sat again, and put five hundred in the fakir's hand.

'There is no curse upon them; a priest stole them. There will be no curse,' said the fakir, counting the notes and folding them. Then he turned his back, and Hussein walked away with a meditative air.

The evening came, and the night came. There was a brilliant moon. In the courtyard of the house next to Sashiya's the fig tree stood as it had stood before for Hussein. There was a strange constriction in his throat as he climbed, his knees felt weak, and he trembled. He was an hour too early, but Sashiya was there.

For half an hour they said but little, holding one another very closely, and talking with no words. And for a long while they said and did nothing that has not been said and done by half the world when it was young.

When this was over, Hussein said, 'Heart's ease, we have waited long enough. Will you come away with me to-night?'

———

'Yes, best-beloved, I will come with you.'

Then Hussein knew that the tale that he had told for himself had come true, and he breathed deeply. In the moonlight he brought out the rubies, and hung them about her neck; they flamed on her honey skin.

The moon moved half across the sky while he explained all things. It was as though they floated on a sea of immeasurable happiness.

They crept down the tree to the place where Jehangir and his men awaited him; Hussein bade the men go before him to Laghat.

Three shooting stars blazed across the sky, and Hussein and Sashiya went away upon Jehangir.
